Praise for

The Neighbor Favor

"[A] warm and welcoming new contemporary. . . . The book breathes easily and pulls you right into its world. Especially recommended for anyone who ships Janine and Gregory from *Abbott Elementary*."

—*The New York Times Book Review*

"Warm, witty, and deeply romantic. Kristina Forest is a fantastic storyteller, with an eagle eye for detail and a knack for crafting lovable characters. It's impossible not to smile while reading this book!"

—Rachel Lynn Solomon,
New York Times bestselling author of *What Happens in Amsterdam*

"*The Neighbor Favor* is the type of charming, feel-good story that reminds me why I love romance. I dare anyone to try reading Lily and Nick's adorably awkward encounters without smiling. Impossible."

—Farrah Rochon,
New York Times bestselling author of *Pugs & Kisses*

"I fell head over heels in love with Lily and Nick. *The Neighbor Favor* is sweet, swoony, and full of heart. I didn't want it to end!"

—Lynn Painter,
#1 *New York Times* bestselling author of *First and Forever*

"This swoony contemporary romance with fully realized characters will have readers hooked from the first page, and the protagonists, who are Black, have deep, relatable backstories."

—*Library Journal* (starred review)

Praise for
The Partner Plot

"A top-tier second-chance romance. . . . Xavier and Violet jump off the page and directly into your heart. . . . Kristina could write my to-do list, and I'd read it faithfully. This fantastic book is no exception."

—Erin Hahn,
author of *Catch and Keep*

"*The Partner Plot* is everything I'm looking for in a romance. Violet and Xavier's swoonworthy second-chance journey stole my heart—a chemistry-filled and thoroughly satisfying exploration of what it takes to turn first love into forever love. I'll read anything Kristina Forest writes!"

—Ava Wilder,
author of *Some Kind of Famous*

"Forest's novel is a sweet portrayal of first love and second chances. Violet and Xavier are memorable, real, and vulnerable as they struggle with career sacrifices and the fear of more heartbreak. Yet they were destined from the start—and Forest's romance never misses a shot. A second-chance slam dunk."

—*Kirkus Reviews* (starred review)

Praise for
The Love Lyric

"*The Love Lyric* is equal parts swoon and *fire*! It has everything I want in a story: soft healing, adorable banter, burning-hot steam, and a plot that's so easy to get lost in!"

—Sarah Adams,
New York Times bestselling author of *In Your Dreams*

"*The Love Lyric* reads like a sexy nineties R & B song—intense, heartfelt, and deeply moving. Kristina Forest has once again proven herself to be a shining star of contemporary romance, weaving a story that's as emotionally resonant as it is unforgettable."

—Regina Black,
author of *August Lane*

"Kristina Forest always delivers romance with the tenderness and heat of the best R & B songs, and *The Love Lyric* is no exception!"

—Alicia Thompson,
USA Today bestselling author of *Never Been Shipped*

"A gorgeous song of a book. At times it reads like a slow jam that will make you grin from ear to ear and kick your feet. And then it's a ballad, pulling on your heartstrings and making you swoon. Clearly Forest's Angel and Iris are made for each other, just like the rhythm and blues that provide a backdrop for this stunning end to the Greene sisters series."

—Myah Ariel,
author of *No Ordinary Love*

"Readers will be rooting for marketing exec Iris and R & B singer Angel to sync up. Their love story is cozy and tender, unfolding with a sweetness that makes their happily ever after feel inevitable."

—Alexis Daria,
bestselling author of *Along Came Amor*

Berkley Titles by Kristina Forest

The Neighbor Favor

The Partner Plot

The Love Lyric

The Summer Girlfriend

The Summer Girlfriend

KRISTINA FOREST

BERKLEY ROMANCE
NEW YORK

BERKLEY ROMANCE
Published by Berkley
An imprint of Penguin Random House LLC
1745 Broadway, New York, NY 10019
penguinrandomhouse.com

Library of Congress Cataloging-in-Publication Data

Names: Forest, Kristina author
Title: The summer girlfriend / Kristina Forest.
Description: First edition. | New York : Berkley Romance, 2026.
Identifiers: LCCN 2025045273 (print) | LCCN 2025045274 (ebook) |
ISBN 9780593956397 trade paperback | ISBN 9780593956403 ebook
Subjects: LCGFT: Romance fiction | Fiction | Novels
Classification: LCC PS3606.O74747 S86 2026 (print) |
LCC PS3606.O74747 (ebook)
LC record available at https://lccn.loc.gov/2025045273
LC ebook record available at https://lccn.loc.gov/2025045274

First Edition: June 2026

Printed in the United States of America
2nd Printing

The authorized representative in the EU for product safety and compliance is Penguin Random House Ireland, Morrison Chambers, 32 Nassau Street, Dublin D02 YH68, Ireland, https://eu-contact.penguin.ie.

For all the Jersey girls

The Summer Girlfriend

Prologue

Heart Beach, New Jersey
1974

The ocean-gray house was two stories tall. The white paint on the window shutters, wraparound porch, and front steps chipped in various places. The top step sank in the middle and wood splintered at its center. The front lawn was unkept, and weeds swayed back and forth in the brisk March breeze.

The house didn't look abandoned necessarily, just neglected. Momentarily forgotten. Especially in comparison with the other pristine homes lining either side of the street.

All in all, this particular house wasn't anything special.

Not yet.

That *yet* was imperative to Jeremiah Smith I. He had a talent for looking at something and sensing its hidden potential. Believing in what could be and believing in *himself* and what he could do for his family were what had gotten him this far. Keys in hand. A **SOLD** sign planted in the front yard. His wife, Minnie, by his side, their six-year-old daughter, Celeste, staring up at the timeworn house with curious, captivated eyes.

"*This* house is where Dr. Thomas vacationed with his wife every summer?" Minnie asked, voiced tinged with skepticism. She wrapped her wool coat tighter around herself as another gust of wind blew down the street, bringing with it the salty smell of the Atlantic Ocean. Minnie's high-volume curls whipped about her face, and she fought to tame them into stillness. She fastened Celeste's knit hat tighter on her head and then she looked up at her husband and waited for his answer.

Jeremiah took a moment to admire his wife, which he did often. With her thick hair, chocolate brown eyes, and smooth brown skin, in his opinion, she was more beautiful than Pat Cleveland, more alluring than Donna Summer. *Pretty Minnie* had been her nickname growing up back in Florida. He and Minnie met almost a decade ago at Riley University in northern New Jersey where Minnie had been a junior on a full-ride scholarship, working at the campus bookstore. And Jeremiah, the same age as Minnie but not a college student, had been an evening-shift custodian. Late-night chats among acquaintances had turned into friendship, then turned into romance. When Minnie mentioned how much she missed the ocean, Jeremiah had driven her an hour and fifteen minutes to the Jersey shore in his battered Ford pickup. Once they reached the beach, Minnie had kicked off her shoes and run toward the glistening waves. Not knowing how to swim, Jeremiah had watched from the shoreline as Minnie dove into the ocean and glided through the water like a mermaid, or a siren.

He'd known then that he wanted to marry her. Known that he wanted to make her happy in every way possible and that he would work hard enough to make it so that she could swim in the ocean whenever she wanted.

Now that day was finally here.

"Jeremiah?" Minnie prompted, her brow arched. He still hadn't answered her question.

"Dr. Thomas said he hasn't been to the house in almost eight years," Jeremiah replied. "Not since before Celeste was born."

"Looks that way," Minnie mused.

Dr. Thomas was Celeste's pediatrician. He was an older, self-made Black man with his own medical practice, and Jeremiah admired him greatly. When Jeremiah mentioned that he was looking to buy a summer home in a beach town that was friendly to Black folks, Dr. Thomas recommended Heart Beach, a barrier island along the coast of the Atlantic Ocean in central New Jersey. The small beach town was founded in 1911 by an affluent Black couple who purchased land and sold plots to others who faced discrimination while trying to purchase vacation homes or open businesses in other parts of the state. Now, over sixty years later, the town had flourished into a thriving, tight-knit community. Dr. Thomas had offered to sell his vacation home to Jeremiah—he hadn't been to Heart Beach since his wife passed in '65. The house had been more for her enjoyment than his own. Without children or other living relatives, Dr. Thomas had no one to leave his home to. He hadn't wanted to sell the house to just anyone. But Jeremiah wasn't just anyone.

"I want you to have the house," Dr. Thomas had said. "You can leave it to your daughter, and your daughter can leave it to her children, and so on. A house like that deserves to be kept in a family for generations."

Now Jeremiah looked up at the house and tried to imagine

the future Dr. Thomas spoke of. He glanced at his wife's perturbed frown and smiled as he planted a soft kiss against her temple.

"Don't worry, baby," he said. "We've got at least three months to fix it up before summer. Come on, let's take a look inside."

Eager to finally explore the house, Celeste skipped up the walkway ahead of Jeremiah and Minnie.

"Be careful on that top step!" Minnie called. Celeste gingerly hopped over the broken wood and paused in front of the door. She spun around to face her parents and flashed a sweet smile, as darling as ever with her round cheeks. She was the spitting image of her mother.

Jeremiah winked at his daughter as he fit the key in the lock and turned the knob. The floorboards creaked beneath their feet as they stepped inside. The spacious foyer was empty. The entire house was empty, in fact. Dust particles filtered through the air and sunlight slanted through the windows. A wide staircase led to the bedrooms upstairs. It was a big house, and there was much to explore. But what caught their eyes immediately was the large bay window in the living room to their right.

The corners of Minnie's mouth lifted in a smile as she walked toward the window with Celeste right on her heels. Jeremiah followed and watched as his wife and daughter peered out the window onto the street. He tried to picture their lives here during summers for years to come. A feeling of warmth and rightness nestled in his chest.

Minnie looked over at him and let out a small laugh. "I can't believe Mama's recipes got us all the way here."

Jeremiah grinned. After college, Minnie had worked as a

teacher, and Jeremiah had continued his custodian work while taking night classes. They got by, but they lived paycheck to paycheck in a one-bedroom apartment. Neither he nor Minnie came from money, so they didn't have a nest egg gifted to them by their parents. Minnie was the second oldest of nine children and had grown up in poverty, and Jeremiah was the only son of a widowed mother who'd worked multiple jobs to keep a roof over their heads. Jeremiah and Minnie knew how it felt to go to bed hungry, or to go without in general. He was determined to figure out a way to spare them from struggle.

His answer arrived when Minnie became pregnant with Celeste. In the evenings, like clockwork, Minnie craved something sweet. But not just anything sweet. She craved one of her mother's desserts that she used to bake whenever they had extra money. Too tired and uncomfortable to stand and make the sweets herself, Minnie dictated the recipes to Jeremiah, who was all too willing to please her. The first dessert that he baked for Minnie was a pound cake. He made some instinctual alterations to the recipe, like adding an extra teaspoon of vanilla extract, adding one less teaspoon of lemon flavoring, and sprinkling in a bit of brown sugar. He sent up a prayer that the cake would taste good. An hour later when he pulled it out of the oven and Minnie took her first bite, she moaned, and her eyes rolled to the back of her head in bliss.

"Jeremiah, baby," she said, mouth full. "Mama would probably slap me silly if she heard me say this, but this is the best pound cake I've ever tasted."

"*Really?*" In disbelief, Jeremiah took a bite of the slice that Minnie held out to him. The fluffy, sugary texture touched his tongue, and as he chewed, he fully understood why Minnie's immediate reaction was to moan. "Lord, this *is* good."

Delighted, Minnie laughed and hurried to cut them each another slice.

Jeremiah baked whatever she wanted. Not just pound cakes, but 7 Up cake, pecan pie, and cinnamon apple pie. Carrot cake, drop sugar cookies, classic chocolate chip. It became a source of joy for Jeremiah, baking whatever his wife desired as their baby grew in her womb. Minnie brought some of his desserts to work to share with her coworkers and students, and soon word got around town about Jeremiah's baking. Requests started pouring in. People wanted him to bake cakes and pies for their birthday parties and holiday gatherings.

Jeremiah quickly realized the business potential that they had on their hands. Most evenings after work, he baked late into the night. And after Celeste was born, Jeremiah kept her swaddled to his chest, whipping batter as Minnie bustled around the kitchen, helping to package his increasing orders. They saved as much as they could, and within a couple years, they had enough money put aside to quit their jobs and rent a storefront and open their own bakery. They coined it Smith's Sweets. A year after that, they bought their very first home.

Now, a few years later, the Smiths had a place of their own to vacation in the summers. They'd come such a long way.

"Can we go see the beach, Daddy?" Celeste asked, tugging on Jeremiah's coat sleeve.

He smiled down at his daughter. "Of course, sweetheart."

The family of three huddled together against the wind as they walked the few short blocks toward the beach. Because it wasn't tourist season yet, the beach was mostly empty, save for the seagulls looking for food. In a couple of months, almost every inch of sand would be overtaken with beach towels and umbrellas, and a tramcar would announce its coming and going as it navigated up and down the boardwalk. But today, it was just the three Smiths walking across the beach, their eyes on the ocean in the distance.

They stopped walking before they reached the wet sand. Jeremiah lifted Celeste to sit on his shoulders, and Minnie leaned her head against his arm.

"It's too cold to swim now, right, Daddy?" Celeste said.

"Yes, too cold today, sweetheart," he answered. "But we'll be back soon when it's warm. And when we're here, you can come to the beach every day if you want."

"Every day?"

Jeremiah angled his head and glanced up, seeing the wonder in his daughter's eyes. *This* was what it was all for. All their sacrifice and late nights. To see that awestruck expression on his daughter's face as she looked at the ocean. To witness his wife's smile and hear her contented sigh. To know that Celeste would never have to want for anything in life, that she wouldn't know struggle the way that he and Minnie had.

"Yes, sweetheart," Jeremiah said. "Every day."

Jeremiah thought of Dr. Thomas's wish to keep their new Heart Beach home in their family for generations to come. In that moment, he had no way of knowing that years later, Celeste would give birth to three children, including a son whom she'd name after her father.

As Jeremiah Smith I stood with his wife and daughter, feet from the ocean in Heart Beach on that cold March day, he felt completely warm inside.

This was only the beginning.

Chapter One

New York City
Present Day

There was an unopened box of Smith's Sweets salted caramel chocolate chip cookies waiting for Noelle Lewis in her kitchen cabinet.

She'd been thinking about the cookies for hours. Earlier at her day job while organizing a new beach reads display, she'd daydreamed about dipping the delicious cookies in milk before taking a big bite as she sat on the couch and searched through movie options on streaming services, pretending to look for something new, only to end up choosing *Brown Sugar* for the billionth time. Unfortunately, though, her date with her favorite cookies and early-2000s rom-com would have to wait. Because tonight was reserved for her side hustle.

In the dimly lit bathroom of Galactic Karaoke in Koreatown, Manhattan, Noelle hastened to unravel what felt like a yard of toilet paper, and she handed it to her client, Sheree, who stood at the bathroom sink, crying tears of anger because her cousin was ruining the joint bachelor-bachelorette party for Sheree and her fiancé, Justin.

"I don't know why she's *here*," Sheree grumbled, accepting the wad of toilet paper. She swiped at the running mascara that now streaked her brown cheeks and looked at her reflection in the mirror. She emitted a weary sigh and turned her tearstained face back to Noelle. "Why bother showing up if you don't even like me or my fiancé? She's drinking up all the liquor that she hasn't lifted a finger to pay for, and she's being a bitch to Justin's friends, but she thinks she's flirting. Lord knows why I let my mom guilt me into choosing her as my maid of honor."

"They say that weddings bring out the worst in people," Noelle said gently.

Secretly, Noelle had to admit that Sheree's cousin Raven *was* a bit much. Earlier at dinner when Sheree had introduced Noelle to the rest of the bridal party; her fiancé, Justin; and Justin's friends, Raven had looked Noelle up and down with pursed lips like she'd just finished sucking on a sour straw. And for the past twenty minutes, Raven had hogged the microphone and was currently making her way through Rihanna's catalog. Her off-key rendition of "Rude Boy" was terrible enough to make someone's ears bleed. It didn't help that she insisted on attempting to dance like Rihanna while she sang. She needed to sit down, expeditiously.

But it wasn't Noelle's job to fan the flames of drama. She was here to smile and seamlessly adapt, all in an effort to make the bride's life easier. It was why she'd pulled Sheree into the bathroom when she'd noticed her eyes brimming with tears.

"Listen, you don't have to let Raven ruin your night," Noelle said, taking Sheree by her shoulders and looking at her head-on. "Think of the bigger picture! In a couple months, you'll be married to the love of your life and living happily ever after. One drunk cousin won't ruin that for you, will she?"

Sheree sniffled and allowed herself a small smile. "I really do love Justin," she said. "I can't wait to marry him."

"Of course you can't." Noelle beamed, satisfied that she'd managed to lift Sheree's mood. She reached into her purse and retrieved a tube of mascara. She always brought mascara, disposable spoolies, and makeup remover with her on nights when she had a wedding or wedding-related event. Brides tended to cry a lot. Noelle didn't judge. Most brides were stressed the hell out and barely sleeping. Also, it wasn't her job to judge.

She instructed Sheree to widen her eyes and look up as she reapplied mascara to her lashes and wiped away the residue of makeup on her cheeks. When Sheree shivered and rubbed her hands up and down her arms, Noelle shrugged off her leather jacket and draped it around Sheree's shoulders.

"No more tears," Noelle said. "Not when you look so beautiful."

Sheree looked at her reflection again and glanced at Noelle sidelong with a smirk. "You're good at this. I see why you have a five-star rating."

Noelle smiled and shrugged, like it was no big deal. But truthfully, she took a lot of pride in her five-star Bridal Bestie rating. Noelle wasn't one of Sheree's oldest friends, and she wasn't a wedding planner or a wedding crisis manager, for that matter. She'd been hired by Sheree to be one of her bridesmaids.

Sheree, a twenty-nine-year-old workaholic accountant who struggled to find time outside of the office to make friends, found herself in a tricky predicament when her outgoing fiancé

Justin wanted all five of his line brothers as groomsmen. Sheree chose three cousins and her old college roommate to make up her bridal party, but she needed a fifth bridesmaid. Through the bridal grapevine, Sheree was made aware of Bridal Bestie, a website where a person could contract a professional stand-in to act as a bridesmaid for their wedding. That was where Noelle came in.

After passing a thorough background check, Sheree was able to sift through the agency's available professionals in the area. There must have been something about Noelle's profile that Sheree liked, because she took the next step, which was to request an agency-arranged meeting with Noelle. They got coffee in order to feel each other out. Then Sheree chose the Ultimate Best Friend package, which meant that in addition to being a bridesmaid in her September wedding, Noelle was contracted to attend tonight's bachelor-bachelorette party, as well as Sheree's bridal shower next month in August.

The story that Noelle and Sheree had agreed to tell was that they'd met a few months prior at a Lagree class and had quickly become close friends. Justin knew the truth, of course. But the rest of Sheree's family had easily accepted the tale because Sheree attended Lagree religiously. Noelle, however, hadn't ever heard of Lagree before meeting Sheree, so she'd watched countless YouTube videos of people bending themselves into pretzels on workout machines just in case anyone asked her a question about the class. So far, Lagree hadn't come up, and it probably wouldn't. But Noelle liked to be prepared anyway.

"Come on, let's head back," Noelle said, urging Sheree toward the bathroom exit. "You've got more singing to do. Maybe you can sing 'We Found Love' if Raven hasn't already."

Sheree laughed and smiled at Noelle gratefully as she followed her out of the bathroom and down the dark hallway back to their private karaoke room. One of Justin's groomsmen had managed to steal the mic from Raven, and he was belting out "Don't Leave Me" by Blackstreet. The other guys were surrounding him and singing backup. Raven stood in the corner of the room with her arms crossed, glaring daggers.

Noticing that they'd returned from the bathroom, Justin rushed over to Noelle and Sheree. He wrapped his gangly arms around Sheree and sported a lopsided, drunk smile.

"Everything good, babe?" he asked. Sheree grinned up at him and nodded. Justin looked over Sheree's head at Noelle. "Thanks for helping her, Nola."

For a second, Noelle considered correcting him. But he was drunk, and it honestly didn't matter if he got her name right. She wasn't a permanent fixture in their lives. She'd been working with Bridal Bestie for almost two years, and sometimes when she got along really well with a client, she wondered what it might be like if they tried to be real-life friends. One of the reasons she was so good at this job was because she didn't struggle to connect with other people. In her high school senior year superlatives, she'd been voted Most Friendly. But it was a lot harder to make friends as an adult. She'd long ago lost touch with anyone from the University of Maryland, and lately she saw less and less of her best friend and roommate, Tati, because she spent most nights at her boyfriend André's place. Noelle was happy for Tati. She was blissfully in love and had finally found her person after kissing one too many frogs. But Noelle still missed her. Both things could be true.

Sheree would probably be cool to hang out with in real life. But these days, Noelle was more concerned about the money.

She'd had various side hustles over the years. Bartending,

cater waiting, walking dogs, babysitting toddlers, walking dogs while babysitting toddlers. Being a hired bridesmaid was *by far* the easiest and highest-paying side gig she'd ever had. With her side gig money, her paychecks from her main job at Hidden Gems Books, as well as doing food delivery and ride-share driving, combined with a bit of financial aid and private loans, she almost had enough money to go back to college and finish her bachelor's degree. *Finally.*

Suddenly, across the room, an argument broke out between Raven and the groomsmen. While Sheree and Justin went to intervene, Noelle checked the time on her phone. 12:03 a.m. Her contract stated that her services were no longer needed after midnight, so her work here was officially done.

When there seemed to be a break in the bickering, she approached Sheree, lightly tapped her on the shoulder, and whispered, "I'm sorry, but it's after midnight, and I'm going home now." She lowered her voice another fraction. "Um, I just want to remind you that the remaining fee for tonight is due tomorrow by twelve p.m. and you can pay directly through the website. I'll send you the receipt to reimburse me for my ride home."

"Oh, of course, of course!" Sheree twisted around and gave Noelle a firm, warm hug. It felt nice. Even if their friendship was pretend. "I'll pay everything asap. Get home safe."

Each Bridal Bestie client was different, but what they had in common was that they needed Noelle's help in some form or another. People with big social circles weren't in need of her services. More often than not, her clients were a little lonely.

Maybe that was another reason that Noelle was good at this particular side hustle. She knew how loneliness could house itself inside your body and sit on top of your heart. Even six years later, she still vividly remembered the emptiness she felt as she'd packed up her junior year dorm room, knowing full well that losing her scholarship meant that she wouldn't be able to return to UMD to finish her senior year. Her ex, CJ, hadn't bothered to say goodbye to her, even though he was the reason she'd gotten into trouble and lost her scholarship in the first place.

But then again, the only person she could truly blame was herself. No one had told her to get mixed up with him and jeopardize her future.

As Noelle stepped outside onto the sidewalk, a group of girls walked by, laughing among themselves as they marched on in their high heels. It was early July, and the air was hot and muggy. People were out and about, enjoying summer. Noelle couldn't remember when she'd last taken time off to do anything that remotely resembled summer fun. Unless she counted the afternoon last August when she'd gone to that run-down indoor water park with Tati, and middle school boys had catcalled them while they'd floated down the lazy river.

Noelle lived in New Jersey, a state lined with beaches, but she hadn't been to the shore in almost three years. Working and saving every bit of money to go back to school was more important.

Her phone vibrated with an alert that her car ride was four minutes away. At the same time, she heard the karaoke bar entrance door open and close behind her. She turned around and came face-to-face with one of Justin's groomsmen, Brian. He was medium height with light brown skin, and he must have come to their outing straight from work, because he was still wearing a suit, although he'd ditched his tie and unfastened the top buttons of his shirt.

Noelle had noticed Brian looking at her across the table at

dinner, and upstairs during karaoke, he'd sat unnecessarily close to her on the couch, "accidentally" brushing his hand across her thigh as he'd reached for his drink.

In her line of side hustle, Noelle was often hit on by drunk guests who were excited to see a new face in their familiar ecosystem. But she held firm on maintaining boundaries with her clients and their loved ones. It was the only way to keep things professional. And on a personal level, she had no interest in dating right now. Why willingly give away what little time and energy she had to someone who more than likely wouldn't bother meeting her halfway? She'd learned the hard way not to set herself up for disappointment in that regard.

"You dipped without saying goodbye," Brian said as he approached her with a lazy smile. His cheeks were flushed, and his eyelids drooped. He was drunk, obviously. "Broke my heart a little."

Noelle forced a smile. If Tati were here, she would have told Brian to fuck off without thinking twice. But Noelle hadn't been hired for an Ultimate Best Friend package in a while. It had been an unusually slow summer for Bridal Bestie. Last summer, Noelle had worked at least two weddings a month. This summer, she'd worked one wedding in May, and the wedding she'd been assigned to in June had been called off at the last minute because the wedding planner had discovered that the venue was hiding a black mold infestation. Noelle had zero weddings lined up for July and August. Weddings were just too expensive now. People were opting to get married at the courthouse or to elope abroad. Noelle needed this gig with Sheree. It was good money, and she didn't want to screw up her payday by cursing out one of the groom's best friends.

"Yeah, I'm just tired," she said, stepping toward the street and putting space between herself and Brian. "I'm heading home now."

He nodded and crossed his arms over his chest. "I'll stand out here with you. This city's dangerous. Somebody might try to snatch your pretty self up."

He winked. Noelle fought the urge to grimace.

Most days, she wore a Hidden Gems Books T-shirt and a pair of jeans and sneakers. When she wasn't working, she wore whatever clothes she bought off the sale rack. For her Bridal Bestie gigs, with the exception of the bridesmaid dresses that were provided for her, she borrowed cute clothes from Tati. Like the sleeveless navy blue bodysuit, high-rise barrel jeans, and silver Mary Janes that she wore tonight. A few days ago, when Tati had last been home, she'd styled Noelle's hair in goddess braids that fell down her back, which Noelle wore loose.

All this to say, Noelle was aware that she looked nicer than usual tonight. And because of her five-foot-three-inch height, she was also aware that people sometimes assumed she couldn't take care of herself. But she didn't leave the house without pepper spray in her purse and she wasn't afraid to use it.

"That's nice of you," she said. "But I'm okay, really."

If Brian heard her response, he pretended not to. "You mentioned at dinner that you work in Jersey City," he said.

Noelle nodded, eyes on the rideshare app. The car was two minutes away.

"I live in Bayonne," Brian said. "We should get together and chill some time."

Damn, was he *really* gonna make her say it? Fine. Better to get this over with now rather than wait until the wedding in a couple months when he inevitably cornered her again.

"Actually, I don't think that would be a good idea," she said.

He blinked and huffed out a surprised chuckle. "No? Why not?"

She was saved from having to answer him as her phone vibrated in her palm. Her rideshare car turned and drove down the street toward them.

"Oh, look, my ride's here. It was nice to meet you, Brian. Have a good night!"

She double-checked the car's license plate and verified that the driver was there to pick her up before diving into the back seat.

"Can I get your number?!" she heard Brian call as the car pulled away.

She let out a grateful sigh of relief and sank deeper into the back seat. It wasn't until they were driving through the Holland Tunnel that she realized she'd left her old leather jacket on Sheree's shoulders.

It was too late to turn back now. She sent a quick text to Sheree about finding a time to meet up soon to get her jacket back.

Of course! I'll bring it to you asap! came Sheree's immediate reply. Thanks again for working with me.

Noelle's phone chimed again with an email from Bridal Bestie, confirming that Sheree had paid for tonight. Seven hundred and fifty dollars. Amazing. Of course, the agency deducted their 20 percent commission. So Noelle took home six hundred dollars. It was the one hang-up she had about Bridal Bestie. Imagine if she was able to keep the entire fee for herself? She *could* do this work on her own, but she liked the legitimacy that the agency provided. By the time this agreement ended in September, Sheree would have paid a total of two thousand dollars, with sixteen hundred dollars going to Noelle.

It all put Noelle one step closer to obtaining her bachelor's degree, and after she graduated, she planned to apply to grad school to get her master's in library and information science. During her first go-round at college, Noelle had spent more time chasing after her ex-boyfriend than she had contemplating her future. Amid one of the toughest times in her life, the library had provided solace and had helped her discover a newfound love of reading. She knew that her goal of becoming a librarian would put her in even more student loan debt, but after six years of zigzags and unexpected detours, at twenty-seven years old, she had discovered her calling. And she wasn't going to give up on herself now.

Noelle hung her keys on the hook by the door and slipped off her shoes as she stepped inside the apartment that she shared with Tati in Brickton, a small town in North Jersey, about a fifteen-minute drive from Jersey City. She and Tati had lived in their apartment for almost three years. The building was only a few blocks away from the apartment building they'd grown up in.

Noelle and her mom had lived on the floor above Tati's family. Now Noelle's mom, Portia, lived in South Carolina with her husband, Bill. They were both middle school teachers who'd met on a dating site four years ago. They'd encouraged Noelle to move with them to South Carolina, but Noelle hadn't wanted to intrude or feel like a burden on their happily ever after. And if anyone deserved a happily ever after, it was her mom. No matter how many years had passed, Noelle's bones still rattled when she thought of the phone call she'd received from her mom's old coworker, shakily telling Noelle that Portia had been in a car accident and Noelle had better get to the hospital. Noelle remembered the bright lights and shiny hospital floors. The chaos of the emergency waiting room, the twist and pull of her stomach muscles as she tried her best not to have a panic attack while her mom was in surgery.

She'd been twenty-one years old then. A frightened recent college dropout who was wholly unprepared for what might happen if things with her mom didn't turn out okay. But thankfully, they had.

Noelle continued to her room and cut on her bedroom light. Her room, with its periwinkle-painted walls, was small. There was enough space to fit a full-size bed, dresser, and a little bookshelf. She hadn't been a big reader most of her life. That hobby had started when she'd needed a distraction while waiting in her mom's hospital room and later at her physical therapy appointments. Noelle read any- and everything. Right now she was in the middle of a suspense novel about an elementary school superintendent who'd been blamed for her husband's gruesome murder.

She placed Tati's silver flats on her floor in front of her closet. She snapped a picture of the shoes and sent it to Tati.

> Back home. Not a scratch on the goods.

Tati replied within seconds, Thank you, ma'am. How'd it go? Any cute groomsmen?

Noelle snorted. Tati was always hoping that Noelle might meet a groomsman and fall in love. Preferably a sexy, gainfully employed groomsman. So far, no dice. And Noelle wasn't looking for anyone anyway.

Nope, Noelle responded. But one of the bridesmaids is kinda crazy and obsessed with Rihanna.

Shine bright like a diamondddd, Tati texted. She sent a GIF of Rihanna tossing her ponytail.

Noelle laughed. Tati was staying over at André's tonight. They'd met a year ago when he'd walked into the hair salon where Tati worked, and she'd given him a haircut before his big paralegal interview. He got the job and promptly took Tati out to dinner. They were full-on crazy for each other and walked around with perpetual hearts in their eyes. They were the kind of couple who gave Noelle the tiniest bit of hope that maybe one day, in the distant future once she achieved her goals and was financially stable with her librarian career, she might find her person too. Despite her current romantic cynicism, she'd grown up as an only child with a mom who loved her but worked all day teaching, followed by evening shifts at a local restaurant, and deep down Noelle had always craved to be part of a unit of some kind. At the various weddings she worked, her heart pricked with longing whenever she watched the happy couples surrounded by their big families.

Maybe one day she'd be part of something like that, but for now she was focused only on getting her degree.

She opened her banking app to check her savings account the way she always did before bed. She needed a little less than seven thousand dollars to go back to college this fall. She wanted to finish her final year at Riley University, the local state college about a forty-five-minute drive south of Brickton.

She'd already met with the admissions and bursar offices. She'd switched her major multiple times while at UMD before finally settling on sociology. Luckily finishing an undergrad degree in sociology wouldn't keep her from applying to grad school for her MLS. Between working at Bridal Bestie, Hidden Gems Books, doing food delivery and car share rides, she was saving every single penny. Her mom and Bill had offered to give her a couple thousand too, but they lived on teachers' salaries, and Noelle hated taking money from them that they needed for themselves. Even with their money added, she would still be far from her goal. She was holding out hope that a couple last-minute wedding gigs might materialize. Otherwise, she'd have to put off completing her degree for another year. So much could change in a year, though. In the past, whenever she came close to having enough money to finish college, something else always happened. Her car engine blew. She fell ill with a bad bout of bronchitis and was left with a hefty hospital bill because she didn't have health insurance. Her car needed a new catalytic converter. (She really needed a new car altogether.) Each incident took a chunk from her savings. She'd already waited long enough to go back to college. The time to get her degree was now before another thing went wrong. Someway, somehow, she needed to figure out how to get the rest of that money by September.

Her stomach grumbled, and she remembered the precious Smith's Sweets cookies that had been patiently waiting for her all day in the cabinet. She'd continue contemplating her money situation in the morning. For now, she deserved some chocolatey goodness.

She rushed to the kitchen and opened the cabinet above the sink where they kept their snacks. The navy blue and white

Smith's Sweets cookie box looked like it was glowing. She grabbed the box and opened the fridge to pour a glass of milk. Noelle loved Smith's Sweets. Had a hard day? You deserved a Smith's Sweets snack. Had a good day? You deserved a Smith's Sweets snack. Growing up, no Thanksgiving was complete without a frozen Smith's Sweets pumpkin or cinnamon apple pie. But Noelle's favorite snack was the salted caramel chocolate chip cookies.

She sat at the kitchen table with her glass of milk and plate of cookies. Realizing that she forgot her phone in her room and she couldn't scroll mindlessly on social media, she opted to read the Smith family story on the back of the Smith's Sweets box—something she'd done a hundred times before.

It all began when Jeremiah Smith started baking for his pregnant wife, Minnie, in their small New Jersey home. In 1965, Jeremiah and Minnie opened their first official bake shop. They developed a full line of traditional baked goods, perfecting each recipe and baking each dessert from scratch. People traveled from all over to try their delicious desserts. Today, Smith's Sweets is a nationally recognized brand, and you don't have to travel to New Jersey to have a taste of the goodness. Our award-winning cookies and desserts are available at dozens of retailers around the country.

Smith's Sweets is proud to be a family-run business. From our family to yours, we hope you enjoy our sweets that are baked with love.

In the bottom-right corner, there was a small black-and-white photo of Jeremiah and Minnie standing in front of the original Smith's Sweets bakery. Jeremiah was tall and broad-shouldered. He had a handsome face with strong features. Minnie was much shorter and very pretty, fashionably fitted in an A-line dress with her hair styled in curls. She smiled at the camera as Jeremiah smiled at her. He looked completely down bad for Minnie, as if the sun rose and set on her.

Noelle dipped another cookie in milk and glanced at the last line on the back of the box again.

From our family to yours, we hope you enjoy our sweets that are baked with love.

She did some quick math. If Jeremiah and Minnie had grandchildren, they were probably around Noelle's age.

She'd bet they were loaded.

Chapter Two

Celeste was calling him again.

Jeremiah Smith II glanced at his phone and lost his train of thought as Mom popped up on his phone's screen, accompanied by a photo of him and his family taken on his eighth birthday. They were at Disney World and he and Celeste were sitting side by side. Jeremiah wore Mickey Mouse ears and Celeste donned Wayfarer sunglasses as they cheesed for the camera. Off to the side, his younger sister, Amara, was a moving blur, mid-run. Seconds before the photo was taken, she'd dropped her ice cream cone on the ground and was more concerned about replacing it than taking a picture. His older brother, Percy, stood partially out of frame to the left of Celeste, the bottom half of his face obscured by the large water bottle he held to his mouth. His grandfather, whom they'd all called Pop, stood behind Jeremiah, resting his hands atop Jeremiah's shoulders. He wore aviator-style sunglasses and his bald head glistened in the sun. His wide smile was filled with love and pride.

Their Grandma Minnie was absent from the photo. She'd passed away a few months prior. Celeste had planned the trip as a celebration for Jeremiah's birthday, but it had also been an effort to bring some joy back to their family. Particularly to Pop, who'd taken Grandma Minnie's death the hardest. In the first few weeks after she'd passed, Jeremiah often caught Pop staring off into space with a vacant look in his eyes. That trip to Disney had reinvigorated Pop. He'd laughed his booming laugh, rode every ride, and walked with Amara perched on his shoulders, even when he grew tired. He'd resumed his role as their larger-than-life hero.

Jeremiah inhaled deeply and rode out the sharp, familiar sting that he felt in his chest whenever he thought about his grandfather and how much he missed him. It had been two years since Pop's death, and it still hadn't gotten much easier.

He was trying his best to live up to the memory of the man he was named after. He was afraid that he was failing miserably.

His phone finally stopped vibrating.

"Sorry, Mom," Jeremiah mumbled to himself. "Can't talk right now."

He had a pretty good idea about why his mom was calling and what she wanted to discuss. It would probably lead back to the stupid lie he'd told in May—a lie he'd instantly regretted, even though it had let him off the hook. If he answered her call now and the conversation went in the direction that he was assuming it would go, he'd be forced to either confront his lie or continue it. And he wanted to do neither.

Stupid lie aside, he really didn't have time to talk right now. For real. He didn't. He'd call her back later. After his meeting. Or maybe tomorrow . . .

He definitely was *not* purposely avoiding his own mother.

He returned his attention to his reflection in his full-length mirror. His charcoal gray blazer and white button-up, just picked up from the dry cleaner that morning, were crisp and wrinkle-free. His fade was fresh. He flashed a smile and winked, trying to conjure up some good luck and charm. Today's pitch meeting *would* go well. He'd speak that shit into existence.

He clasped his hands together in front of him and pretended that he was speaking to Shop Mart's corporate team.

"At Good Boy, our biggest priority is keeping consumers and their dogs happy," Jeremiah said. "We started our company in the online space by providing the best plush toys on the market, and now we're seeking to expand into more big-box stores because we want as many dogs as possible to experience our durable top-of-the-line products. Like our upcoming fall line, featuring a pumpkin toy, which comes with a little pocket for treats, and . . . and . . ."

Jeremiah dropped his hands at his sides as he trailed off. Ah, fuck. What else were they debuting this fall?

Aaron, Good Boy's founder and Jeremiah's old college floor mate, who was also from New Jersey, was one of the hardest-working people Jeremiah knew. He'd started Good Boy only a year after they'd graduated from NYU, making the dog toys himself and selling them on Etsy. Jeremiah admired Aaron's vision and drive, but during the year and a half that he'd spent with Good Boy, Jeremiah had learned that Aaron could also be incredibly indecisive.

He did a quick scroll through his email and searched for the message Aaron had sent him at two a.m. last night.

Subject: Fall toys FINAL

Pumpkin toy and acorn toy for Fall. We're scrapping the turkey toy!

"Pumpkin and acorn toy," Jeremiah finished for his imaginary audience. "We'd love the opportunity to partner with you and provide our products to your loyal customers."

He smiled, hoping that it would dazzle the Shop Mart team right out of their chairs. While Jeremiah loved dogs, he wasn't a dog owner. He didn't trust himself enough to be responsible for another being. His mom and sister also had severe dog allergies, which meant they'd been a cat household growing up. His mom's hairless sphynx cat Caesar was nineteen years old and hated everyone but Celeste. Despite Jeremiah's near lifelong desire to win Caesar's affections, if he even so much as looked in Caesar's direction, the cat hissed. He also liked to pee on people's shoes to mark his territory. Jeremiah didn't mention Caesar during his Good Boy pitch meetings.

In an hour, he'd drive into New York City to meet with the Shop Mart team at their Midtown headquarters. Aaron was the brains behind Good Boy, but Jeremiah was the charmer, the smooth talker. He was good at landing the pitch.

Years ago, Aaron had received a grant from the Smith Foundation, a nonprofit started by Jeremiah's grandfather, which provided grants to Black entrepreneurs and business owners in New Jersey. The grant had helped get Good Boy off the ground, and through the foundation, Aaron was introduced to some investors. Then a year and a half ago, Jeremiah had run into Aaron at a networking event, where Aaron shared that he wanted to branch out of the online retail space into physical stores and he was looking to expand his team. As Jeremiah had listened to Aaron struggle to pitch his own company, he realized that while Aaron had a good thing on his hands, he was shy, and he needed help spreading Good Boy to the masses.

Luckily for Aaron, he'd run into Jeremiah at the right time. He'd recently left his marketing role at his family's company, Smith's Sweets. It was a role that had been handed to him right after graduation, one where he hadn't applied himself enough, especially not in comparison to his siblings. Jeremiah had wanted a fresh start and an opportunity to do something meaningful with his life without fearing how he measured up to Percy. He'd pitched himself to Aaron on the spot, offering to help get Good Boy's name out there. In college, Jeremiah hadn't had the reputation of a hard worker, but he'd been popular and knew how to talk to people. That was most likely why Aaron had agreed to bring him on.

Since Jeremiah joined the team, in a short year and a half, Good Boy toys were now sold in select big-box stores, and the team was moving into the tech space. They were in the early process of developing an app that would work similar to Airbnb, where people could find temporary overnight housing for their pets. Each stay would come equipped with a Good Boy toy.

The app had been Jeremiah's idea. Initially, Aaron had brushed it off as a waste of time and resources. Then he attended a young-entrepreneur conference and offhandedly mentioned the app idea to some tech friends based in Silicon

Valley, who deemed the app a brilliant idea. Suddenly Aaron rushed to make the app a reality. Jeremiah tried not to take offense that his opinion alone hadn't been good enough.

Aaron, as well as the rest of their small team, had already moved their operations to Silicon Valley earlier in the year. Jeremiah would make the cross-country move the first weekend of September once his lease was up. He'd already found an apartment in the same building as a few of his coworkers.

He was trying his best to view his impending move as an extension of his grand plan to carve out his own path and not like he was running away.

His phone vibrated again. Mom. He froze as if Celeste could see him screening her call. The vibrating ceased, and Jeremiah released a sigh of relief.

Then his phone buzzed with a text from Amara.

Dearest brother, please call Mom back. Every time you don't answer, she calls me to say that you didn't answer. How long must this go on, sir??

Sorry, sorry, he responded. Calling her back now.

But he didn't call back like he said he would. He grabbed his phone and made his way to the kitchen. He lived on the top floor of a brownstone on an idyllic, tree-lined street in downtown Jersey City. He'd left New York City proper soon after he'd quit his job at Smith's Sweets. There had been too many distractions in the city, i.e., the people he used to hang around. He'd thought that moving out of the city would help, and it had, coupled with a decent amount of willpower to leave his old lifestyle behind and his decision to take up running again.

He turned on the coffee machine that Amara had bought him for Christmas last year. It was complicated and had a billion buttons, but it made an excellent cappuccino. After he got the machine going, he sat at his kitchen table and stared at the digital clock above the stove. He waited a full minute. Then he took a steadying breath and FaceTimed his mom.

"Oh, my second born has finally deigned to acknowledge his mother's existence," Celeste said, by way of hello. She was sitting in her office at the Smith's Sweets headquarters in Hamilton, about an hour south of Jersey City. A blown-up framed photograph of his grandparents' original bakery hung on the wall behind Celeste's head. Her hair was cut into a short, blunt bob, and she was dressed smartly in a cream sleeveless turtleneck with matching pearl earrings. She tilted her head as she looked at Jeremiah. "Are you done ignoring me now?"

"Heyyy, Ma," he sang sheepishly. "You look beautiful this morning."

Celeste gave him a look, which let him know that flattery wasn't going to get him very far.

"Sorry, I've been getting ready for a meeting," he said.

Celeste arched a perfectly tweezed eyebrow. "And were you getting ready for a meeting yesterday and the day before that and the day before that too?"

Jeremiah winced. "Yes?"

Celeste shook her head on a sigh. "Who's the meeting with?"

"Shop Mart." As a peace offering, he asked, "Any advice for me?"

The corners of Celeste's mouth curved into a smile. She'd respected his decision to leave Smith's Sweets and try to make his way on his own, and she'd reminded him that she'd always be there if he needed her. Now she loved when he came to her for business advice.

"Be yourself, honey," she said. "The Shop Mart team is selective. If they're taking the meeting with you, they've most likely already decided that they want your product and they just want to feel you out in person before saying yes. Trust yourself. You know how to sell."

A natural-born salesman. That's what Pop had called him.

On Jeremiah's first day at the Smith's Sweets office, Pop had walked him around and formally introduced him to everyone. By that point, Pop had long since retired and left the company in the capable hands of Celeste, his only child. But his second grandson joining the family business had been a big deal, and he'd wanted to be present for the occasion.

Unfortunately, as it turned out, if there was an award for Smith's Sweet's Least Motivated, Most Distracted Employee, Jeremiah would have won it easily.

Sometimes Jeremiah thought about his last conversation with Pop before he died, and he wished that he could give himself a lobotomy in order to forget the utterly disappointed look on his grandfather's face as he witnessed Jeremiah stumble into their family beach house after yet another night of partying.

"You know why I'm calling, don't you?" Celeste asked, snapping Jeremiah back to the present.

Behind him, the coffee machine beeped. Jeremiah slanted his eyes at his mom as he grabbed the steaming mug and sat in front of his phone again.

"Mom . . . I won't be able to make it out to the house this weekend," he said. "I'm sorry."

"I'm not willing to accept that answer."

Jeremiah sighed. "Mom."

"*Jeremiah*," she countered.

It was a family tradition to spend the majority of their summers at their vacation home in Heart Beach, New Jersey. Every weekend, beginning with Memorial Day Weekend and ending with Labor Day weekend, the Smiths inhabited the Heart Beach house. As Jeremiah and his siblings grew older and they spent their summers studying abroad or going on vacations with their friends, they came and went from the house as they pleased. But it was a guarantee that on the weekend, the house would be filled with chatter and laughter, and inevitably someone would complain about how there never seemed to be a way to completely get rid of the sand by the front door.

His grandparents had bought the house when his mom was a kid. Now that Percy and his wife, Robin, had their twin daughters and a new baby on the way, the house had seen four generations of the Smith family.

If someone asked Jeremiah to picture his happy place, his brain would immediately conjure the Heart Beach house. Some of his most cherished memories took place there. But his most painful memory took place there as well. He hadn't been to Heart Beach in two years. Not since the summer before last, when he'd stupidly argued with Pop the night before he died.

"You didn't come down at all last summer," Celeste said. "And I let it slide, but two summers away is too long. You've already missed Memorial Day Weekend and the Juneteenth parade. Harper and Ashley keep asking when you'll be here. You're their favorite uncle."

Jeremiah laughed and rubbed his temple. "I'm their only uncle."

He loved his nieces. Loved them so much he made regular visits to see them even though it meant seeing their dad, Percy. For most of Jeremiah's life, he and Percy had been close, even if Jeremiah struggled with being in his perfect older brother's shadow. But their relationship had become strained since Jeremiah's decision to leave Smith's Sweets. Percy was vice president of operations. In many ways, both professional and personal, Percy was Celeste's right hand.

"And what about your sister?" Celeste asked. "You don't think it's going to break her heart that you're missing her birthday barbecue?"

"What birthday barbecue?" Jeremiah said, blinking. Amara was turning twenty-seven next week, and he'd planned to gift her an edition of her favorite novel, *Dracula*, that she didn't already own. Then he'd take her to watch one of those weird indie horror films that she liked at the Angelika theater in the East Village. This birthday barbecue was news to him.

"We didn't do anything for her twenty-sixth birthday last year," Celeste said. Jeremiah was able to read between the lines as to what she wasn't saying. That they'd all been too sad about their first summer without Pop to celebrate much of anything. "So I've decided we'll have a big party to make up for it next weekend."

"Does Amara know?" He'd last talked to his sister on the phone two days ago, and she hadn't mentioned it.

"She knows now because I just told her before I told you."

Jeremiah smirked, shaking his head at his mom. It was a classic Celeste move to ask for forgiveness rather than permission.

"There's a lot going on with the company before I move," Jeremiah said. "I just don't know if I'll be able to make it down before the gala in a few weeks."

Once every summer, the family hosted the Smith Foundation fundraiser gala in Heart Beach. It was a black-tie affair, and all the proceeds went toward investing in Black businesses in New Jersey. They hadn't hosted the gala last summer, mainly because it had been hard to imagine hosting the gala without Pop. But this year, they'd all mutually agreed that they couldn't skip the gala again. Even though Jeremiah was avoiding the Heart Beach house, he couldn't miss the gala. It was too important of an event for their family. Each Smith needed to be there to represent.

"That is my point exactly," Celeste said. "This is going to be your last summer living on the East Coast. Heart Beach is only an hour-and-a-half drive from Jersey City. A six-hour flight from California will be a lot less convenient. At the very least, you can come down for Amara's party and then come back again for the gala."

Celeste was a formidable businesswoman. Jeremiah admired that quality in her. But it also meant that she was a relentless parent to bargain with. Celeste and Percy Sr., Jeremiah's dad, had divorced not too long after Amara was born, and to this day, Jeremiah's dad said that Celeste was the only person who could convince him to do anything that she wanted.

Jeremiah sighed again. "Mom."

"Yes?"

But he didn't respond, because he realized the time and quickly finished his coffee. He winced as the hot liquid burned his tongue and throat. He slipped his laptop into his satchel and slung it over his shoulder. He slid his feet into his loafers and grabbed his car keys off the kitchen island. According to Amara, his last apartment had looked like *the typical bachelor pad from hell*, so he'd hired an interior designer to decorate his new place. Most of his furniture was shades of oat and gray. He'd thought it was a pretty sophisticated look, but Amara said it now looked like he lived in a doctor's office. He should probably stop asking his sister for her opinions on his living space. It didn't matter anyway. His things would be packed up and shipped across the country in a couple months. And he didn't host people at his apartment that often. Not like when he'd lived on the Lower East Side. He'd had people over all the time back then. It had been a different life.

He locked the door behind him and walked downstairs and outside.

"Is this about your new girlfriend again?" Celeste asked.

Jeremiah stopped short as he unlocked his car door.

Ah, yes. His stupid lie coming to bite him in the ass, as expected.

Back in May, before Memorial Day Weekend, Celeste had tried to persuade Jeremiah to come to Heart Beach. Unwilling to tell her the real reason he didn't want to be in Heart Beach unless absolutely necessary, he'd blurted a lie about having plans with his new girlfriend. A girlfriend who didn't actually exist. And because Celeste often made comments about how Jeremiah was pushing thirty but hadn't yet met a nice girl to settle down with like Percy, she'd immediately dropped the Memorial Day Weekend questions, and instead had peppered him with questions about his "girlfriend." Jeremiah had remained evasive, claiming that he didn't want to share too much in case things didn't work out. He'd promised to tell

Celeste and everyone else more about his girlfriend once he was sure that she was the one. In reality, he hadn't gone on a date in almost a year. All part of his grand plan to work on himself. But Celeste had been so relieved that he was finally seriously dating someone, she'd accepted his lie. And she'd accepted it again when he'd told her he couldn't make it to Heart Beach for Juneteenth because he already had plans with his girlfriend.

He couldn't tell his mom the truth. That the thought of being at the Heart Beach house was too painful. Jeremiah didn't want any of his family to know that on the last night of Pop's life, he'd come home drunk, and while everyone else had been sleeping, Pop had waited up for him and given him some tough love and encouraged him to get his life together. Instead of absorbing Pop's words, Jeremiah had taken offense to them and stormed out mid-conversation, like he was some misunderstood victim who needed an escape from his charmed life. He'd planned to apologize to Pop in the morning, but sometime overnight, Pop had suffered a heart attack in his sleep.

Jeremiah was too ashamed to talk about that night. He just wanted to focus on trying to make Pop proud and being a better person, even if Pop was no longer there to see Jeremiah's efforts. It was why he made sure to share information about his family's foundation whenever he came across businesses that could use their help. It was why he volunteered for a youth mentorship program for high schoolers during the school year and bought their uniforms and school supplies, and he fulfilled supply orders for teachers in the state too. Thanks to his grandparents, he'd been put in a position where he could help others, and that was what he wanted to focus on doing—what he always should have been focused on, honestly.

And trying to be a better person was why he'd left Smith's Sweets. He doubted he'd ever be as good for the company as his mom and siblings. They didn't need him. In fact, he'd only ever been in their way. The best thing for him to do had been to step aside.

Going back to Heart Beach this summer for longer than necessary, having no escape from his grief and guilt, would be too hard. It could upend the progress he'd made. He'd mentally prepared himself to return in August for one night for the gala. Next weekend was too soon. He wasn't ready.

And that was why he continued with his stupid lie and said, "Uh, yeah, my girlfriend and I have plans this weekend. We got tickets to a show she's been wanting to see. It's the last show of the run, and she doesn't want to miss it."

"A musical or play?"

Good question. "A musical. *Cats*, I think."

Celeste's brows shot up. "You're seeing *Cats*? When did that return to Broadway?"

"It didn't," he hastened to say. Why the hell had he said *Cats*? It was the only musical he could think of, mostly because the movie version that had scared his nieces. "It's Off-Broadway. An Off-Broadway *Cats* spin-off."

"She must really be something if she's got you seeing a spin-off of *Cats*."

Jeremiah cleared his throat. "Yeah, she's pretty special."

Celeste fell quiet, eyeing him. Jeremiah tried not to squirm.

He placed his satchel in the passenger seat before sitting at the wheel. He was about to tell Celeste that he needed to start driving and he'd have to call her later—at least this was true. But to his surprise, Celeste smiled fondly at him.

"You look so much like him," she said. "Sometimes it throws me."

She was talking about Pop. While Percy resembled and was named after their father, all his life, Jeremiah had been told how much he looked like their grandfather. He had Pop's height and jawline, the shape of his eyes and mouth. When he was younger, he used to make Pop stand beside him in the mirror so that they could point out each similarity together.

"Yeah," he said quietly.

After a moment, Celeste said, "I miss him too. We all do."

Jeremiah swallowed thickly. An image of his grandfather flashed in his mind. Pop smiling over at Jeremiah as they stood waist-deep in the ocean, the waves moving around them.

Jeremiah inhaled and exhaled deeply.

"It was hard after we lost Grandma when you were so young," Celeste continued. "Now Pop is gone too. Heart Beach isn't the same without him, I know that. But we still have each other. I want you to be there with us. We *all* do. Is that so much to ask? Spend some time with us in Heart Beach this summer before you move, Miah. Please."

His mom was a lot of things. Persistent and fierce. Loving and opinionated. And she was even-keeled. She rarely let her feathers get ruffled or openly showed signs of distress. Seeing her shaky expression threw Jeremiah. It made him feel like shit. He was breaking his mom's heart and that was the last thing he wanted to do.

"Okay," he said, deflating. "I can't promise every weekend, but I'll be there next weekend for Amara's party, and then I'll come back for the gala."

Celeste's expression immediately brightened. Instant relief

washed over Jeremiah at the sight of his mom's smile, even if the thought of going back to Heart Beach made his stomach sink.

"Perfect!" Celeste said. "I'll have your room all set up for you. I've gotta go. Good luck at your meeting. Knock 'em dead, honey. Oh! And bring your girlfriend next weekend. I can't wait to meet the woman who's kept you so preoccupied!"

Oh shit. He'd forgotten his girlfriend lie that fast again. "Mom, wait—"

Celeste blew a kiss and hung up.

Damn. He could tell Celeste that he'd lied about having a girlfriend, but that would only make things worse and hurt her feelings. Then she'd push him on why he'd felt the need to lie in the first place. She'd dig, unrelenting, to discover his true reason for avoiding the beach house.

As ridiculous as it sounded, it would be much easier if he continued his lie and somehow brought a girlfriend with him next weekend.

Maybe he could bring a friend and have her pretend to be his girlfriend. Problem was, he was short on friends these days. If the crew he used to hang around could even really be called friends.

Maybe he could hire someone.

Nah, that was stupid.

He started his car. He had a meeting to get to, a pitch to land. And he had to buy Amara's birthday gift. He'd done some poking around online and apparently there was a bookstore right here in Jersey City called Hidden Gems Books that had a nice selection of vintage editions. He was going to swing by there after his meeting.

He'd figure out a plan for his nonexistent girlfriend after.

Chapter Three

"If I wasn't with André, this is the kind of man I'd want in my life," Tati said to Noelle.

Noelle glanced up at the mass-market paperback novel that Tati held in her hands. *The Pirate Captain's Lover* by Clara Crawford. A brown-skinned, shirtless man donned the cover, displaying his perfectly sculpted abs. Tati ran her fingers over the cover and blew the book a kiss.

"You'd want to date a pirate?" Noelle asked, smirking.

She and Tati were sitting pretzel-style on the floor of the romance aisle at Hidden Gems Books. Between them was a box of vintage romance novels that Noelle had acquired for the store from an estate sale. Almost thirty books for a whopping ten dollars. It had first-edition copies of Clara Crawford's Pirates of the Deep series, and a second box was filled with mass-market cozy mysteries and spy novels from the early '90s. The woman who'd owned the house had obviously been an avid reader.

"Why not?" Tati said. "Being with a pirate is probably so much fun. And you know the pirate in this book is probably rich as hell from all that looting or whatever it is that pirates do."

Noelle laughed. "You should read that one," she said, nodding at the book in Tati's hands. "It's about a woman who's running away from her evil husband, and she thinks she's boarding a ship to England, but she accidentally ends up on a pirate ship and falls in love with the pirate captain. It's so good. Wait, actually . . ." She sifted through the box until she found what she was looking for. *My One True Pirate*. "This is the second book in the series. After a shipwreck, one of the pirates gets marooned on an island with a woman who's pretending to be a maid, but she's actually an heiress."

"*Oh?*" Tati gathered her long twists at the nape of her neck and reached for the book. Her makeup was flawless today, as per usual, and her black scrubs hugged her curves. Even Noelle's coworker Kevin, who usually ignored everyone, especially customers, glanced up from his phone as Tati had walked into the store earlier. Tati flipped the book over in her hands and skimmed the description on the back. "Sounds juicy. I'll buy both."

Noelle flashed a satisfied grin. That was at least two sales for the day. Her boss, Harold, entrusted her with sourcing books from estate and library sales, and she was in charge of sifting through the books that people sold and donated to the store. But her favorite part about her job was hand-selling to customers. It never got old. Even if she were only selling to Tati, who worked at the beauty salon across the street. One of Tati's clients had canceled at the last minute, so she was spending her unexpected break on the floor of the bookstore with Noelle as she shelved books.

Noelle was glad she got to see her best friend when their work schedules overlapped. And Harold never seemed to mind when Tati visited. Maybe it was because without Noelle and Tati's chatter, the bookstore was too quiet. This year had been their slowest in foot traffic in a while.

"I wish I could read as fast as you," Tati said. "You read like your life depends on it."

"It kind of does."

Noelle wasn't joking. A kind librarian and a handful of books had saved her life.

Noelle's mom had been the first in her family to go to college, and Noelle was determined to be the second. Because college was so expensive, Noelle applied for as many scholarships as she could. Each year, EmpoWOMENt, a nonprofit in New Jersey, hosted an essay contest for girls entering their senior year of high school. The essay winner received a full-ride scholarship to the college of their choice. In Noelle's essay, she wrote about how her mom was her biggest hero and she was inspired by how hard her mom worked. What she'd written must have resonated with the judges because she won the contest, and the organization paid for her to attend UMD.

At the start of college, she was directionless in terms of choosing her major before she finally settled on sociology sophomore year because she'd already taken a few sociology courses. Then she met CJ at the beginning of her junior year and things went downhill. CJ was at UMD on an athletic scholarship, and talented as he might have been at basketball, he couldn't have cared less about his grades. When he admitted to Noelle that he'd always struggled in school because he'd grown up in a chaotic household with parents who argued constantly, she threw herself into helping him study. She focused more on helping CJ than she focused on her own classes. But she thought that helping him was the right thing to do, noble even. Because she loved him.

Then came the night that he asked her to hide his bottle of tequila in her dorm room. His RA conducted rounds often, whereas Noelle's RA was more relaxed. Noelle and CJ got into an argument because she didn't want to keep his liquor for him. One, she would get into a lot of trouble if she were caught with it. And two, she had a Social Movements final in the morning, and she'd realized a little too late that the time she'd spent helping CJ meant she hadn't spent enough time studying for her own classes. Their argument was starting to get loud, and CJ finally stormed away, leaving her with his bottle. At a loss, Noelle stored the bottle under her bed and planned to toss it in the morning. But that had been the wrong move. Down the hall, her RA had heard bits and pieces of her argument with CJ, namely the words *tequila* and *party*. Her RA came knocking on her door, and Noelle, who wasn't twenty-one yet, was caught with alcohol in a dry dorm.

Later, before her hearing, when she'd realized that her scholarship was on the line, she'd begged CJ to tell the truth and admit the alcohol was his. At first, he said that he would. But then he'd backpedaled. He'd been too worried about losing his own scholarship. Plus, she'd broken up with him, which had made him bitter. It had been her word against his, and there was proof of Noelle having the liquor in her possession. The violation went against EmpoWOMENt's code of conduct, and Noelle lost her scholarship. It was the end of her junior year, and she couldn't afford UMD, or college in general, without financial help. She qualified for some federal loans, but they weren't enough to cover everything. When she tried to apply for private loans, she was denied. And she definitely didn't want her mom to take out loans on her behalf.

Reality hit her like a ton of bricks. She wouldn't be able to return in the fall to finish her final year and graduate. That summer, Noelle went home, embarrassed and ashamed. Portia seemed to be the only one on Noelle's side. She'd wanted to take action and get CJ to tell the truth, but Noelle just wanted to forget that any of it ever happened. At the end of the day, even if the liquor was CJ's, she chose to hide it under her bed. She begged her mom to let it go so that they could move on.

Soon after, just when it seemed like things couldn't get much worse, one day on her way home from work, Portia got into a car accident. Her injuries—three fractured ribs and a fractured pelvis—required multiple surgeries and a lengthy recovery stay in the hospital. Noelle spent most of her days in Portia's hospital room. Portia slept a lot, and the television in her room worked only when it wanted to. Noelle avoided social media because she didn't want to see pictures of the UMD friends who'd quickly stopped responding to her texts once they realized she wasn't coming back. As her mom slept, she was left to sit with her thoughts and failures.

On one of those quiet, forlorn days, a nurse took pity on Noelle.

"There's a library across the street," the nurse said. "Maybe you can find a book to read to pass the time while you're here?"

"Oh." Noelle blinked and glanced at her mom, who had just fallen asleep again after eating lunch.

"Your mom's okay," the nurse gently reassured her. "I'll come back to check on her."

Noelle stood and bit her lip. She didn't want to leave, but she also didn't want the nurse to see her as a problem. They were nice enough to let her stay after visiting hours ended sometimes. She didn't want to lose those privileges.

She walked across the street to the library. The building was large with a dome-shaped ceiling. As she stepped inside, she was hit with a cold gust of air-conditioning. Three librarians were seated in front of computers at the reference desk. Straight ahead was the children's books section with colorful chairs and rugs. Noelle walked farther inside, and to her left, she saw rows of books in the nonfiction section. She glanced up at the second floor and saw even more shelves. She didn't know where to begin her search. She couldn't remember the last time she'd read a book that wasn't required reading for school. What kinds of books did she even like? It was overwhelming. *Everything* was overwhelming. Losing her scholarship. Not going back to UMD. Breaking up with CJ. Her mom's accident.

She felt her face get hot and tears gathered at the back of her eyes as she stood frozen by the reference desk.

"Can I help you with anything?"

Startled, Noelle turned to see a librarian standing beside her. The woman spoke in a soft voice and she wore tortoiseshell glasses.

"Um" was all Noelle got out before she started to cry.

"Oh, honey, it's all right." The librarian walked Noelle to the reference desk and handed her a tissue. "What's bothering you?"

Noelle realized no one had asked her that question yet, and it made her cry even harder. Through tears, she told the librarian about losing her scholarship and her mom's accident.

"It sounds like maybe you need to read something that will help you relax," the librarian suggested gently once Noelle finished talking. "Something immersive to take your mind off things. Do you like fantasy?"

Noelle shrugged and sniffled. "I can give it a try."

The librarian smiled. She brought Noelle to the fiction section and handed her a fantasy novel about warring witch covens. Then she gave her a romance novel about rival coworkers who were competing for the same promotion. Afterward, she signed Noelle up for a library card. She told Noelle that her name was Margaret.

Books in hand, Noelle thanked Margaret and returned to her mom's hospital room. Portia was still sleeping, so Noelle started the fantasy novel. She continued reading until the nurse stopped by to let her know that visiting hours had ended. Noelle was so engrossed in the book, she'd completely lost track of time.

She finished the book two days later, even though it was almost five hundred pages long. She started the romance novel next and inhaled that one too. When she was reading, she wasn't thinking about the stressful state of her life. Reading had helped her relax, just like Margaret had said.

At the end of the week, Noelle returned to the library and asked for more recommendations. Soon she was reading two, sometimes three, books a week. When her mom came home from the hospital and started physical therapy, Noelle read in the car while waiting for her mom's appointments to end. She read everything. Fantasy, sci-fi, romance, suspense, memoirs. Books had become a source of light during a dark time.

A new goal began to take shape in Noelle's mind. She was so grateful to Margaret for helping her, and she wanted to pass on that same joy to more people. She researched the steps required to become a librarian. She wasn't surprised to find that she'd need to finish her bachelor's degree, but she didn't know that she'd need a master's degree too. It didn't matter, though. She knew that she wanted to be a librarian. And that meant she'd need to start saving to go back to college.

Once Portia's health improved and she needed less of Noelle's help, Noelle started looking for jobs. She applied to every bookstore in their area, and the first store to call her back was Hidden Gems Books. During her interview, Noelle talked about how reading *Parable of the Sower* had been a transformative experience, and her boss, Harold, hired her on the spot.

That was six years ago.

"Here, be my model," Noelle said to Tati now.

She motioned for Tati to hold up the books in the Pirates of the Deep series. She also handed her book three, *The Pirate Who Loved Me*. Tati held the books in front of her and smiled.

"Gorgeous," Noelle said. She opened their Instagram page and uploaded the photo, typing out the caption, Any Clara Crawford fans out there? We've got first editions of her beloved Pirates of the Deep series! Stop by the store before they're gone!

"When are you gonna start paying me for being the star of Hidden Gems' Instagram account?" Tati asked.

Noelle snorted. "Once Harold starts paying me more to run the account."

Harold had opened the bookstore almost twenty years ago, and they sold only used books. Harold said more people needed to pay attention to the literature that had come before in order to appreciate what books were being published now. Noelle respected that Harold wanted to maintain the integrity of his store, but because they weren't selling the newer, popular books, they were making less money. She was getting fewer hours. When she was first hired, she'd basically worked full-time. Then it lessened to thirty-five hours. Then to thirty. Now it was a good week if she got twenty-five hours. It was one of the reasons she'd turned to Bridal Bestie and food delivery for more money. She loved working at Hidden Gems Books, and it would probably look good on her résumé when she applied to librarian positions in the future. She hoped her social media efforts might help turn the store's luck around.

"Noelle?"

Noelle sat up on her knees and turned around to see Harold poking his head out of the office.

"Can you come in here for a second?" he asked.

"Be right there!" Noelle stood, and Tati stood as well, stretching her arms above her head.

"I'd better get back across the street," she said. She pointed at Noelle. "I'll be home tonight. We still good for *Married to Medicine*?"

"You know it."

Tati waggled her fingers, and the bell above the door chimed as she left the store.

Noelle did a quick sweep of the floor to check for customers—they didn't have any. But Kevin, who was also Harold's nephew, was standing at the register, staring at his phone. Harold had hired Kevin and his twin brother, George, as a favor to their mom last year. So far, they weren't proving to be great employees. And because they were the only two booksellers besides Noelle, she ended up doing most of the work whenever they were on the same shift.

She walked to the back of the store and stood in the office

doorway. Harold was sitting behind the desk, staring pensively at a sheet of paper. His glasses had slid to the edge of his nose. He ran a hand over his graying beard.

"Hey, you wanted to see me?" Noelle said, stepping into the office.

Harold glanced up. "Yes, Noelle. Please have a seat. How's everything going out there?"

"Fine," she said, sitting down across from him. "Slow, but fine."

"I wanted to thank you again for driving all the way out to Clayton for that estate sale."

"No problem." She shrugged easily and smiled. "All part of the job."

Harold smiled too, and that was the first sign to Noelle that something was off. Harold was a fair boss, but he wasn't a particularly happy person, and he most definitely was not someone who smiled during small talk. The best word to describe Harold would be *curmudgeonly*. Also, his eyes looked sad. Noelle tensed in her chair.

"Is everything okay?" she asked.

"No. Noelle, I have some not-so-great news." His shoulders deflated. "You know we've been having issues with our sales for a while now, and the landlord let me know last night that he's increasing our rent again. I've been sitting here running the numbers all morning." He sighed and shook his head. "I'm sorry, Noelle, but I'm going to have to let you go."

For a second, Noelle simply blinked at him. She repeated his words, once, twice. Even then, it took another full minute for what he'd said to sink in.

"Wait . . . you're firing me?"

"I don't see it like that," Harold hastened to say. "It's more like I'm downsizing on employees."

"Wow," she said quietly. She thought of Kevin and George, who basically twiddled their thumbs for the entirety of their shifts. But, of course, if it came down to firing Noelle or Kevin or George to save money, Harold wasn't going to fire his family.

"I'm so sorry," he said. "You're great, and I hate to lose you. You can put me down as a reference for your next job, and I promise to sing your praises."

Noelle stared at the mug of pens on the desk. She didn't know what to say, what to think. She knew the store had been struggling. She'd anticipated the possibility of losing more hours, but she hadn't anticipated losing her job *entirely*.

She'd been counting on money that she made from her main job here at Hidden Gems Books to go toward her tuition savings. What was she going to do now? She could apply for unemployment, but it would take weeks for her claim to be approved by the state. Recently, she heard that it could take up to a month or more, due to the high volume of applications. She couldn't wait that long. Her stomach filled with thousand-pound stones, weighing her to the chair.

"I get it," she said, swallowing hard. She took a deep breath. "Should I . . . clock out now?"

"No, no," Harold said. "You can finish your shift."

Noelle nodded. He was giving her some grace. For that, she should probably be grateful.

"Thank you."

An awkward silence permeated the room. Harold cleared his throat and stared at his hands. Noelle wanted to leave the office, but her whole body felt like hard cement. She was still in shock. When the awkward silence became unbearable, she forced herself to stand.

"I guess I'd better finish unpacking the boxes from the estate sale."

"All right." Harold's voice was gruffer than usual. He glanced up at her and he looked so sad, there was no way that Noelle could be upset with him.

Quietly, she left the office. She was in a daze as she walked through the bookstore. Kevin was standing at the register, still texting. He didn't even look up at the sound of Noelle's footsteps. She ignored him and gazed around the store. She looked at the staff-picks shelf, the display of beach reads, and the table of picture books dedicated to summer. Those had all been her ideas. She'd poured every ounce of her creative energy into this job and the curation of the books on these shelves. It wasn't only about the money. Hidden Gems Books had been her home away from home for the past six years. And now she was losing it.

Her phone vibrated in her back pocket. With slow, stilted movements, Noelle pulled her phone out and read a text from Sheree.

> Hey! Brian lives close by so he's bringing your jacket to your job. He should be there within the next couple minutes!

Oh, *fuck* this timing.

The last thing that she wanted to do was have another conversation with the groomsman who couldn't take the hint that she wasn't interested. But she wanted her jacket back. *Ugh.* Hopefully this interaction would end quickly.

"I'm stepping outside really quick," she said to Kevin.

He mumbled something that sounded like *okay*. His eyes remained glued to his phone.

It was hot outside. Kids were playing in the park at the end of the block, and the fried chicken sandwich spot next door was busy with customers. Directly across the street, Noelle watched Tati curl her client's hair. Tati said something, and her client covered her mouth as she laughed. Using telepathic best-friend powers, Tati suddenly glanced over and caught eyes with Noelle. *What's wrong?* she mouthed, frowning. Noelle shook her head and mouthed back *I'll tell you later.*

"Noelle! Hey!"

She turned at the sound of her name. Brian was jogging down the sidewalk toward her, holding her jacket. He was wearing a T-shirt and running shorts, like maybe he'd just come from the gym. At least this time he wasn't drunk. She mustered a smile.

"Hey, Brian," she said. "Thanks so much for bringing my jacket. I really appreciate it."

She reached to take the jacket, but Brian kept hold of it. Her brows pinched together in confusion as he sported a wide grin.

"Yeah, I was over at Sheree and Justin's last night, and Sheree mentioned that she'd have to take the PATH into Jersey City to drop off your jacket," he said. "And I told her I could do it since I live so close by. Plus, you and I didn't have a chance to finish our conversation from the other night."

Noelle groaned inwardly. "It was so nice of you to bring the jacket to me. I have to get back to work, though."

She reached for the jacket again, but Brian took a deliberate step back and held her jacket out of reach.

"What're your plans for the weekend?" he asked. "My boy is having a cookout. I'd love to bring you. And I'm not a cheap date either, so you don't gotta worry about that."

Noelle narrowed her eyes. She was finally able to pin down what it was about Brian that rubbed her the wrong way, aside from how he was holding her jacket hostage. His overly confident demeanor and complete inability to read the room or *her* reminded her of CJ. She hadn't known how to look for red flags in college. But she knew how to look for them now. She wanted to tell Brian to take a damn hint, but she was nervous that he'd badmouth her to Sheree and cause her to lose her bridesmaid gig. She needed that job more than ever now.

"I have to work this weekend," she said. With a sting, she realized that was no longer true, at least not for Hidden Gems Books. She'd definitely do food delivery this weekend, though.

She lunged for her jacket again and clasped on to one of the sleeves. With a hard tug, she snatched the jacket from Brian's grip and draped the jacket over her shoulder.

"Damn, girl," Brian said, laughing. "Relax."

God. Universe. Whoever. Please do something before I haul off and punch this man.

And then God, or the universe, or whoever, heard Noelle's plea.

A sleek, silver car suddenly turned onto the street and pulled up right in front of the bookstore. The windows were tinted dark. The car was so shiny, sunlight sparkled off the hood. It looked like a magnificent car from the future. Even Brian fell quiet and openly stared. The driver cut the engine and opened the door.

Noelle watched as a pair of black leather loafers hit the pavement. Then as she raised her gaze, she observed a set of long legs, covered in dark gray slacks. Her eyes traveled higher and skimmed over a well-built torso, until they reached the driver's face. The man, who looked to be around her age, had brown skin and a square jaw covered by a thick but well-trimmed beard. His hair was cut into a fade and his waves looked smooth.

Noelle spared a quick glance across the street. Tati and her client were gaping out the window at the newcomer. Tati made eye contact with Noelle and mouthed, *Who is that?!*

Noelle shrugged. She looked at the man again. She could hardly take her eyes off him. He glanced to his right and left, then down at his phone, before squinting up at the **HIDDEN GEMS BOOKS** sign above her head. Then he looked directly at Noelle and smiled.

Her stomach muscles clenched. Not just because his smile damn near dazzled the wits out of her. But because he looked familiar. Had they met before?

"Do you work here?" the man asked. He had a deep, smooth voice.

Noelle blinked. Her tongue was a frozen block of ice in her mouth. The question seemed so out of place. Surely, she'd misheard him. "I'm sorry?"

He pointed at her shirt, then at the sign above her head. "Sorry, I mean at the bookstore. Do you work here? Is the store still open right now?"

"Oh." She cleared her throat. "Um. Yes. We're open."

"Thanks." He smiled again, and this time Noelle smiled back, transfixed. She felt the warmth of his smile deep in her belly. His eyes were a soft shade of brown, almost sepia. He continued to smile at her as he walked past her to the door. She got a whiff of his cologne. It smelled spicy.

The man cast a brief glance at Brian and nodded in acknowledgment. Brian frowned, most likely out of jealousy, which Noelle found hilarious. Then the man disappeared inside the bookstore, and Noelle stood there feeling like she'd just witnessed an expensive-cologne ad come to life.

"So, about this weekend . . ." Brian said. "What time should I pick you up?"

He was a walking record scratch.

"Brian, please listen to me," Noelle said. "I do *not* want to go out with you."

Brian screwed his face up into a frown. "Why the hell not? It's not like you've got anything better going on." He gestured to the bookstore behind her.

Noelle narrowed her eyes. Maybe she was going to have to punch him after all.

She balled her hands into fists and took a step closer. "Brian—"

Suddenly, the bookstore door swung open, and the handsome stranger stepped outside again. He was looking at Noelle, but this time his smile was even brighter, if that was possible.

"I *thought* that was you," he said to Noelle. He reached her in quick, long strides. "It's been a minute since we last saw each other. You remember me, right? I'm Jeremiah. We met last year at that thing."

Noelle's eyes widened in confusion. Met at that thing? *What* thing?

The man (Jeremiah?) took a deliberate step directly in front of Brian, and Brian shuffled backward and glared at the back of the man's (Jeremiah's?) head. Noelle was instantly relieved to have a buffer between her and Brian, but she was still confused, trying to recall whatever event from last year that this man was referring to. Maybe that was why he looked familiar. He glanced over and eyed Brian, who was hovering off to the side, still frowning. He turned to Noelle again.

"It's really good to see you," he said. "Is it cool if we hug?"

She blinked. Out of the corner of her eye, she could see Brian beginning to back farther away. She pounced at the chance to hopefully get rid of him for good.

She looked at the handsome stranger before her and nodded eagerly. "It's so good to see you too," she said.

She opened her arms, and the man (Jeremiah, he definitely said his name was Jeremiah) reached for Noelle and pulled her into his chest. His body was warm, and up close, his spicy cologne was almost intoxicating.

Noelle was able to confirm that she had *not* met this man before. Because she would *definitely* have remembered a hug like this.

Chapter Four

The hug seemed to last for an eternity. Noelle's lips brushed against his shirt. The fabric felt crisp and smooth. Expensive. What kind of cotton was this shirt made out of? She had no idea what had come over her, but she almost didn't want to let go of this man. Instead of pulling away, she leaned in closer.

His chest rose and fell as he breathed and she could hear the steady pounding of his heart. She peeked her head around the man's arm and saw that Brian had finally walked away. Thank goodness. Brian glanced over his shoulder one last time and puckered his lips in a sour frown. Across the street, Tati was staring out the salon window at Noelle, mouth agape. Noelle could practically see the question marks floating above Tati's head. But she didn't have any answers because she wasn't entirely sure what was happening either.

Reluctantly, she pulled away from the handsome stranger who claimed to know her. He looked down at her and smiled. Again, she was struck by a sense of familiarity, but she still couldn't place him. Maybe she actually *had* seen him in a cologne ad before.

"I'm sorry," she said. "But I actually don't think I remember you."

He chuckled and shook his head. "That's because we've never met." He pointed his thumb in the direction in which Brian had disappeared. "You seemed uncomfortable with that dude and it looked like you needed an out."

Noelle smiled, relieved that she hadn't somehow forgotten meeting Jeremiah before. Maybe she'd seen him on the PATH once, and that was why he looked familiar.

"Thank you," she said. "You saved him from getting punched, so he should be thanking you too."

"We don't need you catching any charges," he said, laughing. "My name really is Jeremiah, though. What's yours?"

"Noelle."

"Noelle," he repeated. He smiled slowly this time, like he was savoring the sound of her name. "Nice to meet you, Noelle."

He held out his hand, and goose bumps spread across Noelle's skin as their palms pressed together. His hand was much larger than hers, and other than the calluses on the inside of his palm, his skin was smooth.

"It's nice to meet you too," she said, gazing down at his long fingers.

"He an ex or something?"

Noelle tore her attention away from their clasped hands and looked up at Jeremiah's face. "No. God, no. He's just some guy I met at my other job."

"Ah." Jeremiah smirked, and a dimple appeared on his left cheek. "So, you were gonna punch him? Let me find out you have a mean right hook. You a boxer?"

He began examining her knuckles, and Noelle shook her head and laughed as he turned her hands this way and that, peering at her skin. He glanced up and looked at her through his lashes. Then he flashed a disarmingly charming smile, and Noelle could do nothing but smile back as a flight of butterflies began a feverish swarm in her stomach.

"I, um," she started, then stopped.

She, *um, what*? She had no idea how to finish her sentence. The butterflies had traveled upstream and were currently discombobulating her brain.

Jeremiah politely ignored her sudden inability to form a complete thought.

He released her hands but kept his eyes firmly on her face.

"I could use your help finding a book—if your shift isn't over, that is," he said. "Would you be able to help me?"

Right. Her job. The one that she'd be losing by the end of the day.

"Oh yeah, of course," she said. "Please follow me."

Jeremiah held the door open for her, and the bell chimed as they stepped inside. Kevin briefly glanced up as Noelle placed her leather jacket behind the register, but he quickly became engrossed in his phone again. Noelle chewed the inside of her cheek and tried to fight her frustration. *This* was whom she was being fired in favor of?

No, she wouldn't let herself get worked up about that right now. She'd finish her shift and think all of her frustrating thoughts later, preferably with a box of Smith's Sweets cookies nearby to help soothe her battered, jobless soul.

She walked back over to Jeremiah. "What are you looking for today?"

He paused by the beach reads display table and picked up a

copy of *How Stella Got Her Groove Back* by Terry McMillan. He turned it over and peeked at the description on the back before placing the book down.

"I'm looking for a vintage copy of *Dracula*," he said. "A few people online said you had a good selection of classics."

Dracula was the last book she'd expected him to say. But so much about Jeremiah and this entire afternoon was unexpected. She might as well just roll with it.

"Sure, our classics are this way," she said, gesturing for him to follow her toward the back of the store. "Are you a big reader of classic literature?"

"Oh, nah, I don't read that much." He sent her a quick, sheepish look as he walked beside her. "I'm sure you hate hearing that."

"Not really. I read a bit of everything now, but I wasn't much of a reader for most of my life. I do think there's a book out there for everyone, though. Maybe you just haven't found yours yet."

"That's a nice thought," he said. He ran his fingers against the spines of several John Grisham novels from the '90s as they passed through the thrillers section. "Makes me feel less uncouth."

Noelle smiled. "There's a word you don't hear often."

He smirked, lifting one shoulder in a shrug. "When my siblings and I were kids, my grandfather had this thing where he would teach us a new word and if we found three ways to use it in a sentence by the end of the week, he'd give us twenty dollars."

"How old were you when he gave you 'uncouth'?"

"Thirteen. One of my sentences was 'Percy thinks I'm uncouth because I get powdered sugar all over everything when I eat funnel cake.'"

Noelle's smile widened. "Who's Percy?"

"My brother."

She laughed, and Jeremiah grinned at her.

"But for real, though, I have read *some* books," he said. "Self-help and business, stuff like that. My sister reads a lot of horror. I'm getting *Dracula* for her birthday gift. It's one of her favorite books. She has a bunch of different versions."

They came to a stop, finally arriving at the classics section.

"I like horror too," Noelle said. "Do you know the names of some of the other books she's read?"

"Umm, maybe. She likes gory shit about vampires and monsters murdering people. You wouldn't know it by looking at her, though. Then again, she does wear a lot of black, so maybe what she reads isn't that surprising. A few weeks ago, she was telling me about this book called *When a Vampire Wakes* or something like that."

"Wait, I loved that book!" In her excitement, Noelle grasped onto Jeremiah's bicep. His muscular, well-developed bicep. He glanced down at the point of contact, lifted his eyes to hers, and flashed an intrigued smile. Noelle's cheeks immediately warmed. She yanked her hand away and busied herself with searching the shelves for last names that started with *S*.

She cleared her throat. "Um, your sister sounds cool."

"Yeah, she's dope," he said.

She could feel Jeremiah watching her, but she couldn't bring herself to look at him again just yet. Her thoughts were loopy and jumbled because she was fighting an internal battle with the butterflies for control of her brain.

She pulled the three copies of *Dracula* they had in stock. A 1986 paperback edition featuring an image of Dracula hovering in the shadows, a 2003 mass-market edition with a painting of Dracula's Transylvania castle on the cover, and a more recent gray and black hardcover clothbound edition, published in 2011.

"Here's what we have," Noelle said, holding the books out to Jeremiah. "Only the 1986 edition is technically considered vintage, but all three are still in pretty good condition."

Jeremiah accepted the books from her and inspected each copy. While his attention was elsewhere, Noelle took a moment to observe him. He had full lips, and his eyelashes were unfairly long. He wore a gold watch on his wrist. She didn't know much about watches, but from the way he was dressed and from the look of his car, she would guess that his watch probably wasn't cheap, even if it was fairly understated. His Adam's apple bobbed as he swallowed, and Noelle found herself admiring his neck muscles, of all things. She wondered what it might feel like to touch his skin there.

Wow. Was she really standing here lusting after a customer?!

"I'll take this one," he said, snapping her out of her thirsty-ass daydream. He held up the hardcover clothbound edition. "I think she owns the other two already."

"Great!" Noelle's voice was a high-pitched squeak. Jesus. She needed to ring this man up and send him on his way so she could think clearly again. She took the *Dracula* editions he didn't want and returned them to the shelf.

Jeremiah leaned his shoulder against the bookshelf, making himself comfortable. "So, you said you read a bit of everything?" he said. "What's your favorite book?"

"That's hard. I have so many. *The Mothers* by Brit Bennett is probably my favorite literary novel. Definitely *Indigo* by Beverly Jenkins. That's a romance novel."

He smiled. "You like romance?"

She nodded and tried not to read too deep into the way the word *romance* rolled so smoothly off his tongue. Had he said it that way on purpose or was she imagining it? Her gaze darted from his throat to his large hands, back up to his brown eyes.

"What's your other job?" he asked.

"Huh?" The butterflies had progressed to full-on chaos. They were gnawing on the wires of her brain and sending sparks flying in every direction. What was wrong with her? She wasn't usually like this around men anymore. But maybe it was because she didn't often meet men like Jeremiah. Men who looked put together and seemed like they knew what they were doing with their lives.

Her reaction to him was also probably due to the fact that she was both touch-starved and sex-deprived. She didn't want a relationship, but she still had needs. The last time she'd hooked up with someone had been over eight months ago—a guy she'd met at a bar in New Brunswick while out one night with Tati. Tati knew him from college (and was able to verify that he wasn't a serial killer), and he was cute, and Noelle had been horny. She'd wanted mind-blowing sex, of course, but she would have been perfectly happy with plain old good sex too. Unfortunately, the guy struggled to find a stroke rhythm and Noelle had ended up faking an orgasm. She'd been in such a rush to leave his apartment, she'd tossed her underwear in her purse and driven home commando. She hadn't gotten any action since. Not that she'd actively tried to get any, though.

"You said you knew that guy earlier from your other job," Jeremiah clarified.

Oh. Right. She considered how to explain her side hustle. Sometimes when she brought up her stand-in job, which wasn't often, people didn't know what to make of it. But at the end of the day, Jeremiah was a stranger, and she probably wouldn't see him again after today.

"Sometimes I work as a bridesmaid for hire," she said.

His brows lifted as his eyes widened. His lips quirked into a smile. "Really? How do you do that?"

"I work for a company called Bridal Bestie. People who need bridesmaids reach out through the website to find someone, and the Bridal Bestie agency connects us. It's kind of like a temp agency."

"Bridal Bestie," he repeated, pulling out his phone. "Do you mind if I google it?"

"Not at all." Honestly, she was surprised that he was taking such an interest.

She watched as he pulled up the Bridal Bestie website. A picture of Clarissa Roberts, Bridal Bestie's founder, was front and center on the home page. Jeremiah read through Clarissa's explanation of how she'd first taken a gig as a bridesmaid for hire from a friend of a friend and realized she wanted to turn it into a business. Jeremiah then looked through the different packages and testimonials.

"Wow, this is brilliant," he said, looking up at Noelle. "Do you like doing it?"

"Yeah," she said. "It's pretty easy. This summer has been slower than usual, though, which isn't great because today's my last day at the bookstore."

"Are you quitting to do bridesmaid stuff full-time?"

She shook her head sadly. "No, I found out this morning that I'm being let go from here."

"Damn," Jeremiah said quietly. "I'm sorry."

"Me too. Especially because I'm planning to go back to

college in the fall, and I was counting on money from this job to go toward my tuition."

She didn't know why she was telling him all of this. It was almost like a taxicab confessional, unloading her life problems onto this handsome stranger who was thoughtfully shopping for his sister's birthday present.

"What are you planning to study?" he asked.

"Sociology," she said. "I have a year left to finish. After that I want to get my master's and become a librarian."

He smiled softly. "Sounds like you'd be perfect for that."

Her face warmed again under his focused attention. She suddenly had the urge to fan herself.

"I'm sure you probably have somewhere to be," she said. "I can check you out now."

She pointed toward the register at the front of the store, and Jeremiah fell into step beside her as they walked through the aisle.

"I'm done with work for the day, actually," he said.

"What do you do?" She glanced over at him, once again noting his sleek yet understated clothes. Clearly, he was doing well for himself.

"Do you have a dog?" he asked.

She laughed, thrown. "No, why?"

"Then you probably haven't heard of Good Boy," he said, smirking. "We're a toy company for dogs, but we're expanding into other avenues. I just had a successful meeting at Shop Mart this afternoon, actually. They're gonna start carrying our products."

"I *do* know Shop Mart," she said, and he laughed. "Congratulations."

"Thank you. We're working on an app now and moved our

operations to Northern California recently to better improve our connections. I'm moving there in September."

"Oh, that's really cool." She smiled even though she felt a confusing sense of disappointment to learn that he was moving across the country.

When they reached the register, Kevin mumbled something unintelligible before slithering away to the back office. Jeremiah watched him, then looked at Noelle and raised an eyebrow.

"Don't even ask," she said.

As she scanned the copy of *Dracula*, Jeremiah leaned against the counter and twirled a bookmark between his fingers. Noelle glanced up at him, once again trying to figure out why he looked so familiar to her.

She gave him the total for the book. "Will you be paying with cash or card?"

"Card." Jeremiah pulled out his wallet and handed her his credit card. The card had a significant weight to it, and she glanced at his name at the bottom. Jeremiah Smith. She paused. Her brain, which was recovering from the butterfly attack, was trying to tell her something.

She placed the book in a paper bag and handed it to Jeremiah, along with his card and receipt.

"Thank you for shopping local," she said.

Jeremiah took the bag and returned his card to his wallet. She waited for him to tell her goodbye and resume what was most likely his very fabulous life. Instead, he continued leaning against the counter, looking at her.

"I'm mad at myself for not coming in here before today," he said. "I don't even live that far. To think I could have been talking to you about books this whole time."

Oh goodness. She sucked in a breath as the butterflies made a surprise reappearance in her gut. *Oh, you thought we were gone?* they taunted. *Think again!*

Spellbound, Noelle found herself leaning down onto the counter toward Jeremiah. He grinned as their eyes locked. There was a vibe here. She wasn't imagining it. She'd read tons of romance novels about characters living their everyday lives and then *boom*, an alluring, smooth-talking stranger materialized at the most unexpected moment and everything changed. Electricity pumped through her veins as Jeremiah smiled at her.

But slowly, inevitably, reality set in. Noelle remembered the mistakes she'd made before with men, and how she'd let herself get distracted and lose sight of her goals. Now that she no longer had her main job, the last thing she needed to do was to start up something new with someone else. It didn't matter that Jeremiah seemed charming and funny and smooth. She had to stay focused.

Plus, he was moving to California in just a couple months.

She cleared her throat and abruptly adjusted her posture, putting distance between them again. For a split second, Jeremiah's face fell. He glanced down, but by the time he looked up at her again, his lips were set in an easy smile. He rapped his knuckles again the counter.

"Maybe I'll see you around before I move," he said.

Despite her reasons for why she shouldn't want to run into him again, she was shocked by how much she wished it might happen.

She smiled softly. "Yeah, maybe."

"Bye, Noelle," he said, backing away toward the door.

She lifted her hand in a wave. "Bye."

Jeremiah slipped out the door, and she watched him walk

to his car. Once he was out of sight, she deflated against the counter. *Goodness gracious.* How were people like him just walking around among the rest of society, beguiling bystanders with their charm and attentive questions?

She reached to grab her phone out of her back pocket, but she stopped herself. No, she would *not* look him up on social media. Well . . . she would at least wait until she was at home and off the clock. How many Jeremiah Smiths were out there in the world anyway? It would probably take forever to find his account if he had one.

Jeremiah Smith.

Jeremiah . . . Smith.

Wait a minute . . .

The image on the back of the Smith's Sweets box flashed in her mind just as the bell chimed above the door. Noelle glanced up and froze as Jeremiah walked back into the store and approached her, sporting a nervous, yet determined expression. Had he come back to ask her out after all? Would she say yes, despite her good sense?

Maybe.

But what Jeremiah ended up asking wasn't something Noelle had anticipated at all.

"Noelle," he said, releasing a deep breath. "I know that you're used to being hired as a bridesmaid, but can I hire you to be my girlfriend instead?"

Chapter Five

"*Excuse me?*"

Jeremiah stared at Noelle's slack-jawed expression and took a second to mentally repeat his words back to himself, trying to imagine how they'd sounded to her. Okay, so maybe his delivery could have been a bit better. But he was just so eager. As he'd walked to his car, the idea had struck him.

Wait. First, for the record, he hadn't meant to start flirting with Noelle before. He just couldn't help it. She was so pretty, it made it hard to think. He could have listened to her talk about books all day and he didn't even read like that. Talking to her made him feel like he was floating in a hot-air balloon, exhilarated, and existing on a higher plane. He'd even blurted out that story about the word game Pop used to play with him and his siblings. He'd been the worst one at that game, and he hadn't told that story in ages. He'd used the word *uncouth* because he'd wanted Noelle to think that he was clever and used words like that regularly, which couldn't be further from the truth. He'd been driven by the desire to impress her.

But back to his idea. He needed a fake girlfriend to bring with him to Heart Beach next weekend. Noelle, with her bridesmaid side hustle, was used to playing a role, and more important, she was losing her main job and needed money for college tuition. Pop had always encouraged Jeremiah and his siblings to help others whenever they could. In this situation, Jeremiah and Noelle could help each other. In exchange for pretending to be his girlfriend, he could pay her and then she'd have money to put toward her tuition. The arrangement made perfect sense to him. And from the way he and Noelle had talked with each other so easily, he felt strongly that they'd be able to spend time in each other's company for a weekend. However, given how Noelle was currently looking at him like he'd sprouted an extra head, maybe she wouldn't see the same value in his proposal.

"Just for next weekend," he added.

"*What?*" she asked, incredulous. "You think just because I'm a fake bridesmaid sometimes, I'd be your fake *girlfriend*? What kind of question is that even? We just met!"

"Please let me start over and explain," he said, mortified at how he was fucking this up. She was right. She didn't know anything about him other than his claims of having a sister who read horror novels and that he worked for Good Boy.

She frowned at him. "I'm waiting."

Her long braids hung loose, and she brushed them away from her face as she blinked at him with her big, almond-shaped eyes. She wore tiny hoop earrings in each ear, which accentuated her heart-shaped face. She was short. He was six feet tall exactly, so he'd guess her height was around five three or five four at most. She had a smooth-sounding voice like an old Hollywood star or a radio talk show host. She laughed by way of a sultry chuckle. Who *was* this girl who'd been working in this bookstore literally a twenty-minute walk from his apartment? And why had he just become aware of her and the bookstore today? Fate, probably. The universe had most likely sensed that Noelle was too good for him, and it had been intent on keeping her hidden. And you know what, the universe was probably right. But Jeremiah didn't see why the universe couldn't allow him and Noelle to spend a weekend together for pretend if it benefited them both.

"Have you ever heard of Smith's Sweets cookies?" he asked. "My grandfather Jeremiah Smith—"

"*That's* why you look so familiar!" Noelle snapped her fingers and pointed at him. "Jeremiah and Minnie Smith from the back of the Smith's Sweets cookie box! You're their grandson? Oh my goodness. *Wow*, you look just like your grandfather."

"Yeah, I hear that a lot." He smiled a little.

She hesitated and lowered her hand back to the countertop. "I'm sorry. Does my saying that make you uncomfortable?"

"Nah, not uncomfortable," he said. He took a mental catalog of his posture and facial expression. His cheek muscles did feel a bit strained. It wasn't that he minded when people pointed out his resemblance to Pop. But with the wounds from Pop's passing still so fresh, the comparison to him only reminded Jeremiah that the man whom he resembled had been a very good man with a legacy that Jeremiah didn't think he could ever live up to. He was surprised that Noelle had read him so easily. He was eager to change the subject and get back on track. "So, is it safe to say you know our family brand?"

"Know it? I eat Smith's Sweets all the time! Just last night, I almost housed an entire box of salted caramel chocolate chip cookies by myself. The only reason I stopped is because my best friend loves them too and I wanted to save some for her."

A regular, everyday consumer singing praises for Smith's Sweets, unprompted? If Celeste were here now, she'd take Noelle by the hands, bring her to the Smith's Sweets headquarters, and have her repeat what she'd just said on camera for the social media team.

"I'm really glad to hear that," Jeremiah said, pulling out his phone. He opened his camera roll and scrolled to a picture of the last time that he and his family were all together in April, standing in Percy and Robin's backyard for Ashley and Harper's tenth birthday party. He showed the picture to Noelle and pointed at each family member. "This is my mom, Celeste; my brother, Percy; his wife, Robin, and their daughters, Harper and Ashley; and that's my sister, Amara."

Noelle leaned closer and peered at the picture. Jeremiah could smell her perfume, a fresh, floral scent. The shiny lip gloss that she wore distracted him. While she observed the picture of him and his family, he became transfixed with observing her mouth and the delicate dip of her Cupid's bow. When she finally glanced up at him, he flashed an easy smile like staring at her mouth hadn't jump-started his pulse.

"You have a beautiful family," she said. "But that doesn't explain why you want to hire me to be your fake girlfriend."

"Right. So, the reason I'm telling you about my family is because we have a house in Heart Beach that we go to every summer. Have you ever been to Heart Beach?"

Noelle's brows scrunched together. "No, I've heard of it, though."

"I told my mom this stupid lie about having a girlfriend, and now she's expecting me to bring my 'girlfriend' to the beach house next weekend for my sister's birthday party—"

"Noelle?"

Jeremiah was interrupted by an older, gray-haired man who emerged from the back of the store. Like Noelle, he wore a blue Hidden Gems Books T-shirt. When he noticed Jeremiah standing there, his steps slowed. "Oh, excuse me. I didn't realize you were with a customer."

Noelle pivoted to the man, then glanced at Jeremiah. "Oh, um, he . . ."

"She already rang me up, sir," Jeremiah said, figuring this man was probably Noelle's boss. He lifted his bag with a smile.

"Oh, good." Her boss hesitated, then looked at Noelle again. "Can I speak to you for a moment?"

"Sure." Noelle walked to meet her boss, and they hovered near the picture books display to the left of the register. They spoke in low voices, so Jeremiah couldn't hear what they were discussing, but it must not have been good because Noelle's shoulders slumped, and she nodded as she listened to her boss. He gently patted her shoulder, sporting a sad frown. He said something else that caused Noelle to summon a small smile before she returned to the register. She wasn't crying, but her eyes were shiny and red-rimmed. Jeremiah felt a sharp tug in his chest. He wanted to do anything to erase her crestfallen expression.

"Is everything okay?" he asked as she typed something on the computer.

"It's slow, so my boss told me that I can clock out early."

"Oh." Jeremiah wasn't sure what to say. He'd never been let

go from a job before—even though he'd absolutely deserved to be. "I'm really sorry."

"Me too." Her mouth formed into that small smile again. "I'd better go and get my stuff."

She picked up her jacket behind the register and started to walk away. Jeremiah worried that this was where their conversation would end. He wanted to ask if they could keep talking, but she probably wasn't in the mood to hear more about his clumsy proposal now, and he didn't blame her. Then, to his surprise, she paused and looked at him over her shoulder.

"Wait there, okay?" she said.

He nodded eagerly, relieved. "Yeah, I'll be right here."

While Noelle walked to the back of the store to gather her belongings, the younger guy who'd been standing at the register earlier returned to the floor and lingered by the beach reads table. His head was angled down as he stared at his phone. He didn't acknowledge Jeremiah's presence or greet the new customer as they entered the store. It made no sense to Jeremiah that Noelle was being let go while this kid and his stellar lack of customer service was staying.

Noelle reemerged from the back of the store with a tote bag slung over her shoulder. She glanced at her oblivious coworker, briefly closed her eyes, and took a deep breath before sporting a strained smile.

"Bye, Kevin," she said. "Today's my last day. I'm not sure if your uncle told you."

"Oh," Kevin mumbled. "Good luck with everything."

"Thanks, you too."

Her boss was this kid's *uncle*? That explained how he was still employed. But damn. Jeremiah knew all too well what it was like to be given a job because of nepotism. And he knew what it was like not to care about the job the way it deserved. He'd judged this kid when he'd been just as careless in the past. How many people like Noelle had been looked over at Smith's Sweets so that Jeremiah could keep his cushy position in the family business? The thought made him sick to his stomach, which was often how he felt when he thought about some of his past actions. He felt even more determined to help Noelle.

She gave a little wave to Kevin and motioned for Jeremiah to follow her outside.

There was a moment of weighted silence between them as they faced each other on the sidewalk. Noelle tilted her chin up and watched Jeremiah. Her expression was unreadable, but at the very least, he inspired her curiosity. He'd better take his chance now and tell her the full story.

"My family has been spending summers at our house in Heart Beach for decades," he said. "I didn't go at all last summer because I've been too busy with work. But next weekend my mom is throwing a birthday party for my sister, and because I haven't been to the house in so long, she wouldn't take no for an answer when I said I wouldn't be able to make it. Back in May, when she wanted me to visit for Memorial Day Weekend, I made up a stupid lie about having plans with a new . . . girlfriend. When she asked if my new girlfriend was the reason that I couldn't come this weekend, I said yeah. But then I felt guilty about not coming, so I changed my mind. Then she told me to bring my new girlfriend too, and I knew that if she found out that I'd lied about the girlfriend, it would cause more problems, so the best thing to do was figure out some kind of situation to save face. Then I met you, and you told me about your fake-bridesmaid side job, and I know being a fake girlfriend is different from being a bridesmaid. We won't be at a wedding, but like the brides you work with, you'd still have to pretend to know me in front of my family. I need a temporary fake girlfriend, and you need money for college. We'd be helping each other."

He paused, gauging Noelle's reaction to everything he'd said. She stared at him silently with a thoughtful expression, teeth tugging her bottom lip.

"Can I buy you dinner so that we can talk about it more?" he asked, desperate.

Noelle glanced back at the bookstore with a slight frown and then averted her eyes to the ground. He wondered what she was thinking. Finally, she returned her gaze to his face.

"This would be a strictly professional arrangement, right?" she said, brows knitted. "You aren't expecting we'll do anything sexual, are you?"

"No, of course not!" he hastened to say. "Nothing like that at all."

She watched him silently again. Then, "How much are you offering to pay me?"

"What's your usual rate for your bridesmaid work?"

"It depends on the package. It can range anywhere from five hundred to twenty-five hundred, depending on how much time it requires. Then the agency takes a twenty percent commission from whatever I make."

"I'll give you thirty-five hundred dollars for the weekend. Friday night to Sunday morning. All yours, straight up."

Her jaw dropped as she gawked at him.

"For real," he said. "And no funny business. Just us pretending to be a couple in front of my family."

She blinked like she was still trying to wrap her mind around how much he'd offered. But the amount wouldn't hurt his pockets. He had his salary from Good Boy, of course. But in addition to that, he and his siblings each had trust funds set up for them from birth. And once he'd turned eighteen, Pop and Celeste had set him up with a financial advisor to make some smart investments, which had helped him build a healthy nest egg of passive income. Pop and Celeste had done the same with Percy and Amara as well. They'd wanted to make sure that money was something Jeremiah and his siblings never had to worry about.

"Okay . . . I'll go to dinner with you to talk about it more," Noelle said finally. "I have questions."

"Yeah?" he said. She nodded. His relief was almost palpable. She hadn't officially agreed to come with him next weekend yet, but at least she was willing to know more. "Wait, I should have asked, are you already in a relationship?"

He didn't know why it had just occurred to him now to ask that question. Noelle was beautiful and just by talking to her, he was able to see that she was smart and sweet. The odds of someone else recognizing those qualities and snapping her up were pretty high.

"No," she said. "I'm too focused on going back to college to worry about dating."

That explained why their flirty vibe had abruptly ended when he'd been about to ask her out inside the bookstore before. But more than anything, he respected her dedication to her goal.

"Good, that makes this easier," he said. "What are you in the mood to eat? I'm fine with anything. There's a steakhouse downtown that I've been to, or we can go to this Italian spot that's supposed to be one of the best restaurants in Jersey. I think we might need a reservation, but I'm sure we can figure something out."

"There's a mom-and-pop Thai place up the street from here," she said, pointing in the restaurant's general direction. "We can walk if you're cool with that."

"Yeah, for sure. Let me just put this bag in my car."

He unlocked his car and jogged to the passenger side, quickly dropping Amara's gift in the seat. When he turned around, he saw a woman standing in the window of the hair salon across the street. She eagerly waved at Noelle and held up her hands and moved her thumbs like she was texting. *Text me!* she mouthed. Noelle nodded and gave a thumbs-up. When the woman caught eyes with Jeremiah as he reapproached Noelle, she quickly dropped her hands and smiled innocently. Noelle herself looked like she was fighting a smile as she turned to him.

"Ready?" she asked.

"Yeah." They started to walk, and he nodded his head toward the woman who was still watching them from the hair salon window. "Is she your friend? You can tell her I'm just taking you to dinner and I don't plan to abduct you."

"She's my best friend and roommate," Noelle said. Her mouth curved into a wry, if not slightly exasperated, smile, like she was thinking of an inside joke. "Don't worry. I'm pretty sure abduction isn't what she has in mind."

Curious, Jeremiah raised an eyebrow. "What does she—"

"So what made you feel guilty enough to change your mind and tell your mom that you'd come to Heart Beach after all?" Noelle asked.

Jeremiah glanced at her, surprised that this was her first

question. Farther ahead, a group of people ascended the steps of the PATH train station, and on either side of the street, people were gathering outside of restaurants for early dinners and happy hours.

"She . . . brought up my grandfather and how we all miss him," he said. "He passed away the summer before last. She wants me to spend time with everyone in Heart Beach before I move."

"I'm really sorry about your grandfather," Noelle said. She lightly touched his elbow, and his skin hummed beneath her fingertips. Before he could analyze his response to the contact, she pulled her hand away.

He cleared his throat and smiled. "Thank you."

They arrived at the Thai restaurant and the host ushered them to an open table by the window. Twinkle lights lined the window frame, and when Jeremiah looked across the table at Noelle, she almost appeared as though she were glowing. She stared back at him intently, and he was so struck by her beauty, he almost forgot what they were doing there together. Then he realized that she was staring at him because their server had arrived and asked for their drink orders.

"Their Thai iced tea is good," Noelle offered. "You should try it."

"Okay." To their server, he said, "I'll have the iced tea, thank you."

When the server walked away, Noelle folded her hands on the table. "You don't have friends you can ask to pretend to be your girlfriend?"

He shook his head and laughed quietly, more so to himself. "Nah. Unfortunately, I don't have a lot of friends these days."

It may have sounded a little pathetic, but it was the truth.

"Other than my best friend, I don't have a lot of friends anymore either," she said. "It's hard to make friends as an adult, especially if you don't have time because of work." She quirked an eyebrow. "Is that the same reason for you?"

"Kind of. I used to live a, um, very different life, and it wasn't all that healthy. To really move forward and change, I had to let go of a lot, including the people I used to hang around." Belatedly, he added, "I do have a best friend, though. His name's Danny. He lives in Philly, and he works even more than me, so we catch up maybe once a month at best. He grew up in Heart Beach."

Noelle nodded, absorbing this information. "Okay, next question. Why not just tell your mom the truth about not having a girlfriend?"

He thought of Celeste and the specific look she got on her face whenever she wanted to know something that you were reluctant to tell her. How she'd stare with her piercing eyes straight into your soul. And then he thought of how she'd look at him once he revealed the true reason that he'd been avoiding Heart Beach, and how she'd look at him with such deep disappointment when he told her about his last conversation with Pop.

"Because I know my mom," he said. "Once she finds out that I lied, she'll dig deeper and want to know *why* I lied, and she'll be unwilling to accept whatever answer I give. She'll think there's a different reason other than the fact that I've got too much work to do. As crazy as it sounds, going along with the lie is actually easier."

"*Is* there another reason that you don't want to be there?" Noelle asked.

Jeremiah pictured Pop sitting in the living room, waiting

for him that night. He'd been wearing one of his favorite T-shirts. It was white with Heart Beach written across the front in faded green letters. Jeremiah blinked and forced the image from his mind.

"Nah, it's just work," he said.

Noelle squinted and tilted her head. She opened her mouth to speak, but she was interrupted as their server arrived with their iced teas. For their entrées, Noelle ordered crab fried rice, and Jeremiah ordered beef pad see ew. Noelle took a sip of her tea and Jeremiah did the same. It was sweeter than he'd expected, but good, like she'd said.

"I still can't believe that I'm sitting here with you," she said. "My mom and I love Smith's Sweets. We have one of your products for almost every occasion. It's really special to us."

Jeremiah smiled. This was exactly what Pop would have wanted, the joy of knowing that another family was enjoying what he and Grandma Minnie had worked so hard to build.

"If you agree to let me hire you, I'll throw in Smith's Sweets snacks for life," he said.

Noelle's eyes widened. "Really?"

"Well, maybe not for life," he said, thinking that Percy would probably have an aneurysm if he discovered that Jeremiah had made such a promise. "But I can definitely give you several boxes of your favorite flavors."

Their food arrived on steaming-hot plates. Noelle lifted her fork and moved the rice around before taking a bite. Jeremiah dug into his food too and snuck glances at Noelle. There was something graceful about her movements. He'd noticed that earlier at the bookstore.

"What would our sleeping arrangements be?" she asked.

"My family will expect us to sleep in the same room, but

you can have the bed. My room there has a couch by the bay window, so that's where I'll sleep."

"And in terms of PDA," she said. "I'm going to assume you aren't expecting me to tongue-kiss you in front of them as soon as we walk through the door."

He almost choked on his pad see ew. He took a sip of his tea to wash down the lodged food.

"No," he said, coughing. "I think some light PDA would be helpful, though, to make it look convincing. Hugging. Holding hands. That kind of thing. A kiss on the cheek if you aren't comfortable with the mouth. And I completely understand if you aren't."

Her eyes lowered to *his* mouth, and his skin immediately prickled with heat as he stared at her mouth too. When she cleared her throat, he quickly lifted his gaze. A pinkish hue flushed beneath her brown skin. He started to smile but checked himself. He shouldn't feel satisfied that he'd made her blush. They were having a business meeting.

"Okay, but what happens after the weekend ends?" Noelle asked. "What if your family expects to see me again? Will you tell them that we broke up?"

"Yeah, that's the tricky part," he said. "In order for this to work, I think it's probably best if they don't like you *too* much."

She frowned. "What do you mean?"

"Something else you should know about my family is that when they like someone, they don't let them go. My best friend, Danny, is basically an honorary Smith. Percy brought Robin to Heart Beach once when they were in college and weren't even official yet, but my mom got Robin's number somehow and started texting her like they were new best friends. You and Amara already have a love of reading in common, and I know she'll want to talk to you about that. Percy will probably leave you be, but Robin will definitely want to get to know you. I'm not saying that you should be disrespectful or rude. Just don't let them endear themselves to you, you know? Don't be *too* friendly."

"But I'm a friendly person," Noelle said, looking troubled. "How can I not want to be friendly with the people who run the company that makes my favorite snacks? I want your family to *love* me."

He laughed. "I'm thinking maybe Saturday night, we can have a dramatic breakup in front of my family. I'll be heartbroken for the rest of summer. They'll leave me in peace, and we'll all move on."

Noelle chewed her food, considering this. "Wait. Don't you want to know more about me first?"

"I would, yes." He set down his fork and gave her his full attention.

"Well, I'm twenty-seven—wait, how old are you?"

"Twenty-nine."

"Okay," she said with a nod. "I live in Brickton with my best friend, Tati. She was the one standing at the hair salon window earlier. I grew up in Brickton and lived there for most of my life, except for the years when I was at UMD. I had to drop out before my senior year, but, um, I'm going back to college soon, hopefully. I told you that already, though . . ."

He wanted to ask why she'd dropped out, but her expression had turned guarded when she'd mentioned it. He didn't want to push her to talk about anything that made her uncomfortable.

"I don't think I've ever been to Brickton," he said instead.

"It's a small town." She eyed him, and the corner of her

mouth lifted in a smile. "Don't you want to run a background check on me or something?"

"Do I need to do that?"

"I mean." She shrugged and held out her hands, palms up. "I don't have anything to hide."

"Then, no. I trust you enough."

"Just like that?" she asked, blinking.

"I've spent time around schemers and grifters. I can sniff them out pretty easily. I can tell that you're not one." Throughout his life, he'd met his fair share of people who befriended him only because they wanted something they thought he could provide, be it money or connections or whatever else. Those people lacked the ability to come across as truly genuine. Noelle didn't give those vibes.

"Okay," she said. She bit her lip again. "Um, I'm sure you've probably realized that we come from different socioeconomic groups. When I do bridesmaid gigs, the dresses are provided for me, and if there are other events that I need to attend, I usually borrow clothes from my best friend. But this situation is different. I don't really own cute summer clothes to wear next weekend around your family." She gestured to her Hidden Gems Books T-shirt and old, faded jeans. "Unless you're okay with me showing up like this."

"I think you look beautiful," Jeremiah said honestly, and her cheeks flushed again as she thanked him and flashed a shy smile. He pulled out his wallet and grabbed one of the credit cards that he rarely used. He held the card across the table toward her. "But if you want to get new clothes, take this. Buy whatever you need."

Noelle stared at the credit card, then looked up at him,

slack-jawed once again. "You're just gonna give me your credit card? What if I scam you?"

"The fact that you asked that question lets me know that you won't do it," he said. "Even if you do, I'll just report the charges as fraud."

When she still didn't take his card, he placed it on the table and slid it toward her. "Please buy yourself whatever you think you'll need, Noelle. If you agree to this, you'll be doing me a huge favor. I don't want you to be worried about what you're wearing."

She stared at the credit card in deep contemplation. Then, slowly, she lifted her gaze to his.

"Thirty-five hundred dollars for one weekend of pretending to be your girlfriend?" she asked.

"Yes," he said.

"We need a contract so that we have our agreement in writing."

"Sure. Whatever you need." He pulled his business card out of his wallet too. "Do you have a pen?" He waited as she fished a pen out of her tote bag. He flipped his business card over and wrote down his personal number before sliding the pen and card across to her. "My email, work number, and personal number."

She studied his business card. "I'd like to have a lawyer look over the agreement first too."

"That's a good idea."

She leaned back in her chair and shook her head, smiling a little, almost in disbelief. Jeremiah leaned back in his chair and observed her as well.

She really was so pretty. And likable. He wasn't worried that anyone might question if they were really together. The Smiths wouldn't care if Noelle hadn't grown up like them.

They weren't the kind of family that cared about status or elitism. Pop and Celeste had made sure of it.

"Okay," Noelle finally said. "I'll do it."

Overwhelming relief washed over Jeremiah. He felt more accomplished about this agreement with Noelle than he had about his successful meeting with the Shop Mart team earlier. "Great. Thank you. You're doing me a real solid."

"You're welcome," she said. "But you'll have to pay half up front."

He nodded. "Done."

"I'll send you the contract after my lawyer looks at it."

"Okay."

She lifted her hand, and Jeremiah held his out too. He felt a spark when their palms met to shake hands. Noelle's eyes locked with his, and when she smiled, he felt the power of it rearrange something in his chest. He smiled too, and somewhere in the back of his mind, a small voice was trying to warn him that he might be biting off more than he could chew.

But, as with most thoughts he didn't want to ponder, he ignored it.

Chapter Six

What I'm doing isn't crazy or stupid," Noelle said. "It makes sense because I'm getting paid a good chunk of money."

It was Friday afternoon, and Noelle was staring at her reflection in her bedroom mirror, giving herself one last once-over before Jeremiah arrived to take her to Heart Beach. She was wearing a red and white gingham tube top with matching capris and red platform sandals. Her braids were arranged in a half-up, half-down style, and she wore matte red lipstick on her lips. She looked fun and flirty, like she was about to enjoy a summer traipsing through Europe. Yesterday, she and Tati had taken the train into the city to shop. She'd bought the gingham set from a boutique in SoHo, along with the other clothes she'd purchased for the weekend. At first, she felt weird about using Jeremiah's credit card, but then Tati reminded her that unless she wanted to show up to the Smiths' beach house wearing her Hidden Gems T-shirt and old denim shorts, she'd better get used to swiping. That realization helped Noelle get over her unease real fast.

"Exactly," Tati said now, appearing behind Noelle. She grinned at Noelle in the mirror. "You're not crazy. You're a businesswoman. An entrepreneur, really."

She spritzed Noelle with a few squirts of perfume. Noelle inhaled the summery, beachy scent as she continued to stare at her reflection. She turned to face Tati.

"I look okay, right?" she asked as her heartbeat picked up pace.

"For the millionth time, *yes*," Tati said. "You look better than okay. You look *gorgeous*. And you have no reason to be nervous! You do this stuff all the time. You play a role and then you get your money and leave. This isn't any different."

"But this *is* different. They're the Smiths! I've been eating their cookies and sweets my whole life. They're a culturally relevant family, and Jeremiah is so . . ."

She swallowed hard and trailed off, not wanting to finish her thought.

Tati smiled slyly. "Jeremiah is so what?"

"Nothing. Never mind." Noelle shook her head and crouched down to zip up her suitcase. Jeremiah would be arriving any minute. "He's my client. That's what he is."

After their dinner last week, Noelle had solicited the help of her "lawyer," otherwise known as André, Tati's boyfriend. He was a paralegal who was applying to law school soon, so he'd be a lawyer eventually. He'd drafted up a contract, roughly based on Noelle's Bridal Bestie contracts. Her contract with Jeremiah outlined the duration of their agreement as well as the payment schedule. André had also added rules of conduct. Like no physical contact that hadn't previously been discussed and green-lit. Noelle sent the contract to Jeremiah and expected him to take at least a day or two to look it over, but he'd electronically signed it and sent it back within minutes, followed by a digital transfer of $1,750.

Noelle tried to picture how she'd look standing next to him as they presented themselves as a couple to his family. Would they buy it? Or would they see through her new clothes and suss out immediately that she was a fraud who'd agreed to this farce because of the money?

No, no. Tati was right. Noelle was overthinking. She knew how to play a role. She could do this. And anyway, she didn't have much of a choice. She needed that second half of Jeremiah's payment.

Just as she took a deep breath and squared her shoulders, Jeremiah texted that he'd arrived.

"He's outside," Noelle said. She grabbed her suitcase and her new cat-eye Ray-Bans and looked at herself in the mirror one last time as Tati squealed and clapped. She grabbed Noelle's suitcase handle and rolled her suitcase into the hallway.

"Come on!" she called. "Rich bitch life awaits!"

Outside, Noelle spotted Jeremiah in the parking lot. He was leaning against his car and wearing a well-fitted, white polo shirt and denim shorts with white sneakers. A pair of sunglasses hung from his shirt collar. His face immediately broke into a smile when he saw Noelle, and she felt the energy of his smile zap her straight in the abdomen. He pushed up off his car and walked toward them. He opened his arms for Noelle, and without a second thought, she stepped into his embrace.

"Hey," she said, letting his arms envelop her. His body was

warm, and his hold was secure. She wondered if anyone had ever told him how great his hugs were.

"Hey." He pulled away and looked her up and down. His lips curved into an appreciative smile. "You look great. I'm digging the red and white."

"Thank you," she said, cheeks warming.

"She does look amazing, doesn't she?" Tati said. "Hi, I'm Noelle's best friend, Tatiana."

Jeremiah turned to Tati, still smiling. "You work at the hair salon across from the bookstore."

"Yes." Tati beamed, clearly pleased that he remembered her. "You should know that if anything bad happens to Noelle, I will hunt you down myself and make your life a living hell."

Jeremiah nodded solemnly. "Noted. She'll be taken care of, I promise." He looked at Noelle. "For real."

"I believe you," she said, nudging Tati in her side.

Noelle wouldn't have agreed to join Jeremiah this weekend if she thought she'd be in some sort of danger. A quick Google search confirmed that he was exactly who he'd said he was. There was his LinkedIn account for one, proving that he was the director of business development at Good Boy, Inc. She'd also found his social media page, which was private, but his profile picture was a candid photo of him taken mid-laugh, and his username was JSmith2. All of the Smiths' social media accounts were private, except for Amara, whose account was devoted to pictures of her paintings. It looked like she was currently working on a series of scenes from popular horror films. Her most recent post from a week ago was a painting from a scene in *The Shining* of Jack Nicholson frozen in the snow.

There were several photos online of Jeremiah and his family, though. Most were taken at fundraisers and events over the years. By all appearances, they seemed like a happy and successful family. She didn't know what they were like behind closed doors, of course, but she was about to find out imminently.

As Jeremiah placed Noelle's suitcase in the trunk of his car, two of her younger neighbors whizzed by on their bikes. The boys came to a screeching halt at the sight of Jeremiah's car, and they gawked in awe. His car definitely stood out in their complex, where most of the parked cars were pre-owned Hondas and Toyotas, including Noelle's used 2009 Honda Accord. One of the boys scooted his bike closer and asked Jeremiah how fast his car was able to drive.

"Pretty fast," Jeremiah said. He closed the trunk and beckoned the boys to come around to the driver's side and take a look at the steering wheel. The boys oohed and aahed, and Jeremiah grinned. Noelle watched him with a slight smirk on her face. As if he could feel him watching her, he glanced up. Satisfied with their exploration, Noelle's neighbors thanked Jeremiah and pedaled away.

"Ready to go?" Jeremiah asked her.

"Yep." Noelle took a steadying breath and turned to Tati. She squeezed her close in a quick hug. "Thank you for helping me shop," she whispered.

"That's something you never have to thank me for," Tati whispered back. "Text me when you get there."

Noelle promised that she would. Then Jeremiah jogged around the car and held the passenger side door open for her.

Huh. Maybe chivalry isn't dead after all.

She shook off that thought, reminding herself that Jeremiah was a client. Him treating her with kindness and respect was to be expected. And more men should open car doors! Why had they stopped doing that?

The inside of Jeremiah's car smelled like his spicy cologne, and his seats were buttery smooth. He drove out of her complex and through Brickton toward the parkway entrance. Noelle checked her phone and saw a text from her mom.

Have fun at the beach this weekend, honey! Love you!

Her mom knew about her bridesmaid side hustle, but this situation with Jeremiah was a bit harder to explain. She didn't want her mom to worry about her or ask more questions, so when she'd talked to her mom on the phone yesterday, she'd told her that she was spending the weekend at the beach with one of her brides.

She responded, Thanks! Love you too!

Then she put her phone away and dug around in her purse for the mini client bible that she carried with her during gigs. She flipped the journal open to her current page about Jeremiah and the Smiths.

"I think it would be a good idea if we went over the details again," she said.

After Jeremiah had signed the contract, she'd FaceTimed him to hear a more thorough rundown on his family. Jeremiah had been sitting at his kitchen table. He'd unbuttoned the top few buttons of his shirt and leaned back in his chair, drinking a can of Dr Pepper. A fancy coffee machine sparkled on the countertop behind him. He'd looked tired as they'd talked, and his voice sounded a bit deeper from exhaustion. But otherwise, he'd been game as he'd answered each of Noelle's questions with as much detail as possible. They decided that they would tell the truth about *how* they met, but they'd lie about when. Their official story was that they'd met in early May at Hidden Gems Books. Noelle had helped Jeremiah browse for books, and he'd asked her out to dinner. They'd been inseparable ever since.

They'd also agreed on levels of PDA. Hand-holding, hugging, and kisses on the mouth with prior warning were approved. She'd gone to bed that night wondering what it might feel like to kiss Jeremiah, which meant she was already starting off on the wrong foot. She couldn't let those pesky butterflies invade her brain again. She needed to remain professional. She shifted in her seat and straightened her posture, journal perched on her lap.

"For sure," he said as he merged onto the parkway. "Shoot."

"Okay, so Celeste is your mom. She's the current CEO of Smith's Sweets, and she likes fancy things and cats, and she'll to want to know everything about me and my life."

Jeremiah laughed and glanced at the open notebook in her lap. "Yeah, that's an easy way to sum her up."

Noelle continued. "Percy is your older brother. He works with your mom and he can come across as standoffish, but I shouldn't take it personally because he's like that with everyone. His wife, Robin, is a child therapist, and she's seven months pregnant with a baby girl. Their twin daughters, Harper and Ashley, are ten years old. Amara is your younger sister and we're celebrating her twenty-seventh birthday this weekend. She's a graphic designer at Smith's Sweets, loves horror novels and films, and she's also a talented painter on the side, even though she sees it more as a hobby. And oh my goodness, I'm just realizing that I didn't get her a birthday gift! I can't show up empty-handed!"

"You won't," he said, keeping his eyes on the road as he switched lanes. "I signed her birthday card from both of us. You helped me pick out her gift."

"I did," she said, relieved. And touched that he'd already thought to include her in that way. "Thank you."

"No, thank *you*." He flashed her a smile that immediately made her heart flutter.

She forced herself to refocus on her notes. On their call, Jeremiah had also shared that his parents had divorced when he was in elementary school, and his dad lived in Seattle with his longtime partner, Vicky. Noelle could relate. She'd told him how her dad lived in Dallas with his second wife, Monica. When Noelle was younger, she used to spend every summer with her dad, Monica, and Monica's sons, Will and Greg, who were older than her. Back then, she'd often felt like the puzzle piece that didn't quite fit anywhere. Jeremiah was lucky to have grown up in a big family where he knew he belonged, without the shadow of a doubt.

He nodded at her notebook and smirked. "I appreciate your analog way of documenting this information."

"Thank you." She closed her notebook and held it to her chest. "I use this for all my jobs."

"How many weddings have you worked?"

She did a bit of mental math, then flipped through her notebook to confirm. "Sixteen."

"Damn." Jeremiah whistled. "You're a real pro."

She smiled and shrugged. "I'd like to think so."

"You'll have no problem with my family," he said. "Don't worry."

She appreciated his confidence in her. If this were any other family, she'd rely on her usual bag of tricks to dazzle everyone and get through the weekend. But the fact that she was spending the weekend with the Smith's Sweets family, *and* that she was supposed to act aloof around them, was throwing her off her game.

It didn't have anything to do with her attraction to Jeremiah, when she'd never had to worry about being attracted to any of her brides before.

They ran into traffic, which was unsurprising. It was the weekend, and a good portion of people in New Jersey were probably headed for the beach.

"You can hook up to the Bluetooth if you want to play some music," Jeremiah said.

"R and B okay?" she asked, and he nodded.

She connected her phone, and "Jaguar" by Victoria Monét started to play.

"Ooh yes, I love H.E.R.," Jeremiah said, snapping his fingers to the beat.

Noelle's eyeballs almost popped out of her head. "*H.E.R.?* What—"

"I'm joking," he said, laughing. He laughed even harder when he glanced over and saw the incredulous look on Noelle's face. "I know this is Victoria Monét. Amara listens to her."

He started to sing along, and Noelle discovered Jeremiah's first flaw. Well, his second flaw. His first flaw was that he didn't mind telling his family a lie about being in a relationship. His second flaw was that he couldn't sing. For some reason, she found this incredibly endearing.

"Don't sit over there judging my singing," he said, grinning at her. "Can you sing any better?"

Noelle cleared her throat and started to sing the song's hook. Jeremiah used his free hand to cover his ear that faced her.

"Damn, girl." He pretended to wince. "You might hurt somebody with that voice."

Noelle snort-laughed, and Jeremiah smiled at her as he turned up the volume. They spent the rest of the drive singing poorly to each other. By the time they turned off the exit for Heart Beach an hour later, Noelle's nerves had mostly evaporated. They drove over a bridge, and the water sparkled in the sun beneath them. Seagulls soared overhead.

"Do you care if I roll down my window?" she asked.

"Nah," Jeremiah said. "Go ahead."

She rolled down her window and inhaled the salty air. Something about the smell of the ocean instantly relaxed her. "I haven't been to the beach in forever."

"Welcome back," Jeremiah said. He smiled at her, but something about his smile was a bit stilted, less carefree than when they'd sung together during the drive down. She wondered what that was about.

As they drove through Heart Beach, Noelle absorbed her surroundings like a sponge. The houses in Heart Beach were definitely nicer and larger than the ones in the beach towns she'd visited before. The front lawns were groomed and pristine. They drove by a country club where people played tennis or lounged by the pool. Kids biked down the sidewalk on beach cruisers, balancing ice cream cones in their hands. Other people were walking down side streets, dressed in bathing suits and cover-ups, clearly having just come from the beach.

Jeremiah made a left onto Hawthorne Street, and he slowed

to a crawl as he pulled up in front of a gray house with white shutters. The house was three stories high, and a veranda wrapped around the perimeter. Rocking chairs were stationed on either side of the front door, and perfectly pruned bushes lined the front lawn. It was definitely a big house, but somehow remained picturesque and quaint. It looked like a beach house from a Hallmark movie.

People in black uniforms were carrying tables and umbrellas from a van parked across the street to the backyard. The driveway was packed with other cars. New cars, like Jeremiah's. Noelle guessed they belonged to his family members.

"They're setting up for Amara's party tomorrow," he explained as he cut the engine and stared up at the house.

"Home sweet home," Noelle said. She inhaled deeply and placed her hand on the door handle, but Jeremiah didn't move. He stared up at the house with furrowed brows, his mouth set in a tight line. He rubbed his hands up and down his thighs. He didn't crack a smile at her home sweet home joke. He probably hadn't even heard her.

"Are you okay?" she asked.

Slowly, he blinked and looked at her, almost like he just was remembering that she was there.

"Yeah," he said, unlocking the doors. "Ready?"

She squared her shoulders and took one more deep breath.

"Ready," she confirmed.

She was officially on the clock.

Chapter Seven

Two summers ago, the night before Pop died, Jeremiah had stumbled up the driveway of their Heart Beach home, tripping over his own feet and struggling to see straight because he was so drunk. Hours ago, Theo, an old friend from NYU whose family also had a home in Heart Beach, had met Jeremiah at the Sand Saloon, the main bar in town. They'd taken shot after shot before switching to beer, and eventually Jeremiah realized that it was almost three a.m. He was an adult and could do whatever he wanted, but out of respect for his mom and grandfather, he tried not to come home too late whenever he was at Heart Beach. A lot of the time, he failed at this endeavor.

He didn't always get as drunk as he did that night. Sometimes he didn't drink at all. Most nights, he was just *out*. Whether it was here in Heart Beach or back home in the city. He was still part of the same friend group from college, and the great thing about those friends was that they didn't expect anything from him because they didn't care. They didn't care about how he fell short in comparison to Percy, who was ambitious and intelligent, or Amara, who was creative and individualistic. They didn't care that Jeremiah stuck out like an inadequate sore thumb among his stellar siblings. When Jeremiah was out with those friends, he didn't have to think about his shortcomings. They cared only that he knew how to have a good time.

At his private high school, Jeremiah hadn't made friends through debate team and Model UN like Percy, or through art club like Amara. True, he did have a couple friends from cross-country and track, and he'd been best friends with Danny since childhood. But Danny lived in Heart Beach, and Jeremiah saw him only during the summer. At school as he'd made jokes in class to distract his classmates from how he struggled with his grades, he'd discovered his niche. If he distracted people with humor, maybe no one would find out that Celeste had hired a tutor to help him a few times a week. Academics just weren't Jeremiah's thing. But in his social life, he thrived. He was the one who everyone invited to their parties because they knew he'd liven things up just by being there.

This strategy followed him to NYU, where he formed an easy friendship with Theo because Theo also knew how to have a good time and was always looking for the next party. Theo and the rest of their friend group never talked about serious things. They didn't discuss life goals or encourage one another to be their best selves. If shit ever went left or if Jeremiah found himself in a real pinch, he knew he couldn't count on Theo or the rest of them to be there for him. Their friendship was surface level, but Jeremiah didn't mind because it was easier that way. Into adulthood, Monday through Friday, thoughts about being the one subpar Smith crowded his mind from the minute he woke up at the crack of dawn to take the NJ Transit to the Smith's Sweets headquarters in Hamilton. There, he watched his mom and siblings thrive in their respective roles, while he worked with the crippling fear that nothing he contributed would ever be up to par with the rest of his family, which resulted in him not trying hard enough. His social life was where he found escape.

Being out with Theo one-on-one could get intense, though. Theo didn't have a drinking limit, and he peer-pressured those around him, which was why Jeremiah was drunker that night than he'd expected to be.

He tried to be quiet as he fumbled for his keys outside the door. Once inside, he tripped over a pair of flip-flops and almost face-planted in the hallway. He regained his balance, kicked off his sneakers, and rubbed his eyes, thinking about the blueberry pie that Celeste had baked earlier that day. He wanted to heat up a slice and eat it with vanilla ice cream.

"Jeremiah."

Jeremiah snapped his head up and froze at the sound of his grandfather's voice. Pop was sitting on the living room couch. His hands were clasped together, and he was looking at Jeremiah with somber eyes.

"Pop . . . I didn't know you were awake," Jeremiah mumbled.

Even in his cloud of inebriation, Jeremiah was aware of how he must have looked to his grandfather. Sloppy, careless, irresponsible. But this was all wrong. No one was *supposed* to be awake right now. Especially not Pop, who'd made a habit of going to bed earlier and earlier lately. Jeremiah didn't want Pop to see him like this. Pop was more of a father figure to him than his own dad.

"What are you doing, Miah?" Pop asked.

"Uh." Jeremiah fought through his brain fog to form a

coherent reply. "I was going to warm up some pie. I'm sorry if I woke you. I couldn't—couldn't find my key."

"You didn't wake me up. I waited for you." Pop walked over to Jeremiah. Now in his early eighties, Pop moved slower than he had before, and he'd lost weight, but his vibrant aura remained. He was wearing an old Heart Beach T-shirt and pair of plaid blue pajama pants that Amara had bought him for Christmas years ago. It was a running joke in their family that Pop never bought pajamas for himself and preferred to receive them as Christmas gifts. Gently, he rested his hand on Jeremiah's shoulder. "I meant, what are you doing with your life?"

Jeremiah stared. His arms fell limp at his sides. This was an important conversation, one he didn't currently feel equipped to have.

"Every weekend, you're out carrying on at all times of the night," Pop said. "Then the next day, you sleep and waste the day away. You're missing it, missing *us*. When you were in your early twenties, I chalked it up to you being young, but you're twenty-seven now. Still young but old enough to start taking yourself more seriously."

"Aw, Pop, come on," Jeremiah said, even though he knew deep down that Pop was right. He dragged a hand down his face. "I don't want to talk about that now."

"Yeah, because you're drunk." Pop crossed his arms over his chest. "When I was your age, I worked two, sometimes three jobs. I worked as hard as I did to make your mom's life and *your* life easier. The world is at your fingertips, and this is how you're choosing to spend your time? I raised you better than this, Jeremiah."

His words were a sharp cut to Jeremiah's chest, because they were true.

Pop had always been Jeremiah's biggest supporter. Pop helped Jeremiah study when he struggled in school. He cheered him on at his track and cross-country meets, and whenever a herd of nerves stampeded over Jeremiah's thoughts before his race began, he'd look into the crowd and see Pop up on his feet, clapping. Then Jeremiah would feel assured that no matter the outcome, everything would be okay. Because Pop was in his corner, and he believed in him.

To be confronted with the reality that Pop was disappointed in him was the worst feeling. Jeremiah was angry at himself because Pop's disappointment was warranted. Every now and then, Celeste had made a comment to Jeremiah about how she thought he was staying out too late, but Pop was the one who saw Jeremiah clearly. Jeremiah was angry at Pop for seeing through him because it was so much easier to hide behind his facade.

"What are you talking about? You act like I'm out here getting into fights or driving drunk," Jeremiah said. "I just had a few drinks, and I walked home. What's the problem? Why are you judging me?"

"I'm not judging you." Pop sighed, and Jeremiah realized how tired his grandfather looked. "My wish is for you to realize your potential and to find your purpose and work toward it, no matter what it is. I can tell you've been unhappy working for the company, and that's okay, Miah. Maybe you need to find what's best for you and your life. But you won't find it by going out every night, especially not with people who don't care about your well-being. Come on, let's get you a glass of water. We can talk about this more in the morning."

"No, I don't want to talk about it more." Jeremiah backed away. He couldn't stand to see the look in Pop's eyes, a mixture of disappointment and fierce love. It asked too much of him. It asked that he be the person whom Pop thought he was capable of being. Jeremiah was terrified that he'd never live up to whoever that was, and he'd let Pop down even more. He didn't want to talk about it then or the next day. He wanted to run away from the conversation entirely. "I'm going back out."

"Miah," Pop called after him, but Jeremiah kept walking until he was out the door. Only when he was walking down the driveway did he realize that he forgot his shoes.

He walked to the beach. The cold, wet sand and the chilly night air helped sober him up. He sat on the beach for a while, breathing in and out and listening to the waves crash loudly against the shore. He replayed his conversation with Pop and felt like the world's biggest asshole for walking out. He needed to go back and apologize. He splashed some ocean water on his face and jogged back to the house. But when he returned, Pop was asleep in his room. First thing in the morning, Jeremiah vowed to talk to Pop and apologize. He went to bed that night and closed his eyes as soon as his face hit the pillow.

In the early-morning hours, he felt someone trying to shake him awake.

"Miah," Amara whispered. "*Miah.* Get up."

Jeremiah struggled to open his eyes. His mouth was dry and tasted of the previous night's liquor. His limbs felt like they were weighed down with sandbags. "W-what?"

"It's Pop," Amara said.

His vision cleared, and he realized his sister was crying. Jeremiah hastened to sit up. His hangover pierced his skull.

He followed Amara to Pop's bedroom. Percy and Robin were standing in Pop's doorway. Robin held her hand to her mouth as Percy rubbed her back in slow circles. They turned to look at Jeremiah and Amara.

"He's gone," Percy said, eyes red. "I don't know what happened, but he's just . . . gone."

Jeremiah blinked, sure he'd misheard his brother. He still didn't believe him, even as he moved past Percy and Robin into Pop's bedroom and saw Celeste standing by the window, wiping her eyes as she talked to the 911 dispatcher.

Jeremiah couldn't move, couldn't think. He couldn't bring himself to look at Pop's bed, where he knew he'd find his lifeless body. He'd just talked to Pop the night before. He'd planned to apologize in the morning for stupidly walking out on him mid-conversation. Pop wasn't supposed to *die*. He was supposed to defy death and live forever. He was infinite. He hadn't even been sick. So how could this have happened?

It wasn't until later that Celeste revealed Pop had been having heart trouble, and that he'd asked her not to tell anyone. He hadn't wanted the rest of them to worry. Because that was the type of person he'd been. Selfless, who cared more about the rest of his family than he cared about himself. At first, Jeremiah had been riddled with sickening guilt that his argument with Pop had caused the heart attack. But from his autopsy, they learned that Pop's heart attack had most likely developed gradually throughout the day with subtle symptoms, which meant that, without medical attention, it had been inevitable.

Pop was irreplaceable, and Jeremiah missed him all the fucking time.

He stared at the house as he and Noelle walked up the driveway. His heart was in his throat. He didn't know if he was ready to step through the front door again. But it was too late to turn back. He was already here with Noelle, who was looking up at the house in awe, and he'd made a promise to pay her.

They walked up the porch steps, and Jeremiah inhaled deeply before he turned the knob and opened the door.

They stepped inside, and errant grains of sand crunched beneath their feet. Flip-flops were scattered in the hallway, and one of his nieces had left a water gun abandoned at the foot of the wide staircase that led to the second and third floors. To their right, navy blue and white furniture was arranged in the living room. The windows were open, letting in the summer breeze.

A sense of belonging and nostalgia washed over Jeremiah. Even if being back at the house was complicated, it would always feel like a constant base in his life.

"Hello?" Jeremiah called out. No answer. To Noelle, he said, "They're probably in the backyard. I'll show you where we'll be sleeping first."

He carried their suitcases upstairs, and Noelle followed behind him, observing the paintings of boats and fish and whales that lined the staircase walls.

"My mom loves a nautical theme," Jeremiah said. He pointed at a painting of two dolphins jumping out of the ocean. "Amara painted that in middle school."

Noelle smiled at the painting. "I love it."

On the second-floor landing, she paused in front of a large, framed photograph of him and his family from many years ago, standing in front of the Heart Beach house. In the photo, Jeremiah, a toddler, squinted one eye and cheesed at the camera. Beside him, Percy held his hands clasped in front of him and smiled brightly like it was picture day at school. His two front teeth were missing. Behind them, Celeste held baby Amara in her arms, and Pop and Grandma Minnie stood on either side of Celeste. The house looked different back then. There had been no wraparound veranda, white stone walkway, or a third story. Those additions had come later when Jeremiah was in middle school.

"Wow, the house went through some changes," Noelle said.

"My grandpa had a lot of work done to it over the years. He initially bought the house for my grandma in the seventies. She loved to swim, and he wanted her to have a place to go where she could be closer to the beach."

"That's really romantic," Noelle said.

"Yeah. He never remarried after she died. I don't even think he dated anyone. If he did, it wasn't serious enough for him to bring them around the rest of us."

At a young age, Jeremiah was able to see the kind of love that his grandparents shared, and it had set an example for him to never settle when it came to love. He'd had short-lived flings over the years with women he'd really liked. But he hadn't felt a deep love connection, not like the one between his grandparents.

He fell quiet, and Noelle glanced over at him. He had a feeling that she was about to ask if he was okay again. He summoned a smile and continued on, past his mom's bedroom, Percy and Robin's bedroom, and the bedroom that Ashley and Harper shared, up to the third floor, which housed his bedroom, Amara's room, a bathroom, and a small sitting room that Amara used when painting.

"Here's where we'll be," he said as he pushed open his bedroom door.

He gazed around the room. His queen-size bed was made, and the large flat-screen television mounted on the wall was spotless. An old LeBron poster from when he'd played with the Cavs was still tacked to the wall, and his old longboard leaned against his closet. He'd originally bought it during one summer in high school when he and Danny had adopted longboarding as their new personalities. This bedroom was a time capsule, a place where Jeremiah preserved the artifacts and phases of his life. Other than the changed bed set and sheets, most of this room had gone untouched since he'd last been here two summers ago.

Noelle gasped and immediately ran over to the bay window and reading nook. She sank down onto the soft cushion.

"Oh my God, I would *kill* for one of these reading nooks!" she said, bringing her knees up to her chest. "Can you imagine reading here for hours, unbothered?!"

Jeremiah laughed, happy that the nook pleased her. He observed her delighted smile, and also took a moment to take in the rest of her too. She looked beautiful. Her pants hugged her hips, and she wore some kind of lotion or body oil that made her skin shimmer in the sun. He'd checked the charges she'd made on his card, and the amount she'd spent had been less than what he'd expected. Earlier, she'd tried to return his card to him, but he told her to keep it until the weekend was over.

He left their suitcases by the closet and joined Noelle at the window, drawn to her. He leaned past her and inhaled the beachy, almost tropical scent of her perfume. He swallowed thickly as he reminded himself that she was here with him for professional reasons and nothing more. He forced himself to look away from her beautiful face and he peered outside into the backyard. Right away, he spotted Celeste showing the event planning team where she wanted the tables placed. She was wearing a white linen top and pants set and a white wide-brimmed beach hat. His niece Ashley ran up to Celeste and bounced on her toes as she spoke. Then she glanced up and saw Jeremiah and Noelle watching from the window.

"Uncle Miah's here!" Ashley said, pointing and waving.

Celeste whipped around. Her eyes were concealed behind her large sunglasses, but she smiled so big, there was no way to deny her happiness. Or her relief. She'd probably been worried that Jeremiah wouldn't show up.

He smiled and waved back. To Noelle, he said, "I guess we'd better get downstairs."

He held out his hand for her, and she let him pull her up off the reading nook.

"I think we should probably hold hands in front of my family," he said. "Is that cool?"

"Cool."

She entwined her fingers through his, and he tried not to pay too much attention to how nice it felt to hold her hand.

Chapter Eight

They hadn't reached the bottom step before his nieces came barreling into the hallway. They wore matching pink sundresses, and pink beads adorned the ends of their braids. They were identical, but Ashley was taller and had a beauty mark beneath her right eye, and Harper wore glasses. They knocked into Jeremiah and tightly wrapped their arms around him.

"Uncle Miah!"

"You're finally here!"

"What took you so long?"

"We're going to the boardwalk! Are you coming?"

"You have to come! Promise that you'll come with us!"

"Okay, hold on, hold on," Jeremiah said, laughing. "First, hi. I'm happy to see you too. Second, I want to introduce you to my girlfriend, Noelle."

The girls spun around to look at Noelle.

"Noelle," he said, "these are my nieces, Harper and Ashley."

"Hi." Noelle stepped closer, smiling. "It's really nice to meet you."

The girls stared at Noelle with big, curious eyes and waved.

"She's your girlfriend?" Ashley asked, looking up at Jeremiah. "When did you get a girlfriend?"

"Remember Mom told us that he was bringing his girlfriend?" Harper whispered. She was the quieter, shier twin. She looked at Noelle again. "I like your outfit."

"Me too!" Ashley abandoned Jeremiah and ran to grab Noelle's hands instead. "What kind of lipstick are you wearing? Our mom doesn't let us wear lipstick. She says it's too grown. Can I put on your lipstick to see what it looks like on me? You don't have to tell our mom, and we'll take it off right after. Are you coming with us to the boardwalk?"

"Uh." Noelle smiled and blinked. She seemed unsure of which question to answer first.

"Miah?" Another voice called. Next, Amara entered the hallway. She wore a black denim sleeveless minidress and black Doc Marten sandals. Her short, coily hair framed her face. She jogged over and hugged Jeremiah. Then she flicked him on the forehead.

"Ow." He winced. "What was that for?"

"You didn't text me back when I asked what time you'd be here," Amara said.

He rubbed his forehead. "I was driving. Since you wanna be violent, I'll withhold your birthday present."

Amara grinned, shaking her head. "No, you won't."

She was right. On his way downstairs, he'd placed the wrapped book and card on Amara's bed.

Amara smiled warmly at Noelle. "I'm his sister, Amara. It's

so nice to meet you." She hugged Noelle, then pulled back and bit her lip. "Sorry, I should have asked if you're a hugger."

"I'm a hugger," Noelle confirmed, laughing. She glanced at the dried blue paint marks on Amara's hands. "Are you working on another painting? I saw some of the art you posted on your Instagram. It's so good. My favorite is the one you painted of Florence Pugh crying in *Midsommar*."

"Thank you! That's one of my favorites too. Her face is so expressive. I'm in the middle of working on a painting that we'll auction off at our family gala in a couple weeks. It's not horror related, though. It's a dedication to Heart Beach."

"That's so dope," Noelle said. "I wish I knew how to paint."

Amara squeezed Noelle's hand. "I can definitely teach you, girl."

"Really?" Noelle asked, and Amara nodded, beaming.

It was exactly as Jeremiah had feared. Amara was trying to bring Noelle into her fold from the get-go.

"Where's Mom?" he asked as he smoothly wrapped his arm around Noelle's waist. She glanced up and leaned into him, resting her head against his arm.

As if she heard him, Celeste breezed into the hallway.

"Hi, hi, hi," she said. She'd taken off her sunglasses and hat, and her linen outfit flowed as she walked toward them. She looked ethereal and radiant.

"Hey, Ma," Jeremiah said, smiling.

"Hi, sweetheart." Celeste kissed him on the cheek and wiped away the stain that her nude brown lipstick left behind. She practically floated over to Noelle, sporting the largest smile. "You must be Noelle. I'm Jeremiah's mother, Celeste. Welcome to Heart Beach!"

Noelle didn't have a chance to respond before Celeste

hugged her. Celeste pulled away, but kept her hands placed on Noelle's shoulders as she took her in.

"Thank you so much for having me this weekend," Noelle said.

"Of course, honey." Celeste turned to Jeremiah as she dropped her hands from Noelle's shoulders. "Miah, you didn't tell us Noelle was so beautiful! I see why you've been spending all your time with her."

"I don't know how I forgot to mention that," Jeremiah said, grinning at Noelle. He returned his hand to her waist. "Her beauty takes my breath away sometimes."

Noelle laughed lightly, but Jeremiah could see the slight flush of her cheeks as his family looked at her.

"My son, the charmer," Celeste said with a smile. "How was the drive down?"

"Fine," Jeremiah said. "We sang lots of songs. Where are Percy and Robin?"

"Robin's napping, and Percy is working at the coffee shop in town. He said he couldn't focus here. He'll meet us on the boardwalk later."

"Oh, I thought he took the day off like everyone else," Jeremiah said.

"I encouraged him to, but you know your brother."

Smith's Sweets was growing. Last year, they'd switched to a larger warehouse, hired new crew members, and changed distribution channels in order to keep up with demand. Celeste had always said that she wanted to retire early at sixty, and she was turning sixty next year. So far, there had been no word on her retirement, but if she did make that decision, Percy's transition to CEO would be smooth. He was the one who poured oil into the Smith's Sweets machine and kept things running efficiently. He'd always been devoted to his work, even as a teenager when he'd sold funnel cakes at Marty's on the boardwalk. Working at Marty's had been Jeremiah's first summer job too. Celeste and Pop thought that it was important for Jeremiah and his siblings to learn the value of earning their own money. Summer jobs were part of the deal. Jeremiah had worked at Marty's because Percy had worked there. Percy was three years older than him, and back then, Jeremiah thought that everything Percy did was worth emulating, even if he wasn't as good at it.

"We're ready to go to the boardwalk now," Ashley said, interrupting them. "Can we leave soon, please, Grandma?"

"Yes, sweetheart. Let me go and wake your mom. She wanted to come too." To Jeremiah and Noelle, Celeste asked, "Will you be joining us?"

Jeremiah looked at Noelle. He was eager to get out of the house. Everywhere he turned reminded him of his grandfather. It was soothing, yet simultaneously painful. He raised an eyebrow, mentally asking her, *Is that okay?*

To his relief, Noelle smiled. "Yes, we'd love to."

"Noelle, can you tell us the story of how you and Jeremiah met?" Amara asked. She rolled her eyes at Jeremiah. "Miah's been very tight-lipped about your relationship."

Jeremiah smiled down at Noelle as she slipped her hand through his, like it was the most natural thing in the world. They were walking down the boardwalk, having just left the ice cream parlor. Ashley and Harper walked ahead of them.

"It's a simple story," Noelle said. "We met at the bookstore where I used to work. I helped him look for a book and he asked me to dinner. We've been having dinners together ever since."

She delivered the story perfectly, smiling in the right places and sending affectionate glances his way. He was impressed, although he shouldn't have been. She was used to doing this at the weddings she worked.

"I didn't know that you liked to read, Miah," his sister-in-law, Robin, said. She'd brought a mini electric fan outside with her and was currently fanning her face and neck. She rested her other hand on her round stomach. Thanks to her pregnancy, she felt overheated all the time. She'd recently chopped her hair into a pixie cut. "What kind of books are you into?"

Well, he hadn't expected anyone to ask him *that*.

"I saw Noelle in the window and made up an excuse about needing a book," he said, thinking fast. "She was so beautiful, I just wanted to talk to her."

He looked at Noelle and made lovesick, puppy-dog eyes. She batted her eyelashes and blew him a kiss. Celeste, Amara, and Robin smiled as they watched the two of them and their PDA.

"So, what do you do for fun up there in Jersey City?" Celeste asked.

He and Noelle blinked at each other. What they did for fun wasn't something that they'd thought to discuss.

"We like to eat Thai food," he blurted.

"Oh?" Celeste said.

"Yeah, we do this thing where we go to a new restaurant every week and try out different cuisines," Noelle said, covering up his blunder. "It's like traveling the world, but through food. The most recent food we tried was Thai."

"That sounds cool," Amara said.

"We like singing together too, right?" Jeremiah said. "We do karaoke. R and B karaoke specifically."

Noelle fought off a grin. "Have you ever heard Jeremiah sing? He has the voice of an angel."

He barked out a laugh, and Noelle squeezed his hand, trying to keep a straight face. He lifted her hand to his mouth and pressed a kiss to the back of it. Only he noticed the stutter of her pulse on the inside of her wrist. They locked eyes, and for a second, he simply enjoyed the privilege of looking at her up close. He almost forgot that they were supposed to be pretending.

"Do you like charades, Noelle?" Robin asked. "You can't escape a summer with the Smiths without playing at least once."

"I haven't played in a while, but I'd be up for it," Noelle said.

Little did they know, after this weekend, they wouldn't be seeing Noelle again.

"What should we do now?" Celeste asked the group. "Play some games? Ride some rides?" She touched Noelle's arm. "There's this one ride that shoots you into the air like a slingshot."

"Games, then rides?" Harper suggested.

Beside her, Ashley pointed. "Look, there's Dad!"

Their group turned. Percy was making his way down the crowded boardwalk. He wore a simple white T-shirt and khaki shorts. He rubbed the bridge of his nose and adjusted his glasses. Jeremiah tensed, wondering which version of his brother he'd get today. Ever since he'd left Smith's Sweets, Percy's default setting with Jeremiah was surly. The level of surliness varied depending on Percy's mood.

Robin waved, and Percy waved back. His eyes widened slightly when he noticed Jeremiah. He'd probably assumed that Jeremiah wasn't actually going to show up this weekend. When he reached them, he kissed Robin and hugged his daughters. He looked over their heads at Jeremiah. He and Percy were the same height. They had the same complexion and shade of brown eyes. They differed almost everywhere else.

"What's up, bro?" Jeremiah asked. "Good to see you."

"Good to see you too," Percy said.

They dapped each other up and hugged.

"I'm glad you came," Percy said as he pulled away. "Thought you might be avoiding us for some reason."

Jeremiah forced a smile. "Nah."

He never straight up avoided Percy, but he didn't make a habit of seeking him out anymore either. Percy thought that Jeremiah left Smith's Sweets because he was being selfish and shirking his responsibilities. But Jeremiah had left because after his last conversation with Pop, he'd realized that he was only making the family look bad by staying with the company but slacking off. Pop had been right—Jeremiah hadn't been happy with the job he was doing at the company and knew he could do better, but when he tried to think of ways to contribute, it became clear that Celeste and Percy had everything under control, and they didn't need Jeremiah. It would be best if he left and stopped ruining the Smith's Sweets image. In the two years since he'd left, he'd gotten himself together more, but whenever he thought about the idea of returning to Smith's Sweets, he still feared that he'd somehow mess things up. It was a fear that he didn't have with Good Boy because at Good Boy he'd started with a clean slate, and it was less personal. However, explaining that to Percy meant he'd also have to explain his last conversation with Pop, and that was the last thing Jeremiah wanted to do.

"Percy, this is my girlfriend, Noelle," he said.

Noelle smiled cordially at Percy. "It's nice to meet you."

"Likewise." The corners of Percy's mouth lifted half an inch in a brief smile before he gave his full attention to Celeste. "I just got off a call with Anthony at the warehouse. Almost a dozen sugar cookie shipments are unaccounted for. That's the second time in two weeks."

"We'll worry about that later," Celeste said. "A few missing boxes won't make or break us this weekend. There's not much we can do until Monday."

"Yeah, babe," Robin said. "Plus, the girls have been waiting for you."

"Can we go to the arcade now?" Ashley asked.

Percy frowned, glancing between his daughters, his wife, and his mom. "It might be a few missing boxes today, but it could turn into a larger issue down the line. I'd rather get this situation handled now."

"I can take you to the arcade," Jeremiah offered his nieces. "I was planning to take Noelle anyway. I wanna win her a bear."

Percy looked at Jeremiah and narrowed his eyes. "It's interesting when you choose to be helpful."

There it was. The ire that Jeremiah had been waiting for.

"You have a problem with me taking them to the arcade?" Jeremiah asked.

"I have a problem with how you pick and choose when to care," Percy said.

"Stop this right now." Celeste stood between her sons. She

looked back and forth imploringly. "You're family. Cut the drama."

Jeremiah and Percy frowned at each other. Jeremiah hated that this was the nature of their relationship now. Percy would always hold it against him that he'd left the family company. And Jeremiah would always wish that he was worthy enough to stay.

Noelle tightened her grasp on Jeremiah's hand. "Did you mean what you said about winning me a bear?" she asked.

She looked up at him, patient and calm. Slowly, his pulse rate regulated. He reminded himself that he was here at Heart Beach to keep the peace with Celeste and to attend Amara's birthday party. Not to argue with Percy.

"Yeah," he said to Noelle. "Let's get you that bear."

"We'll *all* go to the arcade," Celeste said. "Percy, honey, worry about the warehouse issue on Monday."

Percy grumbled something and pulled out his phone, most likely trying to send off one last email.

"You good?" Noelle whispered to Jeremiah. They began leading the group down the boardwalk.

"Yeah," he said. "I'm good. Thank you."

She nudged his arm with her shoulder. "You've got my hopes up about that bear now."

Jeremiah laughed, feeling his mood lift steadily. "I did mean it. I'm gonna win it for you."

"Okay, then," she said, winking.

He brought her hand to his mouth and kissed the back of it again, just because. She looked at him through her lashes and smiled. Maybe thanks to Noelle, he'd be able to make it through the weekend.

Chapter Nine

Noelle smoothed her hands down the front of her satin, sleeveless olive green dress. She'd bought it at the same boutique in SoHo with Tati. The hem fell right below her knees, so it seemed appropriate to wear to dinner. Jeremiah's mom had hired a private chef to cook tonight. He said that Celeste didn't have a ton of house rules, but she preferred that everyone be dressed for dinner. Nothing fancy, but you weren't allowed to sit at the table in your bathing suit or your pajamas.

Noelle had gotten a tan from being out in the sun today, and she wore her braids loose down her back. They'd spent the majority of the early evening at the arcade and the games section of the boardwalk. Jeremiah had tried and failed three times to win her a stuffed bear at the balloon darts booth, but he'd won her a stuffed turtle after playing the spray-and-race game. While accepting the prize, Noelle had kissed Jeremiah on the cheek, and she'd carried the turtle proudly like it was a coveted trophy. His mom and sisters had found this adorable.

Hopefully, she and Jeremiah looked convincingly in love, and when their big breakup happened tomorrow night, his family would understand his heartbreak and he'd be able to drop the girlfriend narrative for good.

So far, the Smiths had been nothing but kind to Noelle. Amara and Robin went out of their way to include Noelle in conversations, and although she found Celeste intimidating, she could tell that Celeste was making an effort to be welcoming to her son's new girlfriend. His nieces were rambunctious sweethearts. After the standoff between Jeremiah and Percy on the boardwalk, they'd avoided each other, and as a result, Percy also inadvertently avoided Noelle. He'd walked away from the group more than once to take phone calls.

Noelle didn't know the source of friction between Jeremiah and Percy, but that also didn't seem like important information that she needed in order to do her job properly. It wasn't her place to insert herself and ask Jeremiah about what was going on. Every family had drama, and she wouldn't be seeing this family after the weekend ended.

She was more concerned about keeping herself in line. Literally. The house was immaculate. Like the kind of house that location scouts picked for movies. Noelle felt like a bull in a china shop here. Every item was placed just so with intention. From the spotless furniture to the wall decor to the sparkling plates and utensils she'd spotted in the dining room. Even the toothbrush holder in the third-floor bathroom was made of white glass. If she broke something, it would cost her a pretty penny to replace it. That was for sure.

She reached toward the bedside table and grabbed the dainty gold necklace with a heart pendant that she'd also bought in SoHo. She'd added it to her overall purchase at the last minute when she'd realized she didn't have jewelry to wear this weekend.

A knock sounded at the door.

"Hey, can I come in?" Jeremiah asked. He'd waited downstairs while Noelle got dressed in order to give her privacy.

"Yeah, I'm dressed," she called.

Jeremiah opened the door and took a tentative step inside. He wore a navy blue polo, tan chinos, and navy blue and white low-top Dunks. He was holding a hand over his eyes, and he pretended to stumble as he walked.

Noelle laughed. "You can open your eyes."

"You sure?" He peeked through his fingers, smiling.

"Promise."

He dropped his hand, and whatever he was about to say died on his lips. He gazed at Noelle and blinked slowly.

"You look beautiful," he said.

She bit her lip, suddenly bashful. She'd felt the same way earlier when he'd said that her beauty took his breath away. It had been a line for his family then. But the way he was looking at her now, like the sight of her made his breath catch, seemed genuine. Especially since he hadn't complimented her for the benefit of any witnesses. Her inner butterflies were trying to break themselves out of prison and flood her brain again.

"Thank you," she said, forcing herself to turn to the mirror. "You don't look so bad yourself. I'll be ready in a second."

She tried to clasp the necklace around her neck, but she kept missing the tiny hole.

"Let me help you," Jeremiah said. He walked over and stood behind her. Their fingers brushed as she released the necklace ends into his hands. Warmth radiated from his skin.

He smelled good too, of course. He probably never smelled bad, even when he sweated.

Great, now she was picturing him shirtless and glistening with sweat.

STOP, brain. Please!

"I like this," he said, focusing on the necklace. "Is it new too?"

"Yeah, but it's not real gold," she hastened to say. "It didn't cost that much."

He just smirked and shook his head. "I told you to buy whatever you needed for the weekend. Real gold or not."

He'd also told her to keep his credit card until the weekend ended, just in case. It was nothing to him. That must be nice.

He finished fastening her necklace, but he didn't move from behind her. She didn't move either. Their gazes held in the mirror.

"How are you feeling?" he asked.

"Pretty okay," she said. "Your family seems to believe us, right?"

"Yeah, I think so." His attention traveled from her face to her collarbone and hovered there, like he didn't want to lower his eyes and openly ogle her. The neckline of her dress was modest, but a bit of cleavage was still visible.

"We look good together," he said, meeting her eyes again in the mirror.

"We do," she agreed.

For a second, she let herself imagine that she was living in an alternate reality where she was Jeremiah's real girlfriend and they were about to have dinner with his family. They'd met at the bookstore weeks ago and had fallen madly in love, hard and fast. She hadn't lost her job, and she was all squared away to start classes in the fall. No, wait. In this scenario she was already a librarian. (Her alternate reality, her rules.) She didn't have to worry about Jeremiah distracting her because she had achieved landing her dream job. He wasn't moving to California anymore either, and on her lunch breaks, he picked her up in his sleek, fast car and they made out in his back seat. In this reality, pigs also flew, she was best friends with Beyoncé, and the sky was purple. Because why not.

It was best to stay grounded in real life, though.

She turned around to face Jeremiah.

"I've decided that if your mom offers me sweets for dessert, I'm going to tell her that I don't eat them," she said with a regretful sigh. "I don't think I've been doing a good enough job at not endearing myself to them. They don't need to know how obsessed I am with Smith's Sweets."

"I'll sneak you some later," he said. "I got you."

"Thank you." She grinned up at him, and he winked.

She didn't know how she was going to manage sleeping in this room with him without wanting to jump his bones, but she'd figure that out later.

"Ready?" he asked.

He held out his hand, and she placed her hand in his.

"Ready."

Palms pressed together, they walked downstairs. She heard the chef and his team bustling around in the kitchen. The voices of Jeremiah's family members drifted down the hall from the dining room. Noelle leaned in closer to Jeremiah.

"We haven't kissed yet today," she whispered. "I thought I'd ask if that's fine with you, or if you'd like to plan a kiss for sometime tonight."

His eyes immediately went to her mouth, and her heart started doing jumping jacks.

"You're right," he said. "We should probably kiss tonight, shouldn't we?"

"For believability's sake, yeah," she answered, trying to remain purely professional. "That way when we break up tomorrow, it will be all the more shocking. And your family will want to give you space because they'll think you're really heartbroken."

He nodded. "True. I like how you think. Let's kiss as we walk into the dining room, before we sit down. What should be our cue? I'll let you take the lead."

"I'll wink at you," she said.

"Perfect."

When they entered the dining room, the rest of the Smiths were already seated around the table.

"There they are," Celeste said, smiling. She was sitting at the head of the table, and she shook her finger at Noelle and Jeremiah good-naturedly. "There's always a couple stragglers for dinner."

"Sorry, Jeremiah was helping me with my necklace," Noelle said. She looked up at him. "Thanks, babe."

Then she winked, giving his cue.

Jeremiah reached up and lightly cupped her cheek. Their eyes locked as he slowly lowered his mouth to hers, like he was giving her a chance to change her mind if she wanted to. But Noelle didn't move. Their lips pressed together, and it sent her rebellious butterflies on a frenzy, rattling around inside her chest and begging for release. The kiss was sweet and chaste. Featherlight with no tongue. But electric currents moved through Noelle, nonetheless.

She pulled away from Jeremiah, ending their kiss, and she smiled easily as she walked to one of the open seats at the table, even though every cell in her body was buzzing. As Jeremiah sat next to her, she was afraid to look at him, afraid for him to see how much their simple kiss had affected her. When she finally found the courage to glance over, she found him looking down at the table, smiling quietly to himself.

"How are things at Good Boy?" Percy asked. He was sitting directly across from Jeremiah, who looked up and blinked, like he was surprised to hear Percy ask that question. Percy glanced at Celeste. "Mom was telling me that you just landed a new deal with Shop Mart. That's dope. Congrats."

"I didn't know that, Miah," Amara said, grinning at Jeremiah from her end of the table. "That's amazing."

"Yeah, congratulations," Robin said.

"Very proud of you, honey," Celeste added.

Harper and Ashley applauded, even though they probably had no idea what it meant for Jeremiah to land the deal with Shop Mart. Noelle didn't know the details about the deal either, but his family wasn't aware of her ignorance. She rubbed Jeremiah's back like a proud girlfriend. It said that this deal was old news to her, and she enjoyed seeing him receive praise from his family.

"Thanks, y'all," he said. His attention lingered on Percy, and Noelle wondered if Percy's praise mattered to Jeremiah the most. He sent a smile over his shoulder at her, and her heart skipped a beat. "I appreciate it."

The private chef, Chef Amir, entered the dining room with his small staff, who placed plates in front of everyone. He explained their meal. Sautéed pork chops, mashed potatoes, and grilled asparagus. For dessert, Celeste baked a blueberry crumble pie from scratch using a Smith's Sweets recipe. Noelle inwardly groaned. She wouldn't be able to have any of that pie. At least not directly after dinner in front of his family.

They thanked Chef Amir and his team, and everyone fell quiet as they ate. A long day spent on the boardwalk made for empty stomachs. The food was delicious. Noelle was savoring the taste of the creamy mashed potatoes and wondering how much it cost to have Chef Amir cook for them tonight, when Celeste broke the silence.

"Noelle, hon, you mentioned that you and Jeremiah met at the bookstore where you used to work," she said. "Where are you working now?"

Noelle's fork froze halfway to her mouth. She glanced around the table. Each of the Smiths was looking at her. Jeremiah's smile was encouraging. She'd told him that she'd planned to lean toward honesty if asked about her job. She was going to say that she wasn't working right now because she was focusing on school, which was technically true in a way. She was focusing on *going back* to school. It was a fair answer.

But when she placed her fork down on her plate, she blurted, "I'm a librarian."

It appeared that without her prior agreement, her alternate reality and actual reality had decided to clash.

"Oh, that's lovely!" Celeste said. She looked at Amara. "We have another book lover in our midst." Amara nodded eagerly.

For his part, Jeremiah continued to smile like Noelle hadn't just thrown a monkey wrench into their lore. She smiled too and rubbed her dampening palms against her thighs.

Why? Why had she lied? She wasn't here to impress anyone. She was just a weekend prop for Jeremiah's story! But . . . she couldn't help caring what Celeste thought about her. And she didn't want Celeste—or any of the Smiths for that matter—to think she was a gold digger who'd hooked her claws into their beloved *Miah*. She wanted to be a librarian so badly. It was the reason she was here pretending to be Jeremiah's girlfriend in the first place. His money was going to help her reach her goal of becoming a librarian. She wished that her lie was true right now. Hopefully it would be true soon enough. Didn't that count for something?

"What kind of librarian?" Percy asked.

Noelle glanced across the table at him. "I'm sorry?"

"Are you a school librarian? A public librarian?" Percy asked. "Do you work at a university?"

"Oh." That actually was a pretty great question. "I, um, work at the public library in Brickton."

"She's good at her job," Jeremiah added, resting his arm across the back of her chair.

"I know Brickton," Robin said, perking up. "My cousin and her girlfriend just bought a house by that park with the gazebo and the lake. Do you know which one I'm talking about?"

Noelle nodded. "That's a really nice area."

"It is," Robin agreed. "Do you live around there too?"

The people who lived on that side of Brickton had corporate jobs in the city and sent their children to private schools. Their roads were better paved, and they put up elaborate decorations outside their homes every year during the holidays. They were like their own separate community. One that Noelle and the people she'd grown up with in Brickton were not part of.

Noelle simply shook her head. "No."

"We have an announcement!" Ashley declared.

Noelle silently thanked Ashley for stealing the attention away. As everyone turned to look at the twins, Jeremiah leaned over to Noelle and whispered, "Are you okay?"

"I'm good, thanks," she whispered back, sparing him a quick smile.

"We're doing the summer talent show this year," Ashley said. "We're going to dance."

"Oh wow!" Celeste said. "That's wonderful. Just the two of you?"

"No, Ciara and Zoe too."

"Ciara and Zoe's family vacations at the home next door," Jeremiah explained to Noelle, and she nodded.

"We still need to figure out an appropriate song for them to dance to, though," Robin said. "We can't seem to agree on anything yet."

"We want to do 'TGIF' by GloRilla," Harper said. "But Mom said no because there's too much cursing."

"And Dad says no too," Percy added. "No way *at all*."

Jeremiah snorted, and Percy shot him a look across the table.

"I'm sure there's a Kidz Bop version of that song somewhere," Jeremiah said.

Noelle covered her mouth to muffle the sound of her laughter.

"How about some dessert?" Celeste asked.

She went to grab the blueberry crumble pie from the kitchen. She placed it in the middle of the dining room table and as she began slicing a piece, Noelle's mouth watered.

"Noelle, since this is your first time in Heart Beach, the first slice is yours," Celeste said. "I used one of my parents' favorite recipes to make this pie. It's also a top seller for us every summer. I hope you love it."

Oh, goodness, here we go.

"Oh, um, I'm really sorry," Noelle said. "But I don't like eating sweets."

The words were physically painful to say.

Celeste looked up sharply. Confusion wiped her face blank. The rest of the family blinked at Noelle. She sat up straighter. In a protective gesture, Jeremiah inched his chair closer to hers.

Celeste laughed lightly. "I'm sorry, hon, we're just a little shocked because that's not something we hear around here very often, but I understand." She looked at Jeremiah. "Miah, big or small slice for you?"

"I'm not gonna have any pie either," he said.

Celeste simply stared at him.

"What? Really?" Amara asked, leaning forward to look down the table at Jeremiah. "Isn't blueberry crumble your favorite?"

"You're the same guy who once fought me over the last slice of blueberry crumble pie," Percy said, laughing in disbelief.

"That happened when I was sixteen and you were nineteen," Jeremiah said, sighing.

"Have you stopped eating sweets now?" Celeste asked, brows raised.

It was like they'd just found out that Jeremiah had decided to stop brushing his teeth or drinking water. Essential things. But then again, maybe being a fan of sweets kind of *was* an essential thing in this family.

"Nah," Jeremiah said. "I'm just full. I'll have some pie for breakfast tomorrow."

Under the table, he gently squeezed Noelle's hand. She realized that he probably did want pie, but he wasn't going to eat it in front of her while knowing that she wouldn't have any herself. He was abstaining in solidarity. It was silly and unnecessary, but she felt touched all the same.

"Okay, the first slice goes to Amara since she's the birthday girl tomorrow," Celeste said. Amara gratefully accepted her plate of pie.

"You know what I was thinking," Amara said, changing the subject as Celeste sliced pie for everyone else. "We should do a horror movie night in the backyard with the projector. We haven't done that since the summer before last."

"You and these scary movies." Celeste shook her head as she sat down and scooped pie onto her fork. To Noelle, she explained, "My dad was a horror film buff. He got the kids into it too."

"That's where my love for horror started," Amara said. "I used to watch all kinds of scary movies with Pop when I was younger. I think I liked feeling scared, but I felt protected too because I knew if Pop was there, I'd be okay."

"*I* don't love horror," Celeste said. "Pop and Jeremiah used to play the worst tricks on me."

Jeremiah smiled and shifted to face Noelle. "This one time we watched *Scream* with Pop. I didn't think it was that scary, more so gory—"

"All that fake blood," Celeste said. She closed her eyes and shivered.

"That summer, Mom took yoga classes at eight p.m.," Jeremiah continued. "So, one night while she was gone, Pop and I bought Ghostface masks from the costume store. And when she came home, we turned off the lights and jumped out and scared her."

"I almost leapt out of my skin!" Celeste said, even though she was laughing.

Noelle smiled and rested her chin in her hand as she listened. "How old you were you then?"

"I think I was fourteen," Jeremiah said.

"No, you were thirteen," Amara said. "Because I was eleven, and that was the same summer that Pop taught me how to water ski."

"He sounds like he was a lot of fun," Noelle said.

"He was," Jeremiah agreed. He fell quiet and stared at his empty plate.

"Celeste, I forgot to tell you that I saw Mercy Webster at the grocery store this morning," Robin said. "She asked if she could bring a plus-one to Amara's party tomorrow. I think she has a new boyfriend."

"Really?" Celeste asked. "What happened to the last guy?"

As the family moved on to another subject, Noelle noticed that Jeremiah didn't join in. He kept his eyes averted, focused on the table. His brows pulled together as he rubbed his forehead. Then he stood abruptly. Everyone looked at him.

"Is anybody else hot?" he asked. "I'm kinda hot. I'm gonna get some air."

"Oh." Noelle began to slide her chair back.

"It's okay," he told her quickly, his expression strained. "I'll be back in a couple minutes."

He left the dining room. Unsure of what to do, Noelle looked around the table at his family. The adults exchanged quiet glances.

"Sometimes talking about my father can be difficult for Jeremiah," Celeste explained quietly to Noelle. Her smile was soft. "Grief manifests itself differently for everyone. Don't worry. He just needs a few minutes."

"Okay," Noelle said, folding her hands in her lap.

She decided that she'd wait ten minutes, exactly. Then she'd go and check on her fake boyfriend.

Chapter Ten

Jeremiah sat in a chair by the pool, his head in his hands. Inside the dining room, he'd started to feel suffocated. There were so many conversations with Pop that he wished he could have. Things he wished he could do over. He wished he could deal with Pop's death normally like the rest of his family. He wished that he didn't carry so much guilt about how his last conversation with Pop had been so fraught.

He didn't know how long he sat outside alone before he heard the sound of someone else's footsteps. He glanced up, and Noelle was walking across the backyard, maneuvering between the party tables and chairs. Wordlessly, she sat down in the pool chair beside him.

"I'm really sorry," he said quickly. "I shouldn't have left you in there alone. I just needed a minute."

"It's okay," she said. "I understand that you're sad about your grandfather." She paused. "Do you want to talk about it?"

He inhaled a deep breath and let it go. He wanted to open

up to someone. Maybe Noelle would be the perfect someone because he most likely wouldn't see her again after this weekend, and he could speak without fearing her judgment. But he didn't want to burden her with his problems. That wasn't why she was here.

"Nah, I'm good. Thank you, though."

She nodded. Silently, they stared at the glowing pool water.

"I'm not sure if you could tell how much it pained me to turn down that pie," she said eventually, "but I really do want to sneak a slice upstairs tonight to eat before bed, FYI."

Jeremiah chuckled softly. "I'll get you a slice. And some salted caramel chocolate chip cookies too. I know we have a box around here somewhere. They're your favorite, right?"

"Yeah," she said, smiling. "Thank you."

They sat by the pool for another few minutes before they went back inside. Amara, Robin, and the twins were settled on the living room couch. It was L-shaped and big enough to fit the entire family.

"Noelle, come sit with us," Amara said, patting the empty seat beside her. "We're about to find a movie to watch."

"Oh," Noelle said. She hesitated and glanced at Jeremiah. Then she bit her lip before turning back to his sister. "I'd better go to bed. I'm pretty tired."

He figured she said this for the sake of keeping her distance.

Amara nodded and smiled. "No worries."

They exchanged good-nights. As Noelle started up the steps, Jeremiah told her he'd meet her in his room after he grabbed the sweets he'd promised her. He was surprised when he walked into the kitchen and saw Celeste and Percy hovering over Percy's laptop at the island. They were speaking in low tones, most likely discussing the missing shipments that Percy had been worried about earlier. They glanced up when they noticed Jeremiah.

"Sorry, just grabbing some pie," he said. "Decided to eat some tonight after all."

"Help yourself, honey," Celeste said.

He grabbed a half-full box of salted caramel chocolate chip cookies from the cabinet and made quick work of slicing the pie.

"Good night," he said to Celeste and Percy.

Percy nodded, and Celeste smiled, looking a little tired. "Good night, sweetheart. See you in the morning."

When he walked into his room, Noelle had already changed into her pajamas. An oversize yellow T-shirt that said I Like Big Books and I Cannot Lie and a pair of old tennis shorts. She sat at the top of the bed by the pillows, a thick paperback novel open in her lap. When she saw the cookies and pie in his hands, her eyes lit up.

"Thank you *so, so, so, so* much," she said. She immediately dug into the pie, balancing the plate on her thighs. With her free hand, she opened her book again.

Jeremiah sat at the edge of the bed and leaned back, resting on his elbows. He peered at the cover of Noelle's book. A woman and a man were caught in a passionate embrace. The man was shirtless, and the woman's breasts were pushed up, displaying her cleavage. The title read *Pirate Daughter in Disguise* by Clara Crawford.

He glanced at Noelle again. She'd looked radiant tonight in her dress, but she looked beautiful now too, relaxed and comfortable in her pajamas with a scarf tied around her braids. When they'd kissed earlier, he'd felt it deep in his bones. Her lips were soft and plush, and he wanted to kiss her again. He wanted to lie down next to her, just to be physically closer. And . . . he absolutely should *not* be thinking about her that way because he was her client.

"What's your book about?" he asked.

Noelle finished chewing and placed her pie to the side. "A woman named Anne grew up on a pirate ship because her dad was a pirate captain, but she's always hated life at sea, so she seeks passage to France and lies about her identity because being a pirate is a crime. When she gets to Paris, she meets an inventor named Timothy and they fall in love, but she's afraid to tell Timothy the truth about who she really is because his parents were killed by pirates, and he despises them."

"Damn, that's wild."

"Right? But the real plot twist is that his parents *weren't* killed by pirates. They were killed by a shady businessman who wanted to steal the patent of one of their inventions. He's the villain in book one. This is book four in the series."

"Wait, wait," Jeremiah said. "Can you start from the beginning, please? What happens in book one?"

Noelle eagerly put her bookmark between the pages, holding her place. "Okay, so in book one . . ."

Jeremiah eased back fully onto the bed and listened as Noelle talked about pirates and drama and sweeping romance. He asked for clarification on certain things, like why one hero wanted revenge on his father, and why one heroine was seeking a treasure map. Noelle answered each question with patient enthusiasm. After she was done catching him up on the series, she asked if he wanted to borrow the books.

"Yeah," he said, genuinely intrigued. "But I wanna be where you are in the story now."

She looked at him and smirked a little. "Do you want me to read out loud to you?"

He nodded, smiling. "If that's cool."

Noelle began to read. Anne was finally admitting her true identity to Timothy. Noelle had an incredibly soothing voice. Jeremiah felt his eyes drift closed as she lulled him into relaxation. It had been a long day. Physically, mentally. He should change into his pajamas. But his limbs felt so heavy.

"Jeremiah . . . are you listening?" Noelle asked.

"Yes." He forced his eyes open. "Timothy just asked Anne to leave, but then he immediately regretted it. Keep going, please."

Noelle laughed quietly and shook her head. "You're falling asleep."

"I promise I'm not."

After a moment, she continued reading. He listened to her honey-dipped voice, and soon his eyes drooped closed again against his will.

Later, distantly, he felt a blanket being draped over him. The bedroom light cut off, shrouding him in darkness. He was lying at the foot of the bed, perpendicular to Noelle, and her feet gently brushed against his side as she got comfortable.

I should get up and go to the nook, he thought to himself.

But instead, he rolled over and fell into a deeper sleep.

Chapter Eleven

"That has got to be the final boss of balloon arches," Noelle said.

She stood in the Smiths' backyard beside Jeremiah and stared up at the helium-inflated masterpiece made of white and gold balloons that arched across the pool. Another set of gold balloons floated in the water spelling out *Happy 27th Birthday, Amara!* This pool was a lot nicer than the pool she'd learned how to swim in at the Brickton YMCA.

Amara's birthday barbecue was officially in full swing. A DJ was spinning. A painter was in the process of creating a live oil painting of the party. Servers maneuvered through the throng of guests, carrying trays of hors d'oeuvres. Other servers carried assorted baggies of Smith's Sweets cookies.

From what Noelle could tell, Amara didn't seem like the type to make a big deal out of her birthday. The dress code was all white, but Amara wore a sleeveless black minidress paired with her Doc Martens platform sandals. She was laughing with a few friends by the pool. Celeste was the one making the rounds, flashing her dazzling smile as she sauntered through the backyard, wearing a delicate-looking white midi dress and tie-up espadrille sandals. Her bob bounced effortlessly as she walked, stopping to talk to many of the guests who were business owners and/or neighbors in Heart Beach.

Through the sea of white, Noelle spotted Ashley and Harper playing with two girls around their age. Noelle figured they must be their friends Zoe and Ciara from next door. Percy and Robin were nearby, talking with another couple. Jeremiah was the only Smith who didn't have friends of his own in attendance. He'd told Noelle that he didn't really have friends other than his childhood best friend, Danny, who wouldn't be in Heart Beach this weekend. He'd said he'd had to cut off his other friends in order to change his lifestyle.

She wondered if that made him feel lonely now.

"Believe it or not, that's average-sized compared to some of the displays my mom has had for past parties," Jeremiah said, looking up at the balloon arch too. "Caesar is gonna hate when the balloons have to get popped later, though. It'll scare him."

Jeremiah was wearing a short-sleeve open-collar white shirt and straight-legged white jeans with white Veja sneakers, while Noelle wore an eyelet white minidress and white open-toe slingback kitten-heel sandals. They might not have been a real couple, but they matched each other's fly. At least Noelle hoped they did. Blending in wasn't an issue for her at weddings because she usually wore a dress that was approved by the bride, and her hair and makeup were done by professionals. But here, standing with Jeremiah in his family's backyard, among people who probably had no idea what it was like to miss a bill or go into credit card debt for buying essentials, she hoped she looked like she fit in.

"Who's Caesar?" she asked Jeremiah.

"My mom's cat," he said, turning to her. "He doesn't like the beach house, so he hides under her bed most of the time. You'll probably never see him, which is for the best, because he only likes my mom, and he might scratch you if he sees you."

"Yikes." Noelle tilted her head and quirked an eyebrow. "So you're telling me he's even able to resist your charms?"

"He likes to resist me the most." The edge of his mouth curled into a slow smirk. "Are you trying to say that you think I'm charming, Noelle Lewis?"

She laughed. "I think we both know that you're charming."

"You said it, not me." His grin made her stomach muscles tighten involuntarily.

This morning, she'd turned over to find him lying beside her on top of the covers. Sometime overnight, he must have moved from the foot of the bed to lie vertically. He was far enough away that they weren't touching. She rested her head against the pillow and observed his sleeping form. He'd been frowning. She'd never seen someone frown in their sleep before. She wondered what he was dreaming about.

By the time he woke up, she'd been reading for almost an hour. He rubbed his eyes and immediately apologized for falling asleep on the bed when he'd meant to sleep in the nook. She told him it was fine, he probably would have hurt his back anyway.

"I don't want to sleep in the bed with you again if it makes you uncomfortable," he'd said, his gaze direct and earnest.

"I wasn't uncomfortable," she'd replied.

In fact, she liked waking up next to him more than she

should have. It felt nice to read quietly in bed while he slept not too far away. If this were a longer commitment, their sleeping arrangement might have presented a bigger problem. But they had only one more night here together. It would be fine if they shared the bed again.

Jeremiah had gotten up and gone down to the kitchen. He'd brought Noelle a cup of coffee, and then he'd left to go on a run.

It was clear to Noelle that all of the Smiths missed their patriarch, but Jeremiah seemed to take his grandfather's death harder than the rest of his family. When she'd found him by the pool last night, he'd been staring despondently at the ground. With her brides, she always made herself available as a sounding board. Someone to listen to their problems and help ease their emotional load. She'd wanted to offer the same opportunity to Jeremiah. She didn't like seeing him so upset. It was why she'd asked if he wanted to talk about his grandfather. But unlike her brides who were usually bursting at the seams to unload their stress, Jeremiah wanted to keep whatever was bothering him close to his chest.

Maybe that was for the best, though. Historically, whenever Noelle asked a man to open up to her, things didn't end well. CJ had been her first and last lesson with a serious boyfriend. She was too focused to let a relationship get in the way of her goals. But there had been others after CJ here and there whom she'd dated casually when feelings of loneliness wore on her. And even with those less serious situationships where her heart wasn't on the line and there wasn't much at stake, men couldn't or wouldn't meet her halfway in simple ways, and it was still disappointing. It had been years since she'd casually dated, though. It was a waste of her time and attention.

Jeremiah was different, of course, because on paper he was nothing like CJ or any of the men she'd dated before. And he wasn't her real boyfriend. He was her client, and they hadn't agreed to exchange emotional truths; they'd agreed to exchange a fee. There was no point in trying to get Jeremiah to open up to her if she wasn't going to see him again after tomorrow. She needed to keep reminding herself of that. Because every time he touched her, an electric current zipped through her veins, and when they'd kissed last night, her skin cells had rearranged themselves. It was confusing, to say the least.

Jeremiah leaned closer and whispered now, "Two o'clock. A lady wearing big-ass sunglasses is making her way over here. Her name's Mercy Webster. She owns a few clothing boutiques in the tri-state area, including one here in Heart Beach."

Noelle waited a second before she discreetly turned her head in the direction that Jeremiah had indicated. A woman with large white sunglasses was walking toward them. Her sunglasses were decorated with white feathers and colorful gemstones. She had medium brown skin and short, dark hair. Her bracelets jangled as she waved at them.

Jeremiah waved back, his smile instantly widening. Guests had been venturing over to Noelle and Jeremiah since the party began, and Jeremiah hadn't said as much, but Noelle suspected he'd chosen their current spot at the back of the party because he *didn't* want to be found or sought out. But once he was approached, he was amiable as he engaged in conversation. Noelle was beginning to tell the difference between his real smile and the smile that he gave when he was putting on a performance. For example, the smile that he gave to

Mercy Webster lit up the bottom half of his face, but it didn't completely reach his eyes.

"Jeremiah, I thought that was you," Mercy Webster said, beaming as she neared them. She pushed her sunglasses up onto her head. "Aren't you a sight for sore eyes."

"Hi, Ms. Webster," Jeremiah said, hugging the woman. "How are you?"

"Perfect as a peach." She glanced curiously at Noelle as she pulled away from Jeremiah. "Who is this lovely date of yours?"

"This is my girlfriend, Noelle. Noelle, this is Ms. Webster. She's a friend of my mom's."

"It's nice to meet you," Noelle said. Mercy shook Noelle's hand in firm, quick pumps. Noelle was realizing that a lot of people here shook hands this way.

"Lovely to meet you as well." Mercy turned to Jeremiah and winked. "We missed seeing you over Memorial Day Weekend. But now I see why you've been so preoccupied."

"Ah, you know how it is," he said. "We're in the honeymoon stage."

He smiled lovingly at Noelle, and for a second, his smile disarmed her. But she quickly remembered her role and leaned into him as he leisurely wrapped his arm around her waist.

"'Summer lovin' happened so fast,'" she sang.

"What's that from?" Jeremiah asked. "No, don't tell me. It's a musical. Um . . . um . . . damn, is it that movie with Meryl Streep and she's on an island with her daughter, and she has three baby dads?"

Noelle snorted. "*Mamma Mia!*? No, the song is from *Grease*."

"Oh yeah, the musical with the surprise sci-fi twist at the end."

"Wait, what?" Noelle's brows furrowed. "I don't think we're talking about the same thing."

"Yes, we are. Danny and Sandy are riding in their convertible and all of a sudden it starts to fly."

Noelle burst out laughing, and Jeremiah grinned in satisfaction as he looked at her, like he was pleased with himself for having made her laugh.

"You two are adorable," Mercy said. "How long have you been together?"

"Two months," Noelle said. At the same time, Jeremiah said, "Three months."

Mercy's brows furrowed as she glanced between them.

"*Honey*," Noelle said, forcing a laugh. Jeremiah's eyes widened as he realized his mistake. "I know it feels like we've known each other longer, but it's only been two months. We started dating in May, remember?"

"Of course I remember," Jeremiah said, easily smoothing over his error. His eyes sparkled as he looked at Noelle. "The day you said you'd be my girlfriend is a day I'll never forget."

He said it so *convincingly*. Her heart stuttered as their eyes held. And for a sweet second, she forgot that they were supposed to be pretending.

"Noelle, do you live in Jersey City like Jeremiah?" Mercy asked, snapping Noelle out of her trance.

"No," Noelle said, clearing her throat. She turned to Mercy again. "But I live close by."

"Lovely. And what field of work are you in?"

This wasn't the first time today that someone had asked Noelle about what she did for a living. It seemed to be a conversation starter with this crowd. Or like a way to determine a person's value.

“I’m a librarian,” she said. She had no choice but to continue the lie that she’d told the rest of the Smiths last night.

“A noble profession,” Mercy said, nodding approvingly. “And how are things at Good Dog, Jeremiah?”

“Good Boy,” Jeremiah corrected, smile unfaltering. “Things are going well. Thank you for asking.”

“Is it true that you’re moving to the West Coast?” Ms. Webster asked. “Your mom mentioned it a few weeks ago. She hasn’t said so, but I know she’s sad that you’re moving.” She looked at Noelle. “Are you planning to move with him?”

“No,” Noelle said. “We’re going to do long distance.”

Mercy frowned, like she thought that was a terrible idea.

“How interesting,” she said. “Jeremiah, you know, I still don’t understand why you left the family business. But these days I guess everyone wants to make their own way in life instead of following in the footsteps of those who came before.”

Mercy’s comment annoyed Noelle, but Jeremiah took it in stride, still sporting his easy, if manufactured, smile. Noelle didn’t know why Jeremiah didn’t work for Smith’s Sweets. Like his beef with Percy, it didn’t seem like information that she’d need in order to do her job. She was curious, of course, but she wasn’t about to pass judgment on his choice, like Mercy. She rethreaded her fingers through his and gave his hand a light squeeze.

“You’ll be attending the gala in a few weeks, won’t you?” Mercy asked. “I remember how much your grandfather loved the gala. You look more and more like him each year. It’s uncanny.”

Jeremiah’s hand tensed in Noelle’s. His first sign of true discomfort.

Chapter Twelve

Jeremiah immediately began looking for a way out of this conversation.

"Ah, yeah," he said, feeling his smile finally crack. "I hear that a lot."

The polite conversation and schmoozing, he could do. He'd been doing it for the past two hours. It was surface-level talk that required him only to smile, listen, and respond. But talking about Pop wasn't an easy, superficial topic. It was inevitable, really, that someone would mention his grandfather today. Now that he thought about it, he was surprised that it had taken this long. He should have better prepared himself.

"Your grandfather loved to dance at the galas," Mercy continued. She smiled as she looked at Noelle. "Did you ever see his grandfather dance?"

"Um, no." Noelle's fingers remained threaded through Jeremiah's. "He passed away before I met Jeremiah."

"Oh, right, of course," Mercy said. "He was one of a kind. A sweet and giving man. He used to—"

"I'm sorry, Ms. Webster," Jeremiah said. "I hate to interrupt, but I forgot that I need to talk to my mom about something. It was good to see you again. Enjoy the rest of the party."

He began to pull Noelle away, and she went with him easily.

"Oh yes, lovely speaking with you, Jeremiah!" Mercy said. "And lovely to meet you, Nolie! Come by the boutique! We have feather sunglasses in a variety of colors!"

"It's *Noelle*," Jeremiah called over his shoulder.

How could Mercy ask someone to spend money at her store and call them the wrong name in the same breath?

"Thank you," Noelle whispered.

Jeremiah nodded, feeling slightly embarrassed about his sudden need to abandon the scene. Maybe he would have been able to deal with hearing Ms. Webster's story about Pop if they weren't here in Heart Beach. If they weren't surrounded by Pop's memory, along with Jeremiah's ever-present fear that he wasn't doing Pop's memory any justice.

As he and Noelle moved through the crowd, people tried to stop him to talk, but he kept up the same excuse that he needed to find Celeste. In reality, Celeste was in social butterfly hostess mode, and Jeremiah probably wouldn't get a chance to speak to her again until after the party ended. But saying that he needed to find her was an excuse that no one would question. He just needed a break from all the conversation. Holding hands with Noelle felt like the only thing anchoring him in place.

He led her around to the side of the house where there were no guests milling around. The music was less loud here. He leaned back against the house and took a moment to hear himself think. He'd once thrived in big social settings, but he'd spent the past two years quietly trying to work on himself. This party was more jarring than he'd expected.

Noelle silently stood in front of him, watching. Waiting. He wondered if she'd ask if he was okay. He half hoped that she would, half hoped that she wouldn't.

"Mercy's sunglasses were kind of ridiculous," she said. "I wonder what it says about me that she thinks I'd want to buy them."

Jeremiah laughed softly. "I think it's more so that she wants someone who looks like you to be seen wearing her stuff."

Noelle smiled as she shook her head. "I'd love to be a fly on the wall at her boutique to see who shops there."

"I've been to her boutique before. You'll suffocate from the perfume spray before you can see who else is inside."

Noelle laughed, and the heavy mental cloud hovering above him began to dissipate at the sound of her giggle.

"How are you doing?" he asked, lightly touching her arm before dropping his hand to his side. "Are you having fun?"

"I am," she said. "And as far as how I'm doing, I guess I should ask you that. Am I being a good girlfriend?"

He was about to tell her that she was doing an amazing job, but then he heard someone call his name.

"Jeremiah, yo, I've been looking for you all afternoon!"

Jeremiah instinctively fixed his face into a smile, but his smile froze once he turned and saw who had discovered him. Theo Cruz, his old friend. The same friend he'd been partying with the night before Pop died. Last he'd heard, Theo lived in DC now, but his family still had a house in Heart Beach.

"Theo, what's up?" Jeremiah said. He swallowed hard and

forced his smile to stay in place. Seeing Theo was a stark reminder of the choices he wished he could remake.

"Nothing much. Just spending time with the fam for the weekend," Theo said, walking closer. He wore a white button-up and white shorts. He lightly punched Jeremiah in the shoulder. "I was in the city back in November, by the way. I hit you up, but you didn't respond."

"Yeah, sorry." Jeremiah scratched the back of his neck. "Work's been crazy. I probably responded to you in my head but forgot to actually text back."

That was half true. Jeremiah had seen Theo's text, and he'd known that Theo would want to go out like they used to. After Pop died, Jeremiah took a hard look at himself and realized that he needed to change. He thought of Pop's wishes for him to find his real purpose and to stop wasting his life around people who didn't care about him. He could be more than just the guy people invited out for a good time. Further driving home Pop's point, after he died, no one in that friend group bothered reaching out to Jeremiah to offer their condolences. It had been Jeremiah's final wake-up call. After that summer, he fell back from that friend group, and he stopped going out altogether. What had surprised him was how quickly he realized that he didn't miss any of it.

So when Jeremiah saw Theo's text come through, he purposely hadn't responded. There was no easy way to explain that he couldn't chill with Theo anymore because the activities that they'd once bonded over were no longer part of his life, and without that, he and Theo didn't have much foundation for a friendship.

"Right, Good Boy," Theo said. "You're killing it. My ex had

a subscription for her mean-ass Chihuahua." He sent a curious glance in Noelle's direction.

"Theo, this is my girlfriend, Noelle." To Noelle, Jeremiah explained, "Theo and I went to college together."

"Hi," Noelle said. She gave a small wave and a smile.

"*Girlfriend?*" Theo laughed in surprise. "Damn. In all the years I've known Jeremiah, he's never had a serious girlfriend, although he definitely had friends, if you know what I mean. Never met someone brave enough to tame him until now, I guess . . ."

Theo trailed off, and an awkward silence permeated the air.

"Noelle is too special for me to not be serious about her," Jeremiah said. He looked at Noelle with a genuine smile.

"Jeremiah swept me off my feet," she said with soft adoration.

"Cool." Theo nodded, clearly uninterested in their expressions of affection. "Listen, a few of us are meeting up tonight at the Sand Saloon. Y'all should come out. Have some fun."

"We have plans tonight, actually," Jeremiah said, nodding at Noelle. "We're gonna have to pass."

"Aww, nah, bro. Change your plans! Bring your lady!" Theo looked at Noelle. "If you're with Jeremiah, I'm guessing you already know how to have a good time. Come on, convince him to bring you out with us instead."

"Nah, we're gonna chill," Jeremiah said, more firmly.

Theo sucked his teeth and waved Jeremiah away. "You got into a relationship and turned boring. I hate to see it!" He laughed, but his laughter abruptly stopped once he saw the irritated look on Noelle's face. "Sorry, I'm joking. I don't have a great sense of humor."

"Clearly," Noelle mumbled under her breath.

"It was good to see you, Theo," Jeremiah said, officially signaling that it was time for the conversation to end. "Enjoy the rest of the party."

"Will do." Theo saluted Jeremiah and smiled guiltily at Noelle. "See you around."

Noelle nodded, frowning as she watched Theo retreat to the party.

"How good of a friend is he to you?" she asked Jeremiah.

"We're not super close."

"Oh," she said. Then, "I don't know if I like him very much."

Jeremiah chuckled, exhausted. "Me neither, to be honest. We didn't have much in common, other than partying. But I don't really do that anymore now, so."

She paused, tilted her head. "Can I ask you something? It's personal."

Jeremiah studied her for a beat. He was a little wary about what she might ask, but he found that he wanted to answer whatever question she had for him. He nodded.

"You said before that you don't really have a lot of friends and that you changed your lifestyle. Why did you decide to make those changes?"

"I, uh, just wasn't surrounding myself with the best people," he said. "And I wasn't really living up to my full potential. I mean, I'm still trying to figure out what my full potential is now, but I wasn't trying at all then. Before my grandfather died, he said some things about how I was living that made me want to change."

That was the most he'd ever admitted to anyone about his last conversation with Pop. He looked over at Noelle, wondering what he'd see in her face. Her brows drew together, and her lips parted like she was about to ask a follow-up question. But then she bit her lip and nodded.

It was easier for him when people didn't poke around in his thoughts and ask for more. But for some reason, he'd hoped that Noelle might have pressed further. Maybe it was because she never seemed to judge him, and he appreciated that.

"About our breakup," she said, changing the subject completely. "We haven't discussed the reason behind it. Something that Mercy Webster said stuck with me, though. What if there's tension between us because you're moving soon, and the thought of being long distance has been stressing us out, and we realized we won't be able to last, so we argue and break up."

"I like it," Jeremiah said, even though thinking about their fake breakup was a reminder that he most likely wouldn't see Noelle after this weekend. "Tell me more."

Secluded away from the party, they huddled together and plotted their fake demise.

Chapter Thirteen

The party continued late into the night and ended with a fireworks display that was more elaborate than the Fourth of July fireworks show that Noelle watched every year in Brickton's memorial park. It was after one a.m. when the last remaining guests said their goodbyes.

Noelle and Jeremiah chose to wait to have their breakup after the party ended, because it was mainly for the benefit of his family, and they didn't want to cause a public spectacle. They stood on the back veranda and observed Celeste, Amara, Robin, and Percy, who were outside, talking by the pool. Ashley and Harper had gone to bed hours ago.

"Okay," Jeremiah said, turning to her. "Ready?"

Noelle inhaled a breath. This was her first time ever enacting a fake breakup, and she was a little nervous, but it was too late for nerves. It was time to deliver. She nodded. "Ready."

He counted down. "Three . . . two . . . one . . ."

"Action," she said.

She stormed down the steps, feet pounding as she crossed the backyard. "Okay, fine, Jeremiah," she called over her shoulder. "If you don't want me to move with you to California, I won't. I don't want to talk about it anymore."

The Smiths turned their heads and stared at Noelle as she charged past them to stand by the now-empty bar setup. She crossed her arms over her chest and narrowed her eyes at Jeremiah, who hurried across the lawn after her. She turned away, showing him her back.

"You told me that you didn't care about the long distance," he said, shaking his head in irritation. "Why do you suddenly care now?"

She whirled around to face him. Mirth flashed in his eyes, but he quickly schooled his features. She fought the urge to laugh. They'd rehearsed this scene while everyone else had been enjoying the party, and they'd struggled to get through it without laughing. But now it was time to be serious. Well, fake serious.

"That is such a lie to say I don't care about being long distance," she said. "Why would I be okay with a three-hour time difference and being separated by a six-hour flight?"

"Lots of people do long distance and they're fine," Jeremiah said. "You just started your job at the library. Your life is here, Noelle."

"So you aren't an important enough part of my life? Am *I* not important enough to *you*?"

Noelle heard the Smiths mumbling to one another as they watched her and Jeremiah from afar.

"Of course you are," he said. "You know that. I care about you so much."

"It doesn't feel that way," she said. "It doesn't feel that way at all, Jeremiah. If you can't even figure out when you'd be able to see me, it doesn't sound like our relationship is much of a priority to you."

Jeremiah began pacing back and forth. Noelle spared a brief glance at his family. They were gawking at the two of them.

"I don't know, Noelle," he said. "I just don't know. This whole thing is stressing me out."

"Maybe we can't survive the long distance," Noelle said. "You need to focus on your job without any distractions, and so do I."

Jeremiah ceased his pacing and paused in front of her.

"So this is it?" he asked, voice shaky. "It's over just like that? You're breaking my heart."

"You broke my heart first, Jeremiah," she said sorrowfully. "I guess it's over."

They stared at each other in their storm cloud of made-up heartbreak. For a split second, Jeremiah's despondent expression cracked, and the corner of his mouth tugged into a smile. Noelle bit the inside of her cheek to maintain her straight face.

"Okay, let's all just take a moment here," Celeste said, walking over. "It's been a long day and it's hot. Emotions are running high." She placed her hand on Jeremiah's shoulder. "Miah, why don't you go for a walk and cool off."

"Yeah, okay," Jeremiah said. He glanced at Noelle and winked discreetly before he strode through the backyard and out onto the street. They watched in silence as he walked in the direction of the beach.

"Percy, can you go after him, please?" Celeste asked.

Percy sighed and nodded before he dutifully trudged off to follow Jeremiah.

"Are you okay, Noelle?" Amara asked as she approached her. She put her arm around Noelle's shoulders and led her back up to the house. Celeste and Robin followed behind.

"Yeah, I'm okay," Noelle said. "It's just an unfortunate situation."

Inside the kitchen, Robin retrieved a cold water bottle from the fridge and handed it to Noelle. Noelle appreciated that they were being so kind to her, and she felt a little guilty that they believed that she and Jeremiah were in need of such care. But after this weekend, they'd move on and eventually forget all about her. She was doing what Jeremiah had paid her to do, and she needed that money.

"I haven't seen Miah upset like that in a long time," Amara said. "He must really like you."

"I agree," Robin mused. "Long distance can be tough, but I'm sure you'll work it out."

Noelle looked up sharply. This was not the reaction that they were supposed to be having. She glanced over at Celeste, who was watching Noelle with furrowed brows.

"You sure you're all right?" Celeste asked.

Noelle nodded. "Yes, thank you."

"I'm going to call Percy and see where they went," she said. "Excuse me."

Celeste left the kitchen, and Amara and Robin got the idea to heat up some slices of blueberry crumble pie and eat it with ice cream. Noelle's mouth started to water. That was her cue to leave. She bid Amara and Robin good night.

In Jeremiah's bedroom, she sat at the edge of the bed and

let out a deep sigh. Well, she'd done her job. She got to spend the weekend in a nice big house, eat tasty food, and attend a fancy party, all while wearing cute new clothes that she got to keep. And now she was going to have thirty-five hundred more dollars to put toward her college savings. Her only regret about this weekend was that she hadn't had a chance to sit on the actual beach or swim in the ocean.

Reality would set in tomorrow once she was back home. She'd need to start looking for another job. But she'd milk these last vacation-esque moments while she could.

About an hour later, she heard Jeremiah's footsteps climbing the stairs.

"Hey," he whispered as he eased inside the room. He closed the door behind him and kicked off his shoes before he walked toward the bed.

"Where'd you go?" she asked.

"The beach. I talked with Percy for a while. I thought he was coming to lecture me about arguing with you in front of our mom, but he ended up trying to give me relationship advice. Then that somehow turned into him going on a tangent about how he's learned to anticipate Robin's pregnancy cravings. Irrelevant to me, but interesting overall, I guess."

He produced one of the assorted Smith's Sweets cookie party bags from his pants pocket.

"Nabbed this for you," he said as he sat beside her.

"Thank you, thank you, thank you!" Noelle grinned and did a little dance, immediately opening the bag.

She bit into a sugar cookie, and her eyes almost rolled to the back of her head. Jeremiah laughed as he watched her. After finishing the cookie, she tied the bag closed and placed it on the bedside table. She pivoted to face Jeremiah again, and when she moved, the bottom of her dress rode up her thighs. He glanced down at her exposed skin, and it made her think of the way he'd looked at her last night in her dress. Her pulse quickened, and she suddenly felt hot all over.

"Thank you for being a good fake girlfriend this weekend," he said, bringing his gaze back up to her face.

"Thank you for hiring me to be your good fake girlfriend."

They fell quiet and stared at each other, smiling softly.

For a moment, Noelle let herself wonder again what it might be like to date Jeremiah in real life. After a long day of socializing at his sister's party, they'd shower and curl up together in bed. She'd rest her head against his chest and fall asleep listening to the sound of his heartbeat as he whispered sweet nothings in her ear.

Her attraction to Jeremiah made sense. She tended to gravitate toward men who were emotionally unavailable or emotionally resistant. Jeremiah was dealing with some emotional issues that he didn't want to discuss. That didn't bode well for a real relationship. Not to mention, their lives were quite literally going in different directions with him moving to California.

However, there was no harm in simply *imagining* what it would be like to have him as her funny, sweet, sexy, generous boyfriend, was there?

"Can I say something?" he asked. His voice had gone husky. It made the hairs on her arms rise in awareness.

She swallowed thickly. "Go ahead."

"Maybe I shouldn't say this because I'm not sure if it's against our rules. But I liked kissing you yesterday. I wish we would have kissed more."

Noelle's heart pounded violently in her chest. She looked at his full lips, entranced.

"Me too," she admitted.

Her words caused the air to change between them. Jeremiah inched closer to Noelle, and she inched closer too. *What am I doing?* He was her client, and they had clear boundaries in place.

But this was new territory. She'd never *wanted* to kiss a client before, never craved their touch.

She reached out and tentatively grazed Jeremiah's bicep with her fingertips. His muscle flexed beneath her hand. His fingers brushed against her knee as his hand traveled higher to rest against her thigh. They drew to each other until they were chest to chest, breathing heavily. They weren't kissing, but their mouths were so close, they may as well have been. She watched his Adam's apple bob as he swallowed. He lifted his other hand to cradle her cheek. His movements were slow, hesitant. She had all the time in the world to move away, but she didn't.

She realized that he was waiting for her to make the first move. She was composed of hunger and desire as she pressed her lips against his. Jeremiah made a small sound in his throat, an exhalation. He kissed her back and this time it was unlike the chaste kiss they'd shared in front of his family. This kiss was open-mouthed and scorching, tongues knocking against each other. It was a kiss filled with the pent-up tension that had been building between them all weekend. Or more accurately since he'd first visited the bookstore. He sucked on her bottom lip and heat pooled between her thighs. His beard prickled against her face, but she liked it. She brought her hands beneath his shirt and skimmed her fingers across the expanse of his stomach. He kissed his way down her throat to her breasts, cupping them in his hands. She eased back onto the bed, and he leaned over her, covering her body with his. She felt the hardness of his erection settle against her thigh. She rubbed her hips against him, and he groaned.

Mayday! Mayday! Earth to Noelle! Abort mission! Abort!

Her brain was flashing a million warning signs. She wanted her brain to shut the hell up and let her body run the show. Where were those destructive butterflies when she needed them?! But she knew that her brain was right. As much as she wanted Jeremiah, they'd already blurred the lines enough. She didn't want them to take things too far.

"Wait," she breathed.

Jeremiah stopped immediately. His face was buried in the crook of her neck. She felt his breath fan against her skin.

"I'm sorry," he whispered.

"No, you don't have to be sorry."

They were still embraced, hearts pounding, breathing heavily.

Jeremiah pulled away and rolled onto his back.

"Fuck, I'm sorry," he repeated. He looked over at her. "Are you upset?"

"No," she said, touched by his obvious concern. He didn't look like he believed her. "I swear that I'm not upset."

He closed his eyes. "I'm paying you to be here. I promised no funny business."

"Yeah, but I kissed you first. And . . . I wanted you to kiss me back."

His mouth curved into a grin, clearly pleased by her admission. But he schooled his features into seriousness again. It made Noelle laugh.

"Either way," he said. "It won't happen again. I'm sorry."

"Like I said, you don't have to be sorry. But okay. I appreciate that."

He let out a weighty sigh. "I'll sleep on the floor."

She blinked at him, but before she had a chance to respond, he rolled across the bed until he reached the edge and landed on the floor with a heavy thud.

"*Jeremiah*," Noelle hissed. "What in the world?"

She crawled to the edge of the bed. He lay on his back with his arm slung across his face, covering his eyes. From this vantage point, she could see that his erection was still alive and well. Unable to help herself, she stared.

"Eyes up here, ma'am," Jeremiah said, peeking an eye open at her.

"Sorry." She laughed quietly as she looked at him. "You don't have to sleep on the floor. That's ridiculous."

"It might help with our breakup story."

"Or your family might think I've physically harmed you because of that loud-ass thud. And that's the last thing I want them to think."

He didn't say anything. She watched his chest rise and fall as he breathed.

"Come back up here," she said. "I swear that it's fine."

"You're sure?" he asked, and she nodded.

He hesitated, but then he climbed back up onto the bed.

"I promise I won't touch you," he said. "Even if you hog the blankets and leave me to freeze and develop hypothermia."

Noelle laughed again and shook her head. "You're crazy."

"Maybe," he said, running a hand over his face as he smiled at her. "Maybe just a little."

Then he hopped off the bed and went to brush his teeth.

In his wake, Noelle felt a persistent fluttering in her stomach. She lifted her fingers to her swollen lips.

Okay, *fine*.

Maybe she did have a bit of a crush on Jeremiah. It was hard not to. But her feelings would fade soon. Years from now, Jeremiah and this whole weekend would be just a funny story.

Chapter Fourteen

In the morning, Noelle woke to a notification from her bank app that Jeremiah had sent the second half of her payment. She sat up in bed and rubbed her eyes. Jeremiah's side of the bed was empty. She checked the time. It was almost ten a.m. She didn't want to get out of bed yet. This bed was a lot more comfortable than her bed at home.

The door opened, and Jeremiah poked his head inside the room. He locked eyes with Noelle and smiled. Butterflies danced across her esophagus.

"Good morning," he said. "I was hoping to leave within the next hour or so. That cool?"

She nodded. "Yeah, I'll get up now."

"Take your time. You want coffee? I just made a fresh pot."

"Sure, thank you." She pulled back the covers and swung her legs to the floor. She glanced up at him.

"Okay." He paused for a beat. "How'd you sleep?"

"Good," she lied. True to his word, Jeremiah hadn't touched

her for the rest of the night, and she hadn't touched him either. They'd secluded themselves to their respective sides of the bed, and she'd tossed and turned for hours before finally falling asleep from pure exhaustion. Keeping away from each other had been for the best, but it had also been torturous. "How about you?"

"Yeah, same," he said. He cleared his throat. "I'll leave you to get dressed. I have to talk to my mom really quick."

"Okay, I won't be long."

He smiled again before closing the door. Noelle let out a deep breath and urged her heartbeat to chill out.

When she returned to the bedroom after showering, there was a steaming mug of coffee on the bedside table next to a new box of salted caramel chocolate chip cookies. Her heart rate increased again as she grinned like a fool. How was she supposed to like him less when he'd taken it upon himself to become her personal snack fairy?

She drank her coffee and ate some cookies while she finished packing, making sure to fit her new stuffed turtle prize in her suitcase, then she made her way downstairs. Robin sat alone at the kitchen table, peeling a grapefruit. Noelle let out a small sigh of relief that she didn't have to face all the Smiths at once. After her and Jeremiah's "breakup" last night, her interactions with his family this morning were bound to be a bit awkward.

"Pregnancy craving," Robin said, gesturing to the fruit in her hand. "Want one?"

"Oh, no thank you." Noelle turned at the sound of music coming from outside.

"The girls are coming up with their talent show routine," Robin explained.

"What song did they pick?"

"'Last Dance' by Donna Summer." At Noelle's surprised expression, Robin laughed and added, "Celeste helped them pick it. After she showed them videos of Donna Summer performing, they decided their entire routine would be disco themed."

Noelle smiled. "I'm sure it will be cute."

"Morning," Amara greeted as she sauntered into the kitchen. She was wearing a high-rise black denim skirt with a black bikini top. A canvas boat tote was slung over her shoulder. "I'm gonna sketch at the beach for a bit. Where's everyone else?"

"Your mom and Miah are in her office, the girls are outside, and Percy's at the coffee shop," Robin said.

Amara raised an eyebrow. "On a Sunday?"

Robin sighed. "Don't get me started on how your brother doesn't know how to take a break."

Amara shook her head, then focused on Noelle. "Jeremiah told me you'd be heading out early." She walked over and enfolded Noelle in a warm embrace. "It was nice hanging out this weekend," she said as she pulled away. "And thank you for helping Jeremiah pick out that copy of *Dracula*. I love it."

"You're welcome," Noelle said, glancing between Amara and Robin. "It was really great meeting you both."

The chances of her seeing them again were extremely low, and that made her kinda sad because she genuinely liked Amara and Robin. She wished she'd had time to get to know them more. Celeste and the twins too. Percy was a little prickly, but his prickliness could be overlooked. If she were Jeremiah, and she had this nice, big family who wanted her to spend time with them at their gorgeous summer house, it would be hard for her to choose to stay away in favor of working. She had to wonder if there was more behind Jeremiah's reasoning. But then again, it wasn't her business.

"I'm gonna wait outside for Jeremiah," she said. Amara and Robin smiled and nodded before turning to each other to discuss their afternoon plans once Amara returned from the beach.

Noelle rolled her suitcase outside and found Harper and Ashley standing in the driveway, along with their friends Ciara and Zoe, whom Noelle had met at the party yesterday. Harper and Ashley seemed to be in the middle of an argument. Zoe and Ciara watched, their eyes volleying between the twins like they were witnessing a verbal tennis match. At eleven years old, Zoe was the oldest and tallest of the group. Ciara, having just turned nine a couple months ago, was the youngest.

Noelle sat on the porch steps and after a couple minutes of listening, she gathered that the twins were arguing about the group's formation for their dance routine.

"We should be in a square shape, and I should stand in front of Zoe, and Ciara should stand in front of you," Ashley argued.

"No, I should stand in front of Zoe, and Ciara should stand in front of you," Harper countered. "Ciara and I are almost the same height! You're taller than her!"

"I don't care if I'm short," Ciara mumbled. "I don't want to be in the front. It's too much attention."

"I don't think it's fair that *I* can't be in the front just because I'm tall," Zoe said.

"Can I offer some help?" Noelle interrupted.

The girls turned to look at her. In middle school, Noelle

and Tati had been part of the Brickton drill team. Her performing days were behind her, but she remembered a thing or two.

The girls nodded, and Noelle walked over to them.

"You don't have to put the shortest in the front if you're in windows," she said. She hovered her hands above Ashley's shoulders. "May I?"

Ashley nodded, and one by one, Noelle moved the girls into a new formation. Harper and Zoe were in the front, and Ashley and Ciara were in the back, but they were standing to the left of Ashley and Ciara, instead of standing directly behind them.

"This way, everyone will be seen," Noelle said. "And halfway through your routine, you can switch spots if you want." She looked at Ciara, who probably didn't want to move to the front. "Or you can stay in the same spot. What do you think?"

The girls exchanged glances, holding a silent conversation. Then they turned to Noelle and smiled.

"This is a great idea," Ashley declared. "Thanks, Noelle!"

She hugged Noelle and the rest of the girls followed suit.

"You're welcome," Noelle said, laughing as she hugged them back.

The screen door opened behind her. She turned around to see Celeste standing at the door watching them with an unreadable expression. She probably now thought of Noelle as the woman who'd broken her son's heart. The girls went back to discussing their routine, and Noelle pushed aside her nerves and walked to the bottom porch step, looking up at Celeste.

"Thank you so much for having me this weekend," she said. "And I'm really sorry about last night. I know it was a bit dramatic."

"That's all right. We were happy to have you." Celeste tilted her head and looked like she was about to say something else, but Jeremiah appeared behind her. He kissed Celeste on the cheek as he slid past her out the door with his suitcase.

"Bye, Ma," he said. "Love you."

"I love you too." Celeste smiled fondly, but there was a hint of sadness in her expression too. "Call me when you get home so that I know you got there safe."

Jeremiah saluted her. "I will."

"You'll forget." Celeste shook her head with a smirk.

"I promise I won't," he said, laughing.

He grabbed Noelle's suitcase and carried both bags to his car. Then he hugged his nieces goodbye. As Noelle got in the car, she caught Celeste watching her with that same unreadable expression. She wondered what Celeste might have said to her if Jeremiah hadn't interrupted them.

Before they left Heart Beach, Jeremiah stopped at a bagel shop and bought them breakfast sandwiches. Once they were on the highway, he asked Noelle to connect her phone to the car's Bluetooth, and she played another R & B playlist. They were mostly quiet as they listened to the music and snuck glances at each other. Noelle stared at his large hands as they rested on the steering wheel. The same hands that had touched her so reverentially. The silence wasn't awkward. It was more like they were giving space to the awareness between them. An understanding. Last night, they'd acknowledged their attraction to each other, but there was no way forward.

All too soon, Jeremiah turned off the parkway exit for Brickton. Then he was pulling into her apartment complex. He parked his car and the engine hummed as they idled.

It was silly. She'd earned her thirty-five hundred dollars.

She should be happy! And she *was* happy. But she didn't want to get out of the car. She wanted to spend more time with Jeremiah, even though that definitely would not be a good idea. She'd had a Cinderella-type weekend, and now her temporary Prince Charming was dropping her off after the ball. Such was life.

"Oh, I almost forgot to give you this," she said, reaching into her purse to grab his credit card. Their fingers brushed as she handed the card to him. She swallowed thickly as goose bumps spread up her arm.

"Ah, yeah. Thanks." He shifted in his seat to face her. It didn't seem like he was in any real hurry for her to get out of his car either.

"I had a nice time with you this weekend," she said quietly. "Thanks again for hiring me."

"Thank you for agreeing to come, Noelle. I . . ." He trailed off and stared pointedly at the floor, frowning. Then he shook his head and laughed miserably to himself.

"What?" she asked.

"Nothing," he said. "Just—I really hope that everything works out for you. Good luck with finishing your degree and becoming a librarian. You deserve all the good things. If you ever need anything—anything at all—I hope you know that you can reach out to me."

The earnestness in his voice almost made her tear up. It was validating to hear someone tell her that she deserved good things, especially when life tried so hard to push her down.

"Thank you," she said. "And good luck with your move and everything you have going on with your job." She paused and bit her lip. "I hope you don't mind me saying this, but your family seems really great. You should talk to them about how much you miss your grandfather. They'll understand. They're your soft place to land. I've always wanted a big family like yours. You're really lucky to have them."

Something flashed across his face, like the thought of talking about his grandfather with his family pained him. But his expression cleared just as quickly.

"Yeah, you're right," he said. "Thanks."

They stared at each other, exchanging small smiles.

"I should go," she said reluctantly.

She opened her car door, and Jeremiah hurried to grab her suitcase from the trunk. When he hugged her, she carved everything about him into her memory. The way he smelled, the even rise and fall of his chest when he breathed, how he securely encircled her in his arms. If she didn't mentally document these things, tomorrow she might wake up and think that Jeremiah and this entire weekend had been an elaborate dream.

"Bye, Noelle," he said. His smile was sad as he slowly pulled away.

She was sure that her smile looked the same.

"Bye, Jeremiah."

With a heavy heart, she watched as her temporary Prince Charming returned to his car and waved before he drove away.

Well. Back to reality.

Chapter Fifteen

The inside of Jeremiah's car smelled like Noelle's perfume. It had always been part of their plan that her commitment to him would last for only the duration of the weekend. So then why did he feel so off without her here? In a short period of time, he'd gotten used to her warm presence. He'd become accustomed to the sound of her laugh and the boost of serotonin that shot to his brain whenever he'd made her smile. His hands had become familiar with the feel of hers as they'd threaded their fingers and pressed their palms together countless times. He hadn't been prepared for how amazing it felt to kiss and touch her intimately. Now he'd never be able to forget the feeling of her smooth, soft skin, or how she'd moaned in his ear last night.

He'd looked forward to the way he'd lock eyes with her around his family, acknowledging their shared secret. Or how her whole face lit up simply because she was excited to eat cookies or talk to him about the plot of the book she was reading. This weekend she'd been by his side, unknowingly grounding him whenever his thoughts had started to spiral. She'd been his partner in crime.

He missed her already.

It took him a moment to realize that the silence was so loud because Noelle had been playing her music. He fumbled to reconnect his phone so that he wouldn't be stuck alone with his thoughts, but he barely had a chance to open his music app because Celeste was calling him. She probably wanted to check in.

Before he'd left Heart Beach this morning, he'd talked with his mom in her office, and she'd told him that she was concerned about him in the aftermath of his "breakup." She'd reminded him that he didn't have to chase after someone who didn't want to be with him, and that if Noelle couldn't see his value, then she didn't deserve him. He'd reassured Celeste that he was okay and that he just wanted to nurse his broken heart in peace and get back home and focus on work. And separately, he'd be able to catch his breath after being in Heart Beach, constantly confronted with his guilt over how he'd left things with Pop before he died.

"Hey, Ma," he said, connecting the call on his car's speaker. "What's up?"

"Are you home yet?" Celeste asked.

He could hear Ashley's and Harper's high-pitched voices in the background. He felt a slight tug in his stomach. Being back at Heart Beach had been hard, but there had been pockets of joy too. Like being with his nieces on the boardwalk and catching up with Amara and Robin at breakfast. Things with Percy were tough right now, and leaving Heart Beach meant that he wouldn't risk getting into it with Percy again. But as

Jeremiah heard his nieces chattering in the background, a part of him wished that he could have handled staying in Heart Beach for a bit longer.

"Not home yet," he said. "Almost. Why? Everything okay?"

"Everything's fine," Celeste said. "I'm calling about Noelle."

"Mom, I'm gonna be okay," Jeremiah insisted, although as he said those words, he got another whiff of Noelle's lingering perfume, and it caused his chest to tighten. He swallowed. "It was a wrong place, wrong time kind of thing."

"I want you to work things out with her and bring her back next weekend."

He almost swerved out of his lane into another car. "I'm sorry," he sputtered. "*What?*"

"I think I was wrong about her."

He blinked, dumfounded. "Less than two hours ago, you said you didn't think she deserved me. What changed your mind so fast?"

"Well, I saw her helping the girls this morning with their routine, and it was just the sweetest thing. My instincts are telling me that I overreacted about how she broke up with you. You're both hurt, and hurt people say hurtful things."

Jeremiah's brain was doing mental gymnastics. His mom watching Noelle interact with his nieces had brought on her sudden change of heart? What had Noelle done, exactly? Teach Harper and Ashley an entire Beyoncé routine in five minutes?

"But it's not just about her helping the girls, Miah," Celeste said. "Aside from the drama last night, you lit up around Noelle. I haven't seen you happy like that since before Pop died. It was nice to see you that way."

Jeremiah paused, falling quiet. He and Noelle had pretended to be in love for the benefit of his family. What Celeste saw between them had been manufactured. But . . . what if Celeste had been able to see past what Jeremiah had struggled to keep in check? That he'd started to like Noelle in a way that was not outlined in their agreement. Now, suddenly, Celeste was invested in him and Noelle getting back together.

Jeremiah rubbed a hand over his face. This was all his fault. He'd buried himself too deep with his lie. Under no circumstances would he admit to Celeste that he had hired Noelle to be his girlfriend in order to back up his story. In an unexpected turn of events, their plan had backfired. More than backfired—it had blown the fuck up in his face.

"The rest of the family enjoyed you being here too," Celeste continued. "Life is short, Miah. We're here one day and gone the next. I'm not trying to guilt-trip you or be unnecessarily morbid, but that's just the truth of it. We're family and we have to cherish each other. Otherwise, what do we have? We *want* you here." She paused, and Jeremiah felt the weight of her words settle around him. "So, patch things up with Noelle, okay? Bring her as your date to the gala. Spend time with us before you're a West Coaster. And please don't tell me that you can't come down on the weekends because of your job. You work hard but you don't work on the weekends, and you're already working remotely. I don't see why you can't work from Heart Beach if need be."

We're family and we have to cherish each other.

Jeremiah grasped on to those words because they were true. He'd wasted years hanging around the wrong people. His family was important to him. Spending more time at Heart Beach with them, keeping his mom happy, was what he should be doing. But that meant a month of weekends with no escape from his complicated feelings about Pop's death. And weekends where he'd inevitably argue with Percy again. Noelle told him that he should talk to his family about his grief over Pop, that they were a soft place to land. He wanted to believe that he could work himself up to that, even if he didn't feel fully capable.

Also, what if agreeing to return to Heart Beach meant that he could continue helping Noelle? She still needed more tuition money. She deserved to go back to college and become a librarian or be whatever she wanted to be. If he brought Noelle back to Heart Beach, they could play the part of a happy couple for a few more weeks, and he could pay her in return. Then, once summer ended and he moved to California, he and Noelle really could go their separate ways, and that would be the end of it.

He could keep Celeste happy and help Noelle at the same time.

Well, that was only if Noelle agreed to extend their arrangement.

He exhaled deeply.

"I—I'll try to work things out with Noelle," he said. "But I can't promise she'll want to come back with me."

"She'll want to work it out. I know she will. She loved being here with you, I could tell. Trust me. Listen, I'm so glad we had this talk, sweetheart. We're heading to the beach now, so I've gotta go. But I'll see you Friday, yeah?"

"Yeah," he said with a sigh. "I'll be there."

The call ended. Jeremiah blinked rapidly as he tried to gather his bearings. Then he turned off the nearest exit and hopped back on the highway in the opposite direction. He called Noelle, and she answered on the first ring.

"Hi," she said. "Did you forget something?"

At the sound of her voice, the tension slowly left his body.

"Nah, I didn't," he said. "Are you still home?"

"Yeah, why?"

"I want to talk to you about something," he said. "Do you mind coming back outside?"

She paused. Then, "Okay."

Fifteen minutes later, he reentered Noelle's apartment complex. She was waiting on the sidewalk in front of her building. She'd changed out of the sundress from earlier and was now wearing an old Hidden Gems Books T-shirt and denim shorts. He felt a strong tightening in his chest again at the sight of her.

She smiled curiously at him as he got out of the car and walked toward her.

"What's up?" she asked.

Better to just come out with it.

"The plan backfired," he said, and she frowned. "My family wants us to work it out because . . . my happiness is important to them, and they thought we looked happy. My mom asked me to spend the last few weekends at Heart Beach before I move, and even though I have a lot going on, I don't have the heart to tell her no, because I *should* be there with them. She wants you to come back with me because she saw you being kind to my nieces and their friends, and despite our dramatic breakup, my family sees something in us and wants us to stay together."

Noelle's eyes widened. "I really didn't think much of it when I helped your nieces. I just figured they needed some guidance. And your sisters did make a couple comments last night about us working things out, but I didn't think they were that invested." She blinked at him. "What are you gonna do?"

"When is your next wedding?" he asked.

"September. I have a bridal shower the last Saturday of August. Why?"

"If you spend the next four weekends with me in Heart Beach, I'll pay you the same rate per weekend," he said. "So fourteen thousand total. No, fifteen."

Noelle's jaw dropped. "Fifteen thousand . . ."

"Is that enough to cover the rest of what you need for tuition and your bills for the month?"

She blinked and nodded silently.

"Okay," he said. If she agreed to extend their arrangement, he wanted to make sure she had everything she needed and then some. He didn't want her to have to worry about anything. "If you say yes, what I'm thinking is that when I move, I'll say we broke up and things fizzled out, and that will be it."

"Jeremiah . . ." Her laugh was half surprise, half confusion. "I'm not going to pretend that this isn't an extremely appealing offer. But wouldn't it be easier and less expensive if you just told your family the truth?"

"Telling them the truth would cause a lot of drama and it's not drama that I have the capacity to deal with right now." He could predict his family's reactions. His mom and sister would look at him with crushed expressions of hurt and disappointment, and Percy would criticize him for being careless and irresponsible. He cleared his throat. "I just want to keep the peace and keep my mom happy. And I want you to have that money, so all your tuition problems will be taken care of."

Noelle stared at him, brows drawn together as she bit her lip.

"If I come back, will I have to act removed from everyone?" she asked. "Because that was hard, and I don't know if I'll be able to keep up with it for a whole month."

"No, there's no point now," he said. "You can just be at the house and enjoy yourself. And pretend to be my girlfriend, of course. That's all I'm asking."

She eyed him silently. He waited, anxious.

"If I do this, I need you to explain to me what's going on between you and your brother," she said. "You don't have to get into the nitty-gritty, but I need the gist of it."

It was a fair request. He just hadn't expected her to ask it.

"The gist of it is that Percy is mad at me for leaving Smith's Sweets," Jeremiah said. "He thinks I did it to be selfish, but I was just trying to grow and see what I could accomplish on my own."

That was one way to summarize the situation. He didn't need to go into the guilt and shame he'd felt about making his family look bad.

Noelle took a deep breath. Then a slow smile crept across her face.

"This is crazy," she finally said. "But you've got yourself another deal, Jeremiah Smith."

He smiled too, filled with relief. And another feeling that he refused to acknowledge just yet. "Yeah?"

"Yeah," she said, smiling wider.

"Send me a new agreement to sign," he said. "I'll pick you up on Friday."

"All right."

He walked backward to his car, facing her. "And call me if you need anything in the meantime."

"I will," she said. She laughed and shook her head. "Crazy!"

His heart pounded a little harder at the sound of her laugh.

He chose not to examine why.

Chapter Sixteen

"The game is called Stone Man," Jeremiah said.

Noelle glanced over at him. Then she looked past him at Amara. It was Saturday morning and ninety-one degrees in Heart Beach, and the three of them were standing knee-deep in the ocean. On the beach behind them, people were lying out, tanning in the sun, or protecting themselves beneath umbrellas. Amid the crowd, Robin was lounging in a beach chair, listening to a podcast with her eyes closed, while Harper and Ashley built a sandcastle. Other kids splashed in the water or swam out on their boogie boards. It was a little after ten thirty a.m., and the ocean was at low tide. The water was expansive and far-reaching. From her vantage point, Noelle could almost imagine that the world was her oyster.

"How do you play?" she asked, turning to Jeremiah again.

"You have to try to stay as still as possible when the waves hit," he said. "If a wave knocks you down, you lose."

"And you can't try to swim into the wave either, because

that's cheating," Amara added. She smirked at Jeremiah. "That's what he always tries to do."

"Lies," Jeremiah said, but he was grinning. His white teeth sparkled in the sunlight. To Noelle, he said, "Wanna play?"

Water droplets glistened on his skin, and Noelle couldn't help but gape at his strong, defined muscles. At the crack of dawn, he'd gone for a run. Apparently, this was something that he did multiple times a week, and his dedication showed. As she looked at him, the hairs on her arms and the back of her neck rose and she involuntarily clenched her thighs together.

She was a hornball. Plain and simple. Last night in his Heart Beach bed, she and Jeremiah had slept on opposite ends without touching. Not even so much as an accidental foot brush. It had been for the best, but now she was starved. Deprived. She knew how amazing it felt when he touched her.

Earlier this morning before they'd left for the beach, Jeremiah had accidentally walked in on her before she had a chance to throw her cover-up on over her new neon pink bikini, another item that she'd bought during that initial shopping trip with Tati. Jeremiah stood in the doorway, dazed, eyes trailing from her head to her toes as she was exposed to him in nothing but her bathing suit. Her first instinct should have been to quickly grab her cover-up and shrug it on, but she didn't immediately move. She blamed it on her own surprise, but the truth was that she liked to be stared at by Jeremiah. Heart pounding, she'd stared back.

"I'm almost ready," she'd said.

He'd blinked. Then, slowly, like his brain was coming back to life, he'd nodded, apologized, and said he'd wait for her downstairs.

Now, as they stood side by side in the ocean, he kept his attention trained on her face like he was trying really hard not to let his eyes drift down to her breasts.

"Yeah," she said, shaking off her hornball thoughts. She kept her attention trained on his face too. "I'll play Stone Man."

The three of them waded farther out. When they stopped, the water hit just above Noelle's belly button. Jeremiah and Amara immediately locked in, planting their feet and holding their arms at their sides, trying not to move as the waves lapped against them. Noelle laughed and copied their stances. A series of waves passed and Noelle squealed when a bit of water splashed up in her face. Before she had a chance to recover, Amara said, "Shit, here comes a big one."

Noelle wiped her cheeks and blinked. A big wave was building toward them, formed from one of the boats driving by in the distance. If she stayed put, the wave would most certainly do more than slightly splash her face. It would overtake all three of them. Jeremiah and Amara were laughing, like this was exactly the kind of wave that they'd been waiting for. Noelle's heart began to pound harder. She knew how to swim but she hadn't grown up playing this game like them. She was going to get knocked over and end up swallowing a shit ton of salt water if she didn't move, and she suddenly remembered that the taste of salt water made her nauseous.

"Actually, I'm done playing!" she announced, the shrill of her voice giving away her panic. She turned and tried to move her legs as quickly as she could back to shore.

"Wait!" Jeremiah called after her. "Don't be scared! I'll protect you!"

"What?!" she called back. She spared a glance behind her and saw Amara lifting her arms in the air, ready to embrace the big-ass wave. Jeremiah was laughing as he tried to catch up with Noelle.

"Here it comes!" Amara shouted.

Oh, fuck.

Noelle squeezed her eyes closed and waited for the wave to knock her over. But then Jeremiah appeared by her side. He scooped her up in his strong arms like she weighed nothing. He carried her as he ran toward the shore, laughing the entire time. If she weren't so shocked, she would have swooned. He was almost to shore when the wave knocked into him, and they both fell over into the shallow water, with Noelle landing right on top of Jeremiah. Her heart pounded as he grinned up at her, trying to catch his breath.

"I guess you don't like Stone Man," he said.

"Not my favorite game." Laughter bubbled up inside of Noelle. Her skin was buzzing from Jeremiah's touch. She wanted him to wrap his arms around her again, even though she *definitely* shouldn't want something like that. Plus, there were children present. She disentangled herself from him and stood up, offering her hand to pull him to his feet. She couldn't help grinning back at him. "Thank you. You're my hero."

He shrugged and winked as he stood. "All in a day's work."

After she'd agreed to extend their agreement last Sunday, Jeremiah had wired the first half of her payment. She'd never see that much money in her bank account at once. (He also told her he'd give her his credit card again so that she could go shopping for new clothes whenever she needed over the next few weeks.) In total, he was paying her *fifteen thousand dollars*. She still couldn't believe it. That amount was significant to her, but clearly not for Jeremiah, since he'd proposed it to her so easily.

Right away, she'd set aside bill money for August, and she'd put the rest of the money in her savings account. By the end of the summer, when Jeremiah sent the second half, she'd have enough money to cover the rest of her tuition for her final year of college, as well as fees and books for her classes, with a couple thousand left over. Receiving this money also meant that she could take her time looking for a new job instead of rushing into the next available opening.

To imagine, none of this would have happened if Harold hadn't fired her.

Yesterday evening, Jeremiah had picked her up and driven her back to Heart Beach. She'd prepared herself for an awkward welcoming, but the Smiths had acted as if her and Jeremiah's breakup had never happened. They'd exchanged hugs and smiles, and they'd ordered pizza for dinner. Afterward, they'd sat outside on the back patio and played charades. Celeste was the only one who seemed to be treating Noelle a bit differently. Noelle couldn't necessarily put her finger on *how*. Celeste certainly wasn't being mean or rude. But Noelle caught Celeste looking at her sometimes, like she was trying to figure her out. She just hoped that Celeste didn't look too closely. Because then her and Jeremiah's lie could go up in smoke. And she also hoped that after summer ended, Jeremiah would try his best to be honest with his family.

"I won!" Amara declared now, as she ran toward them. She was wearing a black strapless one-piece bathing suit. If she owned clothes that weren't black, Noelle hadn't seen them yet. The chic goth look suited her, though. The wave had flattened her curls against her head and the back of her neck. "Now I'm hungry."

The three of them trekked through the sand back to their

spot on the beach. Robin lowered her sunglasses and smiled, still listening to her podcast, and the twins were laser focused on building their sandcastle. Amara opened a bag of chips, lay flat on her towel, and reopened her copy of *Rosemary's Baby*. Noelle sat on her towel too and flipped open to her place in her fantastical thriller novel, *The Apothecary's Secret*. Jeremiah plopped down in front of Noelle. He reached past her and grabbed her old copy of the first book in the Pirates of the Deep series. He'd asked her to bring it so that he had something to read on the beach. He'd started reading last night in bed, and from the current placement of his bookmark, he was getting through it pretty quickly.

Instead of reading her book, Noelle was busy admiring Jeremiah's back muscles, when he glanced over his shoulder at her and caught her staring. She flashed an innocent smile, and he smirked like he knew exactly what she'd been doing.

"Do you think you can put some more sunblock on my back?" he asked.

"Sure." Noelle's pulse hammered as she grabbed the sunblock from her bag. She squirted dots along Jeremiah's back and began rubbing in the lotion. His skin was hot and smooth. She felt his deep inhale and exhale as she moved her hands across the top of his back. She continued down his spine, and his lower back muscles contracted beneath her palms. The longer she touched him, the harder her heart pounded. She was enjoying this *way* too much. She remembered their contract and her bank account, and she snatched her hands back.

"All done," she said.

"Thank you." His voice sounded deeper, gruff. Had he been just as affected as her?

"Look, they're out parasailing today," Amara said.

Noelle leaned to the side to see past Jeremiah and looked where Amara was pointing. Out in the ocean, a boat was pulling two people who soared up in the air. Their feet dangled freely.

"What did you say that was called?" Noelle asked.

"Parasailing." Jeremiah looked at her. "You ever done it?"

She shook her head, still staring at the people being pulled by the boat. It looked fun. "I'd like to, though."

Jeremiah suddenly hopped to his feet. "Let's do it."

"Wait, really?" Noelle glanced at Amara, who'd opened her book again. "Now? All of us?"

"We'll stay, but you should go," Amara said. "Everybody should try parasailing at least once."

Noelle looked up at Jeremiah. He stood, arms akimbo, waiting patiently for her to join him on her feet.

"What about our stuff? I don't want Amara and Robin to have to worry about carrying it back."

"Percy and my mom will be here later," Amara said. "We'll bring your stuff back for you. Don't worry about it."

"Thank you, sister." Jeremiah saluted Amara, and she snorted and shook her head, returning her attention to her book.

Jeremiah pulled Noelle up. She grabbed her cover-up and flip-flops, and she and Jeremiah walked across the hot sand, maneuvering through the other beachgoers.

As Jeremiah drove them through town to the other end of the beach, Noelle once again admired their charming surroundings. They drove by an ice cream shop and a surfboard store. A restaurant called the Cluck House boasted that it had the best chicken tenders in New Jersey. Soon, they pulled up in front of Hang High Parasailing. As they walked inside, an older man with dark brown skin and graying hair glanced up and adjusted his wire-framed glasses.

"Jeremiah Smith!" The man beamed. "I didn't expect to see you here today."

Jeremiah smiled. "Hey, Mr. Drake. How are you?"

"Great, great. I love the busy season."

"This is my girlfriend, Noelle. It's her first time parasailing," Jeremiah said. To Noelle, he explained, "Mr. Drake is the owner of Hang High Parasailing."

"Jeremiah came here all the time when he was younger," Mr. Drake said. "He begged his grandfather nearly every day to take him parasailing."

Noelle smiled and sent a cautious glance to Jeremiah, gauging his reaction to the mention of his grandfather. His smile didn't slip. Actually, his smiled looked a little genuine.

"Well, we have something special for our first-timers." Mr. Drake dug around behind the desk and produced a bright orange sticker that said *I Went Parasailing at Hang High!* "Around here, people parasail for the first time as kids, so they usually love the stickers."

Noelle smiled and placed the sticker on the back of her hand. "Thank you. I love it."

After Jeremiah paid, Mr. Drake instructed them to head out back toward the beach.

"Grady and Ben will get you situated," Mr. Drake said. "Jeremiah, will I see you next weekend at the gala?"

"For sure."

Jeremiah had told Noelle about his family's yearly fundraiser gala that they hosted in Heart Beach. It was a fancy affair, which meant she'd need a fancy dress. Jeremiah said he'd take her to shop for one, and she was grateful that he'd be available to offer a second opinion because Tati and André would be vacationing in the Dominican Republic this upcoming week, and Tati wouldn't have time to help Noelle pick out a dress.

On the beach, Grady and Ben were waiting with Jet Skis. They greeted Jeremiah with warm familiarity. When he told them that it was Noelle's first time parasailing, Ben explained that he and Grady would use the Jet Skis to take her and Jeremiah out to a boat waiting farther in the ocean. She and Jeremiah put on their life vests.

Noelle had never ridden a Jet Ski before, and she was eager to see what the hype was about. In her haste to climb on, her foot slipped on the platform and she fell sideways into the water, swallowing a bunch of it in the process. The next thing she knew, she was being lifted upright. She blinked, eyes stinging as Jeremiah's face came into focus. He was holding her tightly. But unlike when he'd saved her from the wave earlier, neither of them were laughing.

"Fuck, you okay?" he asked, staring at her intensely.

She coughed and tried to breathe. Jeremiah patted her back and she coughed again. "I'm okay," she sputtered out. "Thank you."

He guided her back onto the Jet Ski, frowning as he rubbed her back.

"Are you sure?" he said. "We don't have to do this today."

"I'm sure." The truth was that she felt like she might puke at any second and her eyes still stung from the salt water; however, Amara had said that everyone should go parasailing at least once, and Noelle didn't know when she'd get the chance again. She didn't want to miss out.

Jeremiah looked at her, and seeming to notice the determination in her eyes, he slowly lowered his hands from her waist. "Okay, just please be careful."

Once Ben was satisfied that Noelle was secured in place behind him on the Jet Ski, they zoomed toward the awaiting boat. Noelle wasn't someone who tended to get seasick, but nausea brewed in her gut thanks to the salt water she'd swallowed.

When they reached the small boat, two more people helped Noelle and Jeremiah climb off the Jet Skis. Then they were hooked up into the parasailing contraption.

"How are you feeling?" Jeremiah asked.

"Great." Noelle forced a smile and gave him a thumbs-up. She was supposed to be his fun, fake girlfriend. Not the girl who got seasick at the beach.

Despite her confident answer, Jeremiah reached down and threaded his fingers through hers. Holding his hand helped steady her erratic heartbeat. She tightened her grip as the boat started moving slowly at first, but soon picked up speed. Then she and Jeremiah were released into the air, and they rose higher and higher as the boat drove faster.

Wind whipped past Noelle's face. Staring at the ocean below made her feel only more nauseous. Eventually, they stopped rising higher and hovered at the same height, way up high.

"Parasailing used to make me feel like the king of the world when I was younger," Jeremiah said. He was still holding her hand. He rubbed his thumb back and forth on the inside of her palm in a calming motion. "And it was relaxing. My brain went quiet whenever I parasailed. That's why I asked my grandpa to take me so often."

Noelle tried not to outwardly react at Jeremiah mentioning his grandfather unprompted, although it definitely hadn't escaped her notice. She closed her eyes and tried to let her brain go quiet too. Gradually, her muscles relaxed, and the nausea receded.

"You should open your eyes and take in the view," Jeremiah said softly.

Noelle slowly opened her eyes. From here, she could see the entire Heart Beach boardwalk. The people below looked like little dots in the sand. She could see the roller coasters and the Ferris wheel. And when she looked up, all around them the sky was a stunning, clear blue. When she looked down, the ocean seemed to go on forever. It reminded her that the world was big, and she still hadn't seen much of it. She hadn't even been to Heart Beach before she met Jeremiah, and it was right here in New Jersey.

"I've never been out of the country," she blurted.

Immediately, she wished that she could shove the words back in her mouth. She didn't want Jeremiah to think that she was fishing for sympathy. It was just that being this high above the ocean made her consider the world and her place in it.

Maybe he hadn't heard her over the wind.

"Where do you want to go?" he asked.

Okay, so he'd heard her.

She looked down at her dangling feet and swung them back and forth. "I read a book once that took place in the Scottish Highlands. It sounded like a beautiful place. So, Scotland maybe."

His face lit up. "You and I can—"

He stopped abruptly and cleared his throat. Her stomach tightened, wondering what he'd stopped himself from saying.

You and I can what? But it was for the best that he'd cut himself off. They weren't going to see each other again after this summer. And the only reason that she was here right now was because he was paying her.

"I haven't been to the Highlands either," he finally said. "But I've seen pictures. It looks dope." He pointed toward the beach. "Do you like seafood? There's a really good seafood spot right on the water called the Oceanfront. I'll take you there."

"I'd like that," she said.

"And that building right there is the casino," he said, pointing again. "Me and Danny snuck in there when we were seventeen. The security guard saw us and kicked us out. He threatened to tell our parents, but we begged him not to. Oh, and Danny's parents' bookstore is over there. I definitely have to bring you by. Amara goes a lot too, so I'm sure she'll want you to go with her one of these days. Maybe we should make a list. Things for Noelle to do in Heart Beach."

She smiled. "First on the list: parasailing. Check."

"Second on the list, Jet Skiing," he said, smirking. "Check. I think we've seen all we need to see there."

She swatted his arm and laughed. It was only then that she realized they'd never stopped holding hands. But she didn't let go because holding hands with Jeremiah felt . . . nice.

"I was excited, and I slipped!"

"I'm just glad you didn't break something." He grinned and slunk away as she tried to swat him again. "Tonight I'll take you to get funnel cake from Marty's. They have the best funnel cake on the boardwalk."

She perked up, but then her shoulders deflated. "I told your family that I don't like sweets. I can't eat funnel cake in front of them."

Jeremiah leaned back and closed his eyes as the wind whipped by. "Don't worry. They don't have to know. I'll cover for you."

She liked when he said that. It made it seem like they were on the same team.

She had to remind herself not to get too used to it.

Chapter Seventeen

I'm only doing jazz and tap this fall," Ashley said, as she and Harper lovingly held Jeremiah's hands in a death grip. "I'm tired of ballet, but Harper still wants to do it."

It was a crowded Saturday night as they walked down the boardwalk. Kids whizzed past on bikes and families moved in groups.

"I like ballet," Harper said, wrinkling her nose, causing her glasses to shift. "Ballet takes discipline and patience like our teacher, Ms. Nina said. And you know you don't have any patience, Ash."

Ashley sucked her teeth. "That's not true!"

Jeremiah smiled at his nieces. It seemed like just yesterday, he'd visited Robin and Percy in the hospital after the twins had been born. He'd held Harper, and Amara had held Ashley. Celeste had fluttered around the hospital room, making sure that Robin had everything that she needed, while Percy had sat by Robin's side with a dazed look on his face—happy, but still in disbelief that he was a father of twins at twenty-three years old. But that had been his and Robin's plan after they'd graduated from college. Get married and start a family as soon as possible. Pop had been there at the hospital too, tearing up as he'd held his great-granddaughters. Jeremiah had teased, *Aww, don't cry, old man*, and Pop had laughed as he'd wiped his eyes. Later as they were leaving the hospital, he'd hugged Jeremiah.

Family, he'd said. *That's what life is all about. What really matters.*

The sound of Noelle's laughter lifted Jeremiah out of his bittersweet memory. She was walking ahead of him between Amara and Robin. She was wearing a light purple sundress that showed off the tan line from her bikini. Amara said something that made Noelle laugh again, and she threw her head back as her shoulders shook. Robin nudged Noelle in her side, giggling too. Noelle seemed so much more carefree tonight than she'd seemed when he'd first met her at the bookstore weeks ago. She'd looked beautiful, obviously, but her stress had been etched into her features.

He liked to think that, in addition to the money, being here at Heart Beach this summer might provide Noelle some much-needed relaxation. There had been a childlike wonder in her eyes when they'd gone parasailing earlier. He wanted her to feel that same joy for the next few weeks. Her happiness was important to him, and he knew what that meant. He knew that having a crush on Noelle could end only in disaster for him. She was focused on going back to college, and he was moving. She was here with him and his family because he was paying her. His budding feelings were only complicating things. But it was just too hard not to like her.

"Where's Dad?" Harper asked, tugging on Jeremiah's arm again. "And Grandma?"

Jeremiah glanced around, searching for his mom and brother. He realized that even though they'd all arrived on the boardwalk together, he couldn't remember the last time he'd seen Percy or Celeste. Most of the day, they'd been huddled inside Celeste's office. From what Jeremiah had gleaned, they were experiencing more issues with the new warehouse in Pennsylvania. The gift and curse of company growth was that the margin of error grew as well.

He spotted Celeste and Percy in the crowd, walking slowly, heads bent toward each other as they spoke, sporting serious expressions.

So far this weekend, he and Percy had remained civil toward each other. Granted, that was probably because Percy had been busy working most of today. But their current peace emboldened Jeremiah to approach Percy and Celeste.

"Hey, can you catch up with your mom?" he asked the twins. "I want to talk to your dad and grandma really quick."

Ashley and Harper skipped ahead to Robin, and Jeremiah waited for Celeste and Percy to catch up to him. They were so deep in conversation, they didn't notice Jeremiah until he was standing right in front of their faces.

"Hey, everything cool?" he asked. "Y'all look kind of serious."

He'd said this jokingly, but Celeste and Percy exchanged strained expressions.

"Seriously, though," he said, earnest. "What's going on? Is everything okay?"

"There's just some miscommunication with the new warehouse management," Celeste said, smiling tiredly. She craned her neck, trying to spot the rest of the family. "Nothing to worry about, really. Where's everyone else?"

Jeremiah glanced at Percy, whose features were drawn.

"Is there anything I can do to help?" Jeremiah asked.

Percy frowned. "Like what?"

"I don't know. I can just be here to listen and offer ideas if you need them."

"You have some experience with Good Boy, but Good Boy isn't on the same level as Smith's Sweets yet. I don't think there's much you can do to help." Percy crossed his arms over his chest. "But I appreciate the offer, especially since you willingly gave up your chance to be a helpful Smith's Sweets employee."

Jeremiah bristled and immediately regretted saying anything to his brother. It didn't surprise him that Percy didn't think he knew enough to be helpful, but hearing him say it still stung. Jeremiah had been naive to think the peace between him and Percy could last forever. It reminded him why he wouldn't tell his family about his last conversation with Pop. Percy would only judge him about it forever.

"Why do you have to be like that?" he asked.

Percy sighed and rubbed the bridge of his nose. "Like what?"

"Percy, Miah," Celeste interrupted, giving them stern looks. "Can we please have a peaceful evening?"

For Celeste's sake, Jeremiah decided to drop it. He didn't say anything else to his brother as they caught up with the rest of their family, who were waiting in front of the water ice stand.

"Everything okay?" Amara asked, glancing between her brothers, reading their tense body language.

"Everything's fine," Jeremiah said. Percy gave her a reassuring smile. Until recently, the three of them had gotten along well. This new hostility between Jeremiah and Percy made Amara anxious. The brothers didn't agree on much lately, but they remained protective of their little sister.

Noelle stood next to Jeremiah and wordlessly linked her fingers through his. It might have been for show, but the way she looked at him with her brows pulled together in concern felt real. Feeling their interlocked hands helped ground him.

"What should we do now?" Celeste asked. "Should we see a movie?"

Harper and Ashley jumped up and down, grasping their water ice cups. Everyone began discussing movie options.

"I'm sorry, but Noelle and I are gonna have to miss out on movie night unfortunately," Jeremiah said. "We have date-night plans."

Noelle blinked. This was obviously news to her because they hadn't discussed any date-night plans, but she covered her surprise with an easy smile and nodded.

Celeste glanced at Jeremiah and Noelle's clasped hands, and her face softened. "Okay, we'll see you back at the house."

Jeremiah and Noelle waved goodbye to his family and continued on down the boardwalk.

"Where are we going?" Noelle whispered.

"First, to get you a funnel cake like I promised," he said. "Then I called in a favor from a family friend because you have to find a dress for the gala. Her boutique is in walking distance."

Noelle quirked an eyebrow. "It's not Mercy Webster, is it?"

Jeremiah laughed. "No."

They stopped at Marty's for funnel cake. Martin Sr. had

opened the shop decades ago, and now his sons ran the business for him. His grandson Brandon, an incoming high school senior, was busy flirting with a girl his age when Jeremiah and Noelle approached the register. The girl blew Brandon a kiss as she walked away. Brandon grinned, showing off his braces.

"Yo, Jeremiah," he said, beckoning him and Noelle forward. "I haven't seen Amara yet this summer. Tell her I love her, okay? I may be young, but she should still give me a chance."

Jeremiah raised an eyebrow. "Maybe when you're twenty years older."

"Man, that's way too long." Brandon looked at Noelle and smoothed a hand over his braids. "How you doing, miss?"

Noelle burst out laughing.

"You think you're Romeo or something?" Jeremiah said, chuckling as he put his arm around Noelle's shoulders. "She's spoken for. And also too old for you."

Brandon sucked his teeth. "Whatever. What can I get you, ma'am?"

"Damn, I went to ma'am that fast, huh?" Noelle said, and Brandon shrugged, obviously disappointed that she wouldn't take his interest in her seriously.

Noelle ordered a classic funnel cake, insisting that Jeremiah share it with her. They watched Brandon pour the batter into the deep fryer in a circular motion. Once the batter was cooked, Brandon drained the funnel cake and placed it on a paper plate. Then he dusted it with powdered sugar. Noelle was licking her lips as Brandon brought the funnel cake to them. She had hearts in her eyes as she took the plate.

They let the funnel cake cool off as they walked down the boardwalk ramp to the street. Once the funnel cake was cool enough to eat, Noelle tore off a chunk then passed the plate to Jeremiah. Funnel cakes were delicious but messy. He and Noelle were getting powdered sugar all over their fingers as they ate, but Noelle didn't seem to care. She closed her eyes like she was savoring each bite. An expression of pure pleasure. She'd looked the same way when he'd kissed her neck last week.

No, don't think about that.

"This is so good," she said.

He smiled at her. "You've got a little . . ." He gestured to the powdered sugar on her cheek.

"Oh, I do?"

"Here," he said, lightly brushing his thumb against her cheek. His skin hummed as their gazes held. He felt each distinct pounding of his heart. He forced himself to drop his hand away before he did something ridiculous like cradle her face and kiss her.

"Thank you," she said.

He swallowed hard. "You're welcome."

They reached their destination: Daniela's dress shop. Noelle used a napkin to dust the sugar residue off her fingers. Then she did the same for Jeremiah. He liked the feeling of her hands pressed against his in any way possible. Even if it was just to rid them of sugar.

A **CLOSED** sign hung on the door. Jeremiah knocked and Daniela, the store owner, appeared and unlocked the door. Her thick, curly hair was tied back in a ponytail, and she'd switched into a pair of comfy-looking sneakers instead of the heels that she usually wore during regular store hours.

"Hey, hey, come on in," Daniela said, opening the door.

Noelle peered around at the many gowns hanging throughout the store. Her mouth formed into a perfect O.

"Thank you so much for staying open late," Jeremiah said. "I really appreciate it."

"Of course. You know your mom is one of my most loyal customers. Your family's grant helped my business when I really needed it." Daniela smiled at Noelle. "This must be your beautiful girlfriend, Noelle. I'm Daniela."

Noelle smiled. "It's nice to meet you."

"Nice to meet you too, sweetie. So you need a dress for the gala next week?" She looked Noelle up and down. "You have a great figure. We can probably take a dress off the rack and do minimal alterations."

Noelle blushed. "Thank you."

I agree, Jeremiah wanted to say. *She does have a great figure.* But he stayed quiet and folded his hands behind his back and listened to Daniela with a serious expression.

"What silhouette are you looking for?" Daniela asked.

"Um, maybe A-line with a slit," Noelle said. "A classy slit, of course."

Daniela nodded and took Noelle by the hand. "I've got options."

Jeremiah sat by the chairs in front of the dressing room area and he watched as Daniela and Noelle bustled around the store. If Noelle liked a dress, Daniela hung it up in one of the changing rooms. Once they were finished browsing, Noelle had chosen three dresses.

Before Noelle tried on the first dress, she walked over to Jeremiah, chewing her bottom lip. "These dresses are expensive," she whispered.

"Don't worry about that. Just choose whichever dress you like best."

A wrinkle appeared between her brows. "You're sure?"

"Positive."

"Noelle?" Daniela called. "Come, come, sweetie."

Jeremiah smiled at Noelle as she hurried inside the dressing room.

"Let me know when you're in the gown and I'll zip you up," Daniela said, closing the curtain as Noelle got undressed. Jeremiah could see her feet below the curtain. Her sundress dropped to the floor, followed by her bra. He swallowed thickly and glanced away, trying not to imagine what she looked like right now.

"Okay, I have it on," Noelle said.

Daniela disappeared behind the curtain and presumably zipped up the back of Noelle's dress. Then the curtain opened, revealing Noelle. The dress was emerald green with a beaded bodice. Skinny straps went over her shoulders, and the skirt was made of tulle. She looked like a princess. Daniela instructed Noelle to step onto the platform in front of the mirror.

"You look beautiful," Jeremiah said.

Noelle smiled at him and blushed. "Thank you."

"Doesn't she? The color suits you well, Noelle," Daniela said. "What do you think?"

"I like it." Noelle looked at Jeremiah. "What about you?"

"I like it too." His opinion didn't really matter at the end of the day. He wanted her to choose whichever dress *she* liked, but he was glad that she'd made him feel included.

Noelle observed her reflection, turning from side to side. "I like it," she repeated slowly, "but I don't love it."

"Let's try on the next one," Daniela said, leading Noelle back into the dressing room. She waited while Noelle slipped into the next option, and she popped behind the curtain to zip Noelle up.

This time when Noelle emerged, she wore a low-cut silver gown that displayed a nice sliver of cleavage. Jeremiah sat up straighter.

"I like this one too," he said immediately.

Noelle laughed and shook her head as she looked at her reflection. "You would say that."

"This is one of my most requested styles. Very sexy," Daniela said. "You look gorgeous."

"You really do," Jeremiah agreed.

"Thank you." Noelle bit her lip. "I like it a lot, but I still don't think this is the one either."

"Third time's the charm," Daniela said, whisking Noelle away behind the curtain once more.

It took longer for Noelle to put on the next dress. Jeremiah overheard Daniela mumbling about a tricky zipper. While he waited, he checked the time on his phone. It was almost nine p.m. He wondered if his family had gone to the movies or not. He was opening his text thread with Amara when Noelle finally came out of the dressing room. He dropped his phone in his lap. The gown was satin black and strapless with a slit that went up her right thigh. The dress hugged her body, and her braids were pulled to the side, showing off her elegant neckline and shoulders. She was a classy, sexy bombshell. And she'd rendered him speechless.

"*Va va voom*," Daniela sang, buzzing around Noelle. She gestured to the slit. "You can dance easily in this one. We can take in the hem at the bottom and a little at your waist."

Noelle spun in a circle, standing on her tiptoes as if she were wearing heels. She grinned at herself in the mirror. It did something to his heart to see her look so happy.

"I love it," she declared. She looked over her shoulder at Jeremiah. "What do you think?"

He was too busy staring at her to answer.

"Jeremiah?" she prompted.

He blinked. "You're breathtaking."

Noelle paused and they locked eyes for a heated moment. She smiled softly. "Thank you."

"Is this our winner?" Daniela asked, glancing between the two of them.

Noelle nodded, and Daniela clapped her hands. At the same time, the store's phone started to ring, and Daniela sighed.

"Who would call this late, knowing that I'm closed?" she grumbled. "Noelle, sweetie, let me know once you've taken off the dress and I'll be there in one minute."

Daniela walked to the register to answer the phone, and Jeremiah's eyes trailed Noelle as she slipped back behind the curtain. Next Saturday, he was gonna have to survive an entire night of Noelle wearing that dress. He didn't know how the hell he would do it.

"Oh shit," Noelle suddenly muttered. "Jeremiah?"

He stood. "Yeah?"

"This zipper is stuck." She hesitated. "Can you help me?"

He glanced at Daniela, who was still on the phone. His heart thrummed in his chest as he pulled the curtain aside. Noelle was standing with the zipper halfway down, exposing most of her back. She clasped the front of the dress to her chest to keep it from falling. His pulse thundered in his ears as he was enveloped by her floral perfume. He held his breath as he stood behind her and moved her braids to the side. His fingers brushed against the smooth skin of her back, and his hands tingled. He made himself focus on the reason she'd asked for his help. There was some fabric stuck in the zipper. Slowly, carefully, he began to dislodge the fabric, trying not to rip it in the process.

"I didn't break the zipper, did I?" Noelle asked, sounding stressed.

"No, it's okay. Don't worry."

She held still as he meticulously pulled the fabric from the zipper.

"Um, you should look at the price tag while you're back there," she said.

He noted the price. "It's fine."

When he glanced up at the mirror in front of them, he found her watching him.

"It is?" she asked.

He nodded and refocused on the zipper. He tried his best not to imagine touching her anywhere else or undressing her with his eyes.

"I've almost got it," he said.

When he finally pulled the fabric free, the zipper nicked Noelle's skin a little, and she winced.

"Shit, I'm sorry," he said, rubbing his thumb against the reddened skin to soothe the spot. He kept his thumb pressed there as he looked up and met her gaze in the mirror.

"It's okay," she said.

He let his eyes trail the slope of her neck. He wanted to place his mouth against her beating pulse. He wondered how she would respond if he did. When he met her gaze in the mirror again, she was watching him, her lips slightly parted.

"Okay, I'm back," Daniela chirped. She paused on the other

side of the curtain and chuckled. "I see two sets of feet under there. No funny business in my shop, young people!"

Jeremiah spared one last glance at Noelle before he backed away and stepped out of the dressing room, letting the curtain close behind him.

He held his hands up innocently. "No funny business here."

Daniela laughed as she disappeared behind the curtain. Jeremiah shook his head to clear his thoughts.

Noelle was torturing him.

No, he was torturing himself.

After Noelle redressed and Daniela took her measurements, Jeremiah paid for the gown, and Daniela promised to have alterations finished before the gala next weekend.

"Thank you," Noelle said to Jeremiah as they walked home. "Not just for the dress, but for the whole experience. I haven't tried on dresses like that since senior prom. It was fun."

"I'm glad you enjoyed it," he said. And he meant it. Noelle deserved to be fitted for beautiful gowns and to be told over and over again that she was beautiful. She deserved to have fun, and she deserved a break. From the looks of things, she'd been the heart of Hidden Gems Books, and it hadn't stopped her from losing her job. She'd been given the shitty end of the stick.

He was torn between respecting the professional nature of their agreement and his desire to know more about her. His desire won in the end.

"Can I ask you something?" he said. "It's personal."

Chapter Eighteen

Noelle hesitated as she looked at Jeremiah. Last weekend she'd asked him a personal question about why he'd changed his lifestyle. She figured he was allowed to ask her a personal question in return. Plus, she was intrigued that he wanted to know something personal about her.

"Sure," she said.

"Why did you drop out of college?"

His tone was genuinely curious. She didn't detect any signs of judgment. But the story behind why she'd dropped out embarrassed her, and she didn't love talking about it.

"You don't have to answer if you don't want to," he said quickly, noticing her strained expression. "I'm sorry if I'm being nosy."

"You're not being nosy," she said. "It's a reasonable question to ask."

She could lie and come up with a nobler, less scandalous reason as to why she'd dropped out. But he'd been open with her when she'd asked her personal question. She wanted to be open with him too. Even though they were lying to other people about their relationship, she found that she didn't want to lie to Jeremiah.

So, she told him the truth. She told about winning the essay contest and scholarship money her senior year of high school. She told him about how she'd loved the camaraderie in the dorms at UMD, and how being surrounded by people was something she'd craved back then as an only child. Jeremiah nodded, listening attentively. They walked by a house with wind chimes dangling outside the door, providing background music for their slow stroll. Then she told him about meeting CJ her junior year and everything that happened after her RA found his alcohol in her dorm room. Losing her scholarship and moving back home.

"Who the *fuck* is your stupid-ass ex?" Jeremiah asked fiercely when she finished talking.

She shouldn't have found his anger so endearing, but she did, because he was angry on her behalf.

"Nobody," she said. "He's irrelevant now."

"He's an idiot, that's what he is," Jeremiah huffed. "I'm so sorry he did that to you, Noelle."

"Yeah, me too," Noelle said. "He was young and scared. I'd like to think that he'd make a different decision today, but who knows. Anyway, I would have kept trying to find ways to come up with the money after it happened, but my mom got into a car accident that summer, and she was in the hospital for a while. I thought it was more important to stay home and help her than going back to school. And I realized that I didn't have a real plan where college was concerned anyway. I didn't want to use my sociology degree toward a job. I only knew that I wanted a fulfilling career that provided a stable salary. It took me a long time to find out what I wanted to do."

Jeremiah gently brushed his hand against hers. "I'm really sorry about your mom. Is she better now?"

"Oh yeah." Noelle smiled softly. "She still has back pain sometimes, but thankfully she's doing okay. She got married a couple years ago, and she and my stepdad live in South Carolina now. They're teachers, so they came up to visit me in June once the school year ended. I miss her a lot but I'm happy that she's happy."

They reached the corner of Hawthorne Street. The Smith house was to their left. The beach was to their right. Noelle could hear the ocean from here, like it was calling to her. To *them*. Like the ocean didn't want them to leave the vulnerable territory they'd crossed into. Once she and Jeremiah returned to the house, they'd have to perform in front of his family again. Right now, they were being real.

"Do you want to sit on the beach?" Jeremiah asked.

She nodded, glad that he wanted to prolong this time with just the two of them too.

They walked to the beach, and they took off their shoes and walked barefoot on the cold sand. The beach was empty, and she and Jeremiah sat with their knees pulled up to their chests, facing the ocean.

"So when did you know that you wanted to be a librarian?" Jeremiah asked.

"I started reading a lot while my mom was in the hospital," she said. "I was stressed and scared, and a really nice librarian showed me around the library and recommended books to me. Reading saved my mental health. It changed everything for me, honestly. I realized that I wanted to help people like that librarian had helped me."

"Is that why you do the bridesmaid jobs too?" he asked. "Because you like helping people?"

"Partially, yeah." She glanced down as she ran her fingers through the sand. "But I mainly do it for the money. Once I get my bachelor's degree, I'll have a stronger chance at finding a decent-paying full-time job. And hopefully after I get my MLS and become a librarian, I'll have a stable career that I love, and I won't have to constantly worry about money. Sometimes it frustrates me that I took so long to find out what I really wanted to do with my life, but I'm trying my best to just work toward the goal and not give up on myself. It's hard not to feel ashamed about what happened while I was at UMD, though."

"I don't think you should feel ashamed," Jeremiah said, taking hold of her hand. "The reason that you lost your scholarship wasn't even your fault. Not finishing your degree doesn't take away from your character. You're still you, Noelle. Trying to help your ex—who was undeserving of your help, by the way—was selfless. Staying home to help your mom was selfless too. You've had some setbacks, but that's more to do with the fucked-up distribution of wealth in our country than anything. The only reason I'm in the position that I'm in now is because my grandparents poured their blood, sweat, and tears into making Smith's Sweets a success, despite every obstacle put in their way as Black business owners. They were good people who wanted better for themselves and their family. You're the same, Noelle. You're a good person. I've met plenty of people who've graduated from the top universities in this country, and a lot of them are assholes. I'd choose you over them any day. There's nothing that you should be ashamed about."

She blinked, taken aback by the intensity of his tone. There was a lot that he'd said just now, but of course her brain snagged on, *I'd choose you*.

"Thank you for saying that."

"I mean it," he said. "And I understand what you mean about not giving up on yourself too."

She looked at him. "You do?"

"Yeah, my situation isn't the same as yours, and I don't want you to think that I'm trying to make a comparison there. I'm very aware that my life has been easier, especially financially, because I was born into different circumstances. But what I'm saying is that I understand how it feels to take longer to find your footing. Amara and Percy always knew what they wanted. Amara had her art, and as the oldest, Percy was expected to take over everything one day. Growing up, to most people, I was Percy's less smart brother." He laughed and looked down at his hand that was still pressed against hers. "But I was personable. I made a lot of friends. People knew that if they chilled with me, they'd have fun. Being the life of the party took my mind off thinking about where I stood in my family and whether or not I measured up to everyone else. After college, my mom gave me a job at in the marketing department at Smith's Sweets, but I didn't take it seriously enough." He inhaled a deep breath. "Before my grandfather died, he encouraged me to make something of myself. I guess that's what I'm trying to do now, starting fresh. Even when I was screwing up, I'd only ever wanted his approval. I valued his opinion above anyone else's."

He cleared his throat and averted his face. He pulled his hand away from Noelle's in order to dust sand off his shins.

She had a feeling that this was the most Jeremiah had admitted to someone in a long time, if ever. She realized how important this admission was, how fragile.

"In my opinion, you're just as impressive as your siblings," she said softly. "You were brave enough to branch out on your own. I think your grandfather would be proud of you."

He chewed on his bottom lip and huffed a quiet, humorless laugh. "I hope so."

Noelle felt exposed as she looked at Jeremiah. Like the thin, opaque wall they'd erected in the name of their agreement was slowly lowering.

"Thank you for telling me about college and your mom," he said. "I know you didn't have to."

She smiled, like it wasn't a big deal. But the reality was that they'd made the choice to open up to each other and there was no turning back now. The realization made her heart beat faster and her skin tingle. She rubbed her arms.

"Are you cold?" Jeremiah asked, and she nodded, pretending that was the reason for her sudden chills. He stood and held his hand out toward her. "Ready to go home?"

"Yeah." She grabbed his hand and let him pull her to her feet. Locking hands only made her skin tingle even more, like little lovebugs were crawling across her fingers. The butterflies were trying to make a comeback too, and she reminded them that Jeremiah wasn't her real boyfriend.

It was quiet inside the house when they returned.

"Everybody's probably asleep or in their rooms," Jeremiah whispered.

He started for the stairs, and Noelle was hit with the startling realization that she would have to spend another night with him in the same bed. But this time she'd spilled her guts to him and she'd inadvertently removed the layer of emotional aloofness that she usually kept in place with her clients. Next to him in bed, she'd be left with nothing but her confusing feelings as he lay inches away from her.

This was a *disaster.*

"Wait!" she hissed. Startled, Jeremiah quickly spun back around. "Um, I want a snack."

"Actually, you know what?" he said. "Me too."

"Okay!" she squeaked.

No, no, no. She was supposed to go to the kitchen and freak out about her feelings for him, alone. He wasn't supposed to come with her! But what could she say now? *No, don't go to your own kitchen in your family's house?*

In the kitchen, Jeremiah made a beeline for the cabinet above the sink. Noelle joined him at the counter, and her frazzled thoughts were momentarily forgotten when he produced a box of Smith's Sweets sugar cookies.

Her eyes widened as he lowered the box into her hands. She thanked him, immediately opened the box, and pulled out a handful of cookies.

Jeremiah laughed as he dug into the box for a cookie too. "You're like Sméagol when he sees the ring. But you're *much* prettier, obviously."

Noelle snort laughed. "You've read *Lord of the Rings*?"

"No, just watched the movies."

"I love that you remembered Gollum's real name, but you confused *Mamma Mia!* with *Grease.*"

He smirked. "What can I say? I'm one of a kind."

"That you are." She tilted her head. Her treasonous butterflies made her ask, "So, you think I'm pretty?"

Jeremiah leaned his elbow against the counter and brought his face an inch closer to hers. She stared into his warm brown eyes as her pulse thundered in her ears.

"'Pretty' isn't a strong-enough word," he said. "'Stunning' feels more accurate."

Her breath caught, and she blinked, deliciously overwhelmed by his nearness and his compliment. "Stunning recognizes stunning, I guess," she murmured, and the corners of his mouth lifted in a smile as his eyes sparkled.

Flirting? Unprovoked? When no one was watching? This was *not* part of their agreement. Still, they smiled goofily at each other in the silent kitchen. Noelle briefly tore her eyes away from Jeremiah's face to grab another handful of cookies. At the same time, she heard footsteps in the hall, coming their way. She couldn't get caught eating sweets! Not when she'd lied last weekend about not liking them!

In a panic, she shoved the handful of cookies in her mouth and pushed the cookie box into Jeremiah's hands.

"What the—" he said, fumbling not to drop the box. He whipped it behind his back just as Celeste walked into the kitchen.

"Oh, you're both home now," she said. She was dressed in a black satin pajama set.

Noelle smiled with her full chipmunk cheeks and waved.

"Hey, Ma," Jeremiah said smoothly. "Getting a late-night snack?"

"Yeah, just warming up some funnel cake," Celeste said, going to the fridge.

With her back to them, Jeremiah quickly returned the box

to the cabinet, and Noelle chewed like her life depended on it. Why couldn't her jaws work faster?!

Celeste popped her funnel cake into the air fryer and turned to face them again. Noelle swallowed the cookies, throat dry as hell, as Jeremiah crossed his arms over his chest. They sported matching *nothing to see here* smiles. "Don't judge," Celeste said, misreading their expressions. The air fryer beeped and she took the funnel cake to the island. "I know it's terrible to eat this much sugar before bed, but Marty's is the best. I couldn't resist." She paused and observed Noelle. "Do you eat funnel cake? I know you said that you don't like sweets."

Noelle's stomach grumbled. She decided to make an amendment to her lie. "I do like funnel cake sometimes."

"Here, have some if you want," Celeste said, pushing the plate toward her. "Funnel cake is meant to be shared."

Noelle thanked Celeste as she sat across from her and tore off a piece of funnel cake. It melted on her tongue. Jeremiah started to join them, but he paused as his phone vibrated in his pocket. He squinted, reading the message he'd received.

"It's Aaron," he said. "Gotta handle this."

He hugged Celeste good night and told Noelle he'd see her upstairs. Noelle watched as he left the kitchen with his phone pressed to his ear.

"How was your date?" Celeste asked.

"Oh, it was nice," Noelle said, turning to Celeste again. "We looked at dresses for the gala."

"Did he take you to Daniela's?" she asked, and Noelle nodded. "Good. I'm glad you're coming with him. This will be our first year hosting the gala without my dad. We didn't have it last year. It felt too soon."

Celeste looked away with a twist to her mouth. Noelle

wished she could have met the man who'd clearly meant so much to his family.

"How was the movie?" she asked Celeste when the silence began to stretch.

"We couldn't decide on the same film, so we split up," Celeste said, looking at her again. "Percy and Robin took the girls to see an animated movie, and Amara dragged me to see some ghastly horror film about a demon on the loose." She shuddered. "The things I do for my children."

Noelle laughed. With just the two of them here in the quiet late-night hour, Celeste seemed less intimidating as she enjoyed a snack in her kitchen. Together, they finished the last of the funnel cake.

"I'm sorry that you had to witness that spat between Jeremiah and Percy on the boardwalk earlier," Celeste said quietly. "I'm sure Jeremiah has talked to you about his issues with his brother."

In the simplest terms, he'd explained their issue. He hadn't gone in depth. But Noelle nodded, because as far as Celeste was concerned, Jeremiah liked Noelle so much, he'd been willing to forfeit multiple weekends with his family in order to spend time with her. Of course he would have told her every detail about what was going on with him and Percy.

Celeste sighed. "I'm an only child, so I don't know what it's like to be competitive with a sibling. Percy and Miah have been competing with each other since they were kids. It used to be good fun, but lately . . ." Celeste trailed off, gazing out the window again.

"I understand them both," she continued. "Percy is upset because Jeremiah left the company when that wasn't originally the plan. And Jeremiah is trying to strike out on his own. I've talked to them about seeing things from the other's point of view, but I've learned that sometimes I have to let my children work things out among themselves. When all is said and done, they really do love each other." She looked at Noelle. "Do you have siblings?"

"I do," Noelle said. "Stepsiblings. But I don't see them that often. They live in Texas near my dad. They're a lot older than me."

"So most of the time, you must feel like an only child," Celeste said. "Like me."

"Yeah," Noelle said, thinking of how she'd wished for a bigger family growing up as a latchkey kid, during those nights when her mom had worked late. She'd wanted to be part of a close-knit family, not unlike the Smiths.

Celeste smiled softly. "Well, I hope we aren't driving you too crazy."

"Not at all." Noelle smiled too. "I like being here."

"Good." Celeste patted Noelle's hand. She stood and poured a glass of water. "I'm taking my butt to bed. Sleep well."

"You too."

Noelle remained where she sat. She still needed more time before she went upstairs and faced Jeremiah and her complicated feelings.

Eventually, she left the kitchen and cut off the light. As she reached the second floor, something soft and warm slipped past her ankle, and she heard a distinctive hiss. She held back a yelp as she realized that she'd just made contact with Celeste's elusive cat, Caesar. She couldn't see the cat in the dark, but she heard his claws scraping against the wood floor as he scampered down the hall.

Heart pounding, Noelle ran upstairs and darted inside Jeremiah's bedroom. She was about to tell him how she'd just run into the cat, but Jeremiah was knocked out, still fully clothed on his side of the bed atop the covers.

Noelle gingerly sat on the edge of the bed. She reached up and smoothed the wrinkle between his eyebrows. He breathed a contented sigh, and she felt herself smile.

Clearly, her crush was not going to die as quickly as she'd hoped.

Chapter Nineteen

"Did the Shop Mart guys seem happy, though?" Aaron asked Jeremiah. "Did they enjoy themselves?"

They were on a video call. Last night Jeremiah had taken the Shop Mart buying team out for dinner in Manhattan to celebrate their new partnership. Even though it was Saturday morning now, Aaron wanted a recap. Jeremiah finished zipping his freshly dry-cleaned tux inside of its garment bag, and he glanced around his room, confirming that the rest of his things were packed for the weekend. Well, everything except for his laptop.

"Yeah, it went well," he said. "I think they had fun. They're excited to work with us."

Jeremiah had treated the team to dinner at Le Bernardin. The buyers were based out of Seattle, so afterward they'd asked Jeremiah to show them the best bars. Jeremiah had wanted to beg off. The last place he'd wanted to be was at the bar. He didn't want to risk another awkward run-in, like with Theo at

Amara's party. But declining to entertain the Shop Mart team wouldn't have been good for business, so he'd taken them to Piano Bar in SoHo and had kept a smile plastered on his face the entire time. Luckily he hadn't seen anyone that he'd recognized.

"That's great," Aaron said, leaning back in his chair. He was dressed in golf gear. He'd been part of a golf club at NYU. In the early-morning hours when Jeremiah had been dragging himself back to their dorm after a night out, he'd run into Aaron leaving with his caddie bag slung over his shoulder. "I knew that I could count on you to show them a good time."

Jeremiah huffed out a laugh and nodded, even though he didn't like feeling as though his talents were reduced to entertaining clients. He'd helped expand Good Boy's business in a short period and he was moving across the country to be with the rest of the team, but Aaron still saw Jeremiah as the unserious, privileged kid from college who knew how to charm. Jeremiah couldn't blame Aaron for his perspective, given Jeremiah's past. He just wanted to be given a bit more credit now.

His attention was diverted as his phone vibrated on his desk beside his laptop. He'd received a text from Noelle.

I'm all packed and ready ☺️

Being with the Shop Mart team last night meant that Jeremiah and Noelle hadn't driven down to Heart Beach like usual. It also meant he'd spent a lot of last night's dinner thinking about Noelle. About how she'd opened up to him and revealed the tender, hidden parts of herself. About how he wanted to know more. How he wanted to tell *her* more about *himself*. Once the weekend ended, they returned to their separate worlds, because that was part of their deal. But he wanted to stay in her orbit. What was she doing when they weren't together? What was she thinking about? Was she thinking about him the way he increasingly thought about her?

He could have shoved his feelings down deep and avoided assessing them. But that all went out the window when they'd started texting.

It started on Monday night. He'd texted Noelle to let her know they'd have to leave Saturday morning instead of Friday evening because of his meeting. She'd responded a few minutes later to say that was fine. He'd stared at his phone and wondered if he should try and continue the conversation, wondered if doing so would be a breach of their spoken and unspoken rules. He'd watched as her text bubbles appeared then disappeared. Maybe she'd been wondering the same thing. Encouraged, he'd texted, Wyd? Simple. Not too invasive. Not even flirty. She'd responded, Guess. He'd smiled and texted, Hopefully not riding a jet ski. She'd sent a handful of laughing emojis. Then, Haha very funny, followed by a selfie of her lying in bed with a book on her chest, a murder mystery. An opened box of salted caramel chocolate chip cookies was on the bed beside her. Probably the box he'd given her on Sunday before they'd left Heart Beach. Her braids were wrapped in a bun, and she looked fresh-faced and beautiful. His heart tugged as he looked at the picture. He'd wanted to text back *You look beautiful.* But they weren't at Daniela's dress shop, and this wasn't a situation where Noelle was waiting for his opinion on her appearance. He'd already felt like he'd overdone it last weekend when he'd called her *pretty*, then *stunning* as they'd stood in the kitchen. He didn't want to overstep or make her uncomfortable. So, instead, he'd texted, I have something to tell you. It's a family secret.

What is it??

If you eat too many of our cookies, you actually turn into one. You probably have about five more days left as a human. I'm sorry.

She'd sent the laughing emoji again. Going out as a cookie isn't the worst way.

He'd responded, Lol true. And she hadn't texted back after that.

He'd figured maybe that was the end of it. He hadn't wanted to seem thirsty or annoying by texting a second time. But then on Tuesday afternoon, she'd sent him a picture of a sphynx cat on the cover of *Modern Pets Magazine.*

Is this what Caesar looks like?

He'd laughed, remembering how she'd told him about her late-night run-in with Caesar.

Kinda, but he's older. Then, Where are you? And how did you find that magazine?

I'm at the hair salon with Tati, waiting for her to take her lunch break. They have all kinds of magazines here. What are you doing?

He told her that he'd just finished his lunch break. She'd wanted to know what he'd had to eat, and then he'd given her the backstory on how he ate the same grilled chicken wrap every day from the café across the street during the week because the elderly woman who ran the shop always greeted him with a warm, *How you doing today, honey?* And he was a ham who loved the attention. But mostly it was because he wanted to be intentional about supporting a Black-owned business. Noelle had told him that she loved that, before jokingly encouraging him to try other items on the menu.

They'd continued texting on and off for the rest of the day, and later that night after his run. Their conversation bled into Wednesday, and by the end of the week, it seemed normal, routine even, that a good chunk of his day would be spent texting with Noelle. Every time his phone vibrated, he felt a boost of serotonin in his brain. There were so many times that he'd wanted to text, *I want to see you. Can I come pick you up?* But he hadn't wanted to press his luck or cross a boundary. He was anxious to finally see her in person today.

He texted her back now: See you soon.

He heard his apartment door open and close. It was Amara returning with smoothies.

"Hey, my sister just got back," he said to Aaron now. "I have to head out, but we'll talk Monday?"

Aaron nodded. "Definitely. And tell your mom I'm sorry again that I couldn't make the gala."

"Will do."

They ended the call, and Jeremiah found Amara in the kitchen, fiddling with the strap on her duffel bag. She lived in central Jersey, closer to Celeste, and she'd stayed over last night because she'd gone to an art gallery event in the city with some of her college friends. Jeremiah, Amara, and Noelle were driving down to Heart Beach together.

"Hey, thanks," he said, crossing the kitchen and picking up the smoothie she'd bought for him.

"You're welcome." Amara rubbed her eyes. Jeremiah had been asleep for hours by the time Amara used his spare key to come inside.

"How was the event?" he asked.

"Cool," she said. "It's always fun to be back in that environment. It makes me think of how the art world was my whole life in college."

Even though Amara's passion was oil painting, she'd studied graphic design at the Rhode Island School of Design. Unlike many of her college classmates, after graduation Amara hadn't moved to New York City. She liked being on the Smith's Sweets graphic design team. With her great eye for aesthetics, she had a lot to do with the brand's overall look. She'd always been keen like that. When they were kids, she used to repaint and redecorate her room every other year. And she used to force Jeremiah and Percy to sit for portraits. She'd carried a small sketchbook with her everywhere. When she enrolled at RISD, no one had been surprised. Now she painted in her spare time and sold the paintings to friends of friends, and every year, she created a painting for the gala fundraiser. But mostly, she painted for fun.

"You could still try and get your art in a showcase," Jeremiah said. "You're more than talented enough."

Amara waved him away. "Nope. Once your passion becomes your job, it loses all luster."

Jeremiah smirked, about to tell Amara he didn't think that was completely true. Then his phone vibrated, and he felt a jolt to his system, knowing he'd most likely received a text from Noelle. She'd responded, See you soon 😊

"*Wow*," Amara whistled, grinning at him. "Somebody has hearts in their eyes. I'm guessing that's Noelle texting you?"

He hadn't even realized that he'd been smiling. Of course Amara wouldn't find anything wrong with him grinning at his phone. She thought that Noelle was his real girlfriend. Only he and Noelle knew that in three weeks, their "relationship" would be over. The thought bothered him more and more every day.

"What about you?" he asked, cleverly turning the conversation back to Amara. "You dating anybody?"

"No one worth speaking about," she said, making a face. Amara had a thing for dudes who connected with her on a creative level but had an aversion to commitment. Suffice to say, she hadn't ever dated anyone whom Jeremiah had particularly liked. Then again, he wasn't sure if he'd ever think anyone was good enough for his sister.

She glanced at the time. "We'd better leave before Mom calls asking for our ETA."

They gathered their things, hopped in the car, and drove to Brickton. Noelle was waiting in her usual spot on the sidewalk in front of her apartment. She was wearing a new sleeveless light pink dress and white sneakers.

She waved as they pulled up, and he finally understood what people meant when they said that someone was a sight for sore eyes.

Amara started to get out of the passenger seat so that Noelle could sit up front, but Noelle encouraged Amara to stay where she was. Jeremiah walked around the front of the car to take Noelle's suitcase and put it in the trunk.

He smiled at her, heart pounding. He fought the urge to immediately pull her into his arms without speaking first. "Hi."

"Hi," she said, smiling back.

Then he hugged her and exhaled a deep, pent-up breath.

"I swear you two are just way too adorable," Amara said, rolling down her window.

Noelle glanced up at Jeremiah, almost shyly. He wondered if she felt this thing growing between them too. But asking her would only complicate things more.

Noelle climbed in the back seat, and Jeremiah disconnected his phone from the Bluetooth. Noelle's phone automatically connected. "Summertime Fine" by a singer named Angel started to play.

"Ooh, I haven't heard this in forever," Amara said, as Jeremiah pulled out of the apartment complex.

"We're working through Noelle's R and B playlists," he explained.

Amara glanced between them. "I love that."

Jeremiah caught eyes with Noelle in his rearview mirror, and they shared a smile. He wished she'd sat in the passenger seat. She felt too far away.

"I looked up some pictures online of past galas," Noelle said. "It seems like a lot of fun."

"It is. You'll enjoy yourself," Amara said. "We always do. And it's in the name of a great cause."

"The dance floor is usually packed all night," Jeremiah added.

"Our grandfather loved to dance." Amara pivoted to look at Noelle. "He and our mom were always the first two out on the dance floor."

At the last gala two summers ago, Pop and Celeste had

walked onto the dance floor arm in arm. Pop had started doing an old dance that he'd called the mashed potato. Celeste had covered her face in fake embarrassment as everyone had laughed.

"Jeremiah?"

He blinked to attention and realized that Noelle had been calling his name. He'd been too focused on the past.

"Sorry," he said, looking at her in the rearview mirror. "What did you say?"

"I asked if you're gonna dance with me tonight."

"Of course." He smiled, and she grinned back. "I got you."

It would be hard attending the gala without Pop for the first time, but maybe having Noelle with him tonight would make things easier.

Chapter Twenty

From the outside, the Heart Beach convention center looked like a standard building, nothing too out of the ordinary. But inside, the Smiths and the events team they'd hired for the gala had pulled off something special. An ice sculpture in the shape of giving hands welcomed guests as they entered the lobby. Floral arrangements featuring various white flowers cascaded down the walls. Based on what Noelle had learned from the brides she'd worked with, she'd guess that these arrangements hadn't come cheap. There was a custom-made black-and-white checkerboard dance floor, and smaller flower arrangements decorated the tables.

Guests had arrived in their black-tie best. Noelle smoothed her hands down the front of her gown. Daniela had personally delivered it earlier that afternoon. Thanks to Daniela's alterations, the dress now looked and felt like Noelle had been born to wear it. She paired the gown with the black open-toed heels that Tati had encouraged her to buy earlier this week. She still felt weird using Jeremiah's credit card carte blanche. He was already paying her a lot. But he hadn't so much as blinked when she'd told him how much she'd spent on the shoes. He'd smiled and said, *Okay*, like she'd told him that the forecast didn't call for rain this weekend. It was another reminder that they were from different worlds. But despite that reality, as she and Jeremiah had texted back and forth this week, Noelle had smiled at her phone, feeling ooey gooey at her center, like a warmed-up Smith's Sweets cookie.

If only he wasn't so generous. And so nice to look at. And didn't make her laugh. Or didn't listen to her while she talked. Then she wouldn't feel so completely drawn to him. She wouldn't spend time daydreaming about what it might be like if they were really together. Even though in reality, she couldn't let anything distract her from her studies once she started college again, and he was moving. And he was currently paying her to be his fake girlfriend, of course. What kind of real relationship started on those grounds? She knew she was being delusional, but she kept daydreaming regardless.

She glanced around the room, trying to locate Jeremiah. He'd been standing with his mom and siblings by the door, greeting the arriving guests, but now Noelle couldn't find him.

She felt a light tap at her elbow. She glanced to her left and found Jeremiah holding a glass of champagne toward her. He was always handsome, but tonight he looked downright mouthwatering in his tux. Like a sleek, sexy, Black James Bond. *His* beauty made *her* feel breathless.

"Looking for someone?" he asked with a smirk.

She glanced at his lips and immediately thought of the kiss they'd shared on his bed weeks ago. Did he think about that moment as much as she did?

"Thank you," she said, taking the champagne flute from him. From the way Noelle's pulse jumped when their fingers grazed, he may as well have caressed her in front of everyone.

"You're welcome," he said, his voice a low rumble in her ear, and she fought off the urge to shiver. "I was looking for you too. You look so beautiful tonight. Have I told you that already?"

"Thank you, and yes, more than once." She laughed softly. The moment she'd put the dress on earlier, it was as though she'd mesmerized him. His inviting smile did nothing to calm the harsh pounding of her heart.

"The flowers are so pretty," she blurted, needing to divert her thoughts elsewhere. She pointed at the flowers cascading down the walls. "What kind are they?"

"I think we settled on hydrangeas," he said. "But I can ask to be sure." He looked at her again. "Do you like flowers?"

"Of course. Who doesn't?"

"Do you have a favorite?"

"I like them all," she said. "Sometimes I keep my bridesmaid bouquets and repurpose them as arrangements for our kitchen table."

He smiled. "Would you put these flowers on your kitchen table?"

"Absolutely."

Jeremiah started to ask a follow-up question, but he was cut off by the MC, who asked everyone to take their seats.

"That's my cue," Jeremiah said, winking. "See you in a few minutes."

As Jeremiah joined Celeste, Percy, and Amara at the front of the room, Noelle made her way to their table at the edge of the dance floor. She sat beside Robin, who was glowing tonight, wearing a black gown with an empire waist and tulle skirt.

"My feet are killing me," Robin leaned over and whispered. "Welcome to your first Smith Foundation gala."

"Thanks," Noelle whispered back, and she felt a little prickle in her chest, realizing that this would be her first *and* last time attending the gala.

At the front of the room, Celeste held the mic, and Jeremiah, Amara, and Percy stood behind her.

"Hi, everyone," Celeste said, beaming. Her bob looked chic as always and she was wearing a formfitting black gown with a sweetheart bodice. "It's so wonderful to see your faces. Thank you for being here tonight for our sixteenth annual Smith Foundation gala!"

Applause rang throughout the room. Celeste smiled and waited for the applause to die down before she spoke again.

"The Smith Foundation awards grants to Black entrepreneurs and business owners every year, and it was founded by my parents, two Black entrepreneurs and business owners, who sacrificed so much in order for me to have a better life. My parents instilled in me the importance of supporting community and giving back, and that's something I've passed on to my children." She glanced back at Jeremiah, Percy, and Amara, who smiled proudly at her. Jeremiah winked, and Celeste laughed.

"This is the first year that we're hosting the gala without my father," Celeste said. "Those of you who knew him know that he was a caring, giving, funny, and singular man. Tonight is a continuation of his legacy. Thank you for being a part of that. Thank you for purchasing your tickets, and for bidding on our many auction items tonight, including season tickets for the Sixers *and* the Nets and a custom painting of the Heart Beach shoreline, painted by my talented daughter, Amara. Your generous gifts will directly help many others achieve their dreams. I'd like to call out a few of our special guests who were recipients of grants in recent years. Racquel Miller opened a soul food restaurant in Oaklyn, using her grandmother's recipes. Fred Thomas, who opened a martial arts studio last year, has created a wonderful space for the young people in Paterson. Brianna and Eden Jones are sisters who opened a bakery in Mays Landing that specializes in delicious vegan and nondairy offerings. But they are just a few of our special guests. There are many, many more honored guests here tonight. Will all of you please stand?"

Throughout the room, several people stood to exuberant applause. As Noelle clapped, she wondered if Harold knew about the Smiths' foundation. Hidden Gems Books could definitely use the help.

"From the bottom of our hearts, on behalf of my family and myself, thank you all for being here tonight," Celeste said. "Now, let's eat!"

The crowd clapped again as the Smiths walked to their table. Jeremiah kissed Celeste on the cheek, and she accepted a sideways hug from Amara, followed by another kiss on the cheek from Percy. Jeremiah sat in the open seat beside Noelle and she gently rubbed his back. She'd done it naturally, without even thinking about performing her fake-girlfriend role. She understood how significant it was for him and his family to be here tonight without his grandfather. She wanted Jeremiah to know that she was there for him. He smiled at her gratefully and kissed the back of her hand. They stared at each other, caught in their own little moment, spellbound.

"That was a really wonderful speech, Celeste," Robin said.

Celeste took a sip of her champagne. "Thank you. I don't

know why I feel so nervous tonight." She cast an anxious smile around the table. "Thinking about Dad, I guess."

Amara rested her head on Celeste's shoulder.

"I'm sure he's looking down at us and wondering when dinner will end so that people can start dancing," Jeremiah said with a smile.

Celeste burst into laughter. "That's probably true."

On cue, dinner was served. At most of the weddings Noelle had attended, food was sometimes the weakest link. It was hard to produce well-seasoned entrées en masse for large events. But the grilled chicken, steak, mashed potatoes, and asparagus that they were served tonight tasted delicious.

Not that the Smiths had much of a chance to enjoy their meals. Throughout dinner, guests visited their table in a constant cycle. Jeremiah introduced Noelle to multiple people, and she smiled and nodded, and held her hand out for a shake and tried her best to remember everyone's names. It was more difficult than it should have been thanks to how Jeremiah casually rested his hand against her thigh in the affectionate gesture of a besotted boyfriend. Her brain was zeroed in on that point of contact, making it hard for her to focus.

Eventually, the dinner plates were cleared away, and the DJ started to play an upbeat song as he welcomed people onto the dance floor. Noelle glanced around the room and waited to see who would be the first to get up and dance. Then she realized that everyone was looking at their table.

Celeste stood. A quick glance was exchanged between Jeremiah and Percy. Percy nodded, and Jeremiah stood from his chair. He walked around the table toward Celeste.

"Ma," he said, holding out his arm for her. "Let's boogie."

Celeste chuckled as she looped her arm through Jeremiah's and he led her out to the center of the dance floor. He spun Celeste in a circle and then they two-stepped from side to side. Jeremiah dropped Celeste's hands and began to move around her, quickly twisting his feet with an in-and-out motion. Celeste barked out a loud laugh at his funny dance, and everyone else laughed too, including Noelle. Once Jeremiah completed a full circle around Celeste, he bowed, and she shook her head as she smiled. It almost looked like she was tearing up, which confused Noelle. Why would Celeste be emotional at Jeremiah's silly dance? But then Celeste blinked, and her expression cleared. Jeremiah swept his arms out toward Celeste, and she curtsied. The room applauded, and Celeste turned to face everyone, encouraging others to get up too. More guests quickly joined the dance floor.

"You promised to dance with me tonight, sir," Robin said, nudging Percy in the arm.

Percy stood and adjusted his bow tie as he pulled back Robin's chair and helped her stand. "I'll definitely try my best."

Noelle watched Percy and Robin make their way to the dance floor. She was intrigued to see what Percy looked like when he danced. For some reason, she had a hard time imagining him having any rhythm.

"My mom and grandpa always shared the first dance," Amara explained, leaning across the table toward Noelle. "The little dance that Jeremiah did was one of our grandfather's favorites. He called it the mashed potato."

"Oh," Noelle said. Now Celeste's brief, emotional reaction made sense. Noelle looked out onto the dance floor at Jeremiah, who was still standing with Celeste. They were surrounded by guests, and Jeremiah turned slowly, searching the crowd. Then his gaze landed on Noelle and he smiled. He pointed at her and curled his finger, beckoning her over to him.

"I think I'm being summoned," Noelle said to Amara, keeping eyes on Jeremiah as she stood. "You coming?"

Amara grinned as she glanced back and forth between Noelle and Jeremiah. "I'll be out there soon. You go ahead."

Jeremiah eased his way through the crowd to meet Noelle halfway on the dance floor. When he reached her, he rested a hand against her waist and began an easy two-step. She followed his rhythm. The DJ was playing "Never Too Much" by Luther Vandross.

"That was sweet of you to dance with your mom," Noelle said, knowing now how special their moment was. "You're a smooth dancer."

"Thank you." He shrugged playfully. "People tell me that I'm a smooth guy."

Noelle laughed and stepped closer to him, moving her hips from side to side. He grinned, moving closer as well. She willingly let him invade her space as he brought his other hand to her waist.

Their dance was interrupted by an older man who hugged Jeremiah.

"You looked just like your grandfather out there," the man said, patting Jeremiah on the shoulder. "Spitting image."

"Ah, yeah," Jeremiah said, smiling. "Thank you."

The man continued walking on, and Jeremiah returned his hands to Noelle's waist. But soon they were interrupted again. This time by two women who were Amara's friends from college.

"You literally look just like the picture of your grandfather when he was younger that Amara posted on her page a few months ago," one of the women said. "It's crazy!"

"You are him and he is you," the other friend added.

The women laughed, and Jeremiah laughed lightly too, but Noelle noticed the strain in his smile. After Amara's friends walked away, Jeremiah took Noelle's hand and started to lead her toward the edge of the dance floor, but that didn't stop more people from approaching them and repeating what had already been said—that Jeremiah reminded them so much of his grandfather tonight. No one else but Noelle seemed to notice how uncomfortable Jeremiah looked. Across the room, Mercy Webster waved at them and started to make her way through the crowd. Jeremiah's posture went rigid. There was no doubt in Noelle's mind that Mercy was going to make a comparison to his grandfather.

Noelle gently tugged on Jeremiah's hand. "I need some fresh air. Walk me outside?"

"Of course." He led her through the ballroom to the exit. Once they were outside in the night breeze, he turned to Noelle, eyes searching her face in concern.

"You okay?" he asked. "What's wrong?"

"I'm fine," she said. "But it looked like you needed a minute."

He cracked a small smile. Then he closed his eyes and turned his face up toward the sky, inhaling a heavy breath.

Noelle was already in deeper than she needed to be where Jeremiah was concerned. She should just leave it. She shouldn't ask why the comparisons to his grandfather seemed to affect him so. Nothing about their agreement said that she needed to get involved. But as she looked at Jeremiah and took in his weary expression, she knew that she'd come to care about him too much to stand by and say nothing.

"Why does it bother you when people say that you look like you grandfather?" she asked.

He opened his eyes, but he was quiet for so long, she wondered if he'd heard what she said.

"It never bothered me before," he finally answered. "People have said that to me my whole life. I'm aware of how much I look like him. I was proud to look like my grandfather and share his name. I'm still proud now, but . . . it's also a lot harder to hear lately when people point it out to me."

"Why?" she asked gently.

His gaze dropped to the ground. "Because no matter how much we look alike on the outside, it only makes me think about the other ways I'm not like him. And how he was a much better man than I'll probably ever be."

Noelle frowned, wondering how he'd come to this conclusion. "What makes you think that?"

He continued to stare fixedly at the ground, like he was weighing if he wanted to share what was on his mind. Then he brought his gaze back up to Noelle's face.

"The night before my grandfather died, we got into an argument," he said.

Noelle listened as Jeremiah told her about his last conversation with his grandfather, and how he'd stormed out instead of staying to talk. He told her how he'd planned to apologize in the morning, but his grandfather had passed away.

Noelle pressed a hand to her chest when he finished speaking. Her heart broke for him. "Jeremiah . . . I'm so sorry."

"I wish I could go back to that night all the time," he said quietly. "I wish that I would have sat my stupid ass down and told Pop that he was right. I should have *apologized* when I had the chance. After he died, I wanted to make him proud and turn my life around, even if he wasn't here to see me do it." He paused. "Percy thinks I left Smith's Sweets because I don't care about the company or my family. But I *do* care about them. Caring about them is why I left. My mom and Percy and Amara . . . they're perfect as is. There was nothing left for me to contribute to Smith's Sweets, and I thought it would be best for everyone if I left and figured my shit out. Then I started working with Aaron and Good Boy. I've made a difference there. That's why I've been pouring so much of myself into the company."

There was something a bit hollow in his voice when he mentioned Good Boy, like he was trying to convince himself that Good Boy was where he needed to be. But he'd already revealed so much to Noelle tonight. She'd ask about his job another day.

"Who else have you told about your last conversation with your grandfather?" she asked softly.

"No one," he said. "I've been afraid of what my family will think. You're the first."

Noelle didn't know what to say. He hadn't shared this heavy memory with anyone, until her, which meant that he trusted her enough. In place of words, she hugged him. She heard his rapid heartbeat and his sharp intake of breath. He immediately wrapped his arms around her and held her close.

"I can't believe you've been holding this in for two years," she said. "Maybe you've done some things in your past that you're not proud of, but you've been making an effort to change." She leaned her head back and looked up at him. "I agree that your family is amazing. But, Jeremiah, you're amazing too. You talk about your family like you think they're more worthy of good things than you are, and that's not true. You're just as worthy."

He looked at her silently. His mouth formed into a consternated frown. She didn't know if he believed what she'd said, but at least he was listening.

"I think that you need to try to forgive yourself for the decisions you made in the past and for how you left things with your grandfather before he died." she continued. "You both loved each other, and you couldn't have known what would happen. If you don't forgive yourself, how can you ever move forward?"

"I'm going to work on that," he said. "I promise."

"Okay."

They fell quiet, still embraced, breathing in tandem.

"Part of me thinks I should leave," he said quietly. "The night is going so well, and I don't want to bring down the mood."

"No, you shouldn't leave," Noelle said, pulling away to look at him again. "You should stay here with your family. That's what your grandfather would have wanted." She paused, observing him. "And I think that's what you want too. You just have to believe that you deserve to be here."

His hold on her tightened, and he nodded wordlessly.

"Plus, you promised to dance with me tonight," she said. "And you haven't danced with me nearly enough."

He finally smiled, and it changed his whole face. "I did promise you that, didn't I?"

"Yep."

"I definitely don't want to break my promise to you." He stepped away and dragged a hand down his face again. His smile turned sardonic. "Do I look like I was someone who was outside going through it?"

"No. You look sexy, like James Bond."

He huffed out a laugh and hugged her to him once more. He leaned down and whispered in her ear, "Thank you."

Noelle's skin buzzed. Blood rushed through her veins straight to her heart. Being so close to him this way made her dizzy with wanting.

"You're welcome," she whispered back.

Hand in hand, they returned inside. Most people were on the dance floor doing the wobble. Amara and Celeste were in the front. Robin was trying to help Percy catch on, but he was moving like he had two left feet.

Noelle and Jeremiah joined his family and easily fell into step alongside them. Jeremiah didn't know how to do the wobble either, but it didn't really matter that he was doing the dance incorrectly. What mattered was that he'd listened to Noelle and he'd stayed. He wasn't missing out on this moment with his family. And the Smiths looked so happy, including Percy, who didn't have a rhythmic bone in his body. It was nice to feel part of it all. Even if this family wasn't for Noelle to keep.

After the song changed, Jeremiah took Noelle by the hand and dipped her in a flourish before whipping her back up into his arms. Noelle laughed in surprise and everyone around them burst into applause. But soon she wasn't thinking about anyone else as Jeremiah pulled her close and swayed with her from side to side.

"Everybody is looking at us," he whispered. His eyes lowered to her mouth. "What do you think? Should we kiss?"

"Yes," she answered quickly. She was tired of pretending like she hadn't wanted to kiss him all night.

The world fell away as Jeremiah's eyes fixed on hers. He lifted one hand to softly cradle her face and he rested his other hand against her lower back. He applied slight pressure and brought her closer. She lifted her chin and leaned in toward him. It felt so natural, like they'd done it countless times before. Their lips met, and her body curved instinctively into his. She looped her arms around his neck. Fireworks erupted in her brain, and the butterflies spread in a frenzy from her stomach to each of her limbs. Kissing Jeremiah felt so right, like all the time they'd spent not kissing had been a total waste. Her skin burned hot as his tongue slid across hers, and she was completely lost in him. Until someone whistled, snapping her back to reality.

Blinking, Noelle pulled away. People were cheering around them. Amara clapped and whistled again. Noelle's face was on fire. They'd planned to kiss, not completely make out in front of everyone. *Whoops.*

She glanced at up Jeremiah, and his eyes were glazed over as he stared down at her, like he was still caught up in their kiss too. He smiled, just a slight lift to the corners of his lips. But Noelle felt the force of it hit her right in the solar plexus.

Jeremiah was her client. She shouldn't want more from him. But her feelings for him had progressed far beyond a simple crush.

Her defenses were evaporating. And it was scaring the life out of her.

Chapter Twenty-One

In the morning, Jeremiah opened his eyes to Noelle's sleeping form. During the night, the satin scarf that she'd tied around her braids had come loose. She looked peaceful and angelic, illuminated by the early-morning light.

They hadn't left the gala until almost three a.m. last night. Noelle had been so tired, she hadn't bothered to read before bed. Her book of the week, a memoir about a child actor, sat untouched on the bedside table.

Jeremiah rested his head against his pillow as he looked at Noelle. Yesterday, he'd told her about his last conversation with Pop, and she hadn't judged him. She'd told him that he was just as worthy of good things as the rest of his family. He wanted to believe that was true. But mostly, it meant a lot to him that Noelle felt that way. She'd encouraged him to forgive himself and stay at the gala with his family. She'd told him not to run away. He was glad that he'd taken her advice. At first, it had been hard to host the gala without Pop. He'd felt Pop's absence everywhere. But as the night went on, the gala began to feel more like a celebration of Pop's continuing legacy. And for the first time all summer, Jeremiah woke up this morning feeling lighter, less weighed down by his memories. A lot of that was thanks to Noelle.

He knew that he was moving to California. He knew that she wanted to focus on getting back into college. He knew that a real relationship between them might not go anywhere.

But the plain truth was that he was falling for Noelle.

And their kiss last night on the dance floor . . . he couldn't stop thinking about it.

He wondered if she felt the same way. Sometimes he caught her looking at him like he was the coveted buried treasure that she'd been searching for (he was now on book two of the Pirates of the Deep series). But it would be inappropriate for him to ask her about her feelings. He was paying her to be here, which inevitably created a power imbalance. Whatever was growing between them felt real, but in the event that he'd misread her and she didn't reciprocate his feelings, he didn't want her to feel obligated to pretend that she liked him back out of fear that he wouldn't hold up his end of the bargain. Ultimately, he'd have to wait and let Noelle take the lead.

He slipped quietly from the bed. Noelle rolled over but didn't wake up. He shrugged off his pajamas and threw on his running gear. Then brushed his teeth and grabbed his phone before jogging downstairs. It was a little after ten a.m. Because they'd been out so late, most of his family was still asleep. But Ashley and Harper were sitting on the living room couch, holding bowls of cereal as they watched TV. They were so engrossed in their show, they hardly acknowledged Jeremiah when he said good morning on his way out the door.

He ran through downtown Heart Beach, and the morning breeze helped keep him cool. As a teenager, he used to go on morning runs every day here. It was a special thing to see Heart Beach as it was waking up. He stopped at Timeless Blooms, the florist that they'd used for last night's gala. The head florist, Gabrielle, didn't blink when Jeremiah asked if she could put together a bouquet with the same hydrangeas they'd used for last night's arrangements.

Fresh bouquet in hand, Jeremiah stopped to pick up donuts from Heart Beach Doughnut Shoppe. There were plenty of sweets at home, of course, but there was only one Heart Beach Doughnut Shoppe. It used to be one of their favorite places to visit on Sunday mornings. Jeremiah, Amara, and Percy used to fight over who got to ride shotgun in Pop's car as they drove into town.

Last night, Noelle had once again encouraged Jeremiah to talk to his family about Pop. He knew that she was right, and although he felt better now after sharing the story with her, he wasn't ready to tell his family just yet. He didn't want it to hurt them, and he didn't want to face Percy's judgment in particular. When the time felt right, he'd tell them. He just didn't know when that time would be.

When Jeremiah returned to the house, Percy was alone in the kitchen, pouring a cup of coffee. He nodded at Jeremiah, and Jeremiah nodded back. There'd been an unspoken truce between them last night for the sake of the gala, but today was a new day. Jeremiah was unsure of how to approach a conversation with Percy that wouldn't somehow end in a disagreement.

"I got donuts," he said, placing the box on the table. He figured pointing out the obvious was a safe choice.

Percy eyed the box. "I already had pie for breakfast."

"Ooh, donuts!" Amara said, breezing into the kitchen. She was wearing a vintage *Blacula* T-shirt and black denim shorts. In one hand, she held her sketchbook, and with her free hand, she opened the box of donuts. "Cinnamon sugar, my favorite. You *do* love me, Miah." She beamed, then pointed at the bouquet in his hand with a smile. "Are those for Noelle?"

"Yeah," Jeremiah said. He cleared his throat and looked at Percy again, anxious that his brother might rebuff him. "I got a Boston cream donut for you. I wasn't sure if it was still your favorite."

"It is." Percy stared at the box, contemplating. Then, "Ah, what the hell."

He grabbed the Boston cream donut and took a bite. While this definitely wasn't a heart-to-heart conversation where the brothers put aside their grievances and differences, it was better than arguing.

Jeremiah grabbed a glazed donut and bit into it. Mouth full, he asked, "Where's everyone else?"

"Outside." Amara wrapped her donut in a napkin. "Harper and Ash are working on their talent show routine, and they made everyone sit and watch. I'm headed to the beach to sketch for a bit. I'll be back later."

She waved at her brothers as she left the kitchen. Without Amara as a buffer, Jeremiah and Percy fell quiet.

"Mom seemed like she had a good time last night," Jeremiah said. "Even if Mercy Webster kept cornering her and talking her ear off."

Percy smirked. "Mercy has to be the most talkative person in all of Heart Beach."

"She called Noelle the wrong name and then tried to convince her to shop at her store."

Percy snorted as he grabbed a second donut. "Sounds like Mercy."

Encouraged by Percy's relaxed attitude, Jeremiah asked, "So, you ready to be a dad of three?"

Percy waited until he was done chewing to speak. "I'm both excited and terrified," he said. "Robin and I were just saying the other day—"

Percy's phone suddenly vibrated on the counter, and he paused, peering at the screen. Jeremiah saw an email alert with Smith's Sweets in the subject line. From the pinched look on Percy's face, Jeremiah would guess that he hadn't received good news.

"Another issue with the warehouse?" Jeremiah asked.

Percy glanced up. "No, this time it's an issue at our new manufacturer. It's been a headache and a half." He dusted off his hands. "I have to make some calls. If I don't see you before you leave, drive safe."

"Yeah, you too." Jeremiah tried not to show his disappointment over their positive conversation being cut short.

Percy left the kitchen, holding his phone to his ear as he headed for the stairs. Pop had been adamant about keeping the company family operated. Even though Jeremiah no longer worked for Smith's Sweets, he was still part of the family. Percy might not want Jeremiah's help right now, but in the future maybe he would.

He grabbed Noelle's flowers and walked outside. On the back patio, Harper, Ashley, Zoe, and Ciara were practicing their dance routine. Celeste, Robin, and Ciara and Zoe's mom from next door, Mrs. Davis, were watching off to the side. And Noelle was standing directly in front of the girls, clapping to help keep them on beat.

The girls attempted a move where they grabbed the hand of the person across from them to switch sides. But Ashley and Zoe crashed into each other. After that mistake, the girls struggled to finish strong. When the song ended, they shared matching expressions of frustration.

"Don't look so disappointed!" Noelle said, pulling them in for a group hug. "That time was a lot better! Switching places is tricky, but we'll figure it out."

"Yeah, listen to Noelle," Jeremiah said. "She knows what she's talking about."

Everyone turned to look at him as he walked closer. Noelle's eyes drifted from his face to the flowers in his hand. A pink flush spread across her cheeks as she smiled. He wanted to take a picture of her smiling at him this way so that he'd able to look at it whenever he wanted.

"These are for you," he said, handing her the bouquet.

Noelle accepted the bouquet, and the girls eagerly gathered around her, commenting on how pretty the flowers were.

"So romantic!" Ashley declared, standing on tiptoe to give the flowers a sniff.

"I want somebody to give me flowers," Zoe pouted, folding her arms across her chest.

"Wait until you're older," Mrs. Davis said. "Until then, your dad and I will buy you flowers."

Noelle looked up at Jeremiah. "These are just like the flowers from last night."

He nodded. "You mentioned that you liked them. I asked

the florist who worked the event to make an arrangement for you. Now you'll have some for your kitchen table."

Noelle's eyes softened. She glanced at the bouquet and looked up at him again. "Thank you."

"You're welcome," he said.

Then, before he realized what was happening, Noelle placed her hand on his cheek, stood on tiptoe, and kissed him. The kiss was quick and light. Over within a millisecond. But Jeremiah felt rewired, nonetheless.

Pulse pounding, he stared at Noelle's mouth as she stared back at him. Had she kissed him because people were watching? He glanced at his mom, but she, Robin, and Mrs. Davis, were talking among themselves again, no longer looking at him and Noelle. And the girls had already lost interest in the flowers and were going over their routine.

Unlike last night, no one had witnessed their kiss, but Noelle had kissed him anyway. His heart filled with hope.

"Uncle Miah, can you stop talking to Noelle so that we can keep practicing, please?" Harper asked, her hands on her hips as she came to stand in between him and Noelle.

"Yeah, she's our official talent show team coordinator now," Ashley added.

Jeremiah laughed and looked at Noelle. "Wait, really?"

Noelle nodded. "I'm taking over for Robin. She should be resting."

"And I'm treating her to a spa day soon as a thank-you!" Robin called.

Noelle smiled at Robin and turned back to Jeremiah.

"You know you don't have to do this, right?" he said, lowering his voice. "Amara or Mrs. Davis could do it. Shit, I could do it."

"It's okay," Noelle whispered back. "I want to. Now, thank you for the flowers. I love them. But your nieces are right. I should practice with them a few more times before we leave."

Jeremiah sighed, sporting a fake frown. "Can't I help?"

Noelle laughed and shook her head. "Probably not."

"You're distracting her, Uncle Miah," Ashley said, pushing Jeremiah away.

"Yeah, you have to go." Harper helped her sister push. "Sorry!"

"Y'all are kicking me out?" Jeremiah said, laughing as Zoe and Ciara joined in. All four girls collectively shoved him away. "That's crazy! Okay, okay, I'm leaving!"

He sat down next to Celeste, who was deep in conversation with Mrs. Davis about the renovations that she and her husband planned to make on their house during the winter. Jeremiah was busy watching Noelle, who kept hold of her new bouquet as she coached the girls. Every few minutes, she smiled and brought the flowers to her nose and gave them a sniff. He felt himself grin.

When he glanced over at Celeste again, he found that she was smiling softly at him. Like she was happy to see him happy.

They left Heart Beach in the early evening and hit a shit ton of traffic on the way back to north Jersey. By the time they reached Brickton, the sun was setting, and it was almost eight p.m.

"Thank you again for the flowers," Noelle said. She brushed her fingers against the bouquet that she held lovingly on her lap. She looked at him and bit her lip. "I guess I'll see you next weekend?"

Slowly, she reached for the door handle. Jeremiah experienced a brief moment of distress at the realization that he'd have to go another week without seeing her. When they'd extended their agreement, he'd asked her for four more weekends. Once this weekend ended, they had only two more weekends left.

He did a quick calculation, glancing from the flowers in her hand, to her gown that was zipped up in a garment bag, hanging on the hook in the back seat, and he thought of her suitcase in the trunk.

"I'll help you carry your stuff," he said, opening his door too.

He walked around the car to get her suitcase as Noelle grabbed her dress from the back seat.

"Are you sure?" she asked. "I can figure out how to carry it all up myself."

"I'm sure you could. But you don't have to worry about that because I'm here, and I'm not going to sit by and let you carry everything without any help."

He smirked and gestured for her to hand him the gown.

She looked at him, then glanced at her apartment building. She seemed to take a second to think something over. Finally, she said, "Okay."

They walked through her complex. Kids were running around, shooting at each other with water guns. A few of them called out to Noelle, and she smiled and waved back.

Jeremiah followed her up a flight of stairs to the second floor. They reached her apartment and Noelle unlocked the door. After they stepped inside, Jeremiah closed the door behind them.

Her apartment was small, but cozy. There was a shoe rack by the door, and a comfy-looking dark brown couch and matching love seat were set up in the living room. Magazines were scattered across the coffee table in front of the couch. The kitchen was to their right, and there was enough space for a small rectangular table by the window.

The living room television was turned on. Someone had been in the middle of watching an episode of *Living Single*.

"Tati always forgets to turn off the TV before she leaves," Noelle said, clicking off the television.

She crossed over into the kitchen area and pulled a clear vase from beneath the sink. She filled the vase with water before placing it in the center of the table.

"Where is she now?" Jeremiah asked, admiring Noelle as she added the flowers inside the vase and arranged them with deft movements. "Tati?"

"In the DR with her boyfriend, André," Noelle said. "They're on vacation."

She was smiling as she spoke, but there was a hint of sadness in her voice too.

He thought of how she'd said that she missed her mom, who lived in South Carolina now. And how her dad lived in Texas, along with her stepsiblings whom she wasn't very close with. Tati was the closest thing to family for Noelle here in New Jersey.

"Do you miss her?" he asked.

She looked up at him. Realizing he still held her garment bag and suitcase, she walked over to take them.

"I do," she said. "I'm happy for her. She and André are so adorable, and they're in love, so I absolutely understand why they spend as much time together as they can. But yeah, I miss her sometimes."

She put the garment bag over her shoulder and rolled her suitcase across the living room to the hallway, where he assumed the bedrooms were located. He walked farther into the living room and glanced at a framed photograph of Noelle and Tati on the wall. They were teenagers dressed in graduation robes, looking at each other mid-laugh.

"I've been with you most weekends lately, though," Noelle said as she returned to the living room. "So I think I've been preoccupied with that."

She stood in front of him and lifted her shoulders in a shrug.

"So, this is our apartment," she said. "It's not much. But it's home."

"I love it."

She raised her eyebrows. "You do?"

"Yeah. I can feel the love between you and Tati here, like it's a real home."

She smiled at him, pleased. "Thanks."

He'd helped her carry her things upstairs. There was no reason for him to stay. But he was reluctant to part from her. From the way she stood there, watching him, he wondered if she was reluctant for him to leave as well.

"Do you want to grab something to eat?" he asked.

"I'm kind of tired and don't want to go out again," she said, and his stomach sank. "But I was planning to cook. Do . . . you want to stay for dinner?"

"Yeah," he hastened to say. "Of course."

He followed her into the kitchen. She opened the cabinets

and pulled out a large skillet and some olive oil and seasonings. Then she opened the fridge and pulled out ground beef and bell peppers.

"What are you cooking?" he asked.

"Tacos. One of my few specialties."

Noelle was always doing so much for other people. She was helping him by being his pretend girlfriend and now she was volunteering to help his nieces with their dance routine. Even her other jobs required her to be in service to others. She deserved to relax and have someone else help her.

He took the seasonings from her hands. "I'll cook."

"You can cook?" She blinked at him.

"I can do a little something something."

She smirked, quirking a disbelieving eyebrow. "A little something something like what?"

"Like . . . picking up the phone to order delivery or putting something in the air fryer."

She barked out a laugh. "Very impressive."

"Nah for real, though. I can cook breakfast foods. Bacon. Eggs. Pancakes. French toast. Whatever. I don't cook a lot, but I'm a fast learner. Just tell me what to do."

She tilted her head and looked at him with a soft smile. "Okay. You can start by chopping up the peppers." She put a knife and cutting board on the counter in front of him. "Please don't slice off your finger."

"Damn, girl, give me a little more credit than that," he said, and she laughed as she sat at the table.

He sliced the peppers. Then Noelle directed him to season the ground beef and add it to a pan on the stove.

"Looking good so far," she said as he used the spatula to

break up the ground beef. She took the peppers he'd sliced and added them to another skillet, seasoning them too.

"You're supposed to be sitting down, ma'am," he said, taking her by the shoulders and ushering her back to the table. "I got this. You're insulting me by helping."

She laughed as she sat down again. "Okay, sorry."

When he was finished with the peppers, she directed him to get the head of lettuce and tomatoes to chop those as well. As Jeremiah opened the fridge, he glanced at a picture of Noelle and her mom. It must have been taken on her mom's birthday a few years ago because they were standing in front of Texas Roadhouse and her mom was holding a birthday balloon. He then glanced at another picture of Noelle that looked more recent. She was standing in an aisle at Hidden Gems Books, holding a stack of old paperbacks, smiling at whoever had snapped the photo. Being here with her in her kitchen, cooking her dinner while looking at her photographs, felt intimate. Real.

"Excuse me, Mr. I Can Do a Little Something, Something," Noelle said, bringing him back to attention. "You're supposed to be chopping the lettuce and tomatoes."

"Yes, Chef!"

She laughed as he grabbed the vegetables from the fridge.

Soon, dinner was done. Jeremiah placed the meat, chopped lettuce and tomatoes, and cheese on the table in separate bowls, next to a plate of tortillas. Noelle placed plates and utensils on the table.

He waited as she took the first bite. She grinned slowly as she chewed.

"Wait, this is so good," she said.

"See, I told you." He puffed up his chest, proud to have cooked a delicious meal for the woman he liked.

As they ate, they talked about new music they were listening to and the shows they were watching. She told him she was looking forward to reading a new psychological thriller by an author named Jeanette Stevens. They could have talked about any topic, and Jeremiah wouldn't have cared. As long as it meant he'd be here in this space with Noelle.

After dinner, she took their plates to the sink and ran the water.

"Wait," Jeremiah said, standing. "I'll do the dishes."

Noelle looked like she wanted to argue, but after a moment of hesitation, she acquiesced. "You wash, I'll dry."

They created an easy rhythm as they washed and dried the dishes together. Once they finished, Jeremiah glanced at his phone and noted the time. It was nine thirty. He had work in the morning. And it was possible that Noelle was tired of having company now.

"So," she said, turning to him as she dried her hands. "Do you want to see my room?"

He nodded, relieved. And he was intrigued that she'd *offered* for him to see her room. He followed her down the hallway to the first bedroom on the right. She moved aside and let him walk into her room ahead of her.

Her room was small but tidy. It smelled like the floral perfume that she often wore. A dark purple comforter was draped over her full-size bed. A few pairs of shoes were lined up at the bottom of her closet, and makeup and hair items were situated atop her dresser. But her wooden bookshelf mainly caught his attention. It was short and only came to his waist, but it was stacked to the brim with books.

"Have you read all of these?" he asked, crouching in front of the bookshelf. He recognized some of the books as ones she'd brought with her to the beach over the last few weeks.

"Yeah," she said. "Well, those are the ones I own. I get the majority of my books from the library."

"I'm on book two of the Pirates of the Deep series now, by the way," he said, turning to look at her.

She sat on her bed and crossed her legs pretzel style. "What do you think so far?"

"I think Clara Crawford is a genius," he said, and Noelle laughed. "For real, though. That thing you said about there being a book for every reader is true. Clara Crawford writes with a lot of emotion. It holds my attention."

Noelle beamed at him. "I've successfully turned you into a Clara Crawford fan. My work here is done."

He smirked as he stood, and Noelle moved over on her bed to make space for him. He sat beside her. By this point, they'd slept in the same bed multiple times, but something about sitting together on her bed here in her apartment felt different. More intimate, once again. He wanted to know everything that he could about Noelle.

"When's the last time you saw your dad in Texas?" he asked, leaning back on his elbows.

"Last Christmas. That's usually when I see him and my stepmom. I used to see them every summer for a month when I was younger."

"Was it fun?" he asked.

She squinted and chewed the inside of her cheek. "Sometimes. But mostly, going there gave me a lot of anxiety. My mom had summers off from teaching, so I really wanted to stay home with her, and I felt bad about not wanting to go to Texas.

My dad and stepmom tried their best to make sure I enjoyed myself, but I don't think they really knew what to do with me. And my stepbrothers were older and always out with their friends. I always ended up feeling really homesick. Once I started high school, I begged my mom to let me stay home during the summer. I blamed it on wanting a summer job, but really, I didn't want to go to Texas if I didn't have to. I didn't really fit there."

Even when Jeremiah considered himself the black sheep, he always knew that he was a Smith and that he belonged with his family. He couldn't imagine how it must have felt for Noelle to spend time with her dad while feeling like she didn't fit into his life.

"I'm sorry," he said quietly. "That's a lot for a kid to deal with."

She shrugged and smiled a little. "I think that's one of the reasons I like being around your family. Everyone fits. You've even created space for me."

She glanced away, and Jeremiah's heart squeezed. He wanted to say that there could be a permanent space for her if that was what she wanted. But they had their agreement. He was moving. She was going back to school.

Still, that didn't change how he felt about her.

"Can I ask you a question?" he said, overcoming his nerves.

"Yes," she murmured.

"Why did you kiss me earlier?"

Noelle's gaze lowered to his mouth. He watched her chest rise and fall as she breathed. She licked her lips, and his pulse pounded in his ears.

"Because . . ." She cleared her throat. "I really wanted to."

The pounding of his heart intensified. He replayed her words in his head, making sure he hadn't misheard her.

"I like you a lot, Jeremiah," she said. She looked at him head on, direct and earnest.

He sat up and moved closer to her, blinking. He almost couldn't believe that she was saying the words he hadn't dared hope to hear.

"I like you a lot too," he said, swallowing thickly.

"That's why I kissed you," she continued, not looking away from him. "Because I really like you."

Gently, he slid his hand up her arm until it rested at her elbow. "Okay," he said. "We're on the same page about how we feel. So, where does that leave us?"

She shrugged, at a loss. "I don't know. You're moving, and I'm finally going back to finish college. I don't want to get distracted. Getting together for real would be complicated. And I lied to your family about being a librarian, about everything. How could I explain that?" She bit her bottom lip. "Even though we like each other, maybe . . . we should just agree to be friends."

The balloon of hope in Jeremiah's chest popped and deflated. He stared at Noelle, taking in her distressed expression. If they really tried, he believed they could figure out a way to make things work. Long distance would be hard, and he'd have to be okay with being put on the back burner in deference to her studies sometimes. But that was doable. She had a point about the lies, but they could cross that bridge when they came to it. They *could* see where things went after summer ended if they wanted to.

He wanted to tell her these things. He wanted to ask her to have faith in them and what they could be together. But . . . asking Noelle to see things from his point of view would be selfish, especially after everything she'd been through in order to get to this point in her life. He didn't want her to see him as just another obstacle.

"Okay," he said, releasing a deep breath. Heart heavy, he smiled softly. "Friends."

Her smile in response was bittersweet. "Friends," she repeated.

They fell quiet. Jeremiah checked his phone again. It was almost ten p.m. He definitely didn't want to overstay his welcome.

"It's late, I should go," he said, beginning to stand. But Noelle placed her hand on his forearm, stopping him.

"Or if you don't feel like driving home, you could stay over," she said. In her voice, he heard her reluctance for him to leave. He clung to that because he didn't want to leave either. He didn't like the idea of her being here in this empty apartment alone. He wanted to stay with her, even though he knew they couldn't be more than friends.

"I know it's not as big as your bed in Heart Beach," she said. "But we can both fit comfortably, right?"

"Yeah," he said slowly. "Friends have sleepovers all the time."

She nodded. "They do."

He went to grab his duffel bag from his car, and he changed into a spare T-shirt and a pair of basketball shorts. After washing up, he climbed into Noelle's bed, and the sheets smelled like her. She turned off her bedroom light and slid under the covers as well. Their arms and legs were touching as they both lay on their backs. Then Noelle turned and curled into Jeremiah's side. He put his arm around her, and she rested her head against his chest, right on top of his wildly beating heart. Holding her this way felt amazing. He wished he could go back and undo every night they'd spent sleeping on opposite ends of his bed.

He liked Noelle. She liked him. They were just going to be friends.

A simple decision that felt more complicated than ever.

Chapter Twenty-Two

Noelle's mind was officially all over the place.

When Jeremiah had left her apartment on Monday morning, he'd kissed her on the forehead and told her he'd text her later. She'd been worried that he might act weird toward her now since they'd agreed to be friends—on her suggestion because she thought that would be for the best!—but then he'd stayed over—also on her suggestion because apparently, she was a masochist!—and cuddled with her all night. However, on his lunch break, he'd texted her like he said he would and asked how her day was going. And they'd continued to text throughout the rest of the week. She liked him more and more as each day passed.

Usually, she was so overwhelmed with her various jobs, she didn't have much time to ponder her thoughts and feelings, but for the time in several years, she actually had the chance to hear herself think. She had time to update her résumé, and she had the gift of discernment when applying for jobs. She was hoping to find some kind of office work that didn't require a bachelor's degree. When she wasn't applying to jobs, she went to the park with a blanket and a book and she read on the grass in the sun. She FaceTimed her mom. When Tati came back from vacation, she and Noelle spent hours lying on the couch, watching old episodes of *Insecure*. She finally had the opportunity to take a breath. All because she was pretending to be Jeremiah's girlfriend.

But that didn't feel like much of a job. The pretending part wasn't very hard at all.

She thought about Jeremiah constantly. She thought about him while cooking dinner, recalling how he'd moved so easily around her kitchen like he'd been there several times before. She thought about him while reading a spy novel, thinking of how he looked like James Bond at the gala. She thought about him at the most random times too, like while on a call with Sheree, as she reconfirmed the location and time of her bridal shower in a couple weeks. As Sheree described the tea party theme, Noelle was busy daydreaming about every time that she and Jeremiah had kissed.

They didn't talk about their kisses, though. They texted consistently and talked about any- and everything *but* their kiss. Instead, they asked each other questions. What were their favorite colors? Favorite movies? Favorite memories? She answered: yellow; *Brown Sugar*; she had lots of favorite memories, but one that she thought of often was that time in high school when she and Tati had gotten lost in Central Park and ended up watching the sea lion feeding at the zoo. Jeremiah's favorite color was blue. His favorite movie was *Coming to America*. His favorite memory was when his grandfather taught him how to drive a boat the summer after he turned sixteen.

They shared their weird, irrational fears. Like Noelle's fear that one day she might bite into an apple and see a worm. Or Jeremiah's fear that he might get bit by a spider and eggs would hatch on his skin.

On Thursday evening after work, Jeremiah went to the basketball courts to meet up with the teens he volunteered with during the school year. He told Noelle how he talked to them about their goals for the upcoming semester and asked what school supplies they needed. He told her about how the boys laughed at him every time he discreetly checked his phone to see if she'd texted him back. He told her that he wanted to lie out on the beach and listen to her explain the plot of whatever book she was reading. He wanted to teach her how to make the famous Smith's blueberry crumble pie. He asked what she was most looking forward to about going back to college. He told her that her resilience inspired him. He wanted to know things about her that her brides had never bothered to ask. And their lack of curiosity had been fine with Noelle. She'd preferred the distance before. But the lines were blurred with Jeremiah. She craved closeness with him in a way she'd never cared about with previous clients.

By the time he picked her up on Friday evening, she was so eager to see him, she practically flew out of her apartment to meet him outside. During the drive to Heart Beach, she damn near had to sit on her hands in order to fight the urge to touch him. He didn't try to kiss her. He was kind and flirty and funny, like usual, but he was also a perfect gentleman, keeping his hands at ten and two on the steering wheel.

She knew that he was respecting the boundaries of their situation. He was right to keep his hands to himself and not kiss or touch her. The only time they needed to kiss was if it was for the benefit of people witnessing their fake relationship in action. But at the same time, she wished that he'd pull over so that they could make out right then and there.

Once they arrived at Heart Beach, they had dinner with his family, and afterward they watched a movie outside on the projector. At night, she and Jeremiah slept in his bed together, and even though they stayed up late, laughing quietly as they took turns coming up with the most ridiculous names for Robin and Percy's baby, they didn't cuddle again like they had in her bed last Sunday. It was excruciating. She wished there was a world in which the two of them being together made sense. A world where he wasn't moving across the country soon, and she could trust herself to focus on her own life and goals without getting caught up with the man she was dating. A world where their relationship hadn't started with him paying her. That was another reason she'd suggested they stay friends, even though she hadn't shared it with him out of fear that it would make things awkward. Her feelings for Jeremiah were very real, but she didn't know how they could transition from their arrangement to a real relationship.

"Noelle, are you listening?" Amara asked now.

Noelle blinked and looked over at Amara. They were walking through town toward Heart Beach Books. Amara was picking up a couple preorders, and Noelle was picking up some books that Jeremiah had ordered for her ahead of time. The books were a surprise. He said he wanted to see how well he could nail her taste. Another reason that it was hard to stop liking him!

"Shoot, sorry," Noelle said. "Can you repeat that?"

Amara pushed her black oval-shaped sunglasses up onto her head. "I was saying that I know you have plans with Miah today, so we'll be in and out."

Later that afternoon, Jeremiah was taking Noelle out on his boat.

"You're fine. I don't think he's in a rush."

A couple hours ago, he'd taken Harper, Ashley, Ciara, and Zoe to the rides section of the boardwalk. Noelle had practiced the girls' talent show routine with them earlier that morning, and they were having a hard time getting through the dance without any mistakes. The talent show was in two weeks. Jeremiah had offered to take them to the boardwalk to cheer them up.

"Okay, good," Amara said, smiling. "That'll give us more time to browse."

The sky was overcast, and a few storm clouds hovered in the distance. The forecast hadn't called for rain, but as Celeste had warned everyone before they'd left, beach weather was unpredictable. Amara had invited Celeste to join them on their walk to the bookstore, but she'd stayed behind with Percy to talk about Smith's Sweets. It sounded like they were having another issue at the warehouse.

As Noelle and Amara came upon the bookstore, Noelle noticed an ocean wave painted on the window in front of a display of books about the beach, ranging from picture books to photography books.

"Did you paint that?" Noelle asked.

Amara nodded. "I always paint the windows for them at the beginning of summer."

Inside, the store was bright and cheery. Noelle was hit with a brief wave of longing. She realized how much she missed working at Hidden Gems Books. She hadn't let herself think about it before because she'd switched to survival mode, worrying about where she'd find work next. But now that she had a chance to breathe, it really broke her heart that she'd been let go from her favorite job.

They approached the register, and they both startled when a man suddenly stood upright behind the counter, holding a roll of receipt paper. He was tall with brown skin and tattoo sleeves on his arms. He wore a white T-shirt and black, square-framed glasses. And he was staring directly at Amara.

"Amara," he said, blinking. "Hey."

Noelle glanced at Amara, who'd transformed into a deer in headlights. Pink spots bloomed on her brown cheeks as she stood there motionless.

"H-hey, Danny," she said, flustered. "I didn't know you were in Heart Beach this weekend."

Wait . . . Danny. Jeremiah's best friend? It had to be him. Jeremiah mentioned that Danny's parents owned the bookstore.

"I got here late last night," he said. "My mom ran out to get lunch, so I said I'd help while she was gone." His throat muscles worked as he swallowed. His eyes softened. "It's really good to see you."

Amara smiled and nodded quickly. "You too."

Then neither of them said anything. Amara stared down at her shoes, and Danny gazed at the top of her head like it was the most fascinating thing he'd ever seen. Noelle glanced back and forth between them.

"Hi," she finally said, giving a little wave. "I'm Noelle."

"Oh, sorry, this is Jeremiah's girlfriend, Noelle," Amara said. "This is, um, Danny. Jeremiah's best friend."

Danny spared a glance at Noelle and recognition dawned on his features. He sprang into action and hurried around the register with a quick, loping gait. He shook Noelle's hand with an exuberant grip.

"*Noelle*," he said, grinning. "That's right. Jeremiah told me about you."

"Good things, I hope," she joked, although she was genuinely curious to know what Jeremiah had said. Did Danny know the truth about her and Jeremiah's agreement?

"Yeah, of course," Danny said, nodding. "Only good things."

He stuffed his hands in his pockets and rocked back on his heels. He glanced at Amara again, and her cheeks resumed their fierce blush. She trained her eyes to the floor.

"We have some books to pick up, actually," Noelle said, breaking the silence again, wondering why Amara had suddenly lost the ability to speak in Danny's presence. *So* curious.

"Oh yeah, of course." Danny returned to the register and grabbed their books. There was a small stack of horror novels for Amara, and Jeremiah had ordered the new Jeanette Stevens thriller for Noelle, most likely because she'd mentioned it to him last week. He'd also ordered an urban fantasy novel that she'd heard about a while ago but hadn't had a chance to read, and a sci-fi romance about two humans stuck on an alien planet.

It was like someone had taken the sun and injected it directly into her veins. That was how happy she felt that Jeremiah had picked out these books for her. She felt so known.

Realizing that she'd been grinning like a fool at her books for the past few minutes, Noelle finally looked over at Amara and Danny. Amara was placing her books in her tote bag, and Danny was leaning his elbows on the counter, watching her with keen interest. He murmured something, and Amara glanced at him with a soft smile. Whatever she mumbled in reply caused his whole face to light up.

When they noticed Noelle watching them, Danny stood up straight and Amara cleared her throat.

"Thanks for stopping by," Danny said. He looked at Amara again. "My mom will be sad that she missed you."

Amara smiled. "Tell her I said hi."

"I will." He looked at Noelle. "It was nice to meet you."

"Yeah, same," Noelle said, raising an eyebrow as Danny's attention automatically returned to Amara.

Amara lifted her hand in a wave as they started for the exit. "Bye, Danny."

"Maybe I'll see you later tonight," he hurried to say, coming around in front of the register again. "I told Jeremiah that I would stop by."

"Oh yeah," Amara said. "Okay, see you then."

Noelle got one last glimpse of Danny's besotted expression before she followed Amara outside. Amara let out a deep breath and started walking in the direction of the house. Noelle hurried to follow her.

"Okay, I have to ask," she said. "Is there a story with you and Danny? Did you hook up before? Date?"

Amara laughed miserably. "No, nothing like that."

Noelle blinked, obviously confused. Amara sighed.

"I was in love with Danny for most of my life up until a couple years ago when I realized he'd only ever look at me as his best friend's little sister," she said. "Eventually, I gave up on trying to get him to love me back. Now when I see him it's very awkward, which is what you just witnessed." She winced. "I know that sounds pathetic."

"I could *never* think you were pathetic," Noelle said, looping her arm through Amara's. "But the way Danny looked at you in the bookstore . . . I don't think that's a man who doesn't love you back."

"That's just Danny," Amara said, shaking her head. "He's nice to everyone. It's kind of his thing. We grew up together. I know he loves me. But he's not *in love* with me. Anyway, I hate talking about my past infatuation with him because it's kind of embarrassing. Please don't tell Jeremiah. He doesn't know, and there's really no need for him to."

"Of course," Noelle said. "Your secret is safe with me."

"Thank you." Amara let out a relieved breath as she leaned her head on Noelle's shoulder. "Can we talk about something else? Which books did Jeremiah get for you?"

"I'm going to read this one next," Noelle said, holding up her copy of Jeanette Stevens's book *The Missing Women*.

"What's it about?" Amara asked.

As Noelle and Amara read the book's description together, strolling slowly down the sidewalk, Noelle realized that her friendship with Amara was something else that she'd miss once summer ended. Would it be possible for them to remain friends beyond August when she was no longer Jeremiah's fake girlfriend?

"Oh God, look at your boyfriend," Amara said, laughing. "What's he up to now?"

In the distance, Noelle saw Jeremiah pedaling toward them on a beach cruiser. He steered another bike alongside him. She'd seen both bikes in the Smiths' garage before.

Jeremiah grinned as he pedaled closer. His eyes sparkled as he looked at Noelle.

"Madam," he said when he reached them, "your chariot awaits."

Noelle laughed. "My chariot to *where*, exactly?"

"To the marina," he said. "Robin wanted to take the twins to the mall, but her car is blocked by Mom's car in the driveway. She and Percy are on a conference call and Robin didn't want to bother them, so I told her she could take my car. That means we're biking to the boat."

"You'd better go soon before it starts to rain," Amara said, looking up at the sky. She reached for Noelle's books. "I can take these to the house for you."

"Thanks," Noelle said, hugging Amara. "I'll see you when we get back."

Noelle climbed onto the spare bike, and Jeremiah smiled at her. "Ready?" he asked.

With Jeremiah, she had a feeling that she could be ready for anything.

She smiled back at him. "Ready."

Chapter Twenty-Three

They rode to the marina and parked their bikes at the dock. Noelle followed behind Jeremiah as they walked past rows of boats on either side of them. They stopped at a small, white bowrider boat with a black accent lining. Unlike Jeremiah's car, his boat looked older. There was a wind cover above the steering wheel and a seating area in the back of the boat that was just large enough to fit a small group. Jeremiah stepped onto the boat and turned around, offering his hand to pull Noelle on as well.

"Welcome aboard the *Caesar*," he said. "I'll be your personal pirate today."

Noelle giggled as the boat shifted under their weight. Jeremiah untied the boat from the dock and pulled the rope up. Noelle followed him to the steering wheel and watched as he put the boat in gear and coasted through the marina and out into the ocean.

"Wait, did you name your boat after your mom's cat?" Noelle asked.

"Yeah." He glanced over his shoulder at her and grinned. "That wasn't the boat's original name, though. It was called *Serenity*. You remember Mr. Drake from Hang High Parasailing?" Noelle nodded. "I bought this boat off his brother when I was sixteen after I got my boat license. He put me on a payment plan because my mom and Pop said I didn't need a boat of my own at that age, but that if I wanted one, I'd have to pay for it myself. So, I saved up during the summers when I worked at Marty's, and I saved the money my parents and Pop gave me on my birthdays. I put it all toward paying off the boat. Then on my twenty-first birthday I was able to access my trust fund, and I paid off what was left. I renamed the boat *Caesar*, and that's been the name ever since."

Him mentioning his trust fund reminded Noelle that money was certainly the biggest difference between them. And it reminded her that his money and their fake relationship went hand in hand, and it reinforced her theory that a real relationship between them probably wouldn't work.

But they'd already decided to be friends so there was no point in thinking about that now. Not when she wanted to enjoy their last couple of weekends together.

"I didn't know you worked at Marty's," she said.

"I can make a funnel cake with my eyes closed."

He reached down and laced his fingers through hers and led her toward the seating area.

"Sit tight," he said. "I'll be right back."

Noelle curled up in the corner of the boat and looked out at the water. She inhaled the salty air. A few other boats were cruising through the ocean or idling in place as people fished. The storm clouds had darkened over the past half hour, but it still hadn't rained. Jeremiah returned to sit beside Noelle, and he wasn't empty-handed. He placed an assorted box of Smith's Sweets cookies and a water bottle in her lap.

"For you, my lady," he said, bowing.

"Thank you!" Noelle laughed, delighted, as she opened the box. "Where did you get this?"

"While you were practicing with Harper and Ash this morning, I came here to make sure that everything was okay with the boat. I brought some stuff with me that I thought we might want."

Noelle smiled at his thoughtfulness as she opened the box.

"As you can see, I haven't turned into a cookie yet," she said.

"Give it a few more days." He winked as he took the box from her and grabbed a few cookies himself.

It started to drizzle then, but it was a light mist that didn't yet suggest the threat of harder rain.

"Hold on." Jeremiah hopped up and rummaged around near the steering wheel. He came back, holding two old hoodies, and he handed one to Noelle. It was dark brown and faded from years of wear and wash. *Heart Beach* was written across the front in white letters. His hoodie was the same but navy blue. "I usually leave these here on the boat just in case."

"You've thought of everything," she said, slipping on the hoodie. She pulled the hood over her head and covered the top of her braids. The hoodie smelled salty like the beach. "You said your grandfather taught you how to drive a boat?"

"Yep." He slipped on his hoodie and stretched his legs out in front of him. "He also taught Percy and Amara. We each got our boat licenses once we turned sixteen. My mom has hers too. She used to drive Pop's boat sometimes, but he sold it a few years before he died. He offered the boat to my mom, but she said she didn't want it. Percy and Amara said they didn't want it either. They never liked being on the boat as much as I did. And I already had my own boat, so I didn't need Pop's too. Now I'm wishing that we'd kept it."

"What was the name of his boat?" Noelle asked softly.

"The *Minnie*. He named it after my grandmother."

"That's so sweet." Noelle glanced down at the photograph of his grandparents on the back of the Smith's Sweets cookie box. His grandfather gazed at his grandmother with such obvious adoration.

"Yeah, they really loved each other," Jeremiah said. "On the flip side, my parents' relationship was the opposite of my grandparents'. They fought all the time. It was a relief when they split up when I was in middle school. They're friends now, though. It was like once they were no longer married, they were actually able to like each other."

"My parents divorced when I was young too," she said. "But I was only three, so I don't remember any of their arguments. My mom said they just became incompatible after a while."

Jeremiah nodded as he grabbed another cookie. "I think maybe the key to lasting love is making sure you really like the person *before* you fall in love. That at the end of the day, they're your friend first."

Noelle swallowed thickly. It wasn't until after Jeremiah was done speaking that he seemed to sense the irony of his words. He and Noelle had just agreed to stay friends very recently. He coughed and focused his attention on closing the top of the cookie box.

"I agree with you," she said, after a beat. "Friendship is the best foundation."

He looked at her again with a soft smile. Her butterflies preened their wings for flight.

"Thank you for the books," she said. "They were perfect choices."

"Good. I did a lot of poking around online for research." He smiled wryly. "Book recommendations are all up and down my algorithms now."

She smiled back and held his gaze. She liked him *so* much. But what would talking about their feelings again do? Earlier, she'd been so confused by Amara and Danny and how they'd stared at each other with so many things clearly left unsaid. But she understood their behavior now. She laughed to herself.

Jeremiah leaned closer. "Why are you laughing?"

"Nothing." Her eyes roamed his face, and then a fat rain drop landed right on his cheek.

Jeremiah jerked back and looked up at the sky. More raindrops fell in quick succession.

"Okay, we should go," he said.

They ducked under the cover above the steering wheel for shelter. As Jeremiah steered them back toward the marina, the rain intensified. The wind blew harder, rocking the boat. Noelle experienced a moment of panic where she imagined them getting blown off course and marooned in the middle of the stormy ocean. But that was the kind of thing that happened to paddleboats. Plus, Jeremiah looked assured and in control as he steered. It was really sexy, actually.

Once they reached the dock, Noelle hopped out and tossed Jeremiah the rope and he made quick work of fastening the knot and securing the boat to the dock. Rain was falling in heavy sheets now. They ran to their bikes and pedaled through the downpour. Thunder rolled across the sky. Noelle struggled to see in front of her. Riding a bike through this weather was low-key scarier than being on the boat.

As they pedaled through town, they saw other people running in the rain. Beachgoers, carrying their chairs and coolers. Kids running barefoot, their laughter tinged with a bit of fear. Neighbors welcomed passersby to wait out the storm under the protection of their enclosed front porches. A man who owned a convenience store was handing out umbrellas, free of charge.

When they finally arrived at the Smiths' house, Noelle and Jeremiah rushed up the empty driveway and stashed their bikes in the garage before dashing up to the door. They stumbled inside. Without the sunlight illuminating the house through the windows, everything was dark. They kicked off their wet shoes and left them at the door.

"Hello?" Jeremiah called out. No one responded. He checked his phone and scrolled through his texts, squinting at his screen. "Amara and my mom met Robin and the girls at the mall. Percy's at the coffee shop. They're all waiting out the storm."

"So it's just us?" Noelle asked.

"Just us," he confirmed.

A flash of lightning broke across the sky, and Noelle jumped. "*Shit*," she whispered.

Gently, Jeremiah took her hand in his. "Come on," he said.

She swallowed thickly as he guided her upstairs. Inside his bedroom, rain pounded against the windows. Noelle was so focused on getting out of the wet clothes that clung to her body, she tore off the hoodie, along with her T-shirt and denim shorts without thinking. It was only when she heard Jeremiah's sharp intake of breath that she spun around to face him. He blinked at her, eyes briefly but hungrily sweeping up and down the length of her body. Her heart pounded as she stared back at him. Suddenly, he bent down and riffled through his suitcase. He stood upright and handed her another hoodie, looking away. This hoodie was plain and black with the Nike logo in the center. It was also dry and newer and smelled like his cologne. When Noelle put it on, it covered her torso and fell to the middle of her thighs. She sat on the edge of the bed as Jeremiah pulled off his T-shirt, giving her a glimpse of his muscular body before he shrugged on a new shirt. She stared openly at him, and he glanced up and caught her gaze. The air around them turned staticky. Noelle shivered, even though she was no longer cold. In fact, she was scorching.

"I'll be right back," he said quietly.

Noelle nodded and inhaled deeply, tucking her legs underneath her. She felt like she was standing at the edge of a cliff, and she was either going to jump and hope she landed somewhere soft, or she was going to back away and never know what lay below. She wanted to be more than just friends with Jeremiah. But would trying for more be a mistake? She didn't know what to do.

She grabbed her phone and opened her text thread with Tati.

I think I'm about to do something crazy, she texted.

Tati responded immediately. Hook up with Jeremiah?

Noelle blinked at her phone. How did you know?

Because I know you and I know that
you like him. He's all you talk about
lately.

Noelle bit her lip.

Would it be crazy tho? she asked. Like a big, big mistake?

Girl, no! If anyone deserves a summer romance, it's you.

But we agreed to be friends and he's paying me to be here. What if it gets complicated if we try to make things real?

Talk to him about it. Tell him how you feel. If he cares enough about you (and he'd be stupid not to), you'll work together to figure a way forward.

Noelle smiled at her phone, grateful for her best friend. Thanks for the advice. Love you.

Love you too! I want all the deets after you get the D!!

Noelle laughed and covered her face with her hands. She lowered them as Jeremiah reentered the room, this time holding two steaming mugs.

"We only had peppermint tea," he said, holding a mug out to her. "I hope that's okay. It should help warm you up."

Her heart melted as she gazed up at him. He was so sweet and thoughtful and funny, and despite the walls she'd put up and the reasons she shouldn't want to get involved with him, he disarmed her defenses just by being himself. And she liked him too much to pretend otherwise. She took a deep breath and stepped off the cliff.

"Thank you," she said, taking the mug. But she set it down on the ground. "Jeremiah, I want to tell you something."

"Wait," he said, standing in front of her. "Can I tell you something first? That's the real reason I went downstairs. I mean, I wanted to make you some tea because you were shivering, but I also wanted to practice what I need to say to you."

She blinked as she looked up at him, pulse quickening. "Okay."

He sat on the bed beside her and took her hands in his. "Is this okay?"

She nodded, touched that he'd thought to ask permission even though they'd definitely progressed past hand-holding at this point.

"I know we have our agreement and that I'm paying you to be here with me, and the goal was to pretend for my family's sake that we're in a happy relationship," he said. "And I know we said that we should just stay friends. But last week, I didn't tell you the whole story when I said that I liked you. The full truth is that I liked you from the beginning when I first met you at the bookstore. I would have asked you out then for real, but I had the feeling that you weren't looking to date, and you later confirmed you weren't, so I held back on my feelings and thought they'd eventually fade away and we'd be cool to keep pretending. But my feelings for you have only grown stronger. I think about you all the time. Whenever you're around me, I can't focus on anything else, and I don't want to. I think that you are one of the most beautiful, kindest, genuine people that I've ever met. I care about you so much, and I wasn't sure where you stood, but knowing that you like me too gives me hope that maybe you want to be more than just friends too." He paused and gave her hands a gentle squeeze. "But if you don't, that's okay. *Please* know it's okay. I promise I will shut the fuck up and never bring this up again."

Noelle burst out laughing at his last line, because it was so unexpected. His worried expression eased into one of relief.

"You're laughing. I'm trying to pour my heart out to you, and you're laughing," he said, smiling as he shook his head. "That's crazy."

"I'm sorry." She attempted to school her features and she inched closer to him, brushing her knee against his thigh. "You don't have to shut up, because I feel the same way. *I* think about *you* all the time. Tati said that you're the only thing I talk about anymore." She paused. "But last week I didn't tell you the full story either. I left out one of the reasons I thought we should just stay friends. The money has been a huge help to me, and this is the first time in a long time that I haven't had to work myself to the bone. That's a bigger gift to me than you'll ever know. Being here with you and getting to know you has made my summer so much better. But the money is also one of the reasons that I feel hesitant about us trying to start something real. Not many relationships start with a contract like ours has."

"You're right," he said, grabbing his phone. "They don't. Hold on."

Her brows furrowed as she watched him type something on his phone. "What are you doing?"

"I'm setting up a wire transfer to send you the rest of the money," he said, and she blinked in surprise. "As far as I'm concerned, the terms of the agreement have been met. We've successfully convinced my family that we're in a relationship. I don't want the contract to be something that's hovering over us anymore. You should receive the rest of the money by Tuesday at the latest." He set his phone aside and met her eyes again. His expression was open and earnest. "Now we have the chance to start fresh. No more agreements. No more payments. Just you and me, for real."

"Jeremiah . . ." she whispered, staring at him. She was grateful, of course, that she would now officially have the money she needed for college. But she also felt deeply relieved that this obstacle between them had been removed and that he'd done it so quickly. "I want us to have a fresh start too. Thank you."

"You don't have to thank me. I should be thanking you." He rubbed his thumbs across her knuckles. "What do you want to do now?" he asked softly. "I'm following your lead here."

"I'm not sure," she answered honestly. One obstacle had been removed, but others still remained. "You'll be in California soon, and I'll be focused on school. I don't know what would happen with us beyond summer."

He bit his lower lip, and it drew Noelle's attention to his mouth. "Maybe we don't need to think about what happens after summer ends," he said. "Maybe we just make the most of the time we have together now."

The thought of having Jeremiah for real just to let him go sounded like a very painful plan of action. But what other options did they have? She was realistic enough to know that a new relationship would easily crumble between long distance and busy schedules.

Ultimately, she hadn't felt this strongly about someone before. She liked Jeremiah too much to not have him at all, even if it was only for the rest of summer.

"Okay." She reached up to touch his cheek. His beard prickled her palm.

He turned, bringing his lips to brush against her fingers. He tilted his head and looked at her closely. "You're sure?"

She nodded. Finally, all pretenses were dropped. It was just them and the truth about how they felt for each other. When Jeremiah leaned in to kiss her, there was no voice in the back of her head telling her not to go too far, and there was no one else around them who might interrupt.

Jeremiah pressed his lips against hers and Noelle's heart pounded as she kissed him back. The kiss was deep and languid, and she savored the feel of his lips and tongue. Slowly, they eased down onto the bed, and Jeremiah hovered above her. He kissed his way down her throat and she struggled to yank off the hoodie to give him better access to her skin. She almost elbowed him in the process.

"Damn," he mumbled, chuckling. "Let me help."

She sat up and lifted her arms as Jeremiah tugged the hoodie over her head. Then she unhooked her bra and let it fall to the side. With heavy-lidded eyes, he stared at her breasts. She leaned back onto her elbows and let herself be admired by him. Jeremiah covered her body with his as he kissed her again and she felt his hardness press at the space between her thighs where she was already wet. He kissed his way down her throat again, pressing his lips against her collarbone and lower and lower until he reached her breasts. She moaned when he took her left nipple in his mouth, and she ran her fingers up and down his back, lifting her hips against his. As he moved his lips to her other breast, she reached down between them into his shorts and wrapped her hand around his length. He was hard in her grasp, and he groaned as she caressed him.

"Wait," he said breathlessly. He lifted his head to look at her, lips swollen from kissing. "I feel like this is leading toward sex, which is *very* cool with me, but I need to know first if that's what you want."

"Yes," she said, grabbing at his T-shirt. "That's exactly what I want."

With lightning speed, he whipped his T-shirt off, and when she reached for the drawstring of his basketball shorts, he shrugged them off in record time. After she tugged down his briefs, he kneeled before her, remaining still with taut muscles, breathing heavily. He was completely naked, and it was her turn to admire him. He was so gorgeous, it overwhelmed her.

"May I?" he asked huskily, curling his finger at the waistband of her underwear. She nodded, swallowing hard, and lay down again, lifting her hips as he pulled her underwear down her legs.

He crawled back over her and they were pressed skin to skin. He kissed her slowly and brushed his hand down the expanse of her stomach, leaving goose bumps on her skin in his wake. He rubbed a finger against her clit and around her opening where she was slick. He slipped a finger inside of her, and she moaned as her muscles clenched around him.

"You feel so good," he said, voice low as he added another finger. "You're so fucking beautiful."

He pushed his fingers in and out of her and she moved her hips, matching his steady rhythm. But she wanted more. She reached down and moved his hand from its place between her thighs, took his length in her hand again, and pressed him against her opening, stroking him.

"*Fuck, Noelle*," he whispered.

"Do you have a condom?" she panted.

"Yes." He hurried to crawl across the bed and reached for the bedside drawer. "Shit, I hope I do."

Noelle breathed heavily, drinking in the strong build of his body, waiting as he riffled through the drawer. He finally procured a sleeve of condoms and smiled at her triumphantly.

"They're not expired yet," he said.

She grinned, eager for him to return to her. "Yay."

He rose to his knees and began to open the wrapper, but Noelle moved closer and took the condom from his hands.

"Can I?" she asked.

He nodded and pressed his forehead against hers as she slipped the condom over his length. He cupped her ass in his hands and gave her cheeks a firm squeeze. They kissed again, and Noelle lightly pushed against his shoulders until he rested his back against the headboard. She straddled him and angled him at her opening, slowly, easing down until he was buried deep inside of her. She bit her lip, feeling pleasure wash over her. His hands gripped her waist and he let out a deep groan.

"*Fuck*," he whispered. "I can't believe this is happening."

Noelle smiled, and her pulse thumped erratically as she began to move up and down. He touched her where they were joined, and she moaned as she rode him, closing her eyes and letting her head fall back.

"Come here," he ground out. "I need you closer."

He pulled her to lie against him chest to chest. At this angle, she felt him even deeper. She was pliant in his arms as he gripped her ass and pumped into her. His movements were rough, but she liked it.

"Does that feel good?" he panted.

"*Yes.*"

"Kiss me."

Their mouths and tongues were sloppy as they kissed, trying to get the most of each other as he pounded into her. When the orgasm washed over her, saturating her in pleasure, her moan was so loud and guttural, she was glad that no one else was home. The sound was enough to drive Jeremiah over the edge. His thrusts intensified, and she felt him jerk inside of her as he filled the condom.

They lay there, boneless. Breathing hard and still joined.

"I don't want to sound like I'm exaggerating," he said, breaking the silence, voice heavy. "But I think this might be the best day of my life."

Noelle smiled as she pressed her lips against his shoulder. "You're silly," she whispered.

"Silly, but serious." He gave her ass a light smack and she clenched her muscles around his length that was still buried inside of her. "You okay?"

She nodded and lifted her head to look at him. His expression was dazed. She imagined that she looked the same. "Are you?"

"I'm fucking wonderful."

She laughed and leaned her head against him again. She expected to feel apprehension over what they'd done, about how they'd rewritten the rules of their relationship. But as the rain beat against the windows and Jeremiah ran his fingers up and down her spine, she was thinking only about how good it felt to be in his arms.

Eventually, she shifted her hips so that Jeremiah could slip from inside her and remove the condom. She snuggled under the covers and watched as he padded naked across the hall to the bathroom. He grinned as he returned and slid in bed next to her. She turned on her side to face him and he did the same, resting his hand against her hip. He moved closer and kissed her, slow and deep. Then a loud crack of thunder rolled across the sky, making them both jump.

A meow sounded from the hall, and the next thing Noelle knew, Caesar scrambled into Jeremiah's room and jumped onto the bed. Noelle gasped and pulled the covers up to her neck. Now finally able to get a good look at the cat, she saw that Caesar was pink and wrinkly, and he stared at them with big yellow eyes. Jeremiah reached for Caesar, but the cat hissed in warning and curled into a loaf at the foot of the bed.

"He hates me, but he hates thunderstorms more," Jeremiah explained. "He doesn't like to be alone when it rains."

Noelle raised an eyebrow, and Caesar looked directly at her without blinking. His expression said, *So what if I'm afraid of thunderstorms? I'll still scratch your ass any day.* Seeming satisfied that his threat was received, Caesar turned his head and looked out the window.

Noelle turned to look out the window too, and Jeremiah spooned her from behind. Content and satiated, they watched the falling summer rain together.

Chapter Twenty-Four

Later, after the storm cleared and Caesar retreated to Celeste's bedroom and the rest of the Smiths returned home, Jeremiah and Noelle dressed and joined everyone downstairs. They gathered in the living room to survey the disarray of tree branches in the backyard. Some houses a few streets over had lost electricity, but luckily the Smiths hadn't been affected. Celeste floated the idea of going out for dinner, but everyone agreed that it was too messy outside to leave again. Instead, they ordered pizza and decided to have another movie night. It took them a while to decide on a movie that pleased the adults while also being appropriate for Harper and Ashley. Eventually, they decided on *The Lion King* live action.

Jeremiah didn't really care what they watched because he was barely focused on the movie. Noelle held all of his attention. He kept his arm around her shoulder and held her close as she leaned into his side. He couldn't stop touching her in little ways, massaging the back of her neck or resting his other hand on her knee. All he could think about was the things he wanted to do to her once they were back upstairs in the privacy of his bedroom, and how relieved he was to know that she wanted more than just friendship too, that they were getting their fresh start.

He was willing to remove his arm from around her shoulders only when he went to answer the door for Danny. It had started to rain again as Danny had walked over from the bookstore. He was soaked, and raindrops covered his glasses lenses. He shook out his arms and legs like a wet cat. Jeremiah burst out laughing.

"Bro, why did you walk?" he asked, opening the door wider to let Danny inside.

Danny laughed sardonically and sighed. "I didn't know it was gonna rain again. I wanted the fresh air. Probably should have checked the weather first."

"Yeah, probably." Jeremiah dapped up his best friend. Unlike his other past friendships, Jeremiah's friendship with Danny had always been genuine, and that was the reason it had endured. Danny was born and raised in Heart Beach with parents who'd been born and raised here too. Growing up, Danny was the pride of Heart Beach as everyone watched him excel in school and sports. The people here still saw him as their golden boy with his successful tech engineer career in Philadelphia. Only Jeremiah knew how stressful it had been for Danny to uphold that image when they were younger, and it was one of the reasons that Danny had loved being at the Smiths' house. They were Heart Beachers too, but only three to four months out of the year. Being around Jeremiah and his family had allowed an escape for Danny to simply *be*.

Even though they'd been attached at the hip during

summers as kids, Jeremiah and Danny saw a lot less of each other in adulthood. They hadn't chilled together in months. They'd both been focused on work, and Danny worked harder than anyone Jeremiah knew, maybe even Percy. He was glad that Danny had found time to visit. "How you holding up? How are your parents and the store?"

"Work is kicking my ass, but that's nothing new. The fam is good." Danny smiled and angled his head to see farther into the house. "Is, um, everybody here?"

"Yeah, yeah. We're all here. Come on back."

When they entered the living room, Celeste sat up and gasped. "Daniel Martin, did you walk here in the rain? Are you trying to catch your death?"

"Hey, Ms. Celeste," Danny said, smiling sheepishly. He waved at the rest of the group. He paused when his eyes landed on Amara and Noelle sitting in the corner of the couch. "Hi again."

Amara was snuggled under a flannel blanket, and she lifted her hand in a wave. Noelle, who was sitting next to her, smiled and waved too.

"I want to introduce you to Noelle," Jeremiah said, leading Danny over to their end of the couch. He'd briefly told Danny about Noelle being his new girlfriend, but he hadn't told him about their arrangement because it wasn't something to easily explain over text. Now that he and Noelle were starting fresh, he wondered if he needed to tell Danny about their arrangement after all. Or anyone, for that matter.

Danny sat on the other side of Amara, and Jeremiah reclaimed his seat next to Noelle.

"Noelle and I met earlier today," Danny said. He leaned

forward and smiled at Noelle, who nodded. "She was with Amara when they came by the bookstore earlier."

Amara pulled the blanket from her body and handed it to Danny.

"You look like you need it more than me," she said quietly.

"Thanks," Danny said, giving her a small smile.

"Look," Noelle said, nudging Jeremiah. She immediately distracted him with her beautiful grin as she pointed at the television, "Beyoncé is about to tell the lionesses to fight with her."

Jeremiah snorted. "You mean Nala?"

"Yeah. Nala Beyoncé."

He laughed and wrapped his arm around her again.

After the movie ended, Jeremiah drove Danny to his parents' house. They lived in northern Heart Beach where it was less touristy. When Jeremiah was younger, sometimes he'd wished that he'd lived in Heart Beach year-round just like Danny.

"I'm sorry the rain fucked things up and we didn't do anything tonight," Jeremiah said as they pulled up.

Danny shrugged, one hand on the door handle. "Nah, chilling with you and your family was more than enough for me. You know that." He smiled. "You and Noelle seem really good together. I'm happy for you. I know you've been working on yourself a lot."

Hearing that from Danny meant more to Jeremiah than he could express. "Thanks, bro. I appreciate that."

"Of course. I'll be back next weekend too," Danny said, getting out of the car. "I'll hit you up then."

"Sounds good." Jeremiah dapped Danny up before he drove away.

Once Jeremiah was back home, he bounded upstairs to his room, eager to see Noelle again. She was sitting up in bed with a book open in her lap. *The Missing Women*, one of the books he'd ordered for her. He closed the door behind him, and she tilted her head and smiled as he walked toward her. He lay down beside her and propped himself up on his elbow.

"I just realized that next weekend is supposed to be our last weekend in Heart Beach," he said. "We'll miss Harper and Ashley's talent show since it's not until the weekend after."

Noelle lowered her book and looked at him. "I assumed you'd be getting ready for your move during the weekend of the talent show, since it's the last weekend of August. You're still planning to move the first weekend of September, right?"

"I am," he said, although his move and being away from Noelle was the last thing he wanted to think about right now. "But I'll have time to pack. I don't want to miss the talent show."

"Me neither. Sheree's bridal shower is that Friday afternoon, so we could drive down Friday night instead if that's okay with you."

"That's okay with me." He curled one of the ends of her braids around his finger. "So, two more weekends left in Heart Beach?"

She nodded, smiling as she snuggled her back against the pillow. "Two more weekends."

He loved seeing her comfortable in his bed like this, happy and content with her book. He loved that her being in Heart Beach meant that she had the chance to enjoy a well-deserved rest. He lowered his eyes to her breasts where he could see her hardened nipples through her shirt. She took one look at him and the hungry expression on his face and closed her book.

They drew to each other like magnets, kissing and tugging off their clothes until they were naked again.

"Like this," Jeremiah whispered huskily in her ear after he slid on a condom, positioning Noelle so that she was in front of him on her hands and knees. "I want you like this."

When he entered her from behind, she arched her back and whimpered. Jeremiah covered her mouth with his hand. She felt so good, it took everything in him to stay quiet so that no one would hear them. Grabbing on to her hip with his other hand and thrusting into her like this was too much for him. He felt her muscles clench around him and she bit down on his hand to keep from moaning as she came. Then, only once she was satisfied, did he finally let go too and follow her into bliss.

At breakfast the next morning, Jeremiah couldn't help gazing across the table at Noelle as she talked with Robin about the talent show. He was replaying scenes from last night in his head, how she'd straddled him and teased him as she'd lowered herself onto him inch by delicious inch. When Noelle caught eyes with him, she blushed and lost her train of thought. He grinned and focused on finishing his cereal.

While Noelle and Robin practiced with the girls in the backyard, Jeremiah swam in the pool. Amara waded in the shallow end. Celeste and Percy were locked away in Celeste's office. Again, Jeremiah thought about asking them if they needed help, but he didn't want to intrude. Or worse, ruin the fragile peace that he and Percy had established over the last couple weeks. So instead, he waited for Noelle while she practiced with the girls. They were getting better. Even if they didn't place in the talent show, they'd definitely finish the summer with more confidence, thanks to Noelle.

Afterward, he and Noelle walked to the beach. Usually, he spent most of his time at the beach trying to become one with the ocean. Something he'd inherited from his Grandma Minnie. But today, he lay under the umbrella beside Noelle and listened as she read aloud from *The Missing Women*. He was trying his best to focus, but he was distracted by how lovely Noelle looked in her bikini. Unable to help himself, he lightly brushed his fingers across her belly button. She laughed and gave him a pointed look.

"Are you listening to me?" she asked.

"I'm trying to. I swear," he said. "But your beauty is distracting. I can't help it."

"Hmm. Well, you're not so bad yourself," she whispered, leaning down to press her mouth against his for a kiss. She pulled away and rolled back onto her towel. "Do you want me to keep reading or should I stop?"

"Keep reading." He folded his hands on top of his chest. "I'll keep my hands to myself."

She raised a skeptical eyebrow as she started to read again. As promised, he didn't move his hands, even though he really wanted to. He even closed his eyes so that he could better listen. But after a few minutes, Noelle stopped reading. He peeked an eye open and found her staring at him. The corner of her mouth lifted in a slight smirk.

"What?" he said. "I was listening, I promise."

"I know, but I'm done reading now."

She leaned over to kiss him again, and he laughed and pulled her closer.

Chapter Twenty-Five

They got stuck in bumper-to-bumper traffic on the drive home. Noelle was driving this time. She wanted to know what it was like to drive Jeremiah's car, and as she suspected, it drove smoothly. She barely felt any bumps in the road, and it didn't rattle like her Accord.

"What kind of car is this again?" she asked as she seamlessly switched lanes.

Jeremiah replied with the name of a foreign car brand that she'd never heard of before.

"You like driving it?" he asked. He'd reclined the passenger seat and was watching her with a lazy grin.

"I *love* it," she said, and he laughed.

Once the traffic began to clear up, Jeremiah turned down the radio.

"Do you wanna stay over at my place tonight?" he asked.

She looked at him with a soft smile and nodded. They had

so little time left before summer ended. She wanted to be around him as much as she could.

She took the exit for Jersey City and drove through the downtown area, past Hidden Gems Books and the hair salon where Tati worked. Jeremiah instructed her to make a right on a street that was lined with brownstones. People were walking their dogs and sitting on their stoops. By the grace of the parking gods, there was an open spot right in front of his apartment.

Noelle looked at Jeremiah and grimaced. "This is where you find out that if someone asked me to parallel park or walk barefoot on burning hot coals, I'd choose the coals easily."

He snorted and opened his door. "I'll do it."

Noelle got out of the car and waited on the sidewalk as Jeremiah parallel parked. There was something about the way he flattened his hand against the steering wheel as he backed into the spot and checked his rearview mirror. Why did she find something so simple as him parallel parking to be so sexy?

As Jeremiah unlocked his apartment door, he sent Noelle a nervous glance.

"I don't have people over that often," he said as he turned the knob and stepped inside, holding the door open for her.

From his apprehensive expression, she was expecting to walk into a messy apartment that wasn't ready for guests. However, his apartment was spotless. Gray- and oat-colored furniture was situated throughout the space, and large windows faced the street. Birds chirped happily on the tree branches outside.

"Wow," Noelle said, eyes scanning her surroundings. "I walk by these kinds of brownstones all the time, and I've always wondered what they looked like on the inside." She turned to him. He was standing by the couch. "Your apartment looks like it's straight out of a catalog."

He laughed. "That's probably because I hired somebody to help me decorate. I wouldn't have done this on my own."

"They did a great job."

Jeremiah lived in a cozy, curated apartment of someone who'd planted roots. It didn't look like the apartment of someone who was moving in three weeks.

"Where are the cardboard boxes and bins?" she asked. "Have you started packing anything?"

"Ah, yeah. I've been procrastinating about that." He scratched the back of his neck. "I'll get to it soon, though. Other than the furniture, I don't have that much stuff to move, honestly."

She nodded as she walked to the hallway that led to the bathroom and his bedroom. She paused in front of a photograph that was hanging on the wall. It was a picture of him and his family, taken at Disney World when he and his siblings were kids. She recognized it as the same photo that appeared on his phone's screen whenever his mom called him.

"Look at you and your Mickey ears." She pointed, smiling.

"That was on my eighth birthday," he said, coming to stand beside her.

She looked closer at the picture and noted the similarities between him and his grandfather. There were the obvious physical similarities, of course. But they also smiled alike and squinted the same eye closed as the sun shined on them. It was sweet.

She continued down the hall to his bedroom. Like his living room, his bedroom was filled with matching gray- and oat-colored furniture, tasteful and put together. When she sat on the edge of his king-size bed, she realized that her curious perusal of his apartment might come across as rude or a bit intrusive.

"Sorry, I'm being so nosy right now," she said, biting her lip.

He leaned against the doorway and shook his head. "Nah, I like that you're comfortable looking around. It makes me feel like you're comfortable with me."

"I *am* comfortable with you," she said, as she ran her fingers over the gray comforter. "Your bed is soft." She looked up at him. "Do you like living here?"

"I do. I like being close to my family in case of an emergency," he said. "I like the West Coast too, but I'll miss being a drive away from everyone."

"Why don't you want to continue to work remotely?"

"The rest of the team is in California, and I want to be there too," he said. "I want them to know that I care about the company's success as much as they do. My hope is that once I move to California, they'll see how serious I am."

"Why can't they see that now?" she asked.

Jeremiah shrugged. "The founder, Aaron, knew me in college. I was different then, less motivated. I think he has a hard time separating who I was from who I am now."

"If he can't see how amazing you are, he probably doesn't deserve to have you on his team," she said, frowning.

He laughed softly. "It's a work in progress."

He walked over to his dresser, unclasped his watch, and placed it beside his cologne. He slipped off his sneakers and padded over to his closet. His back was to Noelle, and as she watched him, she realized that she wouldn't have many more opportunities to see him like this. Unwinding at home after a long day. Repeating the small, ordinary acts that stitched together the patchwork of his life. She was already mourning the future they wouldn't have.

"What?" he said, smiling as he turned around and caught her eye.

"Nothing." She forced a smile. They'd been having such a nice day. She didn't want to bring down the mood with her sad thoughts about their eventual separation. "Just admiring you."

He walked back toward her. "I think that's supposed to be my job."

She laughed, which then made her yawn. She wrapped her braids into a high bun on top of her head, and she noticed the way that Jeremiah stared at her exposed skin beneath the hem of her tank top as she lifted her arms.

"I'm tired. I could use a shower." She raised an eyebrow. "Do . . . you want to join me?"

Jeremiah grabbed her hand and pulled her to her feet. She laughed as he led her toward the bathroom.

In the shower, he stood behind her and spread soap suds down the slope of her back. Then, so that her hair stayed dry, he repositioned them so that his back faced the showerhead. He kissed her and slipped his fingers between her folds. She gasped as she kissed him back. He pressed her up against the wall, and the only thing stopping him from lifting her up and burying himself inside of her was that he didn't have a condom.

Once they were back in his bedroom, Noelle lay on the bed, and Jeremiah kissed his way down her body, stopping to kiss her between her legs. She rolled her hips and panted as she gripped the sheets. Breathless, he grabbed a condom from his drawer and wasted no time sliding it on. Noelle stared up at him, dazed as he propped her legs on his shoulders and slid inside of her. He grabbed her hips, and her breasts bounced as he pumped into her. She gasped his name, moaning as she came, and soon the headlong rush overtook him too.

Heart pounding, he collapsed beside her, keeping her wrapped in his arms.

She wished they had more time together. She wished that they had an endless summer before them.

Chapter Twenty-Six

"The only time I worry about not knowing how to swim is when I think about how my options of escape would be limited during an alien invasion or something like that," Tati said, "Otherwise, I don't think about it that much."

Noelle laughed, while Tati smiled, lifting her shoulders in a shrug. They were sitting side by side on the back of Jeremiah's boat. Their feet dangled in the water. Unlike last weekend when Noelle and Jeremiah got caught in the storm, this weekend they'd been blessed with beautiful weather.

Amara was sitting on Noelle's other side, and she leaned forward to grin at Tati. "Do you believe in aliens?"

"I definitely believe that we aren't the only ones in the galaxy," Tati answered. "I mean, how can that be true? The galaxy is so big."

"She makes good points," André said. He was lounging on one of the seats of the interior of the boat deck. He sipped his beer and nodded his head at Tati. "Babe, tell them about what you saw behind the Shop Mart on Route 21."

Tati glanced back at André and narrowed her eyes, but she was fighting a smirk, aware that he was poking fun at her. "I thought I saw a small spaceship, but it was actually an abandoned ice cream truck."

"Wait, I remember this story," Noelle said. "Didn't you take an edible a few hours before that happened?"

"Yeah, but that's not the point," Tati said. "Anyone could have been confused like me."

"I've seen some crazy shit after taking an edible," Danny said over his shoulder. "Happens to the best of us."

Danny was hovering over the left side of the boat with his fishing rod poised in his hands. Beside him, Jeremiah did the same, but instead of participating in their conversation like Danny, Jeremiah kept his eyes trained on the water. Noelle wouldn't have guessed that he'd take fishing so seriously. He said that his grandfather used to take him fishing often. André had originally planned to fish too. He'd even bought new fishing gear for the occasion. But after two hours without any catches among the three of them, André had since given up.

"I can doggy paddle," Tati said. "So, I guess if aliens invaded, I'd be able to move through bodies of water to get to safety." She smiled cheekily. "Or I could steal Jeremiah's boat."

Jeremiah snorted and finally turned to face the rest of the group. "If aliens are invading, you're gonna need a lot more than this boat to get you to safety."

"Don't worry, babe," André said to Tati. "I'll get my pilot's license."

Tati batted her eyelashes dreamily and clasped her hands to her chest. "My hero."

Everyone laughed, and Noelle felt a deep contentment in her bones as she watched her world collide with Jeremiah's. A few days ago, she'd mentioned to him that she felt bad that she hadn't spent much time with Tati this summer, so he'd told her to invite Tati and André down to Heart Beach. Tati and André had jumped at the chance and had arrived earlier that morning. Jeremiah had offered them one of the guest rooms to stay overnight, but they were staying only for the day since they'd promised to take André's mom out for brunch tomorrow morning. Either way, Noelle was glad that Jeremiah had the chance to spend time with her friends. She wanted Tati and André to see the wonderful things about Jeremiah that she saw.

After she spent the night at his apartment last Sunday, Noelle had stayed with him most of Monday too. While he'd worked, she'd applied to jobs. She found a few administrative assistant positions that didn't require a bachelor's degree. Already this upcoming week, she had an interview at a real estate company in Hoboken that was looking for someone to work the front desk.

She'd also visited Riley University's bursar's office and paid her tuition for the upcoming year. The office assistant had smiled warmly and handed Noelle a welcome packet. Noelle had held the packet close to her chest as she'd walked to her car. She was this much closer to achieving her dream. Her last pre-semester task was to schedule a meeting with her academic advisor, Professor Mathis, who'd requested that her final-year advisees choose a time to meet with her during the first week of classes. Her reasoning was that advisees who met with her and discussed goals at the beginning of the school year tended to have more successful semesters. The tricky part was that Professor Mathis had limited time slots during the first week of classes, so meetings were available only on a first-come, first-served basis, and anyone who missed out on the first week would have to wait until Professor Mathis became available for advisee meetings midway through the semester. The other tricky part was that Professor Mathis said she'd email out the scheduling link on Saturday at six p.m. Noelle needed all the help for success that she could get. She had to make sure she secured a meeting.

Throughout the week, she and Jeremiah saw each other as much as they could. She spent every night at his apartment, and every night was date night. On Monday, they went indoor go-kart racing. On Tuesday, they took some of the teens whom Jeremiah volunteered with to the movies to see the newest blockbuster superhero film. Later they went for pizza, and as it turned out, the three rising seniors, Jay, Amir, and Lamont, were avid readers, and they spent most of dinner talking with Noelle about their favorite graphic novels. Jeremiah couldn't seem to get a word in edgewise, but he was smiling through the whole meal, so Noelle didn't think he minded very much. On Wednesday night, she and Jeremiah tried out a new soul food restaurant in Bayonne. On Thursday night, they went to a '90s R & B–themed party in Brooklyn. Each night ended with them wrapped in each other's arms.

She was fully aware that they were conducting a desperate attempt to spend as much time together as they could before he moved. She felt a sharp tug in her stomach every time she thought about it, although she'd gone into this with her eyes wide open. They hadn't really talked about what would happen between them once they were on opposite sides of the country. Would they keep in touch? Would he visit her whenever he flew back? Did she want him to? Would he start seeing other people and fall in love with a West Coast girl? It didn't seem fair to ask him that question when they'd be separated by thousands of miles, and she'd be so focused on school. But the thought of Jeremiah making someone else laugh or them being on the receiving end of his smiles set fire to her veins.

She glanced at him now, and he caught eyes with her and winked. He seemed so much more relaxed now than when they'd first come to Heart Beach weeks ago. Lately whenever one of his family members brought up a story about his grandfather, he didn't tense up like he had before. Instead, he joined in on the conversations, sharing more memories about his grandfather with Noelle. And there was considerably less tension between him and Percy. This morning, she'd even seen them on the back porch drinking coffee together. They hadn't been talking, but they hadn't been arguing either, and that seemed like progress.

"Oh shit," Danny said, suddenly jumping to attention. Something had caught on his line.

Everyone gathered around him. Whatever he'd caught was putting up a fight as he tried to reel it in. Jeremiah leaned over the edge of the boat and peered at the water.

"Damn, it looks big as hell," he said. "It might be a black sea bass."

With keen concentration, Danny continued to reel in the fish. But when he lifted the line from the water, there was no black sea bass, or a fish of any kind, attached to the hook. Instead, they stared at the tangled mass of an old black fishing net. Danny's shoulders drooped on a deep sigh.

"So," Jeremiah said. "I was wrong."

Danny laughed and shook his head. Amara came closer and helped Danny detangle the net from his hook.

"Maybe you'll catch one next time," she said.

Danny's disappointed expression gave way to a soft smile. "Yeah, maybe."

A flush spread across Amara's cheeks, and Noelle glanced quickly at Jeremiah to see if he'd noticed this small interaction, but he was busy putting away his fishing gear. Then he turned around and clapped his hands together.

"Well, we obviously won't be eating any fish today," he said. "Who wants pizza?"

They ate pizza on the boardwalk, and afterward, they took their time walking back to the house. Jeremiah, Danny, and André walked ahead, while Noelle walked with Tati. Amara stayed behind on the boardwalk to hunt down some saltwater taffy, but Noelle suspected she'd used that as an excuse to avoid Danny.

"Okay, so what's up?" Tati asked, lowering her voice. She looked at Noelle expectantly.

"What do you mean?"

"You know." Tati nodded her head toward Jeremiah. "What are you going to do when he moves?"

Noelle blinked and looked away. "I'm going to focus on school and hopefully I'll have a new job to focus on too."

"You'll obviously find a new job, girl," Tati said. "You always do. And I have no doubt that you'll be the best student to ever grace Riley University's campus. But what about your heart? This is the first time that I've seen you genuinely like someone in years."

"I . . ." Noelle looked at Jeremiah, watching as he smiled

and nodded, listening to something that André was saying. She emitted a shaky sigh. "I think I've set myself up for heartbreak."

Tati hummed sympathetically. "That doesn't have to be the case if you don't want it to be."

"But how can something between us work beyond summer?" Noelle asked. "We'll both have a lot going on in the fall. And . . . and it's not like we've been together for years and have the foundation to sustain long distance. I really, really like him, but what if our feelings aren't enough for us to last?"

"Maybe they won't be," Tati said. "Or maybe they will. I think, at the very least, you should allow life the opportunity to surprise you. Don't miss out on something good because you're afraid." Tati lowered her sunglasses and raised her eyebrows. "Girl, he has a boat. You don't let somebody like that get away."

Noelle barked out a laugh. "I'm not with him because of his boat."

"I'm joking, obviously," Tati said, laughing too. "But y'all seem like you have a real connection, and he makes you happy. All I'm saying is maybe you should try and hold on to that connection a bit longer and see where it goes. I think you deserve to give yourself that chance, don't you?"

Noelle let Tati's words marinate. She'd made many points—points that Noelle agreed with. But she had to find the courage to give herself the chance and believe that things wouldn't end in disaster.

"Look at you being all philosophical," she said, wrapping her arm around Tati and hugging her close.

Tati smirked and turned her nose up in the air. "I've always been this way. You were just too busy being distracted by my other amazing qualities to notice. And you know I love you, but it's too hot to hug."

Noelle giggled as Tati scooted away from her. The sound of her laughter caused Jeremiah to glance back at them. He immediately mirrored Noelle's smile. The guys waited for Noelle and Tati to catch up. Jeremiah fell into step beside Noelle and wordlessly entwined his hands with hers. She welcomed the overjoyed butterflies.

When they returned to the house, they swam in the pool for a couple hours. Amara eventually returned too, and she, along with Robin and the twins, joined everyone in the pool. Evening turned to night, and Tati and André decided to begin the drive back home before it got too late. Celeste, who'd been in her office most of the day, sent Tati and André off with boxes of Smith's Sweets assorted snacks and apologies for not being around to properly chat.

"That is one bad bitch," Tati whispered about Celeste as Noelle walked her to André's car. Celeste stood in the doorway, waving goodbye, looking serene and elegant in her pale yellow wrap dress. "I want to be her when I grow up."

Noelle laughed quietly. "Yeah, same."

Jeremiah dapped André up and hugged Tati when they reached the car. "You're welcome back anytime. For real."

"Thanks, bro," André said, taking Tati's bag and putting it in the back seat.

"Yes, thank you, and we'll certainly take you up on that offer," Tati said, winking.

Noelle hugged her best friend goodbye.

"Remember what I said," Tati whispered in Noelle's ear. "Don't miss out."

Noelle stuffed her hands in her back pockets as she and

Jeremiah watched them drive off. *Don't miss out* ran on a loop in her mind.

"You okay?" Jeremiah asked. He placed a soft kiss against her temple.

She looked up at him. Heart full, she nodded. "Yeah."

Before Harper and Ashley went to bed, Noelle helped them practice their talent routine once more. It was a small thing for her to help them. She was essentially there to supervise and give pointers on how to better execute a move or help with their transitions. But they took the routine so seriously because they wanted a trophy, and they were so grateful for Noelle's help. It warmed her heart.

"Will we see you after summer?" Harper asked, tugging on Noelle's arm before they went upstairs to bed.

"Yeah, will we?" Ashley asked. "Promise you'll come to one of our recitals this school year."

"I'll definitely try," Noelle said. She was once again reminded that Jeremiah wasn't the only Smith she'd formed a bond with.

When she made her way to his bedroom, Jeremiah was lying on the bed, fresh out of the shower, wearing a T-shirt and boxers. He was squinting at his phone as he typed quickly.

"I'm emailing Aaron," he said. "Sorry, give me one sec."

"You're fine." She sat on the edge of the bed. From what Jeremiah had told her, Aaron often sent emails at odd hours, like on a Saturday night. To Noelle, it sounded like Good Boy was Aaron's baby, and he treated Jeremiah like the babysitter who could be trusted to make sure that the baby had fun, but he couldn't be trusted to look after the baby's actual well-being. She hoped that Aaron would wake up and see that Jeremiah was an asset and not someone to be overlooked or undervalued.

While Jeremiah wrote his email, Noelle glanced around his room. She'd loved being here every weekend for the past few weeks. She loved being here with *him*. Her feelings for him grew stronger with each passing day. And it was time to face the truth. She didn't want to lose him after summer ended.

Jeremiah tossed his phone to the side and folded his hands behind his head and grinned, giving her his full attention.

"Okay, future librarian," he said, getting comfortable. "What are we reading tonight?"

Noelle smiled a little as the butterflies formed a chain link across her veins. There was so much that she wanted to say to him. She was unsure where to begin. She closed her eyes and pinched the bridge of her nose.

"What?" He sat up, frowning in concern. "What's wrong?"

She took a second to remind herself of a couple necessary facts. It was okay that she'd fallen for him. It was okay that she wanted them to at least try and see where things went beyond summer. It was *okay*. She didn't need to freak out!

"When you move are you going to start seeing other people?" she blurted.

Jeremiah's expression sharpened in surprise. She'd surprised *herself*. That wasn't how she'd intended to begin the conversation.

"No," he said slowly. "That's not even something that I've thought about." His brows drew together. "Why? Do you plan to see other people?"

"No." She shook her head fiercely, frustrated with herself for blundering this. "That's not what I meant to ask. Can I start over?"

Jeremiah nodded. She took another deep breath. He waited patiently for her to find the words.

"What I want to say is that I know that school will be my biggest priority and you'll be busy with work," she said, "but when you come back to visit your family, and if I have time outside of school and work, I'd really like to see you too. I know we said we'd just spend the rest of the summer together, but what if we tried to see what happened beyond that? What if you come back to visit while I'm on a break? I have a three-day fall break in mid-October, and—what? Why are you looking at me like that?"

Jeremiah was smiling huge. His shoulders shook as he laughed quietly.

"Babe, the only reason I said let's see how things go this summer is because I thought you'd feel less pressure that way," he said. "I didn't want to scare you by telling you that I wanted something more." He moved closer to her and took her hands in his. "I thought you might need more time. But I fully intended to have this conversation with you before I moved. You just beat me to it."

She blinked. Her relief manifested itself in a delighted smile. "Wait, really?"

"Yes, really." He squeezed her hands. "I want you to know that I'm always gonna be respectful of your school schedule. If that means flying back to see you while you're on break, I'll do that. Or if you decide you want to spend a break with me in California, I'll fly you out. And maybe it will mean that some days, the most we'll be able to do is FaceTime before you go to bed. I'm not saying it won't be hard. I don't think long distance is ever easy, but you're a priority for me, and I agree that what we have is worth preserving." His expression turned serious as he gazed at her. "When you walk into a room, I feel like the sun is shining right on me. And you don't even have to do anything; you're just being yourself. For two years, I dreaded coming back to Heart Beach, but with you here, I've looked forward to being at this house again. I've been able to spend more time with my family. I miss my grandfather, and I always will, but the pain of his passing eases more and more each day because being here brings me closer to him in a good way. You said I gave you a gift, but you gave me one too."

Her heart melted as she listened to him. She was so touched, she suddenly felt like she might cry. She ducked her head to hide her face, and Jeremiah used his index finger to lift her chin so that she'd look at him again.

"So to answer your question, no, I don't plan on seeing other people when I move," he said. "And I ask that you don't see other people either."

Hope spread from her heart to every corner of her body. It was scary, a little like free-falling, but she wanted to believe that she and Jeremiah could have a future that worked for both of them. A future where they were somehow still together and happy.

"We'll have to figure out how to tell your family the truth about me not being a librarian yet," she said, biting her lip. "We should tell them sooner rather than later."

"True," he said. "Don't worry. We'll think of the right way."

She was hopeful. And she wanted to be happy. That was why she said, "You've got yourself another deal, Jeremiah Smith."

She launched herself into his arms and he laughed as he held her close and kissed her.

"I can't believe you were nervous to tell me that," he said as his lips brushed against hers. "I feel like I've been waiting for you for years. There's no way I'm letting you go that easy."

Her heart pounded. "I feel the same way," she whispered.

Slowly and reverentially, he undressed her. He worshipped her body with his hands and tongue. And later, when he was deep inside of her, she felt the strength of their connection and just how much he cared. She tightly wrapped her arms around him, grateful that she didn't have to let him go, and that he didn't want to let her go either.

In the middle of the night, Noelle woke with a start. She'd forgotten to schedule her advisor meeting with Professor Mathis.

She'd been so caught up in spending time with everyone on the boat and later in the pool, scheduling her meeting had *completely* slipped her mind. *Shit.*

She glanced at the time on her phone. It was a little after three a.m. Heart in her throat, she opened her email and clicked on the scheduling link. Just as she'd feared, there weren't any slots left. She'd have to wait until the middle of the semester, but she didn't *want* to wait that long. She wanted to be one of the students who discussed their goals and set themselves up for success. She needed to do everything right this time around.

She hopped out of bed and began pacing back and forth as she drafted an email to Professor Mathis, asking if there was a way that she could be added to a wait list on the off chance that someone canceled. She was so busy staring at her phone, she walked right into the bed and stubbed her toe against the bed frame.

"*Ouch,*" she hissed, bending down to rub her big toe.

In bed, Jeremiah rolled over, mumbling something to

himself in his sleep. Noelle was in the middle of an academic crisis, and she didn't want to wake him. Better yet, she needed her favorite comfort food to deal with this. And there were some salted caramel chocolate chip cookies right downstairs in the kitchen.

She threw on Jeremiah's T-shirt and her pajama shorts. She paused outside of the bedroom door and listened for Caesar in case he'd decided to make his way up to the third floor again. She tiptoed downstairs, checking her phone every few seconds, praying that Professor Mathis had insomnia and would speedily reply to her email.

As Noelle entered the kitchen and reached for the light switch, she paused when she heard voices coming from the back porch. She squinted in the dark and made out Percy and Celeste sitting in the rocking chairs.

"I don't know. It's a good offer, Mom," Percy said. "You want to retire. I want to be able to spend more time with my family. I want to be there for Robin with the new baby. I've felt guilty all year. At the very least, we should consider it."

Celeste sighed. "I just keep wondering what my father would do. He had other plans for the company. He didn't want us to sell."

"I know," Percy said solemnly. "But Pop isn't here now, and times have changed."

Noelle froze in place, realizing that she'd stumbled into a conversation between Percy and Celeste, and that they were discussing selling Smith's Sweets.

Chapter Twenty-Seven

Noelle was afraid to move. She didn't want Celeste or Percy to notice her hovering in the kitchen. Theirs was a conversation that she definitely should not be overhearing. This was probably a conversation that they didn't want *anyone* to overhear. It would explain why they were talking outside at three a.m. while everyone else was asleep. Jeremiah had mentioned before that his grandfather's desire had been for Smith's Sweets to stay a family-operated-and-owned business. He'd thought that Celeste and Percy were running things fine, to the point that he didn't think they'd needed him. But maybe that was no longer the case.

Hesitantly, Noelle stepped into the hallway, eager to return upstairs. But Percy and Celeste rose from their chairs. Celeste pulled back the sliding glass door as they stepped into the living room. Noelle scurried into the kitchen again and flattened herself against the side of the fridge. She wished that she were invisible. She wished that she hadn't forgotten to schedule a meeting with Professor Mathis, because then she wouldn't be down here, searching for cookies to stress-eat while she waited for Professor Mathis to email her back. She should have just stayed in bed!

"Avid Foods is promising to keep our team and avoid layoffs," Percy said to Celeste as they passed the kitchen. "We won't have to worry about anyone being let go. It's a best-case scenario."

"I hear you," Celeste said. "And I know the past year has been a lot for you, especially with me planning to retire next year. Just let me think about it some more. And we need to talk to your brother and sister. Everyone needs to be behind this decision."

Percy sighed. "Okay."

"Good night, sweetheart," Celeste said.

"Night, Mom."

Noelle listened closely as she heard footsteps ascend the staircase. She waited until she heard their bedroom doors close as well. Once she felt confident that the coast was clear, she finally cut on the kitchen light. Since she was here, she might as well grab those cookies and get the heck back upstairs. But she nearly jumped out of her skin when she heard someone behind her mumble, "Oh."

She gasped and spun around, coming face-to-face with Percy. His brows drew together as he looked at her.

"How long have you been down here?" he asked.

Noelle chewed her bottom lip. Of all the Smiths, she'd spent the least amount of time talking to Percy this summer. He was always busy, and even when he was around, his mind was elsewhere, preoccupied. Other than polite greetings, this was the first time that she and Percy had spoken directly since her first dinner with the Smiths almost a month ago. He was looking at her so intensely now. She felt like a specimen under a microscope. There was no point in lying. If she'd come downstairs after his conversation with Celeste, he would have run into her in the hallway, and she wouldn't have already been in the kitchen.

"Around ten minutes," she answered.

Percy glanced in the direction of the back porch. "Did you overhear my conversation with my mom just now?"

Again, no point in lying. There was no way that she wouldn't have overheard what they'd said in the hallway as they'd passed the kitchen. And Percy was well aware of this.

"Some of it," she admitted.

He dragged a hand down his face and released a deep sigh. He looked exhausted. Most of the summer, when everyone else had been relaxing at the beach or on the boardwalk or swimming in the pool, Percy had been locked away, working. If this was how he spent his weekends, she could only imagine how his weekdays looked. She knew how it felt when work exhausted you, body and soul. In that way, she empathized with Percy.

"Our plans aren't set in stone yet," he said. "But the chances of us selling the company are strong. I want to continue our growth, but with my mom retiring, I don't know if I can do it on my own. It makes more sense to let a bigger team take over."

Noelle leaned her lower back against the counter, curious as to why Percy was sharing this additional information with her. She wasn't sure what to say, but she also realized that he most likely wasn't expecting her to say anything at all. Maybe he just needed someone to listen while he vented, and Noelle happened to be in the right place at the right time.

"Can you do me a favor, please?" he asked. "Don't tell Jeremiah about what you overheard."

Noelle blinked. "I can't make that kind of promise."

This wasn't as simple as her not telling Jeremiah that his sister used to have a crush on his best friend. Percy's secret was way more serious. She was shocked he'd even ask her not to say anything.

"You don't understand," Percy said. "Jeremiah and my grandfather were so close and . . ." He broke off and glanced away. With a deep breath, he turned to Noelle again. "Once Jeremiah finds out that we're considering selling, he'll be upset. My grandfather wanted to keep Smith's Sweets family owned. Even though Jeremiah left the company for whatever reasons he had, there's been an unspoken rule that I would take care of everything . . ." He sighed again. "It's just really complicated, and my mom and I need to tell him in our own way when we're ready."

Noelle understood that there were complicated family dynamics at play. And she knew that Jeremiah and Percy didn't have an easy relationship right now. She wanted to give them a chance to talk things through on their own. But at the same time, she didn't feel comfortable keeping a secret from Jeremiah.

"You have to tell him soon," she said. "That's the only way I'll promise not to say anything to him."

"I will," Percy said, nodding. "We'll tell him soon."

"Okay."

They stood in silence, assessing each other. Percy leaned his hands on the kitchen island as he looked at her.

"I was in Brickton last week," he said quietly. Noelle's stomach muscles clenched. "I had to stop by Robin's cousin's house, and the library was right there. I was feeling bad about how I haven't really had a chance to talk to you much this summer. You're my brother's girlfriend. I should get to know you. So I stopped by the library to say hi, and maybe ask to take you to lunch or something."

Noelle's throat was dry as she swallowed. But she couldn't look away from Percy's focused expression.

"Imagine my surprise when one of the librarians told me that no one named Noelle Lewis worked at their branch," he said. "And that she never had."

Noelle felt the pounding of her heart in her hands and her throat. She didn't speak. She couldn't.

Percy crossed his arms over his chest. "Does my brother know that you're lying to him?"

Even though Noelle was in the hot seat, she refused to throw Jeremiah under the bus, especially without warning. The truth about their initially fabricated relationship was for Jeremiah to share with his family if he so chose. But now that their relationship was no longer a lie, she didn't know if he'd ever say anything.

And as she stared at Percy, she realized he hadn't asked, *Why did you lie to us?* He'd asked if *Jeremiah* knew that she was lying to him. He was regarding her with suspicion because he was being a protective older brother who didn't want his sibling to get played. In that moment, she saw Percy's love for Jeremiah, even if he struggled to express it in words.

"Jeremiah knows that I don't work at the library," she replied. "I said I was a librarian because I wanted to impress you and the rest of your family. I'm in between jobs, and I'm going back to college next month. For the record, I've only ever been honest with Jeremiah."

Percy squinted. Noelle held her breath and waited for whatever he said next. But, be it exhaustion or maybe that he was satisfied with her answer, he didn't press for more.

"All right," he said. He backed up toward the hallway. "I haven't told anyone else about your librarian lie, by the way." He shrugged. "I guess we both have our secrets now. Good night."

"Good night," she said quietly.

Percy turned to leave, and Noelle waited until she heard his bedroom door close upstairs before she let her shoulders relax. She didn't want the cookies anymore. She'd lost her appetite. Between forgetting to schedule her meeting with Professor Mathis and now her conversation with Percy, she was too rattled.

She hurried back upstairs to the safety of Jeremiah's bedroom. He didn't stir when she slipped back into bed. Instinctively, he reached for her in his sleep, and she let herself be enfolded in his embrace.

She hoped that Percy and Celeste would tell him about what they were considering for the company soon. If they didn't tell him over the next few days, she would tell him herself. And she hoped that would be the right move.

And she hoped that Professor Mathis would email her back in the morning.

Chapter Twenty-Eight

When Jeremiah woke up, Noelle wasn't beside him in bed, which was unusual. With the exception of the first weekend she'd spent in Heart Beach, she'd been trying to take advantage of the freedom to sleep late. Most mornings, she even covered her face with a pillow when the sun shined too brightly. Before he fully cracked his eyes open, he reached across the bed, seeking her out, but her side of the bed was empty. He sat up slowly and looked around the room. He heard people moving around downstairs. Noelle's voice in conversation with his nieces.

Twenty minutes later, he stepped outside into the backyard and found her watching his nieces and their friends as they practiced their routine. A hurricane of fierce emotions stirred in his chest at the sight of her. Their decision to give their relationship real legs was more than he could have asked for. He was glad that they were on the same page. With Noelle, he saw potential for them to have the kind of enduring bond that his grandparents had shared. Pop had always said that falling for Grandma Minnie had been the easiest thing he'd done in his life. That was how Jeremiah felt about Noelle.

The realization caused his steps to falter as he walked across the grass. But his feelings weren't something to fear. They were something to embrace. And after what Noelle had experienced in relationships before, she deserved to be adored loudly and without question. He wanted to do that for her. He wanted to take her to the Oceanfront for an early dinner tonight before they drove home. He'd buy her a brilliant bouquet of red roses too.

"Wow, y'all started practice without me?" he joked. He came behind Noelle and wrapped his arms around her waist. He kissed her temple, and she angled her face up to look at him. Her smile was less open than usual. He realized that the difference lay in her eyes. They looked strained, like she hadn't gotten much sleep. Or like there was something weighing heavily on her mind.

"You okay?" he asked.

She nodded first but then changed course and shook her head. "No. I realized that I forgot to schedule a meeting with my advisor yesterday. Now there aren't any slots left and I'm afraid that I'm gonna have to wait until the middle of the semester to meet with her."

"Damn." He pulled back and looked at her head on. A few days ago, she'd told him about how much she wanted to make sure that she scheduled her advisor meeting during the first week of classes. Now her fraught expression made sense. "Is there any way that she can fit you in?"

Noelle shrugged, shoulders tense. "Maybe, I don't know. I emailed her. She still hasn't responded."

"I'm sorry. Hopefully you'll hear back soon." He kissed her cheek, and that seemed to relax her somewhat but not much. He wanted to help take her mind off her stress. Maybe they could go for a long drive around Heart Beach or he'd take her to the spa. "How long are you gonna be practicing?"

"Probably most of the day," she said. She nodded at the girls and lowered her voice so that only Jeremiah could hear her. "They're a little nervous because the talent show is next week."

He was ready to say that he'd stick around for moral support. But Noelle glanced past him, and her expression became strained once more. He turned and followed her line of sight. Percy was standing in the kitchen, pouring a cup of coffee. Jeremiah turned to Noelle again, but she'd gone back to focusing her attention on the girls.

"Uncle Miah, you have to leave now," Ashley said. "This is a serious, *closed* practice."

"You'd better listen to them." Noelle managed a smirk. "I'll come find you later."

He was reluctant to leave her, but he didn't want his nieces to bite his head off either.

"Let me know if you hear back from your advisor," he said, and she nodded.

Officially exiled, he returned inside. Percy was still in the kitchen, and when Jeremiah walked past him, Percy glanced up and opened his mouth like he was going to say something. Jeremiah paused, but Percy cleared his throat and fell silent. Percy might not have been the most talkative person, but he'd certainly never struggled to articulate his thoughts. Jeremiah raised an eyebrow.

"Morning," he said.

Percy cleared his throat again. "Good morning."

Before Jeremiah could ask what was up, Celeste breezed into the kitchen, wearing a cover-up over her bathing suit. Her sunglasses were perched atop her head, and she was holding a thick fashion magazine in her hands. It looked like she was ready to go relax by the pool. But her drawn expression didn't indicate any hint of impending relaxation. With pinched brows she glanced between Percy and Jeremiah. Jeremiah frowned again. What was going on with everyone?

"What time do you and Noelle plan on leaving today, Miah?" Celeste asked.

"Later. I wanted to take her to the Oceanfront for dinner," he said. "Why?"

"I'd like us to have dinner together as a family on the patio tonight," she said. "And afterward, there are some things I want to discuss with you and your brother and sister. Can you change your dinner plans?"

Alarm bells instantly rang in Jeremiah's head. He thought of Pop and the heart problems he'd kept from everyone. He stepped closer to Celeste, eyes sweeping over her in concern.

"Are you okay?" he asked. "What's wrong?"

"I'm fine, sweetheart." She gently patted his cheek. "Nothing's wrong with me, I promise."

Jeremiah eyed his mother. He glanced at Percy, who continued to stand nearby, quietly drinking his coffee.

"Of course we'll stay for dinner," Jeremiah finally said.

Because Amara had locked herself away upstairs to paint, and Robin wanted to spend most of the day sleeping, and Danny had already returned to Philly, Jeremiah spent the majority of the afternoon alone. He went for a run, and afterward, he lay on the beach and tried to read book three in Clara

Crawford's pirates series. The plot was entertaining, and it would have kept his attention if he wasn't so preoccupied with wondering about what was going on with everyone. What did Celeste want to discuss at dinner? Why had Percy suddenly become tongue-tied in the kitchen? And then there was Noelle. She was upset about forgetting to schedule a meeting with her advisor, which he understood. But that didn't explain the way she'd looked at Percy.

Eventually, he put the book aside and went to submerge himself in the ocean. The sound of the crashing waves drowned out his thoughts.

Celeste hired Chef Amir to cook dinner again. The Smiths sat around the outdoor table on the patio and ate together as the sun began to set. Harper and Ashley led most of the conversation, sharing their hopes to place at the talent show. Robin talked about how she took the twins and Ciara and Zoe shopping for their outfits. Jeremiah glanced to his right at Noelle, who ate quietly beside him. She'd been quiet most of today; she still hadn't heard back from her advisor. She'd pulled her braids into a low ponytail at the nape of her neck with a light pink scrunchie that matched her dress. She looked pretty and sun-kissed. She speared a shrimp with her fork and then sent an apprehensive glance across the table at Percy, who didn't lift his eyes from his plate.

"Hey," Jeremiah leaned over and whispered in Noelle's ear. "Did Percy say something that upset you? Do I need to talk to him?"

Noelle quickly shook her head and rubbed his thigh in reassurance.

"No, it's okay," she whispered back. "I'm fine."

She didn't *seem* fine. Neither did Percy. And neither did Celeste, who was hardly participating in the conversation as she focused on slicing her scallops in half.

"Okay, what's up with everyone?" Jeremiah finally asked. "Can someone tell me what's going on?"

Celeste and Percy sported matching expressions of unease.

"I promise we'll talk later after dinner," Celeste said.

Jeremiah shook his head. He'd been stressed over the strange tension all day. He didn't want to be in the dark for a second longer. "Please. Just tell me now."

Celeste hesitated. Her fork and knife were poised in her hands as she looked at Jeremiah. She let out a slow, even breath and placed her utensils to the side.

"So, the first thing I want to share is that I officially plan to retire next year," she said as she looked around the table. "Originally, Percy and I had agreed that he would step into the CEO role after my departure." She paused. "But very recently we were approached by Avid Foods with a lucrative offer to buy Smith's Sweets."

Jeremiah stared, blinking. Confusion clouded his brain. He glanced across the table at his siblings to check their reactions. Percy cleared his throat and kept his attention focused on Celeste, while Amara frowned, eyes wide. Robin gently placed her hand on Percy's shoulder and chewed on her bottom lip. Finally, Jeremiah looked at Noelle, who kept her eyes trained on her hands in her lap.

"You turned down the offer, right?" Jeremiah asked, looking at Celeste again.

His mom inhaled deeply. "We haven't made a decision yet. That's what I wanted to discuss tonight."

"But what is there to discuss?" Jeremiah asked, confused. "We have to turn it down."

"Not exactly," Percy said. "It's a good offer."

Jeremiah looked at his brother. "Of course it's a good offer. Avid Foods is a corporate machine who wants to make a profit, but they won't care about the integrity of the company. Pop wanted Smith's Sweets to stay family owned. Selling isn't what he would have wanted."

Celeste's throat worked as she swallowed. "Miah, it's more complicated than that."

"I agree with Miah, though," Amara said, biting her lip as she looked at Celeste. "How sure are you that you want to sell?"

"*Very*," Percy cut in. But he wasn't looking at Amara; he was looking at Jeremiah with a tense frown. "Why do you deserve a say in what happens? While you've been off with the dog company, I've been taking on the brunt of Smith's Sweets expansion as Mom has started setting herself up to retire. I'm exhausted. Robin has been dealing with this pregnancy on her own, and I feel terrible. I've barely been able to spend time with my family." He gestured to the twins, who anxiously looked back and forth between their father and Jeremiah.

"Girls, why don't you go inside and eat your dessert in the kitchen," Robin said.

"But, Mom," Ashley started to protest. However, at Robin's stern look, the twins rose from the table and walked back inside.

Jeremiah waited until the girls were out of earshot before he spoke again.

"I know I don't work for the company anymore," he said slowly. *I wanted to stay out of your way*, he almost added. "But I'm still part of this family. How long have you known about this offer?"

"A week," Celeste said.

He looked at his mom. "A week? Why didn't you say anything sooner?"

"You're such a hypocrite," Percy said, shaking his head. "Like you haven't been withholding information too."

Jeremiah narrowed his eyes. "What are you talking about?"

"You've been lying to us about your girlfriend all summer," Percy blurted in frustration.

Jeremiah's stomach dropped. He looked at Noelle, who stared back at him with round, wide eyes, wringing her hands together.

"What are you talking about, Percy?" Celeste asked, glancing between Jeremiah and Noelle.

Percy cleared his throat, looking guilty. Like he was aware that his anger had led him to say something he hadn't meant to reveal. But it was too late now. Everyone was looking at Noelle with fixed curiosity.

"It's nothing," Percy said, sighing. "I just found out that she isn't a librarian like she said she was, and Miah knew. But, look, that's irrelevant to our current conversation."

Jeremiah was relieved that Percy wasn't aware of the full scope of his relationship with Noelle or how they'd originally lied about being together. But he was still confused about *when* Noelle and Percy would have talked about her not being a librarian.

"He asked me about it last night," Noelle said quietly, as if she could read Jeremiah's thoughts. She leaned closer to him, expression uneasy, still wringing her hands together. "I didn't want him to think I'd been lying to you."

Her behavior today toward Percy made so much more sense now. Jeremiah hated to see her look so stressed, but he was confused as to why she hadn't said anything to him about it until now.

"You should have told me," he said quietly.

She bit her lip and nodded.

Celeste rubbed her temples. "What in the world is going on?"

Jeremiah turned to his mom, ready to enact some sort of damage control because now she, Robin, and Amara were looking at Noelle with suspicion. He and Noelle had just decided last night that they wanted to keep dating long term and that they were going to tell his family that she wasn't actually a librarian yet. But they hadn't had a chance to formulate a plan. The conversation wasn't supposed to happen this way. However, before Jeremiah could think of what to say, Noelle answered Celeste first.

"Percy is telling the truth," she said. She glanced around the table. "I'm not a librarian. At least not yet. I used to work at a bookstore, but I got laid off. I'm going back to college in the fall to finish my bachelor's degree, and then I plan to apply to grad school to get my master's degree in order to become a librarian. I lied because I didn't want you to think I was using Jeremiah. And because I wanted to impress you. I'm really, really sorry."

"I see," Celeste said quietly. Amara and Robin sported matching expressions of hurt. Percy crossed his arms and focused his gaze on the table.

"You didn't have to lie to us about your job," Amara said softly. "We wouldn't have cared about that."

Noelle's throat muscles worked as she swallowed. "I realize that now."

"Just so everyone is aware, I never cared about what she did for work either," Jeremiah said. "It wouldn't have made a difference to me or change how I feel about her."

He put his arm around Noelle, wanting to shield her from everyone's eyes. He felt the tension in her shoulders. He glared at his brother, angry that he'd inadvertently put her on the spot.

"Don't look at me like that," Percy said. "I didn't mean to tell them about Noelle, but the point I wanted to make is that you shouldn't judge me when you've got your own secrets too. Just because you think you were Pop's favorite doesn't mean you get to dictate our decisions now that he's gone. You didn't give a shit about the company when he was alive, so don't pretend that you give a shit now."

"Fuck you, Percy," Jeremiah spat, standing. Percy immediately stood too.

Noelle grabbed Jeremiah's forearm and attempted to keep him still, but as Percy rounded the table toward him, eyes blazing, Jeremiah's anger flared hotter, and he shrugged Noelle off. This fight between him and his brother had been brewing for months. *Years*, even.

"Stop!" Celeste said, shooting out of her chair.

Suddenly everyone was scampering to intercept the brothers, but Jeremiah lunged at Percy, and they scuffled on the patio, rolling into the grass. Celeste, Amara, and Noelle shouted for them to stop. It took all their strength to pull the brothers apart.

"Have you lost your minds?!" Celeste cried. "We're family! You can't fight each other like this! What's wrong with you!"

Jeremiah stumbled to stand. His T-shirt was covered in dirt and grass stains, and his jaw ached from Percy's right hook. Percy was doubled over, rubbing his stomach where Jeremiah had kneed him. As the adrenaline wore off, Jeremiah began to see how stupidly they'd acted. But he couldn't let Percy's comment about him not giving a shit slide.

"Come with me," Noelle said, appearing at Jeremiah's side. She grabbed his hand and pulled him away. He let her lead him around the house to the front yard, and down the driveway to the street.

"Just take a deep breath," she said, looking him in the eyes as she placed her hands on his shoulders.

Jeremiah listened and inhaled and exhaled deeply. He just couldn't believe that his mom was even considering selling. The thought of taking Pop and Grandma Minnie's legacy and handing it to someone else made Jeremiah's stomach turn. It felt like another way of losing Pop. But he'd parse through those thoughts after he made sure Noelle was okay.

"Tell me what happened between you and Percy," he said, removing her hands from his shoulders and holding them instead. "Is that why you've been so quiet all day?"

She nodded and let out a slow breath. "Last night while you were asleep, I went downstairs to the kitchen for a snack, and I ran into Percy. He told me that he'd stopped by the library where I said I worked because he wanted to take me to lunch in order to make up for how he hasn't tried to get to know me better this summer. That was when he discovered that I didn't work there. He was concerned that I was lying to you or trying to play you, so I told him you knew that I wasn't a librarian."

"Damn," Jeremiah said quietly. "Okay."

"But the reason he brought up the librarian lie is . . . because I overheard him and your mom talking about selling Smith's Sweets," she said. "Percy realized that I'd overheard them, and he asked me not to tell you. I didn't want to keep something like that from you, but I also felt it was important for you to learn that information from your mom and brother directly instead of hearing it secondhand from me. I thought they *owed* you that. I told Percy that I wouldn't say anything to you as long as he told you soon. But I didn't think it would happen like this."

Jeremiah stared at her, unblinking. The thing was, he understood her logic. If the roles had been reversed, he probably would have made the same decision. She'd been thrust into the middle of a convoluted family matter, and it was true that he deserved to hear the truth straight from Celeste and Percy. But he and Noelle had been on the same team all summer. He'd asked her multiple times today if she was okay when it was clear that something was bothering her, and she'd told him only about forgetting to schedule her advisor meeting. All the while, she'd also been stressed about knowing that his mom and Percy were considering selling Smith's Sweets.

"I'm so sorry that I waited to tell you," she said quietly. "I knew that if you heard it from me first, it would be worse. And I promised myself that if they didn't tell you in a few days, *I'd* tell you. I was trying to protect you the best way I knew how."

"I mean, I understand why you didn't tell me," Jeremiah said. "But I'm disappointed that you thought you had to carry that burden for me, especially when we've been so locked in." He dragged his palms down his face. He was starting to get a headache. "And I'm upset that you somehow got in the middle of all this because that wasn't fair to you. I'm sorry too."

Noelle took a step closer. She was back to wringing her hands again. "I . . . I should probably go home."

Jeremiah snapped to attention. "Wait, what?"

Chapter Twenty-Nine

Noelle's stomach tied itself in knots as Jeremiah stared at her in distress.

"There's so much that you and your family need to talk about, and I'm in the way by being here," she said. Jeremiah's brows furrowed as he shook his head in confusion. "I'll take the bus home. At least one that will get me to Newark. I can figure out my way to Brickton from there."

Her mind buzzed as her thoughts clambered over each other. She'd opted not to tell Jeremiah about Celeste and Percy's plans because she thought it was best that they told him themselves. But in an effort *not* to insert herself, she'd still done so anyway. Now Jeremiah and Percy had fought. And she'd intended to tell his family the truth about her job, but she hadn't wanted the truth to unexpectedly land like a bomb in the middle of dinner. Her chest tightened as she recalled Celeste, Amara, and Robin and their hurt expressions. She wished that she could go back to their first dinner together earlier this summer and make it so that she'd never lied. She'd barely known the Smiths then, and she'd been so intimidated. She'd had no way of knowing how little they would have cared about her job, and how much they'd come to care about her.

But she wasn't just stressed about the situation with Jeremiah's family. All day, she'd been berating herself for forgetting to schedule her meeting with Professor Mathis. *How could she have forgotten?* But she knew how. Yesterday, she'd been busy running around with her head in the clouds and hearts in her eyes. How could she not view this as a bad omen? How many more things would she lose sight of while her heart was focused on Jeremiah?

"Noelle, you're not in the way." Jeremiah searched her face, his gaze imploring. "How could you think that? Did I make you feel that way?"

"No, of course not," she said. "You haven't done anything wrong. The truth is that I just feel really overwhelmed right now. It's already enough that I lied to your family about my job, but the *way* they found out makes it worse. I feel so embarrassed and guilty. And then there's the situation with my advisor meeting. I can't believe I missed the sign-up. I don't know. I think I just should go."

She didn't want to leave, but she *had* to. She needed to be alone in order to think clearly. Because right now she was smack-dab in the middle of the Smiths and their drama, and she was afraid that she'd done the very thing she'd been determined to avoid for so long: lose focus on herself.

Jeremiah's face fell. He nodded, resigned. "I understand if you want to go home," he said quietly. "I do. But I'm not letting you take the bus. I'll drive you."

"*No*, you need to stay here and talk to your family," she said.

"What Percy said to you about not caring wasn't fair, but he was right about one thing. You *do* have secrets, Jeremiah. You haven't told your family the real reason behind why you left the company because it means you'll have to tell them about your last conversation with your grandfather. You've let Percy think you left because you're selfish, but you're not. I hate that he has the wrong idea about who you are, all because you're afraid to tell your family about what happened. And you should tell them the real reason you avoided coming to Heart Beach before you brought me here. That it was about your grief."

"Okay," Jeremiah said. "I'll tell them. I will. But I can tell them later after I drive you home."

"No, please stay here." She hated the hurt look on his face, but him staying and talking to his family was way more important than him giving her a ride home. The last thing that she wanted to do was hurt Jeremiah, but right now, he needed to be with his family, and she needed to put herself first.

She walked back inside, and Jeremiah was right behind her. Celeste and Amara were hovering in the kitchen entryway, while Percy and Robin stood by the staircase. From the way they each turned their heads to look at Noelle and Jeremiah as they walked inside, it was clear that his family had been waiting for them.

Noelle tensed, shrouded in guilt over her lie. She was eager to get out of Dodge and call less attention to herself, but Percy cleared his throat and said, "Noelle, wait. Please."

She turned to Percy sharply, surprised that he'd singled her out. He looked at her sheepishly with slumped shoulders. Jeremiah stepped around Noelle and placed himself between her and Percy. He stared his brother down with suspicion.

"I owe you an apology, Noelle," Percy said. "It was unfair of me to put you on blast in front of everyone like that, especially when I told you that I wouldn't say anything. I shouldn't have involved you, and I'm sorry." He paused and rubbed his jaw. "For the record, I personally don't care if you're a librarian or not either."

Noelle blinked, caught off guard by the sincerity of Percy's apology. He glanced apprehensively at Jeremiah, who continued to stare him down.

"Thank you," Noelle said. She wished Percy hadn't exposed her lie the way he had, but she could tell that he'd said it in a fit of frustration directed toward Jeremiah. And anyway, she'd chosen to lie in the first place. How could she be mad at Percy for telling the rest of the family, whether it was intentional or not? She looked around at the rest of the Smiths. "I'm really sorry again for lying to you about my job. I wish that I could go back and redo that night and tell you the truth. I know there's a lot that you all need to discuss, so I'm going to go home now. Thank you for being so welcoming to me this summer."

"Noelle, that's not necessary," Celeste said, confused. "We have a lot to talk about, yes, but you don't need to go home." Amara and Robin nodded in agreement. This would be so much easier for Noelle if they weren't still being so kind to her after everything.

"No, it's okay. You need to deal with this as a family," Noelle said. "Thank you again for letting me be here."

Before they could persuade her to stay, Noelle jogged upstairs. She heard Jeremiah's footsteps right behind her. In his bedroom, she made quick work of folding her clothes and stacking her books in her suitcase. She focused singularly on the task, not wanting to think about how happy she'd been here with him these last several weeks and how everything had so quickly gone to shit.

"Noelle, can you just talk to me for a second?" Jeremiah asked. "Wait a minute, and I'll pack my stuff."

"No, please stay and talk to your family, Jeremiah," she said, turning around to face him. "I'll figure out my way home. This is where you need to be."

He stared at her, visibly torn like he was fighting his desire to not let her out of his sight and his realization that what she'd said was right. He *did* need to stay here with his family.

His shoulders deflated. He pulled Noelle into his arms, and her heart hammered as she instinctively hugged him back.

"I'm not letting you take the bus," he said. "I'll order a ride."

She looked up at him, ready to protest but he shook his head. "That's not up for debate," he said firmly.

"Okay," she murmured.

He carried her suitcase downstairs. Celeste, Amara, and Robin were still standing in the hallway, but Percy was nowhere to be seen.

"Get home safe," Celeste said. "Let Jeremiah know once you're there, okay?"

"I will," Noelle said, and then to her surprise, Celeste, Amara, and Robin each hugged her goodbye. Her relief at their continued kindness was overwhelming, and simultaneously made her feel guiltier.

She and Jeremiah waited for her ride outside on the sidewalk. Noelle looked up and down the street at the beautiful houses around them. She never imagined that she'd have access to a town like Heart Beach. This whole summer had been like a dream.

"I know tonight was a lot," Jeremiah said quietly. "But I need to know if we're okay."

"We're okay." She swallowed thickly as she gazed at him, afraid of saying anything that might hurt him. "I wasn't lying when I said that I'm not mad at you. But . . . I need a bit of space to think."

"Space?" He blinked, repeating the word like it burned his tongue. "I'm moving soon. All we're going to have is space once I'm in California."

The pained look on his face pierced her heart.

"I know," she said, voice shaking. "But my head is all over the place right now, and in order to be a good girlfriend to you, I need to be able to think clearly. I just need a few days to get my thoughts straight. And I'll call you when I'm ready. If that's okay."

Jeremiah stared at her in worry. Thick silence enveloped them. Noelle could almost hear the pounding of her heart.

"Of course it's okay," he said finally, voice low. "I respect that you want space after everything that happened tonight. Just know that I'm here, and I'll be waiting."

"Okay," she whispered.

Her ride turned down the street and pulled up in front of them. Jeremiah placed his hands on either side of Noelle's face and kissed her deeply, almost desperately, like he was unsure if he'd get the chance to kiss her again. Noelle closed her eyes as she kissed him back.

She loved Jeremiah. The truth was startlingly clear to her now. And that was why this situation was so scary. Whenever she fell in love, she lost herself, and she was afraid that might happen again. She was trying her best to hold on to her heart and protect it. Because now she knew that Jeremiah and his family had the power to break her heart irrevocably.

When their kiss ended, Jeremiah placed another soft kiss on her forehead. He held her close like she was the most precious thing in the world. He was making it so much harder for her to leave.

"I'll text you when I get home," she said, forcing herself to step away from his embrace.

He nodded and stuffed his hands in his pockets. "Okay."

The Uber driver placed Noelle's suitcase in the trunk, and she climbed in the back seat. Jeremiah watched them drive away. He lifted his hand and waved as they turned the corner. She craned her neck and looked at him out of the rear window until she couldn't see him anymore.

By the time she got home over an hour later, her nerves were frayed. She'd left Brickton on Friday feeling like she was floating on a cloud. Now she'd crashed back down to earth.

To her surprise, Tati was home. She was sitting on the couch, watching *Living Single* again.

"Hey," she said, sitting up and pausing the show. "You came home just in time. I just got to the episode where Nia Long is dating Kyle." Tati frowned and looked closer at Noelle. "What's wrong?"

The comforting and familiar sound of her best friend's voice made Noelle realize just how tired and sad she felt. She kicked off her shoes and left her suitcase by the door. She joined Tati on the couch and rested her head against Tati's shoulder. Tati wrapped her arm around Noelle and angled her face to look at Noelle more closely.

"Tell me what happened," Tati said softly.

Noelle poured out her heart and told Tati about everything

that had happened in Heart Beach this weekend. When she was done speaking, she felt raw and empty.

"It's gonna be okay," Tati said, hugging Noelle close.

Sometimes there was nothing better than a hug from your best friend exactly when you needed it.

Noelle realized that she'd forgotten to let Jeremiah know that she was home. She sent him a text.

I made it home safe. Thank you again for my ride.

He responded immediately. Good. And you don't need to thank me.

I hope everything goes okay when you talk to your family, she texted.

Thank you.

She bit her lip as she read his message, unsure of what to say next, or if she should say anything more at all. Then a follow-up text came through.

I'll be here whenever you're ready.

Chapter Thirty

After Noelle left, a block of ice lodged itself inside Jeremiah's chest. Numbly, he went upstairs to his room and sat on his bed. He understood why she'd left. But her no longer being here still fucked him up. He felt her absence everywhere.

Usually on Sunday night, the Smiths were packing and leaving Heart Beach to go back to their separate homes and prepare for the upcoming week. But for some reason, everyone had stayed. It was as if there was an unspoken agreement that no one could leave Heart Beach until some kind of resolution took place.

Jeremiah thought of how Noelle had encouraged him to tell his family about what happened the last time he spoke to Pop. His fear over telling them about that conversation had caused so many problems. It had led to a strained relationship with Percy, who thought he'd left the company for selfish reasons. It had led to him avoiding Heart Beach for an entire summer because he hadn't wanted to be confronted with his painful memories. It had led to his lie about having a girlfriend. If it weren't for that lie, he wouldn't have brought Noelle to Heart Beach, and he wouldn't have fallen in love with her. Because he did love her. He knew that with every ounce of his being. That particular lie had brought him and Noelle together. But it was time to come clean to his family now.

He left his room and went downstairs. His mom and sisters were sitting on the living room couch, each holding bowls of pie and ice cream, watching *The Best Man*. His nieces must have gone upstairs to their room.

"Hey," Celeste said softly. "Did Noelle get home okay?"

He nodded, chest tightening at the thought of Noelle. "I want to talk to everyone about something," he said. "Where's Percy?"

"Upstairs." Robin grabbed her phone. "I'll text him and tell him to come down."

"Okay, thanks," Jeremiah said.

Minutes later, Percy walked into the living room. He looked at Jeremiah, uneasy. "What's going on?" he asked.

Jeremiah was still angry with Percy, but he didn't want to lose track of what he needed to tell everyone now.

"There's something that I should have told you years ago," he started. He inhaled a deep breath, then let it go. "The real reason that I left Smith's Sweets is because I felt like I was a failure to our family. It's not a secret that while I was there, I wasn't the best employee because I wasn't my best self at that time in my life. I didn't take my job seriously enough. Compared to the rest of you, I didn't see how I could add anything of value, so I didn't bother trying. I didn't want to stay with the company and ruin the family image, but I wanted to do better with myself and my life. That's why I left. I started working at

Good Boy with Aaron because I saw it as a chance to start over and really make something of myself." He looked at Percy. "I let you believe whatever you wanted to believe about me leaving, because I wasn't ready to tell you the catalyst behind *why* I realized that I needed to do better."

He paused, pulse thudding in his ears. His family stared at him, waiting. He was afraid for them to look at him differently once he told them about his last night with Pop. But he remembered Noelle's words. *They'll understand. They're your soft place to land.* He pushed forward and told his family about what he and Pop had discussed the night before he died. He told them about how Pop had called him out on his lifestyle, and the shame he felt for lashing out at Pop and storming out when Pop was just trying to help him. He told them how he'd worked hard to get himself together since Pop's death and how that was also why he had a hard time coming back to Heart Beach. Sharing this while standing in the living room, the same place where his worst memory took place, was difficult as hell. But the final weight that had been sitting on his chest for the past two years slowly began to lift. He'd always regret not handling that conversation with Pop better. But he was trying his best to be the kind of person who would make Pop proud, and that wasn't nothing. He was a work in progress, and he would keep working on himself. And he was lucky enough to have one of the best men in the world as an example to follow.

When he finished speaking, his muscles tensed as he waited for his family's reaction. Percy watched him, brows knit together. Amara pressed her hand over her heart, and Robin bit her lip, giving Jeremiah a sympathetic look. It was Celeste who spoke first.

"Why didn't you ever tell us, honey?" she asked. She didn't sound judgmental. Instead, she sounded like she was sad that Jeremiah hadn't said anything sooner.

"I was embarrassed," Jeremiah admitted. "And ashamed. I didn't want any of you to know how awful our last talk was. I didn't want you to know how disappointed he was in me before he died."

"You know he said those things because he loved you, right?" Amara said. "Maybe he was disappointed in some of your behavior at that time, but not in you as a person."

"He would be so proud of you and how hard you've worked and the things you've done with your life," Celeste said. "Just like how I'm proud of you. But what's this about you thinking you couldn't contribute anything of value compared to the rest of us? Why did you think that?"

"I just . . ." He glanced at his siblings, who watched him, awaiting his answer. "The rest of you are so amazing and good at what you do, and you've always been that way. It was hard for me not to compare myself. It's taken me a lot longer to find my footing."

"Honey, you contribute something of value, just by being yourself," Celeste said. "I hate that you've felt this way."

"It's not a competition to see who's the best Smith," Amara said. "We're family. We all bring something to the table."

Beside Amara, Robin nodded in agreement. Percy continued to watch Jeremiah in quiet contemplation, like he was viewing the last few years through a new lens.

"Thank you, that's true," he said, in reply to his mom and sister. It was a relief to hear them say these things, a real balm to his soul.

But he wasn't done sharing the truth yet. Maybe it wasn't

necessary to tell the full backstory about how he and Noelle had gotten together. But he didn't want to hide any more lies. Coming completely clean was the only way to move forward.

"I lied earlier this summer about having a girlfriend who I was spending time with because I needed an excuse not to come here," he said. "There was no girlfriend. I'm really sorry for lying to you."

The four of them sported matching frowns of confusion.

"But . . . what about Noelle?" Celeste asked.

"She was pretending to be my girlfriend at first," Jeremiah said. "We really did meet at a bookstore. That part was true, and I did like her when I met her. But she came here and pretended to be my girlfriend as a favor to me. I didn't want you to know that I was purposely avoiding the house or why I was avoiding it. And then I realized that telling you that I lied would hurt you and make things worse, and I didn't want to do that. At the end of summer, Noelle and I were supposed to go our separate ways, but our feelings for each other became real. She really is my girlfriend now."

And he hoped it would stay that way.

"Wow," Celeste said quietly, brows furrowed. Amara, Percy, and Robin stared at him with renewed surprise.

"I deserve your anger for lying," he said. "But please don't be mad at Noelle. She was always encouraging me to be honest with you."

"This is *a lot* to process," Celeste said slowly. "I *am* angry that you lied to us, but mostly I'm sad that you felt you had to lie because you were ashamed to tell us the real reason that you didn't want to come to Heart Beach." Celeste sighed, shaking her head. "Honey, Pop loved you. And *we* love you. You never have to hide anything from us. Don't lie to us like that again. I'm serious."

"I swear that I won't," Jeremiah said quickly, grateful to still have his family's love even though he'd kept things from them. "Again, I'm sorry. You don't have to worry about me lying again ever. Not even for simple stuff, like if I like the food you cooked."

That got a smile out of Celeste, Amara, and Robin. But Percy didn't smile. He leaned forward, resting his elbows on his knees.

"Us getting in a fight wasn't right," Percy said. "I'm sorry that I accused you of not caring."

"I'm sorry about the fight too," Jeremiah said. "I understand why you were mad at me for leaving, especially because you didn't know the real reason why." He looked at Celeste. "But I don't think you should sell. I stand by that not being what Pop wanted. What can I do? How can I help?"

"We'll table the selling conversation for now, okay?" Celeste said. "Today has been a lot. We can talk more at a later date. For now, can we just watch a movie together as a family?"

Jeremiah wanted to convince Celeste and Percy that selling wasn't the right thing to do. But he recognized that it had been a long day for everyone, and he was exhausted too.

"Okay," he said.

Jeremiah sat down on the couch to Celeste's right. They continued watching *The Best Man*. And even though today had been hard, the fact that they still were able to watch a movie together spoke volumes. After everything, his family was his soft place to land, just like Noelle had said.

Later, alone in bed, he stared at Noelle's reply text to him saying he'd be there whenever she was ready. She'd texted, Okay. He respected however much time she needed. He hoped to hear from her soon, though. She was his soft place to land too.

As the new week started and the days passed, by Wednesday, Jeremiah still hadn't heard from Noelle. He was wrapping up a pitch meeting with Wellman's, a chain grocery store primarily located in the western part of the country. Months ago, Jeremiah had suggested to Aaron that they reach out to Wellman's, but Aaron had dismissed the idea, choosing to focus on pitching Good Boy to bigger prospective clients, even though western states had the highest percentage of dog ownership. In the end, Wellman's reached out to Good Boy because the CEO's daughter loved Good Boy's products. A few members of the Wellman's team were in the city this week for a conference and they'd requested a meeting. Jeremiah met the head buyer, Cara, and her assistant Ian at Serafina's in Midtown for lunch. It was a meeting that could have happened months ago if Aaron had only listened to Jeremiah before.

"We'll definitely be in touch soon," Cara said. "Aaron was confident that you'd be able to talk us into an agreement."

Cara and Ian laughed. Jeremiah forced a chuckle. He'd been right about Wellman's being a great client, so why didn't he feel good about landing this potential partnership? His gaze drifted to the fall toy merchandise that he'd brought to the meeting. Anyone could be good at this job if they tried hard enough. If they didn't mind feeling underestimated by Aaron, or like they didn't have enough wiggle room to progress. Aaron had brushed off Jeremiah's business instincts time and time again. Was this how their working relationship would continue to be once he moved to California?

Maybe he was just overwhelmed, still thinking about the offer from Avid Foods to buy Smith's Sweets. He was also feeling stressed about his move. Movers were coming next weekend to pack up his things, and he still didn't have a single thing prepared.

And he couldn't stop thinking about Noelle. Since Sunday, he'd checked his phone every five minutes to see if she'd texted or called him. She hadn't. This was the longest they'd gone without speaking to each other since they'd met. He missed her so damn much. Even though she'd said everything between them was okay, it was hard not to fear that everything was ruined.

"We've gotta head back to the conference," Cara said, checking her watch. "We're looking forward to working with you."

Jeremiah stood and shook Ian's and Cara's hands. "Likewise."

"By the way, I love your family's cookies," Ian said. "The salted caramel chocolate chip is my favorite. I always keep a box in my kitchen."

"And we just started carrying Smith's Sweets at Wellman's earlier this year," Cara said. "You've got quite the family legacy."

Jeremiah glanced down at the dog toys again. *Legacy.* What a weighted word. He'd thought he'd been ruining his family's legacy, so he'd left Smith's Sweets. He'd thought that maybe he could take part in Good Boy's legacy and help build something else. But it was clear that Aaron wasn't willing to make room for Jeremiah in that capacity. And that was fine. Good

Boy belonged to Aaron. He could make the rules. He didn't have to take Jeremiah's input if he didn't want to. So Jeremiah had to ask himself, What was he still doing there? Was it worth the move across the country? Especially when it was clear that his family might need him more now?

Hours later, back in Jersey City, Jeremiah sat in his apartment and still couldn't bring himself to begin packing a single thing. Instead, he went for a walk. He found his way to the Thai restaurant downtown where Noelle had taken him for dinner all those weeks ago. Foolishly, he hoped to run into her. Maybe then they'd have a chance to start over. Begin truthfully and not based on a lie. But when he stepped inside the restaurant, Noelle wasn't there, of course. With a heavy heart, he ordered his dinner to go.

On his walk back, he passed by Hidden Gems Books. The same teenager was at the register, eyes locked on his phone. Noelle's old boss was restocking books on the shelves. Other than the two of them, the store was empty. Jeremiah saw the remnants of Noelle's influence. The summer beach reads table, and the staff picks on the wall. She'd put so much of her heart into her work. It sucked that she'd been let go because the store was failing. It sucked that the store was failing, period.

But Jeremiah realized that there was something he could do about it. Something he should have done a while ago.

He stepped inside the bookstore, and the bell chimed above his head. The teen at the register didn't react, but Noelle's old boss glanced up.

"Welcome in," he said. "Is there anything that I can help you with today?"

"Um, yeah," Jeremiah said, walking toward him. "Well, actually I was hoping that *I* might be able to help *you*."

The man raised an eyebrow. "Wait, you look familiar. You were here earlier this summer."

"Yeah, I was. I'm Jeremiah Smith. I'm Noelle's boyfriend." His stomach squeezed, thinking of her.

"I'm Harold," the man said. "How's Noelle doing?"

Jeremiah didn't know how to answer that question because he hadn't talked to her in days. But he pictured Noelle's beautiful face, grinning at him as they relaxed on the beach. At this very moment, he didn't know how she was doing, but he knew that she'd been able to rest this summer, and she was going back to college, achieving her dreams.

"She's doing well," he said. "She told me that she was let go from her position here because the store was struggling financially."

Harold sighed. "Yeah, I was sad to let her go too. We've been struggling even more without her. She really helped make the store what it is now." He cast a disappointed glance at his nephew. "Noelle was a good egg. I'm happy to hear she's doing well. I wish I could hire her back, but we just don't have it in the budget."

"That's actually what I wanted to talk to you about," Jeremiah said. "My family has a foundation that offers grants to Black-owned businesses in New Jersey. I'd be happy to put you in touch with the right people to get your store in better financial standing." Jeremiah pulled out his business card. "Please feel free to give me a call if you're interested."

Harold slowly took Jeremiah's card. "Thank you," he said. He eagerly shook Jeremiah's hand. "I'll definitely give you a call."

Jeremiah smiled. "Great, looking forward to speaking."

"Oh, and tell Noelle that I said hi. And that I'm proud of her."

Jeremiah swallowed thickly. He didn't want to admit that he was unsure of how soon he'd be able to deliver his message to Noelle. But he nodded and said, "I'll tell her."

His Thai food had gone cold by the time he returned to his apartment. He placed the food on his kitchen table and plopped down on his couch. The truth struck him then: He didn't want to move. Now that he was being honest with himself, he'd never really wanted to. A lot of that had to do with a reluctance to be so far from his family. But he also realized that he'd been chasing the idea of the kind of life that he thought he'd wanted and he thought maybe he'd find that fulfillment in California. Meanwhile, he'd been slowly carving out that life right here in this apartment, where he'd found peace and growth.

His gaze landed on the framed photograph of him and his family at Disney World all those years ago. He looked at Pop's overjoyed expression. He'd been so proud of his family, even with Amara moving out of frame and Percy complaining about the heat. And Jeremiah surely hadn't been a saint that trip. He'd begged Celeste to buy him almost every toy in sight. Pop had loved them each unconditionally, like always.

Over the past couple days, Jeremiah had been frustrated,

thinking about how crushed Pop would feel to know that Celeste and Percy were considering an offer to sell. But what Jeremiah hadn't thought about was how Pop had never put the company before family. Jeremiah and Percy had apologized to each other in Heart Beach, but they hadn't talked since. They differed in many ways, but they were brothers, and nothing could change that. They had to make things right.

He stood and grabbed his car keys.

Percy and his family lived about a forty-minute drive west of Jersey City in Montclair. Jeremiah pulled up in front of their Victorian-style house. Percy and Robin's cars were in the driveway, and the lights were on inside their home. Jeremiah rang the doorbell and heard Harper's and Ashley's voices on the other side of the door.

"It's Uncle Miah!" one of them shouted.

The door yanked open. His nieces looked at him with big, curious eyes as Harper grabbed his arm and pulled him inside.

"Whoa, hi," he said, laughing.

It smelled like something savory was cooking, and Jeremiah belatedly realized that he'd most likely interrupted their dinner. They were a shoes-off household, so he untied his sneakers and left them by the door.

"Are you here to argue with Dad again?" Ashley asked.

Jeremiah winced. "No. And I'm sorry you had to hear that argument last weekend."

"You and Dad would have filled up Mom's swear jar," Harper said.

Robin came into the hallway then. She hugged Jeremiah.

"This is a surprise," she said. "Is everything okay?"

"Yeah, I'm not bringing drama. I promise," he said. "I just want to talk to Percy. He busy?"

"He's always busy." Robin smiled softly. "He's upstairs in the office."

Jeremiah made his way upstairs and paused outside of the office. It was quiet on the other side of the door. He knocked gently.

"Come in," Percy said.

As Jeremiah opened the door, Percy, who was seated at his desk, turned around. His eyes widened, clearly surprised to see his brother.

"Yo," Jeremiah said.

Percy blinked at him. "Yo."

Jeremiah stood there for a second, and Percy continued to stare at him. Then he gestured to the empty leather couch by the bookshelf. Jeremiah sat down, and the brothers observed each other.

"I think I've been jealous of you," Jeremiah said quietly.

Percy frowned, eyebrows lifting in surprise. "*You've* been jealous of *me*?"

"Yeah," Jeremiah said. "You always knew what you wanted. You were driven. People respected you, and you didn't have to try hard to earn their respect. I felt like I had to overcompensate with friendliness in order for people to overlook the ways that I fell short. You never had to worry about that. I've spent a lot of my life wishing I could be more like you."

Percy shook his head. "Little do you know, I wished that I could be more like you. Do you know how much easier my life would be if I was more personable? If I could talk to people as easily as you do? People are instantly comfortable in your presence. That's honestly one of the reasons that I don't think I'll be able to fill Mom's shoes once she retires. You see how she owns every room that she walks into. I'm not like that. I'm not like y'all. Or like Pop." Percy glanced down. "You're more like him than I am."

"That's in your head," Jeremiah said. "We're all like him in different ways. I might resemble him the most, but you're a natural leader like him. You're smart and dedicated. Amara and I couldn't have had a better older brother growing up."

Percy rubbed his eyes. "Thank you for saying that," he conceded. "But I think that's part of my issue. You and Amara were given the freedom to do what you wanted, while I felt like Mom and Pop depended on me to hold down the fort. Even though I loved having the responsibility at times, that doesn't make it fair."

"You're right," Jeremiah said. "That wasn't fair. And the way that I left the company wasn't fair either. I wanted to move out of your way. I thought you and Mom were doing such a good job running things, and me being there was only making the family look bad. I showed up, but I didn't work hard. And that wasn't fair to you either." He ran a hand over his head. The decision that he'd been subconsciously working himself up to finally crystalized. "Working with Aaron at Good Boy seemed like a great opportunity at first, and it's been an important part of my journey. But Aaron doesn't take me seriously enough, and he probably never will. I'm not moving to California anymore. I'm gonna stay here."

Percy blinked, eyes widening. "Good. I support you if that's what you think is best."

"I'm sorry that you've been so overwhelmed with the

company's expansion and that you haven't had time to spend with your family. I know that Mom wants to retire, and that leading the company on your own feels like too much. But I do think we should keep the business in the family."

Percy sighed. "Miah—"

"What if I came back?" he asked. He was offering more than just working with his brother. He was offering his heart on his sleeve. "What if I came back and helped you out in any way that you needed and made it easier for you to be there for Robin and the girls and the new baby? I could work closely with Mom while you're on paternity leave, so I'll be ready once you're back. Would that change your decision to sell?"

Percy sat up straighter and stared at his brother. "I don't know," he said hesitantly. "What makes you feel like you're ready to come back now?"

"I've always cared about this company and our family's legacy," Jeremiah said. "But I didn't think I was good enough to be part of it, so I focused on trying to help build something else. It took me some time to figure out where my place should be, and it's right here with our family. With Smith's Sweets. And it won't be like before. I'll dedicate myself day and night. No slacking off. No laziness." At Percy's continued hesitation, Jeremiah added, "What will it take to prove it to you? Should I interview formally? Because I'll do that."

That got a laugh out of Percy. "No, you don't have to interview." He drummed his fingers against his knees as he observed Jeremiah. "You're serious about this?"

"As hell," Jeremiah said.

Percy studied Jeremiah, brows knit together. Slowly, the corners of his mouth lifted into a smile.

"Yeah, okay. Let's set up a meeting with Mom tomorrow."

Jeremiah grinned, flooded with relief and the feeling of rightness. "Great."

Working with Percy didn't mean that their relationship would magically become perfect overnight. They were bound to have more disagreements and tough discussions. But that was true for any family. This, at least, was a positive step forward. And it was what Pop would have wanted.

Percy stood and stretched his arms. "You wanna stay for dinner?"

Jeremiah thought of the untouched Thai food on his kitchen table. "Yeah, I'm starving actually."

They left Percy's office and walked downstairs together to the dining room.

"How's Noelle doing?" Percy asked.

"I don't know," he said truthfully. "I haven't talked to her since Sunday. She wants space and I'm trying to respect that. Sunday was a lot for her. And you putting her on the spot like that didn't help."

Percy winced. "I'm sorry, Miah. For real. I will literally tell her I'm sorry every single time I see her if that makes anything better."

"Here's my question, When you found out that she lied, why didn't you say anything to me or anyone else?"

"You looked happy with her," he replied. "And I knew you were smart enough to not be involved with her if she was a real problem. When I brought it up to her last weekend, she said that she'd been honest with you, and that she was *always* honest with you. That was what I cared about."

Jeremiah felt a tug in his gut. "I love her," he said quietly.

Percy nodded. "I figured that. You look at her like the sun shines out of her pores, which is how I look at Robin."

Jeremiah laughed, but quickly sobered again. He needed advice, and who better to ask than his big brother who'd been with his amazing wife for over a decade.

"What should I do?"

"Fight for her," Percy said simply. "Fight for what you have. If it's worth anything to her too, you'll be okay."

Jeremiah had to hope that Percy was right.

Chapter Thirty-One

I miss you. I know you need space. I just wanted to say again that I'll be here whenever you're ready.

It was late Thursday afternoon. Noelle glanced at her phone for the millionth time, checking the text that Jeremiah had sent last night. She'd received it while sitting on the couch with Tati, trying to focus on an episode of *Insecure*, trying her best not to feel so sad and confused about him and her future.

"So we'll get your paperwork checked out and you should be able to start on Monday," Connie said, smiling.

Noelle quickly stuffed her phone in her purse and smiled back. "That sounds great."

Connie was the office manager at Wilson and Woods Realty in Hoboken, and she'd just finished giving Noelle a tour of the office. She'd interviewed for the front desk assistant position on Tuesday afternoon, and Connie had called the next morning to offer her the job and invite her back for a tour and to sign paperwork. Noelle would work Monday through Friday from nine a.m. to three p.m. Because she'd signed up for evening classes, her new job wouldn't overlap with her course schedule.

Professor Mathis had emailed Noelle back on Monday night. As it turned out, several advisees had emailed her asking to be added to a wait list for a first-week meeting. Professor Mathis admitted that sending out the schedule link on a Saturday evening in August wasn't exactly fair, because most people wouldn't have been concerned with checking email then. She extended her office hours, and Noelle was able to schedule her meeting during the first week after all. Professor Mathis reassured Noelle, and the other advisees who'd freaked out, that forgetting to schedule their meeting was a minor mistake, for which she was partially to blame, and that they shouldn't worry about it. Noelle was relieved to know that she hadn't been the only one who'd forgotten and that her advisor wasn't going to hold it against her. She could finally stop beating herself up about it.

Classes were starting next week. She should feel happy. She *was* happy. But . . . summer was officially almost over, and she couldn't help feeling sad. She hadn't felt sad about summer ending since she was a kid. But now it was like she lived in a constant state of melancholy.

"I'll take you out for lunch on your first day," Connie said as she walked Noelle to the exit.

"I'm looking forward to it," Noelle said. "See you then."

Noelle waved at Connie before walking to her car. Connie seemed sweet, and Noelle was looking forward to working at a company where she wouldn't have to worry about her hours getting cut. From what she'd witnessed during her tour through the realty office, the agents were busy with clients.

It made Noelle think about Harold and how Hidden Gems Books had struggled. She hadn't been back since she'd been let go. The thought of returning made her too sad. But Harold had been her reference for Wilson and Woods Realty. He'd sung Noelle's praises to Connie and had helped her secure the new job. Noelle might not be able to visit the store in person, but at the very least, she wanted to call Harold and thank him.

She called Harold when she got into her car, putting her phone on speaker. He answered on the first ring with a gruff, "Hidden Gems Books. We're closing soon."

She laughed quietly to herself. She'd hoped that Harold had at least *tried* to improve his customer service since she'd left.

"Hey, Harold," she said. "It's Noelle."

"Noelle, hi." His voice immediately brightened—or brightened as much as Harold's voice was capable of brightening. "How are you?"

"I'm doing okay," she said. "I wanted to thank you for being a reference for the assistant job at the realty office. I got hired. I start next week."

"They would have been fools not to hire you," he said. "And anyway, I should be thanking *you*."

Noelle blinked, confused. "What do you mean?"

"Your boyfriend, Jeremiah," he said. "When he came by yesterday and told me about his family's foundation that gives grants to Black businesses, I almost couldn't believe it. I called him up this morning and he's already put me in touch with a representative from the foundation. I was afraid that we might have no choice but to close our doors by the end of the year.

But thanks to your boyfriend, it sounds like maybe we won't have to."

Noelle was stunned into silence. Jeremiah had done that?

"Yeah, that's pretty amazing," she said quietly.

"Isn't it?" Harold sounded as awed as she felt. "Who knows, maybe I'll get enough money to hire you back. Maybe for some weekend shifts if you want."

"Yeah, maybe," she murmured.

Harold said that he had to finish closing up the store for the night, and Noelle promised that she'd stop by soon.

She drove home in a daze. She wanted to call Jeremiah and thank him for helping Harold. But at the same time, she was afraid to talk to him just yet. This upcoming weekend was the talent show. Harper and Ashley had worked so hard on their routine, and Noelle wanted to be there. But she didn't know if she could handle returning to Heart Beach and risk digging herself even deeper into such a complicated situation. Plus, she was still so embarrassed over how they'd found out she'd lied about her job. And Jeremiah had most likely told them how they'd initially lied about their relationship too. How could she face his family now?

Last weekend had shaken her because it made her realize how much she loved Jeremiah, and she was afraid of getting too caught up in him and making the mistake of not focusing on herself when she needed to the most. Even though Professor Mathis said that forgetting to schedule a meeting was an honest mistake, it had still spooked Noelle. She was so close to being back on track. And after what she'd gone through the first time around at college, she didn't want to risk anything. She didn't want her love for Jeremiah to overpower her ability to think sensibly.

No matter how much she missed him, she still wasn't ready to talk to him yet.

Instead, she FaceTimed her mom and Bill and told them how eager she was to start her new job.

Friday afternoon, she attended Sheree's bridal shower at Alice's Tea Cup on the Upper West Side in Manhattan. Guests had been encouraged to wear their afternoon-tea best. Noelle wore a pink floral-print dress with puffy short sleeves. Last night she'd taken out her braids, and now she wore her naturally coily curls in a slicked-back low bun. She'd also found a matching pink fascinator at a vintage thrift store.

She sat with the other bridesmaids, including Sheree's cousin Raven, who was pouring champagne into her teacup. The other guests in attendance were Sheree's mom, her aunts, and older relatives. They played games and drank tea and ate finger foods and sweets. Noelle was required only to smile and make casual conversation with Sheree's loved ones. Surface-level topics like the weather and music. She said enough to be engaging but not too deep.

She used to not mind this kind of talk. She'd preferred it, actually. But the more that she spoke with Sheree's guests, the more that she wished there were someone here who she shared a real connection with. The Smiths and the connection she'd built with them were the reasons for this change in her mindset. She missed Jeremiah, of course. Missed him so much. But she also missed hanging out with Amara and Robin, and simply being in Celeste's presence. She kept thinking about Harper and Ashley and wondering if they felt ready for the talent show tomorrow, feeling guilty because she didn't know if she could bring herself to go back to Heart Beach and see them perform. She wondered if Percy had realized that he deserved to take a break. She even found herself thinking about Caesar, who probably didn't care whether she lived or died.

It was a Friday afternoon, and usually around this time she'd be heading to Heart Beach with Jeremiah. Now they were all probably at the house without her.

After the group finished playing a game of wedding word scramble, Noelle excused herself to go to the bathroom. She looked at her reflection in the mirror and let out a deep sigh. Would she ever be able to take on another Bridal Bestie gig and not feel disappointed by playing pretend?

She startled as someone stepped out of the stall behind her. She immediately brightened her expression when she realized that the other woman was Sheree. Her white fascinator hat had a dramatic net that covered half of her face.

"Hey!" Noelle said. Even if she was in her feelings right now, she still had a duty as Sheree's bridesmaid. "Are you having a good time?"

"I am!" Sheree said as she washed and dried her hands. She tilted her head as she looked at Noelle. "I haven't had a chance to talk to you much today. You okay?"

"Absolutely. How's wedding planning going?"

"Stressful," Sheree said. "I'm ready for this wedding stuff to be over. I just want to be married." She smiled. "It must be busy season for you. How many other weddings are you working right now?"

"You're the only one left this summer actually," Noelle said. "I had, um, another long-term commitment."

"Oh, nice." Sheree checked her makeup in the mirror. She turned to Noelle, and her expression became serious. "Also, I meant to apologize about Brian. When he told me how he tried to talk to you outside of your job, I got so upset. Turns out, he was bothering Raven too and wouldn't stop texting her, even after she cursed him out multiple times. We kicked him out of the wedding party, and he won't attend the wedding, period. You don't have to worry about running into him."

Noelle *hadn't* been worried. She'd figured if Brian refused to take the hint again, she'd hit him with a good dose of pepper spray. But it was good that Sheree and Justin were thinking about everyone else's well-being.

"Oh, I would say I'm sorry to hear that, but . . ." she said.

Sheree laughed. "The other reason I bring that up is because we already paid the venue for our guest count, and with Brian's seat vacant, we have space for another person. Do you want to bring a date? You'll know the least amount of people there, so I wanted to offer that option to you first."

"That's really sweet of you," Noelle said. She bit her lip and glanced away. She would have loved to bring Jeremiah as her date. But . . . "The person who I'd bring will be across the country by then."

"Oh." Sheree frowned. "Long-distance partner?"

"Something like that."

Sheree leaned her hip against the sink, looking at Noelle with intrigue and care. "Is everything okay with y'all?"

"It's a bit complicated." Noelle paused. "You don't need to listen to me talk about my problems! It's your bridal shower! You should get back out there with your guests."

Sheree waved her hand, dismissing this.

"You were there to listen to me when I needed it, so now I'm here to listen to you." She gently placed her hand over Noelle's. "Tell me what happened."

"Okay . . . well, remember the long-term commitment I just mentioned having this summer?"

Sheree nodded.

"A guy—his name's Jeremiah—paid me to pretend to be his girlfriend for a weekend with his family, but it turned into a lot more than that."

Sheree's eyes widened. She squeezed Noelle's forearm. "Damn, girl. Tell me the rest!"

So, Noelle spilled everything about what happened with her and Jeremiah this summer, and how everything had unraveled on Sunday night. It felt good to tell the story to someone who was unfamiliar with it. Although Tati had been supportive and attentive, Noelle could tell that she was beginning to drive her best friend crazy with the number of times she'd brought up Jeremiah this week.

"Well, it sounds to me like you had a little drama, but it's ultimately something you can work through," Sheree said, after Noelle finished explaining.

"Maybe," Noelle said. "I'm sure it's something we could overcome. But I don't know if we should."

"Why not?" Sheree asked.

"I'm afraid now," she said. "I really love him. But what if I put in the effort and our relationship fails? What if I end up wasting my time and my heart and get too distracted from my own goals? I've done that in the past, and I don't want to make that mistake again."

"Even if you've made mistakes in the past, you've probably learned from them and grown, right?" Sheree said. "From what

I've seen from you, you're professional and on the ball. Maybe you aren't giving yourself enough credit now. If we spend too much time thinking about the what-ifs, how can we ever accomplish anything? And isn't love always a risk, regardless? Justin has never given me a reason to doubt him. That doesn't mean that something might not go wrong down the line. You never know. But I have enough trust in him and our relationship to believe that we'll be okay. I mean, shoot, I'm marrying him, aren't I?"

She laughed, and Noelle laughed softly too.

"What I'm trying to say is," Sheree continued, "don't take yourself out of the game before you've really had a chance to play. You might be surprised by how well everything turns out."

Sheree's advice was not dissimilar to Tati's advice to not miss out.

Noelle realized that, in a way, she'd been punishing herself for the things that had happened to her when she'd dropped out of college. She'd held on to the embarrassment and shame, and those negative feelings had pushed her to work hard and get back on track. But she didn't need those negative feelings to drive her anymore. She'd grown since then. And she needed to give herself grace about forgetting to schedule her advisor meeting. Because, as Professor Mathis said herself, who would be thinking about something like that on a Saturday night during summer?

Noelle *wasn't* giving herself enough credit, like Sheree said. And she wasn't giving Jeremiah enough credit either. She had no reason to believe that he'd try to interfere with her studies. Look at how he'd respected her desire for space this week. Yes, they'd experienced a brief rough patch, but not giving their relationship a chance would be the real waste. Why couldn't she be dedicated enough to keep her eye on the ball and graduate, while also maintaining a relationship with Jeremiah if that was what she wanted?

"I think you're right," she said softly. Sheree smiled and nodded.

The bathroom door opened, and Sheree's mom peeked her head inside. "Sheree, everyone's looking for you. It's time for the toast."

"Okay, I'll be out in a sec," Sheree said. She turned to Noelle. "You coming?"

Noelle nodded. "Yeah, I'll be right behind you."

Sheree began to follow her mom out into the hall, but then she doubled back. "Hey, once all this wedding stuff is over, do you want to hang out for real?"

Noelle's smile took up her whole face. "Yeah. I'd love that."

Chapter Thirty-Two

Okay, so she needed to get to Heart Beach.

Every minute not spent in Heart Beach was a minute wasted. The man she loved was *moving across the country* soon, and he was in Heart Beach. She needed to haul ass and get to wherever he was.

Once Noelle pulled into her complex, she rushed inside her apartment and kicked off her heels. She ran into her bedroom and dragged her suitcase out of her closet. She didn't have time to change, so she'd have to keep on her afternoon-tea outfit. She haphazardly threw clothes into her suitcase. She needed to stop and get more gas before she hopped on the highway, and there would definitely be traffic on the parkway because it was rush hour and everyone was getting off work and driving to the beach. But whatever, she'd dealt with worse things than traffic in summer.

She slipped on her flip-flops as she dragged her suitcase

behind her into the living room. She sent Tati a quick text, Driving to Heart Beach! Then, with a pounding heart, she called Jeremiah.

He answered on the first ring. "Noelle?" He sounded breathless.

She closed her eyes. Relief and joy washed over her at the sound of his voice. She missed him so much.

"Hey," she said softly.

"Hey, I was just about to call you. Where are you?"

"I'm home right now, but I'm about to leave for Heart Beach. That's why I'm calling. I know we have a lot to talk about, and I haven't called you this week, but I'd rather we talk in person, and—wait, you *are* in Heart Beach right now, aren't you?"

It didn't occur to her until that very second that Jeremiah might be somewhere else. Maybe he was in the city for a meeting. What if he'd left for California early? Oh God.

"No, I'm not in Heart Beach," he said, and her stomach sank. "Funny you ask, though. Can you come to your door?"

"Huh?" She blinked. "My door?"

"Yes, please."

Confused, Noelle did as he asked. When she opened the door, Jeremiah was walking up the staircase to the second floor right toward her. His hands were filled with several items: a bouquet of white hydrangeas, a stuffed teddy bear that looked very similar to the prize bears at the games section of the boardwalk, a paper plate covered with aluminum foil, and a box of her favorite Smith's Sweets salted caramel chocolate chip cookies.

"Oh my goodness," she whispered, heart pounding.

"Hi," he said, coming to stand in front of her. The scent of funnel cake wafted up her nose from beneath the aluminum foil. "I didn't know if you were still coming to Heart Beach for the talent show, so I wanted to bring Heart Beach to you. I brought your favorite flowers from Timeless Blooms, a bear from the boardwalk, a funnel cake from Marty's, and last but definitely not least, your favorite cookies from our house."

"Oh my goodness," she repeated. It seemed to be the only thing that she was capable of saying. The butterflies attacked her brain as she gazed up at him. A giddy laugh bubbled up inside of her. "Thank you! I don't even know what to say!"

He smiled. "Can I give them to you?"

"Yes, of course!" She took each of the items and hurried to place them on the kitchen table. Then she ran to meet him in the doorway again, like she was afraid that he'd delivered his gifts and would now disappear into thin air.

"I know you wanted space," he said. "And if that's what you still want, I can leave. But there's something I need to say to you first, because I want you to know that I'm fighting for you, fighting for us. It's been one of the hardest weeks of my life not being able to talk to you. I know it's only been one summer, but you live deep in here now, Noelle." He placed his hand over his heart. "I love you. I love you *so* much."

She stared at him, speechless, near ready to swoon. There were so many things she wanted to say, but he'd started in the right place by saying what really mattered.

"I love you too," she said softly.

His smile was huge, contagious. His shoulders sagged as he sighed in relief. Then he pulled Noelle into his arms and kissed her with all the pent-up passion and love that he'd been holding on to all week. By the time they came up for air, Noelle was breathless.

"That's . . . that's so great to hear," he said, chest heaving as he leaned his forehead against hers. "That you love me too. I'm sorry about everything that happened last weekend. It was dramatic and sometimes my family can be dramatic, but I promise for the most part, we're chill. Not perfect, but normal in our own way. I told them about my conversation with Pop, and they didn't judge me. They were really understanding. And I admitted that I'd lied about having a girlfriend in order to avoid Heart Beach. I told them the truth about how we started too."

Noelle winced. "Were they mad?"

"They definitely didn't love that I lied," he said sheepishly. "But they were forgiving. I promise to shield you from any drama in the future."

"I know you will," she said. "The real reason that I wanted space is because while everything was going on last weekend, I realized how much I love you." She swallowed thickly as he pressed his hand against her lower back. "And that scared me because I was afraid that being in love with you at this point in my life might upend everything I've worked so hard for. I freaked out about not getting that meeting with my advisor. Even after I was able to schedule a meeting and everything turned out fine, I still hesitated to call you this week because I was worried about getting too caught up with you—with us—and losing sight of my goals, but I know I won't let that happen again. And I know you won't let that happen either."

"Of course I won't," he said. "I'm not gonna get in your way. I'll be right behind you, supporting you."

She nodded, heart melting. "I know we'll be okay. Even if we're three thousand miles apart."

He laughed softly. "Right. I haven't had a chance to tell you yet. I'm not moving."

Her eyes popped. "You're not moving?"

He shook his head. "I'm going back to Smith's Sweets to work with Percy. Working with my family on our legacy is where I belong. We're not going to sell."

Noelle threw her arms around him and squeezed him close again. "You're going to work with your family! And you're not moving! That's amazing!" She abruptly pulled back. "Wait, are you sad about leaving Good Boy?"

"Not at all." He rested his hands on either side of her waist, keeping her close. "What happened with your interview this week?"

"I got the job," she said, and his lips split into a grin. "And thank you for helping Harold with the grant for the store. That was so kind of you."

"You don't have to thank me," he said. "I'm sorry that I didn't think to tell him about the grant program sooner. I wanted to help him. But I mainly did it for you. I know that store means so much to you."

God, she loved this man. She kissed him again, and Jeremiah cradled her face in his hands. He placed soft kisses on her cheeks, on her forehead, like he was cherishing her and this moment.

"You look pretty," he said, finally taking a chance to look at her outfit. "Why are you dressed so fancy?"

"I was at an afternoon tea–themed bridal shower for one of my brides. She gave me a plus-one to her wedding next month, by the way." She tilted her head. "Will you be my date?"

He grinned. "You don't even have to ask. Just tell me when and where."

"Uncle Miah!"

Noelle whipped around and saw Harper and Ashley standing

at the foot of the steps. They were wearing matching purple sundresses and purple beads at the ends of their braids. Noelle blinked in surprise.

"Is Noelle coming to Heart Beach with us?" Ashley asked.

"Did she say she loves you back?" Harper asked.

"Sorry we couldn't wait in the car!" Ashley said. "We got bored! We need to know what happened!"

Noelle laughed and turned to Jeremiah, raising her eyebrow in question.

"So about that," he said, smirking. "I didn't come here by myself. Everyone else insisted on coming too."

"Everyone?"

The next thing she knew, Amara and Robin and Percy walked up behind the twins. They waved at Noelle, and she let out a surprised laugh as she waved back. Then Celeste appeared, carrying several red and pink heart balloons.

"Are those for *me*?" Noelle asked in shock.

"Yes," Jeremiah said, sighing. "I told her the balloons were doing way too much, but she insisted."

"I almost got letters to spell out Noelle's name, so this is me scaling back!" Celeste shouted, beaming up at them.

Noelle laughed and shook her head in awe. She was overwhelmed but in the absolute best way.

"So, Noelle," Jeremiah said, taking her hands in his again. "Are you coming back to Heart Beach with us?"

She looked at him, and then she looked down at his family who'd come all the way here to support her and Jeremiah. They were the big, close-knit family she'd always wanted. And they wanted her too.

"Yes," she said, smiling. "I'll come back with you."

Jeremiah grinned and kissed her, and his family cheered.

Noelle jerked as she heard a loud popping noise, and she glanced down to see Harper and Ashley holding confetti poppers.

She and Jeremiah jogged down the steps and were embraced by his family. Percy apologized to Noelle for last weekend and said he'd keep apologizing every time he saw her, even though she assured him that wasn't necessary. Robin and Amara wrapped Noelle in a sister sandwich, Harper and Ashley tugged on her hands, eager to talk about the talent show, and Celeste hugged her and kissed her on the cheek as she struggled to keep hold of the balloons. It was all so chaotic, and Noelle had never been happier.

"I love you," Jeremiah said, wrapping his arms around her.

She smiled up at him, her heart bursting with joy. "I love you too."

Then he leaned down and kissed her, right there surrounded by his family.

There was no place else she'd rather be.

Epilogue

Ten months later

In one word, this house was special.

That was how Noelle would describe the Smiths' Heart Beach home. It was Memorial Day Weekend, the official start of summer. It was also a bit of a celebration. A few weeks ago, she'd graduated from Riley University. Celeste had tried to convince Noelle to let her throw a graduation party in the backyard, but Noelle remembered the extravagance of Amara's birthday party last summer, and she didn't want all the fanfare. She was happy to go out to dinner with her mom and Bill, Jeremiah, his family, and Tati and André, which was what they'd done. As a compromise, Noelle promised Celeste that she could throw her a party in two years once she earned her MLS degree. She was starting the Rutgers program in the fall on a merit scholarship.

For now, she wanted to focus on summer.

After the sunset, Noelle gathered with the rest of the Smiths in the backyard. They each held a cream-colored wax candle. Robin used a lighter to light everyone's candles. Then she stood by Percy, who held their nine-month-old daughter, Minnie, in his arms.

"Where's Miah?" Celeste asked, glancing around for her missing son.

"He went to grab a hoodie for me a few minutes ago," Noelle said. "But I'm not sure what's keeping him."

Amara smirked. "Miah would be the one to randomly disappear before we start, even though this was his idea."

Just then, Jeremiah came bounding out the back door and across the patio, holding an old hoodie in his hands for Noelle.

"Sorry, sorry," he said, winded. "I got caught up giving a snack to Caesar."

He handed the hoodie to Noelle and used her candle to light his flame. Noelle shrugged the hoodie over her head, and he handed her candle back to her. He smiled that charming smile of his, and it still had a way of setting butterflies loose in her stomach.

He kissed her on the cheek. "Warm?"

She smiled back at him and nodded. "Yeah."

Tonight marked almost three years since his grandfather had passed away, and it had been twenty-two years since they'd lost their Grandma Minnie. Jeremiah told Noelle he'd been thinking about how funerals were always so sad, and he wished the family could do something to honor their grandparents to serve as a celebration of life. That was what they were doing tonight. They'd tossed around different ideas. Lighting sky lanterns or setting balloons off into the sky, but both ideas were terrible for the environment. Candles were the best alternative, and they created a peaceful aura.

"For Mom and Dad," Celeste said, lifting her candle.

Everyone else raised their candles as well.

"For Pop and Grandma Minnie," Jeremiah said.

Noelle glanced around at the Smiths. This time last summer she couldn't have guessed how important this family would become to her. And while she was ten toes down in her relationship with Jeremiah and had built loving relationships with his family over the last several months, she hadn't lost sight of her own goals. She'd graduated with a 3.8 GPA, and just last month she'd been voted employee of the month at Wilson and Woods Realty. She didn't plan to be there forever, of course, and Connie was well aware that Noelle had dreams of becoming a librarian. But the whole team was supportive of her, and she appreciated that. They'd even given her a raise after six months, and she'd officially quit Bridal Bestie.

While Percy was on paternity leave last year, Jeremiah dove right into work at Smith's Sweets, learning under Celeste, who was still planning to retire at the end of the year. Jeremiah and Percy worked well together. They didn't agree on everything, but between Jeremiah's charisma and salesmanship and Percy's level-headed steering, the company was thriving. They were even introducing a new gingersnap flavor soon.

After Jeremiah and his family had surprised Noelle at her apartment last August, Noelle took the chance to finally admit just how much she actually loved sweets. She revealed that Smith's Sweets were her favorite sweets of all, and she'd been eating them in secret all summer.

"I was wondering where all the cookies in the kitchen cabinet kept disappearing to," Celeste had said, raising an eyebrow. Noelle had bit her lip, wondering if Celeste was upset.

But then Celeste had continued, "Would you be open to doing a testimonial for our social media page?"

Of course Noelle had said yes.

For the new gingersnap flavor, Noelle, Tati, and her mom, along with a few other die-hard Smith's Sweets fans, had been invited to their factory for a special taste test. Salted caramel chocolate chip would always be Noelle's favorite, but gingersnap was now a close second.

During the school year, Noelle also got to see more of how Jeremiah dedicated himself to volunteering with the local youth mentorship program. The high school students thought he was so dope, and they loved when he came to cheer them on at their cross-country and track meets. He said he remembered how seeing his grandfather in the crowd always helped him, and he wanted to be able to do that for someone else.

He also continued working with his family, identifying more Black-owned businesses in the state that could benefit from their foundation. Harold had been able to keep Hidden Gems Books open. He'd offered to hire Noelle back for some weekends but working at the realty office was enough, thankfully. However, Harold did listen to Noelle about selling frontlist books too. Every few weeks, she stopped by and organized a few displays. Jeremiah thought that she had an eye for marketing and joked about having her work for Smith's Sweets too if she ever decided not to be a librarian.

Lately, he'd been trying to convince her to move in with him. He said that if they lived together, he could put her on his health insurance. It was a tempting offer, and she would move in at some point, especially because André was planning to propose to Tati soon. But for now, she wanted to enjoy living with her best friend before they moved on to the next phases of their lives. Jeremiah respected her choice. He'd insisted on taking her to Scotland later toward the end of summer. It would be their first vacation together abroad. She couldn't wait.

"I wish you could have met Pop and Grandma Minnie," he whispered to her now. "They would have loved you."

Noelle smiled softly at him. She gazed around the circle at the rest of the Smiths. She hadn't been looking for them, but they'd found her when she'd least expected it, and they had been exactly what she'd needed.

"I wish I could have met them too."

Later this summer, she would start practicing with Harper and Ashley for this year's talent show (they hadn't placed last year and were determined to remedy that), and her mom and Bill were planning to visit, and Tati and André too, along with Sheree and Justin. A really beautiful friendship had developed between Noelle and Sheree since her wedding. (And Noelle actually did attend a Lagree class with Sheree. It was *so* hard.) Noelle wanted to ride a Jet Ski again and not fall off. She wanted to go on bookstore walks with Amara, and sit out by the pool with Robin and Celeste. She wanted to enjoy her newfound friendship with Percy, who turned out to be a really interesting person to discuss books with. (He read only non-fiction, but with time, she would turn him into a Clara Crawford fan too.) She wanted to eat steaming-hot funnel cake and share it with Jeremiah. She wanted to wake up every weekend morning curled up next to him while the sun rose and the seagulls called in the distance.

There would be time for all of that. Heart Beach had a way

of making summer feel endless. She leaned her head against Jeremiah's shoulder, and he kissed her temple.

"I love you," he said quietly.

"I love you too," she whispered back.

They had time for everything.

This was only the beginning.

Acknowledgments

A huge thank-you to my agent, Sara Crowe, and my editors, Angela Kim and Cindy Hwang. I was intending to write a very different book and then I randomly pitched *The Summer Girlfriend* to the three of you on the fly during a phone call, and I'm so glad you all were immediately on board. Thank you for your continued support and enthusiasm!

Thank you to the larger team at Berkley: Ariana Abad, Anika Bates, Elise Tecco, Lila Selle, Lynsey Griswold, Christine Legon, Sammy Rice, Heather Haase, Brittney West, and Emma Tamayo.

Thank you to Julia Jacob for the stunning cover!

Thank you, librarians and booksellers, for all that you do and for inspiring Noelle's career goals and love for books.

Thank you to my friend Alison Tergis, who read an early draft and provided very insightful and helpful notes, as always.

Thank you to my family and friends for the continued love and support, and thank you specifically for all the random and planned beach trips over the years. Throughout my life, I've spent many summer days at the Jersey Shore, walking the boardwalk, eating funnel cake, lying on the beach and listening to music, or reading a book, or simply staring out at the ocean. Who would've thought it would all be inspiration for a book series one day?

Thank you so much to the readers who show up for me and my books! Your support means everything to me. I'd also like to give an extra-special shout-out and thank-you to my readers from New Jersey!

Author photo by Cassie Vu

Kristina Forest is the *USA Today* bestselling author of romance books for both teens and adults. She earned her MFA in creative writing at The New School, and she lives in New Jersey, where she can often be found rearranging her bookshelf.

Visit Kristina Forest Online

KristinaForest.com

KristinaForest_

KristinaForest

KristinaForest1